The Keepers
Land of Angels, Part I

JJ Hull

Paranormal Crossroads & Publishing

The Keepers, Land of Angels, Part I

Table of Contents

Dedicated to...

My Mom, Barbara Hammers,
for supporting my dream.

Sylvia Browne,
for showing me the way.

Jennifer Toms,
for inspiring me.

The Keepers
Land of Angels, Part I

JJ Hull

The Saga begins...

CHAPTER ONE

Marvin

My memory of her began as one of curiosity. I spent many evenings in bed, wondering who she was and what she was doing. I never fully believed in love at first sight, until her memory overtook all sensibility and replayed again and again in my head. If I only had known where it was to lead, I now wonder, would I have changed anything. It all started innocently.

For my entire life, I happily spent every Tuesday evening with my uncle. Today my training had finished behind schedule, leaving me rushed for my Tuesday night commitment. I hurried to his home, only to discover a note stating he intended to take a stroll towards the Administration Complex. Due to the fact he never put anything before what he called our guy time, I thought this was out of character for him. So, I pursued him.

It was a perfect 75 degrees with golden sun beams shining down on my olive skin and a slight breeze rustling the leaves of the trees. I almost passed my uncle by as I strolled down the lane leading to the Complex. I caught sight of him crouching in the tree line. He appeared to be waiting and watching a doorway. He hardly acknowledged me as I walked towards him. I too tried to blend in to the massive pine and oak trees beside him. He seemed entirely preoccupied with his own thoughts and reason for being there, seeming to be a million miles away. His face, which normally was vibrant and showing a sense of youth, seemed unusually stressed showing the true maturity of his age. His body appeared to be rigid and tense as we stood in perfect silence. I began to realize we would not be having any type of conversation.

I was observing him intently gaze at the door when I noticed his gaze move to a small garden which stood in-front of the building. He began to move, like a cat sneaking up on its prey, down the tree line towards the garden. I tried to follow him and move through the dried leaves and twigs quietly. The grace of a cat certainly was not mine. I could hear the dried landscaping rustle, snap, and break beneath my feet. I was eager to get a better look at the two people I could now see standing in the garden who seemed to be the focus of my uncle's evening.

As we crept closer, I noticed her. My heart leapt! No other word would describe her except stunning. She was petite with long, deep brown hair that flowed around her shoulders. She had delicate, pale features with a hint of color in her cheeks. Her eyebrows were subtle and the light bounced off her eyes. I wished I was closer to peer into them and make out their color. Her flawless lips formed a perfect, radiant smile. The garden was nothing compared to her beauty. It was only after I became aware of my staring, that I startled my uncle whose eyes were focused on her too, by whispering, "Do you know her?"

"Never been introduced," he said in a cool tone suddenly acknowledging my presence. I watched every muscle in his body tighten.

Moving my focus, I could not help but believe my eyes were deceiving me. Was she standing with Albert Solliday, the very old and wise leader of the Keepers? Training books quoted and pictured him. I assumed creeping so close to him would not be possible as he was inclined to be heavily guarded. His stance radiated confidence. The robes he wore fluttered in the breeze. He stood taller than I had imagined and in my astonishment I asked, "Uncle, is she with Albert Solliday?"

"Yes," he whispered with a hushed, hardened low tone that I knew meant be quiet.

I kept my eye on the enchanting girl as she smiled at Mr. Solliday while gathering her long hair in her hands and pulling it up away from her slender neck. She then whirled around and I watched as he withdrew something shiny from his pocket. Was it a locket? He placed it around her neck, fastening it. This motion made my uncle gasp with his whole body shuddering. He clasped his hand across his mouth. At no time had I ever seen him react in this manner, leading me to wonder if I had overlooked something significant. Mr. Solliday suddenly spotted us with his and my uncle's eyes meeting. They seemed to hold a conversation without a word being spoken. My uncle turned to me, "Marvin, it is time we go."

I, still mesmerized by her, desired to find an opportunity to make her acquaintance. I remained in place and persistently stared as she removed from her wrist what appeared to be a watch. She deposited it in Mr. Solliday's outstretched hand. The old man pulled her head to him and kissed her on the forehead. He reminded me of someone who was saying goodbye. Was she going somewhere? They then exchanged a long look while a pale, young man with messy spiked hair appeared. She placed her delicate hand in his while a broad grin crossed his face as he led her into the large Administration Complex. She disappeared from my view.

"Marvin lets go," said my uncle in an impatient, annoyed, and urgent manner.

Reluctantly, I followed him with her still on my mind. Who was she and how could I bump into her to make her acquaintance? A couple quick steps enabled me to match my pace to my uncle's.

I was submerged in thought when he began, "I really expect you not to speak of what we just witnessed to anyone."

This statement caught me off guard. Had I witnessed something other than the most angelic young woman my eyes had ever seen? He stepped right in-front of me, turned to face me, and caused me to stop abruptly.

"I know you have questions due to my sneaking about in the shadows spying," my uncle began. "When the time is right, I will explain."

Of all the people in my life, I completely trusted my uncle. I could now see the intensity in which he was demanding my agreement to silence which was unnecessary since he knew I would keep any secret he asked me too. Although, I couldn't help but wonder why was he being so harsh? I now noticed him intently staring at me, dreading, but anticipating my response, "You know you can trust me. Tell me who she is."

"Marvin, she is trouble and no concern of yours!" He responded with a pleading look for me not to ask further questions. "I promise you, when the time is right, I will tell you."

CHAPTER TWO

Elizabeth

With one big gasp of air and a jolt, my eyes opened. I found myself sitting in the middle of an emergency room clutching the arm of a chair and rubbing between my fingers a locket that hung around my neck. The waiting room was filled with the sound of children crying, adults shuffling, magazine pages turning, and the news playing on the television. This waiting room was massive in size with many rows of identical white chairs which all seemed to be stiff and extremely cold. There were no windows and I could not see out through the sliding glass door that lead outside due to the crowd of people standing in-front of it. An overwhelming sense of coldness swept over my body as I looked at the bleach white walls, plain tile floors, and a plain white ceiling.

My attention now turned to the swinging doors beside the nurse's station that had burst open with a young man appearing. He stopped suddenly, fidgeted with an item in his coat pocket, and seemed to have taken a wrong turn getting lost. He was tall and slender with messy, brown hair, standing up on the top of his head in spikes going every direction. His skin was very pale with deep, brown eyes. He looked very fashionable wearing a nice black jacket with a collared shirt underneath. Jeans and crisp leather shoes finished his look. Realizing that I was staring and oddly drawn to him, I blushed and turned away. Who was he? And why did he keep casually looking at me? I began to squirm in my chair. He kept glancing at me as though waiting for me to acknowledge him. I ignored the expectancy in his eyes. He seemed disappointed and vanished back through the swinging doors.

Startling me, the crowd around the sliding door all cheered loudly, "Jessica!" They were hugging a young lady that had made her way inside. I was taken back by their loud hoots and hollers which seemed to be out of place for an emergency room in a hospital. The group all seemed to be related. They looked alike and this seemed to be a reunion. I now noticed the electronic sign above the door that now read, "Welcome Home Jessica." As I watched, the sign changed to a young man's name and he soon appeared through the door quietly, meeting a friend it seemed. The name changed over and over as people walked through the door and the crowd around the door seemed to change along with the changing of the names. What a strange sign announcing incoming patients.

I could no longer sit in my chair, the coldness was numbing. As I paced the length of this massive room trying to warm myself, I kept passing a huge clock that was hanging beside the nurse's station. At first glance it seemed like any other gold framed clock with the hands ticking away keeping time. Stopping to really look at it, I noticed it had several rings that had an odd numbering system.

Pacing and watching patients whom were called to the nurse's desk, I noticed they were each given a bag that appeared to have their name printed on the side of it. Some quickly dug into the bag as if looking for a treasured lost item while others just held on to it looking just as confused as I felt. As the patients were then shuffled through the swinging doors, I wondered what did the bags contain? The longer I sat, stood, or paced the colder I felt.

The nurse behind the desk was middle aged with the most stunning red hair swept up under her white cap. Her eyes seemed black against her blotchy pale skin, long nose, and maroon lip stick. Her face was long and narrow and she seemed to look over the patients in an impatient, judgmental manner. She was wearing a scrub top, scrub pants, and nursing shoes that were all stiffly white which seemed to be as frigid as this environment.

Giving up pacing, I took a seat next to the nurse's desk. I could feel the nurse staring deeply at me as she spoke, "My dear, I have called you several times. Have you forgotten who you are?"

Stunned I did not answer. In fact, I had no idea who I was or what I was doing here.

"Oh, yes. I see it in your blank face," continued the nurse. "Don't worry, this often happens with re-entry." She then said again into the microphone on her desk, "Elizabeth Cantrell."

I approached the nurse's station and stood squarely in-front of the window. I could clearly see a bag coming down a tube located just beside the desk. The nurse thrust the bag into my hands and I could see the name printed on the side of it was Elizabeth Cantrell. I opened the bag, only to find it to be empty. I did not recognize the name Elizabeth.

The nurse, who was staring at her computer screen, frowned saying, "Elizabeth, I will need you to take a seat in the waiting area and I will be right back for you." Before I could object, ask what was wrong, or where she was going, she turned and disappeared through the door behind her.

Returning to a cold chair to wait, I cuddled myself in my arms for warmth. Elizabeth...? She seemed to believe my name was Elizabeth. No spark of recognition was coming to me. This name seemed as unfamiliar as the chilly hospital waiting room where I was seated. The sound of the news on the television caught my attention because I was now certain the news was repeating the same segment again and again.

The nurse reappeared and called, "Elizabeth Cantrell".

I arose. Standing before her, I could clearly see the nurse's expression had changed. She looked oddly pleased with a smirk on her face that she knew something that I did not.

"I see you are late. You were due for re-entry a full twenty-four hours ago," stated the nurse. "This must be what is causing you a great deal of confusion. If you will come through the doors, I will take you to the Keepers."

I started to ask, "Keeper..."

The nurse quickly exited her chair and disappeared through the door behind her desk. She then appeared at the swinging doors, holding one of them open for me. As I walked towards her, the terms Keeper and re-entry were swirling in my head. I didn't comprehend them.

Entering the hall, I was baffled to find a very long corridor filled with offices. The lighting was much softer than the bright lights we just left behind and made me feel instantly warm. I wondered where the doctors were as we passed the offices. In their place, gentlemen with white suits sat behind the desks. Opposite sat one person each and they seemed to be reviewing a file. Outside each office set a bench and most of the long seats were filled with people waiting. In-front of one office, I recognized the crowd of people waiting on the bench. Through the door of the office sat Jessica, looking at a file.

The nurse stopped abruptly in-front of me and I bumped into her because I really was not paying attention to her as we walked. I now noticed the nurse did not appear to be a nurse anymore. Her hair was no longer pulled up under her white cap but flowing around her face. Her white clothes were now black slacks and a bright blue, button up blouse. Her professional, white shoes were now black sandals. Confused about her change of attire and amazed, I blurted out, "Nurse?"

"Oh, don't call me nurse," she answered. "I only appear to be the nurse in the hospital wing. Newly re-entering souls need a sense of familiar surroundings and calmness, so they don't over react. Let me introduce myself, I am Mrs. Mary Ann Farris."

"It is nice to meet you," I answered in a robotic manner. I shivered due to my not understanding the majority of what she just said.

"I suppose you are still having trouble remembering?" She questioned with an amused but satisfied smile creeping back onto her face.

"Yes." I hesitantly answered. "May I ask you where I am and what I am doing here?"

Mrs. Farris gave a calculating smile which screamed she knew a secret that I did not. Motioning for me to follow, we began to walk as she continued, "You have re-entered Home after living a life on the Earth Plane. You are a Keeper and it is my assumption you have lived only one earth life."

What? My head was swirling and my thoughts seem to spill out of my mouth, "A Keeper?"

Mrs. Farris looked very pleased at my lack of memory. "A Keeper assists others when they are learning their life lessons on the Earth Plane. Some call Keepers guardian angels or guides on the Earth Plane. Before you can help others in the capacity of Keeper, you must first live an earth life of your own to develop compassion for those you are helping." She paused smiling at me and continued, "My dear, you've crossed over!"

I gasped! My heart started to rapidly beat inside my chest and I could no longer breathe. I felt nauseous and sat on the nearest bench and tried to regain my composure. Once I found my voice I asked, "I am dead?"

Another voice interrupted our conversation, "No, not dead! Alive and Home. Standing before us was a very large, middle aged lady. Her gray hair and pale complexion were in contrast to the huge, red glasses she was wearing. Her red print dress was equally as loud with huge orange & purple circles spread throughout the print. Definitely nothing I would wear. She extended her hand to shake mine as I rose from the bench. She was wearing red, fuzzy house shoes. "Good Afternoon, I am Head Professor Allene Rae Presnell and I am in charge of the Hall of Knowledge. You have arrived behind schedule and we need to hurry along to orientation."

"Yes, I already know I am late," I said softly while still in shock from the confusion. I felt relieved that my chest no longer ached due to the accelerated beating of my heart.

"Well if you already know, then maybe you could elaborate as to why you were not punctual," snapped the professor.

I shrugged my shoulders. I didn't have any memory of how I arrived here and no clue as to why I was late. However, I did know I didn't intend to break the news to her that I remembered nothing. I sat quietly as her eyes seriously studied me and her foot impatiently tapped the floor. The professor seemed intolerant of any disrespect. I asked in a low voice, "What do you learn in the Hall of …?"

"The Hall of Knowledge," the professor corrected in a short tone. "Really, Miss Cantrell! Job training!" My nausea was back. A job? Me? Who would hire someone who didn't recognize their own name? Yes, it was definitely a fact to keep to myself. The professor then turned to Mrs. Farris. She tipped her head down to peer over the rim of her glasses and condescendingly stated, "Your services are no longer needed. Thank you."

"Miss Cantrell, if you will quickly follow me," demanded the professor as she spun around and advanced at a brisk pace down the rest of the corridor which ended with a choice of a hallway going to the right and one to the left. I followed behind her, turning briefly, giving Mrs. Farris a short wave goodbye. I wasn't sure I really wanted to go with the professor as she continued around the corner into the right hallway.

Once I could visually see the choice of the two hallways, I could see at the end of each stood a door. I halted for a moment. It felt as if the left hallway was calling me down it. It seemed familiar and the plain wooden door at the end seemed inviting to me. I instantly felt curious as to what existed beyond the door.

Again, the professor seemed to interrupt my thoughts. "Miss Cantrell, keep moving. Please! Must I remind you that you are late?"

The golden door at the end of the right hall was very ornate with symbols I did not recognize. A feeling in my stomach made me believe I had never walked through this door before. There was no handle to open it. I watched as the professor stepped up to the door, waved the top of her hand in front of a huge symbol of a tree, and it swung open. How exactly had she done that? I wished I had paid closer attention. Turning one last time to look at the simple wooden door standing at the other end of the hall, I sighed.

The professor glared at me, swishing her hand for me to enter. "Quickly, quickly, the whole group is waiting."

I found myself very small compared to the airy foyer of the large building I was standing in. Looking up I was in awe of the massive paintings on the ceiling of this room. My eyes traveled across the room to the far wall. There stood huge mahogany double doors with massive gold handles. It seemed more fitting that these doors should be the entry for a massive castle. To the left and right of the mahogany doors were staircases made of white marble, leading to the second level. The walls were a soft white color and the floor was different shades of white and beige marble which were laid in a pattern to create the same symbol as I had seen on the ornate door when we entered this building. I turned to look at the wall behind me. It had four elevators doors, one plain wooden door, and one golden door which led to the Hospital. The second level had white marble railing all around the edges of the foyer, allowing a view of the lower level from all sides. A chandelier hung in the middle of the room, leaving the massive room illuminated. I felt a since of awe! There was no doubt I had entered the land of angels and it sure was impressive!

The professor crossed the room, opened one side of the mahogany door, and turned to look at me with an impatient expression. As I moved across the foyer towards the door, a man stepped through the door shaking his head when spying me. He was as different as anyone I had come in contact with on this strange day. He appeared to be middle age, balding, and was an entire head taller than the short, plump professor. His eyes were vibrant blue and his salt and pepper mustache was long and curled at the edges. He was wearing what appeared to be an ancient school uniform which probably belonged to him when he was in school. It was thread bare and he looked as if he was bulging from every seam. I really felt very sorry for him because he projected an image I was sure he did not intend to.

He now spoke, "Where is her watch?"

"Miss Cantrell, where is your processing bag that you were given at the property desk in the Hospital when you re-entered?" Asked the professor.

I held up the bag I was still clutching and answered, "Sorry, it is empty."

The professor turned red with her veins in her neck pulsating and her temper starting to flair showing her impatience. She quickly turned to the man, "She can borrow one of mine." I watched as the two of them walked back across the foyer, disappearing through the office door which set beside the ornate, golden door, which minutes before we had walked through. Seeing how easy the professor seemed to get angry, I felt as if I were right about my first impression of the professor and I would be cautious around her.

The mustached man reappeared and rushed back across the foyer, never acknowledging me. As he exited the office door, he left it slightly ajar. Tiptoeing, I peered through the cracked door. The door led to an office in which the walls and upholstery were a repulsive red, leaving no doubt in my mind who this office belonged too. I tried to breathe noiselessly. I could overhear the end of a conversation taking place between someone I could not see and the professor who stated, "Well, it is the best we can do under the circumstances."

"I agree, she will know the importance in time," responded a deep, diplomatic voice, which seemed to be somewhat familiar to me.

"Thank you for your visit, I must go because the group waits," said the professor. I could hear the desk drawer close with a thud. What was that about? My gut seemed to answer my own question.... me.

"Very Well," responded the deep voice as I heard the legs of a chair move across the wooden floor as it was pushed back. I tried to quietly distance my-self a few steps from the door of the office.

The professor exited the office and handed me a watch which I placed on my wrist as we walked back across the foyer to the massive, mahogany door. I was sure, since the professor's wrists were bigger than mine, the watch to be too big. To my surprise, I found the watch fit my wrist perfectly. Out of curi-osity, I asked, "When should I return this to you?"

"There will be no need to return it to me," the professor said. Once Again the huge mahogany door opened.

What was this magnificent hall I just stepped into? It was very different compared to the airy foyer. The vaulted ceiling was beige with four large rect-angles each containing a different coat of arms painted within. The desks ap-peared to be wooden, but all painted perfectly white. They stood in rows, and were individually lit with their own brass desk lamp. A massive, white podium stood facing the desks while the wall behind it was covered with white wooden bookcases which contained thick books that appeared to be ancient with layers of dust settled upon them. The walls were limestone blocks which seemed to be old and complimented the massive doors. The walls were covered in deep blue banners that seemed to have different dates and titles on them, leading me to believe they were awards of some kind. The floor was dark wood and polished like a mirror. Lighting in the room came from the desk lamps and wall sconces which hung all along the sides of the hall.

The room was full of studious individuals whom all appeared to be about my age and were already sitting at their individual desks. They all seemed to be extremely attractive and wearing a uniform that consisted of a white collared shirt and white pants. How odd, not an ugly or miss-kept person in the room! I glanced down at my own attire and instantly felt as if everyone in the room was staring. I blushed at my own homely attire, a T-shirt and sweat pants fin-ished off with flip flops. My hair was pulled back into a pony-tail. Touching my face with my fingers, I couldn't remember or feel if I was wearing makeup. I was sure my beauty just did not compare to the others in this room.

As I walked down the rows to find a place to sit, I saw others chewing their nails, fidgeting in their chairs, and one seemed to have the nervous giggles. The air in this room left a suggestion of uncertain tension, making me un-comfortable. Almost everyone I passed had nervous looks. Their faces and actions seemed to acknowledge the anxious feeling as well.

I finally reached the only empty chair in the room. Next to it sat a girl who did not look nervous but seemed to be enjoying the tension in the room. Her long exposed, slender legs were crossed at the knee. She playfully kicked a high heeled shoe loosely on the end of her right toe. Her face belonged to a model and it was haloed with her sandy brown hair. The wavy long layers, which were choppy, flew about with movement looking wild and unkept. Her big hoop earrings dangled beneath her hair. A black necklace swooped around her neck. Her uniform's white shirt was purposely unbuttoned revealing a black, leather top underneath. She was not wearing white pants but a white pleated skirt which in my opinion was a little too short. Her high-heels were over the top. As I reluctantly sat down, the girl turned to me saying, "Hi, my name is Tilly."

I nodded and smiled while I fiddled nervously with my desk lamp hoping not to be forced into a conversation with her. I didn't seem to be able to figure out how to turn it on. She leaned over and pushed the button located on the front side of my desk. "And you are?"

"Um..., I'm Elizabeth. Thanks." I responded to her inquiring eyes.

"No problem," she replied while smacking her gum loudly. "Boy, you really know how to make an entrance. I am a little jealous."

"Jealous?" I repeated wondering what was there to be jealous of. I didn't remember anything about myself. I looked frightening. Everything, this place, the people, the events were all foreign to me. Worst of all, everyone seemed to know me and something about me that I did not.

Looking at me strangely, like she could see my internal struggle and green with envy, she replied, "If only I had thought of being late. You know, Professor Presnell paced for at least thirty minutes, back and forth. She has a reputation for not appreciating or tolerating any deviation from the normal routine. Oh, it was great to see her squirm!" She seemed to gage my expression and with delight whispered, "Squirm like a worm!"

"Great," I replied as Professor Presnell made her way to the podium at the front of the room. Silence fell. To my dismay, the boy seated the other side of me was tapping his pencil on his desk attempting to gain my attention. Once my eyes flashed his way, he clenched a folded piece of paper and slid it onto my desktop. "For Tilly," he said under his breath while his hands motioned for me to pass it on which I reluctantly did.

The professor hit a large red gavel on the podium to gain everyone's attention. "Welcome, new trainee class! I am Professor Allene Rae Presnell and I am the head professor here at the Department of Knowledge. In addtion, I represent the Department of Administration. While the other professors begin to hand out our entrance exams and pencils, let me remind you that there are not to be any other items on your desk during the test. This exam is the most important test you will take here at the Department of Knowledge because it will determine which department you will work for during the remaining of your working years." I now understood why everyone else looked so nervous and horrified. I wondered how I could take a test when I didn't even recognize my own name. I began to silently panic.

My panic was soon interrupted by a crackling paper sound. Nobody seated around us could deny that Tilly had finished reading the note when she loudly wadded it up and shoved it into her bag. I looked up to see if the sound had carried to the front of the room but met no returning stares.

Professor Presnell continued, "The professors will wave their hand as I introduce them. First, Professor Kendell Bungard with the Department of Ghosts." I instantly recognized him as the balding man whom had reminded Professor Presnell that I needed a watch. He gave a huge grin to the group which made his mustache further curl as he waved his hand wildly above his head.

I could see out of the corner of my eye Tilly trying to peer around me. I leaned as far back in my chair as I could without falling over backwards.

"Thank you Professor Bungard. Second, Professor Faye Ann Kegley, Department of Records." She was a mousy woman with big teeth and long blond hair that was pulled up into a bun on the back of her head. She was wearing a black dress that covered every inch of her skin and slightly dragged the floor. Her attire left only her hands, neck, and face exposed. I felt she looked very sheepish and nervous while raising her hand. She seemed to be a little klutzy, and while waving, she dropped all of the remaining test papers onto the wooden floor. Professor Presnell gave her a displeased glance and a sigh, stating, "Thank you professor. Last, Professor Ruben Zirak, Department of Keepers." He seemed to stand taller than the rest and his posture left no doubt he had confidence in himself. He tipped the tall hat he was wearing and did a small bow to acknowledge the room.

The boy beside me was making efforts to peer around at Tilly, obviously anticipating a response to some outstanding question. She seemed to be enjoying his attention and then I saw it. She winked and blew a kiss to him. I absent mindlessly let the legs of my chair fall back to their place on the floor with a thud! At the same time, the redhead seated on the other side of the boy coughed loudly. Her face spoke volumes. She appeared jealous, angry, and just plain shocked. I didn't know what her problem was. I just hoped her loud coughing covered my chair falling back into place.

The professor continued, "Thank you Professor Zirak. Directly after your tests, you will be divided into your halls and there unpack and settle your belongings into their proper places. We realize all of you have recently re-entered and the majority of you have not had the opportunity to visit with your families. So, tomorrow you will be given a one week pass to visit your families to celebrate your return and your new career." My head was beginning to throb. What family? I had no recollection of my family!

Tilly interrupted my thoughts as she leaned over and in a hushed voice said, "My Mother's a record keeper and my Father works for the Council. Yours?"

"Er..." I could not think of an appropriate response to this question. I was blank. I had no idea. "Why do you ask?"

"Just wondering," she said with a deep sigh. "Both of my parents hope I will follow in their footsteps. I hope to be in Ghost Relations because I would love to see the shocked look on their faces."

I smiled at her to acknowledge her thoughts not fully understanding Ghost Relations. The professor spoke from the podium, "Does everyone now have their tests? You will have three hours, begin please."

I sat looking at my blank test. The only thing written on my paper was my name. Even that did not look familiar. I could hear the scratching of pencils on paper all around me with pages turning as others flipped one page and then another. The professor's paced up and down between the desks. Their footsteps creaked as they walked across the wooden floors and echoed off the walls. They looked sharply at me each time they passed. I would lay my head down to sleep. However, I was certain I was already asleep and this was a nightmare.

The day's events kept replaying in my head. I could not shake the feeling they all knew something I did not. I was haunted by the conversation I overheard, the way they all look at me as they pass, and the nurse. I knew the nurse from the Hospital seemed to have answers! I wish I could have stayed at the Hospital and asked my questions. Then, there was this outlandish girl which I was seated beside. She was outgoing and friendly in an odd sort of way. Was there another side to her beyond her wild girl persona? No one else in this large room would sit next to her.

Having nothing else to do, I studied the watch on my wrist. It was a small version of the clock on the wall in the Hospital. The band was interlocking gold links, with a face framed in gold. The hands ticked away keeping the time. The watch had several rings that had an odd numbering system. The outer ring had the six small numbers evenly spaced around the outside edge which represented 1-144. The second ring had the numbers 1-24 that went consecutively around. The third ring had the numbers 1-8 that went consecutively around. It had three big gold letters, E. H. D., engraved in the center. None of this made any sense as to how to keep time with this watch. Where were the familiar settings, 1-12? Noon, midnight?

Time finally passed. Professor Presnell clapped her hands and stated, "Time is up. Pencils down. As I call your name, you will bring me your paper." Professor Bungard and Professor Zirak were pushing a bulky item under a sheet to the front of the room and halted next to the podium. Professor Presnell said, "Thank you professors," and removed the cover, revealing a strange machine. I could see big wheels attached to a round board, making the base for the machine. There were two poles attached to the base and between the poles there was a metal box. The professor turned it on, it beeped a few times, and she continued, "As I record your test scores, I will tell you which department you will work for. Please go stand behind the professor who leads your department's training."

The first name was called and a nervous young man with blond hair handed his paper to Professor Presnell who put the paper into the machine. I watched as the paper slowly was sucked into the box of the machine and then simply disappeared into thin air. Professor Presnell announced, "Welcome to the Hall of Records." The boy looked very relieved and made his way to the back of the room while the room was filled with applause. This scenario was repeated again and again with most seeming pleased with their department.

Eventually, the professor called, "Mathilda Bradford." The girl beside me said, "Don't wish me luck, because I don't want any." She marched up like she owned the whole room and handed in her paper and waited while loudly blowing pink bubbles with her gum. I noticed the other girls appeared to look coldly upon Tilly with disapproving scowls. The boys in the room looked as if they were enthralled with her but trying to be evasive with their thoughts in front of the other girls. The professor was clearly annoyed but had a look of astonishment on her face, "Miss Bradford, I would not have thought it. Department of Keepers." The whole room seemed to be caught off guard by this statement as they stared at her. With no applause, she took her place behind Professor Zirak. I felt as if I had missed the joke.

Several others were called and then the moment I dreaded. Professor Presnell called, "Elizabeth Cantrell." I hesitated for a minute wondering how I was going to explain my blank paper. My legs seemed very heavy as I walked towards the front beneath the stares of the others. I handed my paper to the professor and my eyes focused on my feet, hoping to ignore the look on her face. To my surprise, the professor said, "Department of Keepers." Instantly I looked up, questioning. My test? Does she realize my test was blank? The professor seemed to read my face and responded, "Yes, Miss Cantrell, you have a question." I could not speak because I was too shocked. After a long pause, the professor ordered, "If you do not, please get in your department's line."

Stunned, I found myself standing next to Tilly who was beaming as she whispered, "We are going to be room mates!" I did not answer because this was just more than I could comprehend. I felt exhausted by the day's events which had only served to confuse me further.

The newly formed training group was now following Professor Zirak into the foyer and up the stairs. I noticed that Tilly and I seemed to be pushed to the back of the group and I actually found relief in this action because I felt too tired to hold a conversation. Once standing on the second level, I looked down over the marble railing down into the foyer still feeling the building was impressive but unfamiliar before today. As I looked around the second level, I could see that behind the marble railing was an open walkway that went entirely around. Off each corner of the hall was an archway, leading to a long corridor.   The magnificent, domed archway we were standing under had a plaque that read, Department of Keepers. The other archways had plaques above them. Each was different, announcing an individual department. Two of the other groups had already disappeared into their corridors.

I could see the last group climbing the stairs following Professor Presnell. At last, I hoped soon there would be a warm bed to crawl into, letting the exhaustion of the day overtake me. Tilly leaned over with a hand muffling her mouth and whispering, "The Department of Administration. Look at them, they are already strutting around like they own the place, they think they are royalty!"

I saw only one person strutting around. Was she blind or exaggerating her views?

As the group passed, a girl with long curly black hair and perfect skin who looked more like a life size Barbie then a trainee said, "Well silly Tilly, I'm still waiting for the day you'll say or do something intelligent. How did you get into this group?"

Her friend, who was also flawless with her blond hair and doll-like features taunted, "You are only suited to hunt ghosts. No actually, you should be on the Earth Plane, a true Humling."

I could see that Tilly knew them and obviously the dislike was mutual as she wasted no time giving them a dirty look. What in the world was a Humling?

I was the last one through the arch leading into the corridor and I felt warmth enticing and caressing my face. The corridor was bright with the last rays of sunlight coming through the tall windows that lined each side. This corridor ended with our choice of doors; one door to the left, right, and straight ahead. Our group was entering the door straight ahead. I stopped to ask Tilly, "What's behind the other two doors?"

"The other two houses or dorms are for training Keepers," Tilly replied stepping through the door.

I followed her as we entered a smaller, dark hall. Would this trek through hallways ever end? To the right, I could see through the glass of a small office that over ran with papers. To the left there was a closed door. Then we approached two glass windowed, small conference rooms each having a black board and one large table in the middle surrounded by chairs. Anything accomplished in those two rooms, I was sure would involve work. The hall then opened into a comfortable, large room with a sitting area containing three large couches. On the other side of the room was a long, wooden dining table with a pile of luggage surrounding it. At the end of the room was one large kitchen.

Everyone filed in while the professor now spoke, "Please find a place to sit." I was still walking behind Tilly as we moved together and found a place to sit on the floor in-front of the kitchen island. "Good Evening, I am Professor Ruben Zirak. I am in charge of your training while you are here at the Department of Knowledge. You are standing in Keeper House. Many have passed through Keeper House and it is an honor for you to be placed under her roof. I expect each of you to strive to do your best in your training, to honor yourself and those who came before you." He paused as the group sat in anticipation of him finishing his introductory to Keeper House. "Training to be a Keeper is an honor in itself. Not one soul goes to the Earth Plane without first selecting a Keeper to protect and help them along their journey. They entrust their soul to you. Being selected for this honored position ensures that I, as your professor, will have high expectations for you during your training. I personally will look at the results of every training session, whether taught by the other professors or myself. I expect each of you to excel in all subjects."

Tilly turned to me and rolled her eyes at this. I was trying hard not to notice, actually to ignore her.

The professor continued, "I have strict house rules to follow at all times. Rule One. If you make the mess, you clean it up. Each of you is starting your own journey into adulthood and there will be no one here to pick up after you. Rule Two. Gentlemen are not to be in the rooms of the Ladies. Ladies are not to be in the rooms of the Gentlemen. This includes all fellow trainees and visitors. You are welcome to have company only in the common area of this house. This should be all I need to say about this subject."

"Ouch!" I flinched. Tilly was nudging me firmly with her bony elbow. The professor seemed to glance our way. Pressing my lips together and tightening my jaw, I turned to her annoyed. She didn't seem to notice. Tilly had begun scanning around the room looking at our fellow trainees.

The professor continued, "Rule Three. You are to be in the complex by sunset nightly. I know you are young adults, but your parents have entrusted me with your safety. There will be no exceptions to this rule."

I, as well as everyone else, could not ignore Tilly's huge, loud sigh and whisper, "Might as well be in prison!" This caught the professor's attention. He glared at the two of us. His long fixed stare didn't faze her. She started blowing pink, snappy bubbles with her gum.

"Behind the door to the left, off the entrance, you will find a staircase. At the first landing are the bathrooms. Ladies, at the second landing you will find your rooms. Gentlemen, at the third landing you will find your rooms. Please remember, two people to a room. One more note, you are not the only trainees in Keeper House as others are finishing their studies. Their rooms are marked as taken by the names on the outside of the doors upstairs."

To my dismay, Tilly leaned over and whispered, "Great, the good rooms are probably already taken."

Although I was sure he could hear it, the professor chose to ignore the comment, "I expect that each of you will recognize your bags. Please get them, divide yourselves up in pairs, and pick your rooms upstairs. Thank you."

The group seemed frenzied to get their luggage and head up the stairs. I purposely stood and watched hoping whatever luggage was left would be mine. Every single bag disappeared from the pile, leaving me no luggage. I found this was very disheartening. Had no one from my family cared if I had clothes?

My thoughts turned to the thumping noise above my head and decided to join the group and venture up the stairs. The stair case went up six steps and the bathrooms were to one side. Then the steps went up another six steps and I found a long hall with ten doors leading off of it, and then the steps continued upward. I had not thought about my room mate until this moment. Then I saw Tilly standing next to the last door on the right side of the hall waving and motioning for me to come on. I did not know whether to feel glad or sad. I appeared to be developing a friendship or a horrific nuisance.

Nearing Tilly, she beamed and yelled out over everyone, "Elizabeth, I got the best room for us." I made my way past all the luggage and strangers and peered through the door. The room seemed longer and more inviting than I thought it would be. Tilly, looking devious, continued, "I kicked two of the other girls out of here." I now knew what the big echoing thumps on the floor were! I was sure the two exiles would not be too happy or friendly. "I do have to tell you, I was hoping to have big trees with lots of branches closer to the building. I checked each room and none of the trees were close. So, I opted for the room with the most windows!"

I was quite glad the trees were not any closer because I was certain that Tilly had plans to use them as an escape route for adventures. I answered, "Great thinking. Windows are great."

It looked as if Tilly were a caged animal. She paced waiting to explore their surroundings, "Well, you get settled. I am going to check … I'll be back." My gut feeling said she was going to look for trouble.

The room did indeed have four windows. No light was coming through matching the gloom I felt. Darkness was engulfing this new world. There were two magnificent wooden, carved beds with fluffy dusty rose bedding. The head board was detailed, surrounded by the same wooden carved detail as the foot board. Standing at the foot of each was a trunk of dark wood with a floral design carved into it. Between the beds was a night table and setting on the table was a very bright orb lamp. On both sides of the door set a desk with its own intense lamp that looked identical to the white desks downstairs. Directly in-front of the windows set two big, comfortable looking chairs which had a floor light in between them.

I sat down on the bed that did not have Tilly's luggage tossed about on top of it. Tilly's luggage included six extremely large suitcases. I wondered what she had packed in all of them! It must have been her luggage the professor helped carry up the stairs. I, on the other hand, was without luggage. I decided just to crawl into bed hoping to be asleep before Tilly reappeared and I would be forced to explain my lack of luggage. Especially since I knew how much Tilly had brought. I placed the only possessions I had; my watch, locket, and hospital processing bag on the night stand and pulled the covers up over my head.

"So where are you returning from?" Uncovering my eyes and startled at the elevated voice, I shifted my eyes to the door and my new room mate. There was Tilly moving through the door.

I answered "Well, I don't really know."

"You don't know?" A glimmer of interest crossed her face as she continued, "Well, don't worry. Mother told me sometimes there is a memory fog upon re-entry. I'm sure it will pass."

"Lets' hope," I replied with a small shrug of my shoulders. I pulled the covers back up.

Tilly stood there looking at me expectantly. "Aren't you going to ask where I'm returning from?"

The expression on her face led me to believe she would tell a grand story. I asked politely, "Where are you coming back from?"

"Missouri," answered Tilly with a smile, hiding a chuckle. "My parents forced me to go. However, they could not write my chart for me. I charted a course and lived a great life on the edge doing everything they would never let me do."

I knew this was only the beginning of her story. She probably lived on the edge, well beyond my imagination. Tilly drifted into deep thought. I didn't understand what a chart was. However, I was not going to ask tonight. I relaxed into my soft bed and once again I heard Tilly comment, "You know you should check out a chapter on yourself."

All I yearned to do was sleep. I was beginning to feel highly irritated pondering why Tilly would not take the hint. A chapter? Another term I did not understand. I inhaled a slow, deep breath and thought to myself, be patient. I questioned, "Check out a chapter?"

Tilly replied, "Sure, at the Hall of Records."

I shrugged my shoulders once more as Tilly, flabbergasted, sat down onto her bed and for the first time seemed unable to chew her gum. My lack of knowledge intrigued her. She questioned, "The Hall of Records? You know about the Hall of Records, surely?"

I shook my head no, watching the astounded look on her face as she paused a minute, then saying, "My, you really do have a fogged brain and don't remember anything, do you?"

"No," I said firmly as once again I could see Tilly deep in thought.

"Okay, were do we start," Tilly said with a sigh as she removed her high-heels and tossed them into the floor. "A chapter is a book which contains information of what you did during your one life on the Earth Plane. The chapters are kept in the Hall of Records."

"And a chart?" I questioned as I watched Tilly open one of her suitcases, beginning to dig through it.

"Charts are how we plan what lessons we will learn during our life on the Earth Plane," Tilly responded.

"A Humling?" I questioned as she stopped digging in her bag and looked directly at me with the shock returning to her face.

"A Humling is referred to on the Earth Plane as a human. At Home it refers to someone who lives many lives on the Earth Plane," Tilly replied.

"So Keepers are never referred to as Humlings?" I questioned.

"Not normally," Tilly commented.

"One more question," I stated as she sat looking intently at me. "Who were the girls in Professor Presnell's group?"

"The black curly hair, Tiffany. Her sidekick, the blond, Janelle," growled Tilly. "Just keep your distance from them. They live and breathe to cause trouble." She seemed once again to drift and lose herself in her thoughts. I was glad to have the silence as I pulled the covers up to my nose. She bounced back to reality and happily said, "I'll go tomorrow morning before I leave and check your chapter out for you. You can look at it over during the holiday and read about yourself. That should jog your memory!"

I should have said thanks, but I did not answer because I did not want to continue the conversation. The warmth of the bed over took me and I fell peacefully asleep.

CHAPTER THREE

Tilly

What is that beeping?! We were just about to kiss and the beeping! Go away. Blasted beeping! Ruined everything. I took a deep breath to awake my body. Yes, the beeping was my wrist! The alarm my mother insisted be placed into my watch. I could almost hear her rattling on, "Tilly, you need to take some responsibility for yourself." The threats of authority. "Tilly, if you oversleep one more time!" Repeatedly I told her my hatred for the blasted thing. I adamantly refused to use it just to remind my mother of her lack of true power over me.

This morning was different. I had never chosen to use the alarm before. Today for the first time, it had a purpose. I had made the decision to rise early due to my new room mate. I didn't need a tag along. My assessment of her was right on. She could sleep through anything! The alarm was loud enough to wake the dead! Hmm. Technically, we were dead. How fitting. I felt a chuckle escape me.

I stood. In this mess of luggage, how was I too find the perfect outfit? My mother had been insistent that my clothes brought to training needed to be more modest. BORING! I tossed in my choices fast before she could inspect my luggage leaving her little time to alter my choices. However, she had managed to stuff the dreadful green, floral dress she shoved into the outside pocket of my suitcase. It was her favorite. I would remember to burn it if we should have a bond-fire during training! I dug knowing the outfit must be perfect. I couldn't take a chance meeting any guy if I was not stunning to look upon! Really… I don't know what type of guy would be out this time of morning. Most I knew preferred to sleep in. However, I couldn't take a chance!

Now happy with my perfect hair, short skirt, and black stockings I slipped on my chartreuse high-heeled boots. Ever so quietly, I left the room. Better escape routes than the front door is what I would need. I didn't plan to answer questions about my adventures. I stepped down the stairs quietly. I needed an escape route! I would need to talk with Trevor about this. Once through the door, I briskly went to the lift. During my life on the Earth Plane, we had called them elevators. Your mind on the Earth Plane just didn't work right!

This new room mate of mine, Elizabeth, had guts! She was also good under pressure. When I observed her step through the door of the hall, wearing sweats and flip flops I knew she was different. She had nerves! First impressions are hard to overcome. Looking under dressed was her unique statement. The others looking upon her didn't effect her disposition. The girls in the room were gossiping and spreading the official verdict handed down by the self-proclaimed princess, Tiffany, who whispered, "White Trash." It was clear, this poor girl who was instantly judged not good enough, was to be an outcast! Tiffany was always the start of anything catty. I never understood why numerous girls followed her lead. Brainless nit-wits!

Princess Tiffany held the capacity to be in the rebellious category too. She was sneaky, feline mean to anyone receiving more attention than her. Professors steered clear of her path. They were cowards avoiding her! With every pace of Professor Presnell's entrance, it was evident Tiffany's catty nature was incensed. When Elizabeth arrived, Presnell had to flaunt her lateness before everyone with their dramatic entrance. I personally envied sweat pant girls' ability to score a success with this stunt. We weren't so different. Anarchy! She and I were going to see eye to eye on this point.

Stepping off the lift, I took a deep breath. The familiar and calming smell of books filled the air. Standing in the Hall of Records, past memories were flooding back to me. My mother, the workaholic, had been employed here since her training. Much of my childhood vanished within this hall. Time ticked away as I played hide and seek beneath the desks and pulled pranks while waiting on my mother. Nothing had changed! The same ladies were employed here and were versed in my methods for disruptions. Needing to unearth, unmask, and unveil new ways to irritate them and cause them chaos fostered my creativeness. I was forever in their debt for molding me into the person I am today.

"Good morning, Tilly," stated Mrs. Summors who stepped up from somewhere behind me.

"Good morning," I responded as we began to walk.

The expression on her face made me feel warm, just as it always had. She truly had a kind spirit and time after time had looked beyond my stunts. She always encouraged me and often sang my praises to others. Generally, the praise wasn't warranted. She asked, "What are you doing here so early?"

My gut began to tighten. Although I knew she would take me at my word, lying to her would be painful. I pointed to the history books stating, "I have next week off. Figure I better brush up on my studies."

"Hmm," she replied as she intently peered at me. She knew as well as I did, studying had never been a priority of mine. She sighed and told me, "Bring up what you want to check out."

With a quick nod, I turned to move towards the card catalog. I could feel her eyes staring through my back. The guilt was instant. Geez, I'm lying to the only adult who has ever been nice to me. Confiding in her over the years, I knew she was patient, kind, and understanding. Most important of all, she was trustworthy. Not much I did ever gave me this foreign, gut-wrenching feeling. Guilt sucks! However, telling her my real reason for visiting wasn't something I could do. Elizabeth's needs were not mine to share.

I looked into the card catalog. Cantrell, Elizabeth, to be assigned. Oh, no! The chapter was brand-new and hadn't been shelved yet. My mind drifted back remembering Presnell calling Elizabeth to turn in her exam. Her feet appeared bolted to the floor. As if with each movement, she was pulling the boards up with her feet and taking them along with her. It appeared that each step got heavier. She stood staring at the floor while her test was recorded. That was it. The test had been recorded! I slammed the card catalog drawer with a loud thud! I rushed up to the front desk trying to ignore the disapproving eyes upon me. Why did everyone need to be so uptight? So what? I made a little noise! "Mrs. Summors, may I look at the recorded tests?" I enthusiastically questioned.

"Tests?" She responded with an inquiring glance.

"Our entrance exams," I responded as I popped a piece of gum in my mouth.

"You should only look at yours," she qualified, looking over the top of her wire rimmed glasses.

"They're all together aren't they?" I innocently questioned.

"Yes," replied Mrs. Summors cautiously. "Why do you want to see them?"

"I don't know what to study if I don't know what I got wrong," I replied. I blew a big, pink bubble and popped it trying to appear cool and collected.

"I wouldn't get this for anyone but you," Mrs. Summors stated. "It's restricted." She paused to stare, looking for any hint of deception before scolding me, "Don't pop your gum in here." My gut said she was suspicious as she disappeared into the restricted section.

When she reappeared, I thanked her and quickly vanished out of her sight to a small lonely table in the back of the room. Flipping through, pretending to look for my test, I came across Elizabeth's exam. Blank! Crossing my mind was the look on Elizabeth's face when Presnell announced, "Keeper House." Fogged. Totally fogged! She knew the exam was blank. Presnell questioned her before instructing her to her line. Poor thing. Hmm... The Professors must have taken pity on her and placed her in Keeper House. She's a misfit. A challenge. Let's face it, Elizabeth needs my help! I would be the one to answer the call and discover who she was. To know nothing about herself and carry on was a sign of bravery. Now I needed to find her chapter in those that hadn't been shelved yet.

I returned the exams to Mrs. Summors as I moved to position myself behind the check-out desk. Now standing alongside her I said, "Thanks for letting me look."

"Did you find what you were looking for?" Mrs. Summors asked while stacking chapters to be restocked on shelves. Her question hinted of her knowledge that my rummaging through the exams had more reason than I told her.

"Sure did," I replied careful not to catch her eye.

She gathered a stack of chapters saying, "Glad I could help." She then ventured off to restock the chapters in her hands. Once she was safely away, I whirled around to look into the bins containing the new chapters which were waiting to be processed and shelved. I scanned the spines of the chapters in the top bin behind the desk. Nothing. I grabbed the bin and set it on the floor. Next bin, no chapter. Again, I stacked it on the last bin. Scanning the third bin, there it was. Elizabeth Cantrell. I re-stacked the previous two bins and placed Elizabeth's chapter under my shirt. This part of my plan lacked a little planning. I hadn't considered how tight my shirt was. It allowed you to see the chapter which I was trying to conceal. Slinky, tight shirts are great to attract guys but not for hiding chapters.

Inspiration from Elizabeth swelled inside of me. She was brave. Anyone who could plow through and know nothing about themselves was brave. That was exactly what I needed to be. Crossing the room without being noticed is all I needed to do. It was now or never! I crossed my arms across my stomach, summoned the courage from deep inside. I walked casually past the study tables and rows of shelving. Then I darted for the lift. With the exhilaration of the moment, I could feel my body fill with adrenaline. Pure energy took over. My increased heart rate only served as a reminder. I was actually borrowing… okay, stealing a chapter! One of the most prized possessions to the Hall of Records.

I heard Mrs. Summors call, "Tilly, where are you going in such a hurry?"

I never turned to look at her as I replied, "Sorry, just remembered something I was supposed to do!" I made it to the lift as the door was closing. I placed my hand in between the doors with them reopening to my cue. I pushed to the back of the lift where I couldn't be seen by Mrs. Summors. I exhaled the breath I had been holding loudly. I growled at the midget running the lift, "Push the button! Push it now!"

He turned to give me a dirty look at my hurried expression. He stood glaring at me when all I needed him to do was push the button so the door would close. Why must I do everything myself? I pushed him aside and held down the button until the door began to close. I did it! I felt amazing until I noticed everyone in the lift was now giving me a sour look. Okay, maybe not my best plan. No one would ever understand the rush I receive when causing chaos. But, I did it! The thought that I was not unlike Elizabeth, brought a smile to my face. She was setting new standards for me to keep up with. I would do a few favors for her. Then she would cover for me when I needed to slip out! We were going to be two peas in a pod! Heavenly havoc!

CHAPTER FOUR

Elizabeth

The sound of birds chirping outside my opened windows awoke me. Staring at the ceiling, I pondered my own memories of yesterday and where I was now. I turned to see if Tilly was awake only to find her bed unmade and empty with all of her luggage strung around the room. By the looks of our room, I must have been dead to the world and freight train Tilly. On the night stand beside me, I noticed a book, which Tilly referred to as a chapter. It appeared Tilly had already left, and as she promised, had checked out the chapter for me. With the chapter in my hand, I propped up the pillows and fluffed up the blankets around me. I was prepared to sit and read. I found the whole thing odd; to be reading about a life you once lived and could not remember.

The glossy, white cover had nothing on it except the black printed name, Elizabeth Marie Cantrell. I opened the chapter and the first page was dedicated only to a blank, black line with the word Keeper printed underneath leaving me to believe the Keeper's name was missing. The next page was the same with one black line containing a long number, with the words Keeper Identification Number printed underneath. I assumed this number identified my Keeper that guided me during my earth life. I turned the page anticipating my tale. It was blank with nothing to read. So was the next page and the page after that. The whole chapter was empty.

I had let myself prematurely get excited when I saw the chapter setting on the night stand. I didn't know what I really presumed to find out. Who was I and what had my previous life been about? The blank pages were a disappointment. I would be able to ask my family questions over the holiday. As I placed the chapter back on the night stand, I wondered who the Keeper Identification Number belonged too. It was the only clue to my past.

The agony of knowing nothing about myself resettled in my gut. I slowly crawled out of bed knowing I must now figure out what to do about my lack of luggage. Standing, I noticed Tilly had left on the trunk at the foot of my bed, a change of clothes. I held them up finding them more modest than I had expected. I felt extremely thankful for her gesture. Tilly must have redeeming qualities underneath the ruff exterior. I grabbed my watch and locket carelessly, snagging my locket on the edge of the night stand. I stopped to visually examine it. It was surely broken. To my surprise, the locket was fine but had opened. Why had I not thought of opening the locket?

On the inside cover the initials E. M. K. were engraved. A picture was in the other half and I recognized a much younger version of myself staring up at me along with those I assumed were my family. My father was tall with dark, short brown hair. He had sharp facial features but his smile seemed warm and friendly. He stood behind me and my mother with one hand on my shoulder and the other around the back of my mother whom appeared to be very happy. She looked as if the photo was taken mid laugh and I felt I could almost hear it. My mother resembled me with a round face, deep brown eyes, and deep brown hair which looked almost black against the white backdrop of the photo. I was seated and holding a little girl. My sister? I assumed. The girl on my lap did not appear to be as happy as the rest. She resembled my father with the same sharp features, but her eyes looked black and distant. I had the most alarming sensation of animosity towards her. I looked at the faces of my parents and their happy faces looked so familiar. Sudden warmth and emotion overtook my eyes. I snapped the locket closed.

It was time to explore this new world. After dressing, I exited the room and walked down the hallway. It was eerily empty. I began to wonder where my newly discovered family was. Since opening the locket, my excitement had been rising. I now had a picture of my family in my mind. Once down the stairs, I found myself watching Professor Zirak entering the door. He grinned at me, "Good morning Miss Cantrell! Please come into my office. I need to speak with you."

I followed him into his office. The view from the inside was much different from the hall. From the hall your eyes are drawn to the top of his desk which a messy assortment of papers littered. I expected the rest of the room to be the same chaotic mess. To my surprise, I found it to be curiously all in order. The rooms lighting caused me to feel warm and comfortable. He motioned for me to sit down. Once he was seated across from me he said, "I was just visiting with Professor Presnell and she has informed me you have no family coming."

I felt as if my heart sank all the way to my feet, "No family coming, why?"

He leaned back in his chair, "I am sorry. I only know they are not coming. I can see you are disappointed."

"Yeah," is all I could get out as I stared out his window, biting my lip, and holding back the urge to cry.

Professor Zirak broke the awkward silence, "Let me suggest you spend this free time getting to know your new surroundings."

I turned to glare at him. "Great." My only desire was to see the people in the locket.

Professor Zirak continued, "Next week, you will begin your studies on Transportation Law. It is my task to ensure each trainee in my department has success. I would like to assign you fifty questions! Answer these over the next week in preparation for the class."

I instantly wondered if he was trying to fill my time! Did he know how blank my test was? The professor dug beneath a pile of papers and retrieved an old, ragged looking book. He pushed it across the desk towards me. I took the book and started to stand. The professor waved for me to sit back down which I reluctantly did. "I have also been informed you have no luggage, meaning you have no uniforms. I have arranged for the uniform shop to measure you this week and deliver your uniforms the day before class starts."

Politely I said, "Okay, thank you!" I quickly stood and moved towards the door being careful not to make eye contact with the professor.

"Oh, one more thing Miss Cantrell." I stopped and stiffened my neck and back before turning to look at him. He extended his hand, "This letter came for you."

I took the letter and left the room before he could drop another emotional bombshell. Once beyond his view, I leaned against the wall and could feel a tear rolling down my face. My left hand turned into a fist and I banged it against the wall on which I was leaning. Why didn't my family come for me?

Why had they not bothered to ensure I had uniforms? Why had they abandoned me? Mary Farris came to mind. I would ask her.

I stomped up the stairs, tossed the book on my bed, and plopped into the warm chair under the window. The envelope in my hand did indeed have my name on the outside. Upon opening it, I discovered Mary Farris was having a dinner party and had invited me to come to dinner. This lifted my spirits and I sat enjoying the sun as it heated the room. This invitation was perfect! It would allow me the opportunity to ask the questions in my mind. However, I had a few problems to work out before I could go.

To begin, what was I to wear? Then I spied my room was full of luggage. Tilly seemed like the type of person who would appreciate all the rules I was about to break! Borrowing another outfit of hers would not offend her! She probably would feel honored! Searching through several bags I found myself in disbelief. Did Tilly think she would be able to wear any of these items while in training? Her luggage contained many short skirts, way too revealing shirts, and faded jeans which all seemed to be worn with holes. One monstrous suitcase held only high-heeled shoes in a variety of colors and one contained nothing but make-up and nail polish. With relief, I finally found a suitable green dress with flowers embroidered along the bottom of the skirt which was scrunched up and shoved into the outside compartment of the smallest suitcase. It looked nothing like anything else she owned. It was definitely not Tilly's style. She obviously hated it due to its wrinkled, wadded, and pushed condition.

I then needed a plan to handle Professor Zirak's rule to be in Keeper House before dark. I needed someone or something to sleep in my bed for lights out, just in case the professor decided to check. I turned to my bed and flung off all of the fluffy bedding onto the floor. It landed with a thud! The transportation book landed beside my bed. What a dreaded assignment to read! I kicked it under the bed. All of the clothes I had dug out of Tilly's luggage, I haphazardly piled onto my bed and then patted them until it resembled someone lying in the bed. I placed the fluffy, dusty rose bedding over it. I sat on Tilly's bed marveling at my work. Not bad!

I pondered my greatest obstacle to attending the dinner party. How did the hospital door open? I had no answer. It reminded me of a jig saw puzzle. I would keep calm and figure it out.

Leaving Keeper House, I found myself enjoying the warm corridor leading to the pathway. The boy with spiky hair from the hospital waiting room was reading a paper and walking towards me. He brushed my shoulder as he passed and I could smell the oddest, musky cologne. I took a deep breath with my eyes closing. Intoxicating! I wanted to turn, follow him, and keep sniffing the delight.

I could no longer hear the clicking of his hard soled shoes against the marble floor. I turned seeing he had paused and was looking at me. When our eyes met, he seemed frantic to get out of my sight and quickly walked away. His pace got faster as he disappeared into the Department of Administration archway. He seemed odd and in a hurry. Something inside me had stirred when I inhaled his bizarre but familiar scent. I pondered his uniqueness and mystery. Why was he avoiding me?

I could hear the beating of my heart pounding in my ears as I reached the foyer knowing that going to the Hospital would not be acceptable to the professors. I was standing at the marvelous golden door leading me into the hospital corridor. I straightened the borrowed green dress and closed my eyes. I thought to myself, am I really doing this? I whispered, "Yes." I opened my eyes, and glanced around one last time. I relaxed and exhaled. I was alone in the foyer! I waved the back of my hand in front of the symbol. Nothing! Now, clearly standing in front of the symbol, I could see it was a tree in which the ends of the branches were hands all arranged in different visual sign patterns which had no meaning to me.

Suddenly without warning, noises pierced the silence. I heard voices as someone stopped short of coming out of Professor Presnell's office to finish their conversation. Waving more frantically as my heart accelerated to the point I was sure anyone standing near me could hear it, I tried it again. When my watch waved in-front of the door, to my surprise, the door opened. I quickly moved through into the hallway and shut the door behind me quickly and quietly. I placed my hand across my chest and exhaled the breath I had been holding. That was close!

I was now facing the plain, wooden door at the other end of the hallway. It seemed so inviting and familiar. A group rounded the corner from the hospital corridor I watched as the merrily chatting group happily went through the door. I felt as if I understood their giddiness, as if I understood what was on the other side of the door. This just strengthened my resolve to ask Mrs.

Farris the questions burning in my mind.

The long corridor was filled with people waiting on benches, offices filled with men in white suits, and the single person who sat across from them. I sat down on the last bench feeling the warmth from the lighting and watched as many happy people rounded the corner all seeming to feel the same contagious excitement I seemed to have. The anticipation of what mysteries existed behind the door consumed me.

While I fidgeted, I began to believe I had been forgotten by Mrs. Farris. Finally she came around the corner giving me a huge grin stating, "I hoped you would accept my invitation." She leaned over and hugged me. I instantly had a very unpleasant feeling while wrapped in Mrs. Farris's arms. My gut screamed for me to excuse myself from her presence as my skin crawled. To my relief, our hug was brief and Mrs. Farris asked, "Shall we go?" Ignoring my internal feelings, I warily answered, "Yes." I arose and followed her to the wooden door.

I waved my watch in-front of it and it zapped me! I jerked my hand back quickly and found myself rubbing the burning sting with my other hand. Mrs. Farris looked curiously at me with a slight smirk, "You are a keeper! Your watch doesn't work on this door." She pushed past me and proceeded to wave her own watch in front of the door with it opening. The moment had come. What was beyond the door? I closed my eyes, inhaled a deep breath, and stepped through the door feeling a sensation of truly going home.

My eyes opened and to my disbelief. I was standing on a large, dingy subway platform. Overhead, a large round tunnel loomed covered in white tile, dim lighting, and huge banners hanging from the ceiling stating Hospital Station. Concrete benches lined the walls and I could see no exit from this station other than the door we had just come through. This drafty platform was not what I had envisioned. A bit of disappointment gripped me.

Mrs. Farris and I made our way to separate concrete benches because there were no seats together. I enjoyed sitting, watching the crowd, and not even the coldness of the benches could stiffen my delight. Unlike those I had encountered in the Hall of Knowledge, no one here seemed to be dressed strangely and they were all enjoying the company of those they were with. Even though the platform was not what I had expected, I still felt a since of home. I could now see the round lights besides the rail flashing and in the distance the light of the silver subway train. Mrs. Farris was now coming towards me. I felt the swish of the wind off the train, "Come! We are going to Stonehenge Station."

Mrs. Farris entered the door of the train first. I watched curiously as she stopped and said into the air, "Stonehenge Station." She disappeared into the subway car. The person beside me stepped through the door, stopped, stated their destination station, and passed into the car. I felt the person behind me nudge me forward. Once in the door, I tried to continue to walk further into the car, but felt an invisible force stop me. I spoke as I had seen those before me do, "Stonehenge Station." The feeling of the barrier was removed and I continued into the crowded, noisy train and sat a few seats behind Mrs. Farris. The train filled quickly and the doors closed.

I sat next to the window. I assumed a child was seated behind me as I could feel their foot kicking the back of my seat. As the train began to move, I expected to see the different stations as we went along but found when the train moved all I saw was blinding, bright lights streaming outside the window. An abrupt stop caught me off guard. Everyone stood and I wondered what was going on. I looked around and no one else seemed alarmed. The child behind me looked up and smiled at me. Everything appeared to be fine.

I noticed Mrs. Farris was making her way to the door and got off when the doors opened. I followed quickly in pursuit, making my way to the open door. I watched as a man who stepped through the door ahead of me seemed to disappear into thin air once through the door. I paused and thought to myself, where did he go? I could see Mrs. Farris waving at me to come through the door and feel those behind me slightly pushing me towards the door. So, I stepped out. Although the train I had just exited was full of people, when I looked back it appeared empty. I was horrified, what had happened to all of the other passengers?

Mrs. Farris was now standing beside me and obviously could see the horror on my face. She put a hand on my shoulder. I asked, "Mrs. Farris, what happened to everyone else on the train?"

"Elizabeth, when you enter the train you state your destination. Everyone states a different destination and everyone gets off the train in one stop. Each person steps off to their own destination."

I thought a moment, "So, unless they were coming here, we would see them disappear as they stepped off the train or no longer see them after we step off the train ourselves."

Mrs. Farris answered me, "Exactly."

A since of relief overtook me. As I began to look around I thought the Stonehenge Station appeared to be newer and better maintained than the Hospital Station. It was lit by natural light that came through the glass station roof and hanging from the glass roof were pale green banners with Stonehenge Station embroidered on them. The tunnel itself seemed to be circular and made of large, polished stone blocks below the glass roof. The platform I was walking across was a darker version of the stone blocks. I passed wooden benches all with adjacent stone planters filled with vibrant flowers and vines. The station was not full of people. Just a few individuals were passing through and it seemed very quiet and formal.

Another subway train had arrived on the opposite platform. We made our way to the staircase leading out of the subway. I could hear someone calling, "Mrs. Farris." As we both turned, a very tall, slender lady approached us. Mrs. Farris turned away from me and clearly did not want to introduce me to her. They began to talk with their backs to me, ignoring me. I felt offended but followed them up the staircase disappointed I did not have the full attention of Mrs. Farris. I needed to find time to ask her the questions that were burning in my mind.

CHAPTER FIVE

Elizabeth

I felt highly irritated about spending what was left of the afternoon sitting watching Mrs. Farris's neighbors working in their gardens out her living room window. I couldn't help notice odd things about the houses and people on this street. In every yard a person was gardening and attending to the already immaculate yards that were filled with yard ornaments, flower beds, and manicured lawns. I believed the man across the street was measuring the length of his grass with a ruler and cutting shreds of grass with the yard shears in his hands. Since stepping through the door of this house, I hadn't seen Mrs. Farris. I could think of better ways to spend this beautiful afternoon. Out of boredom, I began to form an opinion about her house. It was cold and stiff reminding me of the hospital environment.

The glass of the french doors of an adjacent room was frosted allowing no vision into the room. I felt intrigued by the closed off room. A surge of adrenaline and curiosity filled my body. I tiptoed quietly over to explore it. Turning the knob and pushing the door open quietly, I stepped inside. I found it to be a musty, smelly study. Dark paneling covered the ceiling and massive book cases filled with a wide variety of books covered the walls. The strangest part was there were no windows. Who would want a room with no windows? The furniture in this room was all dark upholstered. The room was a stark contrast to the white glazed furniture in the other rooms. A wooden desk set in the middle of the room with a well used chair pushed under it. The flooring was dingy looking brown carpet. I was certain Mrs. Farris wouldn't tolerate such a pit and had not put her touch on it! This room was not airy like the other rooms. It must be her husband's man cave I told myself.

I thumbed through the books, choosing a book labeled Art History. It was incredibly heavy for such a small book and I struggled to lift and carry it across the room. I found I was out of breath moving it the short distance to place it on top of the desk. Opening the book in the middle, I began to turn pages and soon realized the more pages I turned, the more appeared. It was as if there was an invisible rolodex containing thousands of pages inside this one book which seemed to have only a couple hundred pages showing at one time. I continued to turn the pages hoping to find the last page. I was surprised to see words continuing to appear on the last page before my eyes as though they were being typed as I read.

The door of the study opened. A round, gray haired man entered and appeared startled to find an individual in his study. As he limped on a cane towards the desk, he inquired, "Miss Cantrell, are you enjoying my history books?"

I acknowledged him with a nod of my head as I closed the book. I attempted and struggled to place the heavy book back onto the shelf quickly.

"I am Wendell Farris and you have wandered into my library," Mr. Farris stated.

"So sorry! I did not mean to intrude," I answered. I shouldn't have stepped one foot into this room which was so clearly shut off. I shuffled from one foot to another in embarrassment. When my guilty eyes flickered to him, he gave me a fatherly grin. I was caught with my hand in the cookie jar.

"No, you are more than welcome to read my books." He stated looking pleased. "I was actually interested in who Mary brought home. I saw you coming up the street. She has not brought anyone home in a long time. So, do you like them? The books?"

I answered, "Oh, Yes, they're very fascinating. Can you tell me about the new writing on the last page? How is someone doing that?"

"Miss Cantrell, you must know there is current history still being written on the Earth Plane. The books are updating themselves. I am very blessed to have such a rare, up to date, extensive collection of works." He smiled and lovingly stroked a row of book jackets. "This is actually my great love, knowledge. Mary is gracious to let me have this room all to myself. She is the one who likes gardening. No one here ever seems to be interested in my books."

"Mr. Farris, you said they are rare. How did you manage to acquire so many?" I inquired.

A quiet pause and then he stated, "That is a very long story. I'll just say they were a gift from a great man." I felt he seemed eager to talk about his books when he continued, "Is there anything else you would like to know about them?" I also felt he was clinging to the opportunity to demonstrate his great knowledge of history. I remembered the face which graced the cover of the Art History book. I asked, "Who is the man in the large photo on the front of the art book I was scanning? I mean, why him on the jacket?"

"Well, he was extremely popular after his death as an artist. On the Earth Plane his paintings are worth a lot of money." He grinned and shook his head. "We all have a laugh about it! People on the Earth Plane…"

"Humlings?" I interjected kind of proud I remembered the term.

"Yes! Humlings waste so much money on them! Leo, the artist is Home and now paints and shares freely with anyone who would like one!" Mr. Farris chuckled. I smiled and thought he seemed genuine and warm hearted. His amusement was infectious.

A very loud buzzing bell sounded through out the whole house. "I think we had better go see who has arrived. Shall we?" Said Mr. Farris chuckling and pointing the way.

As we entered a room across the hall, I could see it was filling with other guests.

The other guests were older and ignored my attempts at conversation. I tried to mingle from group to group with hardly anyone acknowledging my existence. At a loss for understanding, I settled to listen to a group of ladies talking about gardening. To my relief, I was rescued and ushered away from the trio by Mrs. Farris.

"Elizabeth, I have someone I would like you to meet," said Mrs. Farris with a devious smirk on her face. When we stopped, I was instantly aware of butterflies fluttering in my stomach. I stood awestruck! It was the young man with spiky hair from the hospital wing. I cringed when I remembered in horror how he had distanced himself from me. Instantly my palms started to sweat as I took in a deep breath. His unique smell delighted my senses and his eyes were almost mesmerizing. Even though I could since the intensity behind his eyes as he looked at me, he did not appear to share my feelings. He stood frozen. He looked as if he really wanted to run but was trapped by Mrs. Farris. He crossed his arms and nervously glanced back and forth between Mrs. Farris and myself. She seemed to have a satisfied look on her face saying, "Dustin, I would like you to meet Elizabeth Cantrell."

I extended my hand to shake his. He didn't reciprocate. His arms continued to be crossed across his chest with his body tensing at the thought of shaking my hand. The realization that he was not going to return my greeting, I lowered my hand half embarrassed. Dreamy as he was, he was also aloof and rude. My face was blushing. I looked fixedly at him as the silence became more awkward. Mrs. Farris responded, "Elizabeth, this is Dustin."

He nodded his head looking like the cat that ate the canary and said, "Elizabeth, sorry about not shaking your hand. I just don't like to shake hands. That's all." His stance had not changed. His voice seemed so familiar to me. I did not like the sudden attraction and excitement I felt concerning him! He definitely had no like attraction for me. However, eerie as it seemed, I could hear his thoughts screaming. He wanted to run and get as far away from me as possible. I was embarrassed.

"Dinner is about to start. I wanted to introduce the two of you since you will be seated across from each other at the table," explained Mrs. Farris as her eyes flickered at Dustin.

He rolled his eyebrows and bit his lip. Dustin and Mrs. Farris glared at each other. "Shall we then," stated Dustin as he lowered his arm from the tight fold across his chest and held it out in the direction of the dining table while never removing his eyes from Mrs. Farris. I could swear her face reacted as if Dustin said or did something that satisfied her.

I nodded. Then I moved towards the table without him acknowledging me. My seating place card loomed directly across from Dustin. I tried very hard to ignore him through dinner. I found myself unable to function normally. I clanged my silverware, dripped soup over my potatoes, and dropped my napkin. He made me jittery. However, his presence was electrifying. I couldn't help but think that I was a moth being drawn to his flame. He did not eat a single bite and looked ghastly ill in my opinion. I was caught off guard when I heard his voice …

"You know I am only here because Mom made me come. I will never do what you have requested," Dustin stated to Mrs. Farris.

I glanced up and could see him intently, darkly staring at Mrs. Farris. He leaned forward, dropping his fork loudly onto his plate. Startled, the other guests looked at him. He didn't seem to notice. His eyes never left Mrs. Farris.

"Don't call her that!" Growled Dustin's voice. "Her name is no longer Kaswell or…

He was growling these words to her but his mouth made no movement. I looked around the table and all the others had gone back to merrily chatting about gardening and eating. No one else had heard the conversation. Who was Kaswell? What was this conversation about? Why could I hear his thoughts?

"Well of course she's not the normal return!" Replied Dustin in an exasperated tone.

I continued to watch as their explosive facial expressions changed with each reply. They seemed to be holding a conversation the rest could not hear. My hearing the conversation was the exception. Mrs. Farris was clearly enjoying their debate. Dustin seemed to be the opposite.

"My dear aunt, you do not know what you think you do!" Said Dustin with tone of certainty in his voice. "You must leave this alone!"

Her unspoken and unheard response made his lips clench tightly and his jaw set intently. The stare from Dustin intensified and turned dark and menacing towards Mrs. Farris. His energy washed over my body like a shock wave. He was strong, protective, and apparently brutal.

"Maybe I should tell… Kaswell about your little proposal for me," Dustin threatened.

Dustin bit his lip. Mrs. Farris smirked. I couldn't hear her thoughts, only Dustin's. His hands suddenly balled into fists. He slammed them on either side of his plate. Everyone once again looked at him. As before, neither acknowledged anyone else at the table. Their eyes were locked on each other.

"I am fully aware I have more to loose than you!" Dustin screamed!

My eyes caught his. He swiftly looked away, threw his napkin upon his plate, and excused himself from the table silently. Mrs. Farris gave him a little wave goodbye with a victorious look on her face. It was at this moment, I realized I had indeed heard half of a conversation between them in my head. How did I do that? The other guests only heard the clink form the loudly dropped fork and Dustin's fists thumping the table. I don't even think they felt his electric energy.

Sitting across from his empty chair made me uncomfortable. My stomach was in knots and my food no longer appealed to me. I pushed the food around on my plate. Eyeing the empty chair, I thought about the conversation and it led me to the conclusion that Mrs. Farris had invited me to cause Dustin anguish. They seemed to have known me long before this dinner party. Mrs. Farris was using their shared knowledge to compel Dustin do her bidding.

The rest of dinner I was lost in my thoughts. Dustin spoke of the name Kaslow. I wondered who that was. The name intrigued me. The dinner party altercation sparked my interest. What did Mrs. Farris know about me? What was Dustin's hang up with Mrs. Farris? More importantly, why did Dustin find me so repulsive?

CHAPTER SIX

Elizabeth

I was relieved to escape from my exhausting adventure with Mrs. Farris beyond the plain, wooden door. I spent the majority of the following week relaxing in my room and exploring the hall and grounds. I had decided to disassociate myself with Mrs. Farris feeling she was not trustworthy. I felt darkness existed in her personality.

On this morning, I felt as if the plain, wooden door was once again calling me. I had risen early and found it to be quite a task to escape the Hall of Knowledge. Professor Zirak had sought me out to ask if I had any questions about my assignment which I had not begun to complete. The book had hibernated under my bed all week never seeing the light of day. I told the professor I didn't have any questions.

I ran into Dustin who pretended not to know me. A small pang of envy stabbed my stomach. He was holding hands with Tiffany. She was staring at him like a love sick fool. In my opinion, she seemed to be enjoying his company much more than he was enjoying hers. She noticed my glances at them and cuddled up to him putting on a show for me. I assume she was trying to make me jealous. It was working! The two of them embracing and cooing was sickening.

I followed an elderly couple through the plain wooden door and found myself standing on the subway platform wondering where I should go for the day. A place popped into my mind. Today, I should go to Lakeland Station. As I waited for the subway train on the concrete bench, I wondered how I conjured up Lakeland. Where in my mind did it spring up from? I mindlessly followed the crowd towards the train hoping Lakeland was an actual place. Stepping into the subway train doorway, I felt the invisible force before me. I spoke, "Lakeland." The feeling of the invisible barrier was removed and I stumbled towards the center of the car. My doubt had been answered! Lakeland was a destination.

The subway car was crowded, noisy, and a stale aroma filled the air. There were no empty seats so I found myself standing and gripping one of the poles to stabilize myself as the train began to move. The familiar blur of lights out the window was followed by the sudden screeching stop. Everyone immediately stood to make their way to the door. Stepping out onto the Lakeland subway platform, I found myself looking through a plate glass window that ran floor to ceiling all along the outer wall. An amazing crystal blue lake lapped gentle waves where the platform and glass ended. The platform was a sandy mound. The entire station probably would have been very dark if not for the huge glass wall and overhead atrium which let in the natural light. Leading up the gradual sandy slope on either side of the platform were wooden stairs that looked well used. This station had no seating. A worn banner hanging against the wall behind the tracks said, Lakeland Station.

As I made my way up the creaky stairs, I could see that the lake was surrounded by a pathway. To one side I could see grassy gradual slopes leading to the edge of the water. Houses and shops dotted the other side of the path as far as I could see. The lake side was full of geese, ducks, children playing along the edge of the water, and dogs being walked along the path. The houses were all very individual with different paint colors, size, and yards. Unlike Stonehenge, where Mrs. Farris lives, everyone here seemed to have a warm smile. They nodded, waved, or as they passed said, "Hello."

Searching for the center point in the town, I came to a noisy farmers market with several stands containing fruit, vegetables, flowers, and various other items. Walking through the farmers market I noticed a stand selling… Routebegas? Was this spelled correctly? I stood watching a young man step up and help himself to the rounded vegetable. He looked at it puzzled and began questioning the farmer while waving the vegetable around in the air. He stepped back turning it over and over, carefully looking at every aspect of the vegetable as if it were a puzzle.

An older lady pushed her way past me shaking her head and mumbling, "Tourists." She stepped up to the young man, grabbed the vegetable, and slammed it upon a piece of metal on the side of the farmers table. The routebega was cored! In the middle of this core was a thin piece of paper.

The young man thanked the older lady while unfolding the piece of paper which grew with each unfolding. I could now see it was a map! The farmer glared at the older lady. She had ended his enjoyment of the joke of the mysterious 'routebega'! How did a map that big fit into that vegetable?

I noticed I was not the only person interested in viewing this. A young lady standing a few steps away looked to be my age and about my height. She had sandy brown hair, pale, freckled skin, and seemed to be very earthy. When I glanced back at her, she extended her hand, "Hi, I am Emma."

"It is nice to meet you, I'm Elizabeth," I said while shaking her hand.

"I seem to have forgotten my watch today," said Emma, as she held up her empty wrist. "Could you tell me what time it is?"

I held out my wrist and watch to her and mumbled, "I would love too if I knew how to tell time with this watch!" The curious look on Emma's face was visible. I knew I needed to say more quickly so I gave the only explanation which had been given to me, "I recently re-entered. I can't seem to remember how to read it."

"That happens sometimes," said Emma as she waved her hand in a gesture as if to say, no big deal. "A couple of years ago, our neighbor came back and couldn't remember her name for a couple of days."

"Then maybe there is hope for my memory yet," I said as I smiled and continued to hold out my wrist for Emma to read my watch.

She seemed to be intrigued it and looked at it much longer than I felt was necessary. She stated, "My time for shopping has ended. My kid brother wants to take a hike this afternoon." She rolled her eyes and I knew she wasn't looking forward to it. "If you would like to walk with me, I will give you a quick watch reading lesson as we go along."

"I really do need to figure out how to tell time with this monstrosity," I replied. Having no plans, I thought why not go with her and let the day lead where it would. So, I walked with her on the pathway offering to carry one of her two shopping bags for her which she gladly handed over.

"Your watch is very ornate," Emma began. "The first ring of your watch is numbered 1-144 and keeps track of time on the Earth Plane, with each number representing one hour.

I peered at the watch and listened. "The second ring of your watch is numbered 1-24 and keeps track of our time here at Home," continued Emma.

My thoughts spilled out my mouth, "So, for every one hour of Home time here is…"

"Six hours of Earth Plane time," Emma finished my thought. "Or simplified, every minute of our time is six minutes of Earth Plane time," stated Emma. I watched as she looked like she had more to say. She hesitated and began to wrap the end of her long hair around her fingers.

"Yes, I get it." I stated excitedly. "It's an equation watch. But what does the third ring project?"

She tentatively smiled, "What surprises me about your watch is how rare it is."

"Rare," I repeated.

"Oh yes, very rare," said Emma as she shrugged. "A watch like yours is generally a Keeper's watch."

"A Keeper's watch?" I repeated. I felt I needed to be very careful not to reveal my secret for some reason.

"Definitely, because of the third ring," said Emma. "Only Keepers worry about keeping the time of the Dwellers."

I placed my hand over my eyes, "My memory must be really fogged." My hand slid up across my brow and pushed my hair back off my forehead. I shook my head, "Who are the Dwellers?"

"They are the people beyond the Black Arch… you know, the dark souls," whispered Emma. I thought this topic made her act and look a little anxious. "I don't really like to focus my energy or thoughts on them." A silence fell between us as we continued to walk.

Emma leaned over whispering, "Humlings don't know a lot about Dweller life and time. I believe the third ring equates three hours of Home time to one hour of Dweller time. Their time is faster."

"Less time for them to plan," I automatically said as my thoughts spilled out my mouth. Looking at the watch the initials, E.H.D., now made since. Earth Plane, Home, Dweller.

I once again could tell she had more to say. She nervously wrapped her long hair around her fingers in thought, "My mom once had a friend who had a watch like yours. It was given to her by a Keeper. I am sure that yours too was given to you or someone in your family by a Keeper."

"I am sure you are right," I said.

"Here we are," said Emma. We were standing in front of a small, fenced, white one story home. A porch rambled along the front. To the right side of it, a swing hung with two cats sleeping on its slanted seats. The grass in the yard was splotchy and overgrown in places with wild flowers cropping up. Two mature trees were filled with squirrels playing about the trunk and limbs. Birds on branches were chirping while the leaves about them were gently waving their hands in the breeze. A cracked concrete sidewalk led from the porch to the wooden fence. Two small dogs scampered about the enclosure wagging their tails.

As we moved through the gate, two boys appeared on the porch. The older of the two seemed to be a little put out. With his arms firmly folded across his chest and a stout stern voice said, "Emma, where have you been? I was beginning to get worried."

"I'm sorry Anthony," Emma said in a sincere manner. "I forgot my watch and lost track of time. When I realized how late it was, I came right home." His gaze then turned towards me. Emma continued, "This is Elizabeth. I met her at the Routebega stand."

This seemed to make them both faintly chuckle. He uncrossed his arms. "Hello, Elizabeth. It is nice to meet you!" He moved down the sidewalk to extend his hand. "I'm Anthony."

"Nice to meet you too," I said while shaking his hand. He was no taller than me with dark black hair. He was short for a boy I thought to myself! He had vibrant hazel eyes, very warm hands, and displayed a tan muscular build in his muscle shirt.

"And this is Daniel," Emma said as she pulled her little brother from behind Anthony. Daniel was a smaller version of Anthony with dark hair and the same vibrant hazel eyes. His one exception was his chubby cheeks freckles, and dimples.

"Hi! Anthony promised to take me for a hike this afternoon. Want to come?" Said Daniel with a child's smile pulling on Anthony's shirt tail.

Emma sighed, "I really hoped you would forget."

Anthony responded in a taunting manner, "We could always go to Hospitality Row in The City for dinner!" His smile was devious as he turned to me and explained, "My favorite place to eat at Home."

"If that is a dig about my cooking," barked Emma as she squinted at him. "You will be cooking yourself."

Anthony rolled his eyes at Emma's last comment. She continued, turning her attention back to me, "We would love to have you join us on our hike. However, won't you need to ask your parent's permission?"

"Oh, of course, ask my parents," I stated actually feeling a little disappointed and caught off guard. I wrestled the pros and cons of going quickly in my head. My mind was made up in an instant. The pros of my mind quickly told me this was living the adventure. After all, I was dead already, what could happen? What parents did I have to care? I crossed my fingers behind my back. "Oh yes! I don't think my parents would mind as long as I'm back by nightfall." I uncrossed my fingers for the lie I had just told.

"Maybe you can ride one-way and take the subway back," Anthony responded.

"Great," I stated. "Wait, ride? I thought we were going hiking?"

Emma motioned for me to give her the shopping bag as Anthony waived for me to follow him with a grin that filled his whole face. I followed him around to the back of the house where I saw a white dune buggy with four seats parked on a path that wound through the forest behind their home.

"What do you think?" Anthony questioned in a playful manner. "Isn't she a dream?"

"Wow, she is really something," I said. My hand traced its body as I walked around it. The first type of automobile I had seen at Home.

Anthony followed close behind me. "We'll take a short cut through the forest to the Silver Woods Walking Trail," stated Anthony. "If we take the pathway, it's longer and we can't drive the buggy on it."

I looked out into the forest which was silently calling us. The ride would be fun. Anthony held open the door for me. I climbed into the back and strapped myself into the harness that surrounded my bucket seat. Emma took the seat beside me. The boys jumped in the two front bucket seats. The rumble of the starting engine made my blood rush through my veins. I could feel excitement that could be measured by my increased heart beats. Emma leaned over, "Hold on."

We barreled through the forest with the buggy sliding around all of the corners with mud flying out and hitting the bushes and trees surrounding the path corners. It wasn't until we happened upon a low water bridge that I began to feel jittery. The bridge itself looked ancient and dangerous with huge cracks and holes running in the concrete and the missing rubble protruding from the creek bed. It was apparent we would not be able to cross without it crumbling. We stopped. Anthony revved the engine several times giving me an opportunity to ask over the engine noise, "We are not going over the bridge are we?"

Anthony glanced back and looked amused. He returned his gaze forward and glanced at me through the rear view mirror apparently feeling no need to answer. The buggy then advanced towards the steep drop off next to the bridge that led to the water. I braced myself. He wouldn't really drive over this steep drop off, would he? My thoughts were answered when the front tires went over. I instantly grasped the seat in front of me in terror. Then the back tires went over with a jarring swift thump.

Then, all four tires were gripped to the steep drop off and he braked roughly. I braced myself with my feet planted firmly on the back of Daniel's seat. We were planted on the steepest incline. The buggy's nose was almost straight down. If I were not strapped in, I was certain I could stand with my feet on the back of Daniel's seat as if it were the ground. I was grateful the buggy had sturdy roll bars. I was certain at any moment we would just flip right over. My face was flushed and fear gripped me. I then observed Anthony gazing at me through the rear view mirror with a huge grin on his face. Obviously, stopping there was for his benefit. He wanted to view the shock on my face. The expression on his face reminded me of the devious look that graced Tilly's face when I thought she was looking for trouble.

He revved the engine a couple times and then gassed it! We flew down the drop off and into the stream bed. I screeched a blood curdling scream. We glided across the water without my feet even getting wet. The other side sloped up gradually leaving us free to forge ahead following the path. The rest of the ride was enjoyable with the wind blowing through my hair. The buggy ride passed so quickly. Anthony braked and killed the engine. However, I was relieved it was over. Anthony was a dare devil!

I glanced about. We were parked in an open field in the middle of this forest. I could see a singular road entrance and a trail head with a wooden arch stating, Welcome to the Silver Woods Trail. A small sign stating subway stood next to it with an arrow that had lost its tip. "There is a subway stop here?" I asked.

"Oh yes, over the hill. The Silver Woods Trail has its own subway stop," Said Emma. "We are lucky to live in a town that has two subway stops."

"No, we are lucky to have this buggy and not have to walk everywhere!" Corrected Anthony as he handed Emma her backpack. "The escalator to the platform is just over the hill." He passed Daniel his backpack and started walking towards the trail head as he put his on. "If you go on many of these adventures with us Elizabeth, you will need to get a backpack."

"I'll remember that for the next time," I assured him as we entered the trail head which was a well worn dirt path meandering across the forest floor.

"No, if you come again, we will do something girly," Emma said softly and quickly to me under her breath.

"Emma, Dad always said fresh air is good for us," Daniel retorted. He and Anthony then shared a mischievous look.

Emma pointed to the escalator which appeared suddenly. The subway entry was a dark, cave-like pit. A moving stairway disappeared down into its sinkhole like opening. Disembarking passengers coming up just seemed to pop up like an array of summer flowers and entered our path congesting it. Emma took my arm so as not to lose me in the crowd. She reassured me, "The path will branch out a little farther on. Then, we can split off from all this foot traffic!"

"Be sure and keep up," Anthony told me as he placed his hand on Daniel's shoulder to ensure they weren't separated.

This forest was dazzling with its many types of trees, foliage, and natural wild flowers springing up from the ground. The path was climbing a slight incline. Anticipation of the marvelous views at the top seemed to be the shared subject spilling out of the mouths of strangers on the path.

We made our way to the top and stopped at a sign designating a look-out point. The view was breathtaking! We set on huge boulders to rest. Daniel found a group of children playing marbles in the dirt. To my surprise, he pulled out his own marbles and began to play with them. All of his orbs were white, gold, and silver and glistened like stars. What a strange thing to bring on a hike. I then turned my attention to the forest and surroundings. To our right was a huge, transparent dome.

"Emma, what is in the huge enclosure?" I asked as I pointed to the dome.

She lowered her water bottle and looked over, stating, "The keepers."

"Hmm," I sighed as Anthony handed me a water bottle from his bag. "Why is it separate?"

Anthony looked over at me like I had asked a very stupid question. He rolled his eyes up and backwards in response, not saying anything.

"She just re-entered and doesn't have her memory back," Emma replied to Anthony's surprised and annoyed look. "Be patient Anthony! Perhaps we can jog her memory." When she turned her attention back to me she gave me a polite smile which I was certain she meant to be reassuring. She began to twirl her long hair around her fingers as she continued, "This is what we have been told. When our parents were children, the dome didn't exist as it is today. Keeper City existed."

I interrupted, "Keeper City?"

"The Keeper Dome was called Keeper City before the dome was built around it," Anthony responded.

"Anyway," Emma continued. "The Keepers came and went with fewer restrictions using the subway at will. They freely mingled among us and traveled to work."

"Humlings like us were welcome on their turf inside Keeper City," Anthony added with a wag of his index finger pointing towards the dome. "Dad had great memories of visiting the massive, inspiring buildings inside."

Emma gave Anthony a smile. She was obviously appreciating his interest in giving her support to retell a story which made her nervous and appeared to be old news to him. As she turned back to me she continued, "However, the Keepers favorite mode of transportation was their lockets. Simply rubbing their lockets and stating their destination would send them instantly to the destination they stated. The locket is a portal."

"Can you imagine?" Daniel's voice popped up from behind us. "Poof! What a way to travel!"

"Poof!" Repeated Emma with a grin.

All three of them seemed to have the same thought. Anthony repeated the word, "Poof!" He spread his hands across the air in a magical gesture to please Daniel. As Daniel smiled in childlike wonder, he returned to his game of marbles.

I suddenly felt the locket beginning to weigh a ton around my neck as I remembered sitting in the Hospital wing rubbing my locket between my fingers upon arrival to Home.

"The Dwellers, another sect occupying dark land beyond the Black Arch, always wanted to rule the Earth Plane. They see the Keepers as their obstacle in fulfilling their desires," Emma stated as she continued to twirl the end of her hair around her fingers at a more rapid pace.

I was puzzled! Emma had explained earlier that the third ring on my watch kept track of Dweller time. Dwellers were dark souls. Why would I want to keep track of the dark souls and their time? How did this all fit together? I asked, "Dwellers? Explain!"

"You don't remember who the Dwellers are?" Anthony asked astonished at my lack of memory. I shrugged my shoulder as he glanced over at Daniel who was in the shooting position in his game and clearly out of hearing range. Anthony moved to sit on my other side which would allow him to continue to see Daniel but to muffle his voice. Guess it wasn't something for little ears, I thought. He explained in a low voice, "The Earth Plane is where we go to learn lessons to perfect our soul." He held his hands up to gesture everything around us. "Home, or here, is where we Humlings and the dome where Keepers live in the eternal light when we return from the Earth Plane. The Black Arch, or dark land, is where the Dwellers return to live from the Earth Plane. The Dwellers are dark souls who create havoc and spread evil on the Earth Plane and here if given the opportunity."

"Okay… Got it." I stated not wanting to appear stupid in Anthony's eyes.

He continued, "The Dwellers believed they could rule the Earth Plane and here at Home if it weren't for the Keepers."

Emma piped in, "When our parents were children, a number of Keepers disappeared."

"Not just disappeared, "Anthony corrected. "During the event, The Keepers and their lockets vanished! A mode of transportation as well as those Keeper's souls were lost!"

"Souls and a way of life just disappeared?" I questioned in disbelief.

"Yes," Anthony replied. "It took awhile for the Keepers to realize what was happening. It was like a creeping plague that morning. One soul disappeared, then a family, and then a group who worked in the same office."

"How did they figure out it was the Dwellers?" I questioned.

"The Keeper Sentries caught a Dweller who took credit for the act. However, he wouldn't tell how his group succeeded in pulling it off!" Gasped Emma in a nervous shiver. "It shocked all of Home to the core!"

"What happened to the Keepers who disappeared?" I asked as their eyes flickered to each others. There was more to this story! "Did they find them?"

"There are lots of theories, but nothing concrete about the tale," said Anthony as he stared off past the look out towards the dome.

"Can't they track them through the locket portal?" I asked. "Isn't all travel here recorded?"

"From the tale I've heard, they wanted too. However, travel by locket in untraceable," Anthony said. "In fear of further annihilation, Keepers isolated themselves inside that quickly erected dome and destroyed their lockets."

Emma leaned over and whispered, "Since then, the Keepers have been suspicious of us Humlings, suspecting we were allies of the Dwellers. Like any Humling in their right mind would help a Dweller. The event changed Home."

"A Humling?" I started to ask rolling the strange word off my tongue.

"A Humling is a person who lives many lives on the Earth Plane and returns to Home in between," piped up Daniel as he skipped up to get a drink from his water bottle. Daniel had an innocence about him with raw child-like wonder seeping out of every pore of his skin. He smiled as he bounded past me and back to his game.

"So, do I have this correct? Keepers never go outside of the Keeper Dome?" I asked to cement how many rules I had broken today in my mind.

"Not normally," said Emma. "I don't think I have ever met one."

Well, she had met one she just didn't know it. I wondered if the locket around my neck was a Keeper's locket or just some family keepsake. Did it really work? Could I just go 'poof' like a magician?

Daniel wandered back over. The other kids seemed to be gathering their marbles as mothers' voices in the distance were calling their names. Daniel joined us and plopped down on the rock between Anthony and myself and pulled his legs up beneath him. "The look out sure reminds me of Mom. I miss her!" It was easy to listen to him and not remember he was a child. He had an old soul quality to his being. An aura of light emanated from him.

"We share your thoughts, Buddy," said Anthony rubbing Daniel's hair wildly and then putting his arm around Daniel's shoulder. "This was her favorite spot."

"Emma, if you don't mind me asking, where is your parents?" I asked.

"They are on a self-improvement sabbatical. Both have just started a life on the Earth Plane," sighed Emma. "Anthony and I were left here to watch and care for Daniel. We will join them later on the Earth Plane after Daniel has finished his extensive training."

"How long will that take?" I asked.

"Too long!" Stated Anthony. "I just want to return there quickly so I can enjoy some real food!"

"Honestly Anthony, all you think about is food! All that eating you do down there, it's distasteful and disgraceful," responded Emma pretending to gag and cough.

"It is not distasteful," said Anthony as he turned to look at me. He whispered, "I always write into my chart to be a competitive eater! I love earth's coconut crème pies!"

"It's not pies and cakes. It is eating innocent animals I'm referring too," frowned Emma.

"Stuff it Emma," retorted Anthony. "The food chain is how the Earth Plane is set up to feed its inhabitants. It is your choice to be a vegetarian." He looked at my gapping mouth and seemed to think perhaps he had said too much and shook his head. He rolled his eyes with a retort, "Girls!"

Daniel seemed quick to bring back the subject of his choice, "I am just glad Mom and Dad let us stay by ourselves. No baby-sitters this time!"

"Yeah, Mom wanted us to stay with our aunt," added Anthony. "This time we asserted ourselves and insisted we were old enough to take care of ourselves and Daniel."

"Do you worry about them while they are on the Earth Plane?" I asked out of curiosity.

"No." Answered Anthony. "They were assigned wise Keepers to watch over them and their charts were full of great learning opportunities."

"Did you meet the Keepers?" I asked.

"We didn't, but Mom and Dad did," Emma replied. "You always get to meet your Keepers before you go."

"They always help you with your chart," Anthony added. "What about your parents?"

"Yeah, just like yours! There off and gone too. Poof!" I replied while I waved my hands mimicking their earlier expression. They grinned. I was not sure mine were missing for the same reason theirs was or even why they were.

"Well, we all get several opportunities to learn on the Earth Plane. It's a good thing!" Anthony stated. "This is their free time from us. I have used my space from them wisely! Aren't you enjoying your bit of freedom from your parents?"

"Yeah," I replied simply. I was relieved they seemed to think my parents were on the Earth Plane. I did not have to tell them I had no idea where they were or who they were.

Anthony stood up and slipped his backpack on. Emma and Daniel followed suit. "You know, I think we had better head back down the mountain."

"No, I want to go to the swinging bridge before we go back down," Daniel whined.

"Go on, I can make my way back down," I said trying to sound reassuring.

"I'll go with you!" Emma chimed in secretly wishing to ditch her brothers.

"Emma, I can't let you go down on your own," Anthony stated. "We gave Mom an oath to always travel together." For the first time today he seemed to show a maturity I had not yet seen.

"There is a group going down now," I said as I pointed. "I will walk with them."

One family who introduced themselves as the McErens were turning to trek back down the incline. Their children had played marbles with Daniel. I promised Anthony to stay with them until I reached the subway stop. I turned and waved goodbye as I descended the path accompanying this family.

The new friends I just left behind... Emma, Anthony, and Daniel made me feel peaceful. There was a sense of familiarity as if I had known them for an eternity. They had listened intently sitting on the boulders above and listened to me tell of my lonely holiday and my upcoming classes. Meeting them filled a void in my memory loss existence. They seemed tuned in to me on a level that even I didn't know. They invited me back to stay with them the next time I was having a holiday!

Halfway down the hill my fingers went to the locket. The possibility of going poof was on my mind. If I rubbed it, would I end up at the destination of my choice? Intriguing! I didn't have the nerves to test it, so I let the locket fall back to my skin. I would ride the subway back. A bit of sadness gripped me. I felt at ease in Lakeland. This was the home I had envisioned beyond the plain wooden door. It was a home with friendly people set within a peaceful community. I really did not want to return to Keeper House where everything seemed so unfamiliar, unfriendly, and everyone seeming to have a hidden agenda.

Arriving back to my dorm room, I could hardly wait to crawl in my bed and rest my weary legs. A charlie horse was annoying one of my legs. Too much walking! As I reached to pull the dusty rose comforter away from my pillow, something fell onto the floor of my room. I could see it was a beige envelope. I bent down to retrieve it. Scrolled across the envelope was my name in gold lettering. I propped my pillows against my head board and sat down to open it. I slid out the crisp, plain paper which wrapped a smaller piece of yellowed paper. The yellowed paper appeared to be a journal entry?

Journal Entry #12

Today I officially finished my training and I am a guard, one of the elite! I haven't been assigned anyone to guard yet. Deward is now my boss and assures me I will one day guard someone important. Geren seems oddly proud of me today as he welcomed me as an official member of Venema House.

I remember when he came for me as a small child. I was seated, alone, in a hospital and was very cold. He came to sit next to me and explained that he was there to take me home. He placed a large locket around my neck. I remember how heavy it seemed then, but I have now grown into it.

My first memories upon arrival to Venema House are of the family that I am now apart of. Deward and Piper, his wife, placed me in the guard quarters with Geren and Inge until I was old enough to start my training. Still to this day, I am surprised Geren and Inge never ended up together with all the time they spend together as Deward and Piper's guards. Everyone else always came and went. Tonight I have been given my own living quarters, my own bachelor pad! All the uncertainty about me and my future became a worry of yesterday.

Did the journal entry have significance? I turned the plain, yellowed piece of paper over in hopes of finding who had left this for me. It left no hints of its origin. I turned the beige envelope over looking for a return address. There was none! Who sent this? What were they trying to tell me? Who were Deward, Piper, and apparently the unwanted child? Why had they pawned the child off on Geren and Inge, their guards? Someone had gone to a lot of trouble to place it upon my pillow. Hmm, if they were in my room, they must be someone in training or a professor. What pertinence did this entry have concerning me?

CHAPTER SEVEN

Elizabeth

Tilly had nothing on me. I discovered I had traveled and broke just about every rule associated with how and where I could travel as a Keeper. I learned the reason behind the restrictions from Emma. However, the fifty questions from the professor summed it all up for me. I could almost hear Tilly call me a rebel. I didn't want to give her any ideas about repeating my little escapades. I decided to keep my adventures a secret.

Earlier in the day, I handed in my questions to Professor Zirak who seemed pleased as he glanced over my work. I had been measured for my new uniforms and a slew of white blouses, white slacks, and white sweater vests had arrived. I tidied up our room and the mess I had made. Tilly's luggage and contents were all over the room. I borrowed several outfits over the week, hoping she would not mind. I carelessly had them strewn about the room. She did not deserve to come back to such a mess. I had busied myself with chores.

Upon Tilly's arrival back to Keeper House, I found myself overwhelmed by massive boxes containing wooden shelving. It arrived while I was out. She hoped to install it above our beds and along the wall beside my bed. It was all Silver Woods Oak and matched the wooden bed and desk nicely. Tilly felt the trunks at the foot of our beds would not be sufficient to hold all of our clothing. I found it amusing because all I owned was one set of sweats and a couple of school uniforms. She on the other hand, had been on a shopping spree! Bags of clothing from fashionable stores were stacked in the narrow hall outside our door.

Interesting enough, she showed no interest in wanting to install the shelving or unpack her new purchases. Her focus was on my chapter. She was insistent the chapter about me needed to be returned to The Hall of Records. Agreeing with her, we left the room's mess with intent to return the chapter. I was now happily listening to her chatter about her week; the shopping, boys, and how she managed to irritate her parents. As we turned the corner, leaving our Department of Keeper arch, we bumped directly into Tiffany. I was carrying the chapter. It fell to the floor with pages scattering. Tiffany was staring at it and to my horror stated, "My mother said this chapter was stolen from the Hall of Records."

Before anyone could answer, Tilly and Tiffany squared off. Both were scowling, eye to eye. Then their eyes moved to the chapter on the floor. Just as suddenly, they both lunged to the floor with each trying to get their hold on it. Somewhere down the hall someone yelled, "Cat Fight!" Others came running. I held my breath as they tumbled round and round on the floor with the chapter between them. Although I could not tell who had the important chapter, my mind knew it made no difference at this point. We had been caught red-handed. Two of the thrill seeking hallway crowd pulled the two of them apart. Tiffany came up with the chapter spewing, "My lucky day. Not often do I get something so juicy to tell Professor Presnell!"

The only thing that could make this worse seemed to stroll down the hall towards us. Anything but this! Dustin walked swiftly over to Tiffany. He placed his hand across her back, asking her, "Are you okay?"

"I'm fine. No, I'm great!" She screeched. The chapter shook wildly while she grasped it tightly in-front of her body. "I have the proof in my hands."

Dustin placed his hand on the chapter and her hands to steady them. You could see the rage and disgust spread across his face when he read the chapter title. He instantly knew exactly what she meant. He looked from her to me and I noticed his hands were balled into fists while his eyes glared at me.

His mind seemed to say, "Great. Just great."

"Don't get so upset, they didn't hurt me," Tiffany said in response to Dustin's angry demeanor. She placed her free hand of fingers on his chest and walked two of them up his chest as though they were little feet. Smiling up at him she gloated, "I'm going to turn it into Professor Presnell."

Why did I always feel nauseous when she touched him?

"Maybe someone will adopt you, Tilly, after your parents find out and disown you," taunted Janelle over Tiffany's shoulder. Tiffany turned to look at

Janelle and they exchanged a catty, victorious smile. They were powerful and their negative energy seemed to intimidate the crowd like a sweeping mist. You could see why no one ever stood up to them. They both spun on their heels and promptly and quickly strutted off towards Professor Presnell's office. Dustin called, "Tiffany, wait!" She gave him no reply.

"Can I speak to you," Dustin asked as he firmly clutched my arm and started to pull me down the passage. *"I can't believe it, she stole a chapter,"* I heard him *think.* We passed under the Department of Keeper Arch. Dustin appeared to be tense when he growled under his breath, "What were you thinking?"

I pulled my arm from his grip while I glanced back. Tilly looked stunned. Turning back to him, I could not imagine why he cared.

Looking directly into my eyes, he demanded, "Tell me. You were thinking?"

I peered at him and solemnly responded, "Tilly brought me the chapter. I didn't realize it was stolen."

"That story won't get far with Presnell, even if it is true", his mind stated as he slightly *shook his head.* His fists appeared to once again be balled into fists. He paced a moment. Five steps forward and four steps back as though assessing the predicament.

I responded to his unspoken thoughts, "Dustin, I honestly didn't know the chapter was stolen."

"Tilly is trouble," he stated as his skin tone started to flush red from anger.

"And who in their right mind becomes friends with Mathilda, Tilly, Bradford. She is always in trouble." His mind screeched.

I could not help wonder, where was this sudden burst of anger coming from? "You know, I actually like her," I contradicted him, holding my head high.

"Great," he rolled his eyes, whirled around, and walked off. I watched as he struck the wall in passing. As I stood dumbfounded, Tilly rounded the corner. Her eyes were wide with questions. I held up my hand, "Don't ask. We have other concerns to worry about."

Before the day was over, we were all three seated outside Professor Presnell's office and Tiffany continued to taunt us. Tilly and I agreed we would not address any comments Tiffany might make, knowing she would twist anything we said to benefit herself.

"I always new you were a thief," spouted Tiffany with a satisfied look on her face while straightening her posture. She waited, shaking her head from side to side, expecting Tilly to answer in response. "Your poor parents! What do you think they will do when you are kicked out?" She smirked at the lack of response, "I've got my act together. You need to focus on making your life amount too something! Like me!"

I could see the blood rising in Tilly's face. It would not be long before Tilly would give in to her impulse to reciprocate the comments. Our plan was about to falter.

To my relief the door opened "Ladies, please come in," demanded Professor Presnell. Her face held a friendly smile for Tiffany but only a glare for us.

I followed behind Tilly as we entered the professor's office, finding the room to be full of staring faces. Professor Presnell sat across the desk from the two empty chairs we were to occupy. The three chairs that lined the wall were filled as well. Sitting in the first was Professor Zirak. Sitting in the remaining chairs had to be Tilly's parents. Her father appeared tall. He was so skinny I was sure standing he must be a bean pole. Her mother was an older version of Tilly. The same wavy hair, body type, and eye color. Her strong attitude appeared to equal Tilly's demeanor. I could not help but notice and wonder why my parents did not seem to be present.

"Ladies," said Professor Presnell as she slid the chapter across the desk towards us, "I would like to know how you came to have this chapter?"

"I borrowed it from the Hall of Records for Elizabeth to read," Tilly stated proudly as she held her head high. "We were on our way to return it when …"

"Elizabeth, did you ask Tilly to remove the chapter from the Hall of Records?" Interrupted Professor Presnell.

I opened my mouth to answer but did not have a chance too before Tilly again stated, "No, I did It all on my own. Again, we were on our way to return it when…"

"Miss Bradford, I do not care when you planned to return it. Your mother works for the Hall of Records. I believe out of everyone in the room, you should be fully aware you are not to remove chapters from the Hall of Records," said the professor sternly with an undertone of anger.

"Well the book is about Elizabeth!" Tilly barked. She leaned towards the desk challenging Professor Presnell. "What real difference did it make if she read it sitting in the hall or our room? Some rules are meant to be broken!" With a quick lip action she blew a tiny pink gum bubble and just as quickly popped it in front of Professor Presnell's face. It was a sheer act of defiance.

"Mathilda!" Reprimanded Mrs. Bradford as she leaned forward, placing her hand on Tilly's shoulder. Tilly's body tensed under her mother's touch with her energy no longer focusing on the professor. "That is enough, Tilly!" Then turning to Professor Presnell Mrs. Bradford glared and continued, "You can see Miss Cantrell has been a very poor influence on my Mathilda. Miss Cantrell convinced her to borrow the chapter. I must request you no longer allow them to be room mates. That should be a suitable punishment."

"Mom," said Tilly as she stood, stomping her foot on the ground. "I am an adult. You can no longer choose my friends for me." Stomping her foot? Did she realize this action made her look like she was three?

"Have a seat Miss Bradford and spit out the gum!" Commanded Professor Presnell visibly angrily as she pushed those bright red glasses up her nose. The veins in her neck indicated her anger might boil over at any time.

A small knock came from the door behind Professor Zirak's chair which prompted him to get up, move his chair, and open the door. Presnell acknowledged the guest with a look of shock. She tugged at the edge of her red jacket trying to calm her disposition. The older gentlemen standing in the doorway was tall with pale, rosy cheeks and radiated confidence. "Mr. Solliday, to what do we owe this honor?"

"News of this meeting reached me," he stated as he clasped his hands together and slightly bowed. "Thank you for keeping me informed. I hear the misplaced chapter has been found."

"Well, yes." She was visually surprised as to how he would be privy to this information. Hmm... It was obvious, she hadn't sent for him.

"May I join you?" He asked as he glanced my way giving me a warm smile.

"Be my guest," she said as she gestured for him to sit in her chair. "We have the parties responsible here." She pointed to Tilly and I. "They were found in possession of the chapter and Miss Bradford has not denied taking it from the Hall of Records. I was just about to punish…"

Mr. Solliday raised his hand and Professor Presnell instantly fell silent, although she still looked to be steaming with much more to say. I could see her trying much harder to appear professional.

"I would like to hear from Miss Cantrell," he stated as he inquisitively peered at me. "Can you tell me, did you know how Miss Bradford intended to come into possession of the chapter for you to read?"

I glanced at Tilly wondering whether it would be better to tell the truth or to go down in the blazing ball of fire with her. "Miss Cantrell?" Mr. Solliday interrupted my deliberating.

"No sir, I did not," I truthfully stated as I looked down at my feet. Tilly had so bravely stood up to Professor Presnell and her parents. Even in telling the truth, I felt I had left her out on a limb by herself.

"Did you know chapters are not to leave the Hall of Records?" Mr. Solliday questioned.

"No sir." I simply replied as I glanced back at Tilly. She seemed to be confident as ever with my comments not affecting her defiant disposition.

"Very well," he continued. "I do not believe Miss Cantrell had any influence over Miss Bradford."

Everyone could hear the gasp coming from Mrs. Bradford. "With all respect Albert, I just won't except that Mathilda did this without Elizabeth's input."

"Mathilda," said Mr. Bradford as he leaned over Mrs. Bradford's lap towards Tilly. He looked at her eye to eye. "If you are protecting her, you need to say so now."

"Dad, I'm not protecting her, I did it!" Tilly bluntly replied to her father's face. She turned away and casually withdrew another piece of gum from her pocket. She unwrapped it, popped it into her mouth, and instantly started smacking it in her mouth. I wondered if this was a nervous tick.

"Mr. Solliday and Professor Presnell, may I request you no longer allow them to be room mates," said Mrs. Bradford who now looked flushed with outrage.

"Mom, I already told you I am not a child. I should be able to be room mates with whomever I want." Tilly said with her displeasure of authority ringing crystal clear.

"I believe they should be allowed to continue to be room mates," stated Mr. Solliday while Tilly's parents were visibly exasperated, getting angrier by the minute.

"What!" They half yelled and started to interrupt him again.

He held his hand up as if to say, let me finish. "Due to her honesty, I do not believe Miss Bradford had any malicious intent when she simply borrowed the book and gave it to Miss Cantrell for a little light reading." I thought Professor Presnell's legs were going to buckle underneath her. In the heat of the passing moment she had remained standing. "I would like to remind both Miss Bradford and Miss Cantrell, as Miss Bradford has pointed out, they are adults. As adults from this point on, they will suffer the adult consequences for their actions." He looked Mr. and Mrs. Bradford in the eye stating, "I am granting them early adult status." Then he turned to us, "Do you both understand?"

We both nodded and I knew I needed to find my voice. "Thank you, sir," I stated despite the tension in the room. Tilly looked as if she instantly gained a new independence which her parents could do nothing about. I was sure Tilly's parents had just cemented our friendship in Tilly's eyes.

Mr. Solliday was intently looking at me. His eyes appeared to be searching for something and then turned his focus to Professor Presnell. "Professor, is there anything else you would like to add?"

"No, I think you have summed it up for all of us," Professor Presnell stated in a strained voice. Both Professors, Tilly's parents, and Tiffany all seemed to share the same look of anger and bewilderment upon their faces.

"Ladies," said Professor Zirak. "I would like the two of you to go directly to Keeper House and wait for me there."

We both nodded and stood as we left the room. "That sure went well," I sarcastically said as we walked across the foyer. "How much trouble do you think will be awaiting us with Professor Zirak?"

"Did you see the look on my parents face? I got them!" Tilly smirked and ignored my question. "I may be a disappointment to them, but they are to me too!"

For the first time since making her acquaintance, I looked at her and could see through the façade she kept. Somewhere deep inside, Tilly's parents had made her feel imperfect, a disappointment on a psyche level. "Well, I am sure you made them proud when you became a member of Keeper House," I stated to try to remind her about her positive new career.

"Nothing I do ever pleases my parents," retorted Tilly.

"Did they find something wrong with Keeper House?" I asked sensing a weird mood swing in Tilly.

"Well, I had always told them I would work for the Department of Ghosts. They consider the job to be low class. My parents are all about appearances, which is something I find to be nonsense. Keepers are Keepers and everyone, no matter what job they do, has value." She replied as her thoughts seem to trail away. "They react only to shock treatment from me. The look on their faces is the only response I ever get from them. I bite them. They bite me."

I could not imagine having a relationship which seemed so cold and poisonous. But then, I really didn't know what type of relationship I had with my family. I reminded myself again they did not show up to defend me in Professor Presnell's office. Their neglect seemed to form a list which only grew as the days went on.

As we entered the door of Keeper House, Tilly quickly climbed the staircase. You might think something was burning in our room by the way she dashed off! Once on our landing she gave a small knock and disappeared through our door. Someone was in our room! She stood guard as I entered to ensure no one followed me through. I was greeted by the boy with the note, whom I sat next to during our initial exam. What was he doing in our room? He tentatively smiled at me as he stood by the window. Tilly shut and locked the door behind me. His grin turned serious as he asked "Tilly, are you alright?"

"No big deal." Tilly responded looking a little self conscious in his presence. She plopped down on her bed.

"Gum?" He questioned with a got you look. She acknowledged his questions with a slight shrug of her shoulders while her eyes rolled. Her guard was down. He too could see past her tough presence. He leaned over Tilly and swept her hair away from her ear, tickled it with his finger, and began to smile. "I found this and I thought it was yours." He pulled a hoop earring from his pocket. The stud was bent on it.

"Thank you!" She held it up in her hand and stated, "Another victim of the demon in curls."

They both seemed to share a chuckle. She leaned towards him, whispering, "Thanks for the shelves."

He had been my focus, but now glancing around I saw an overwhelming amount of shelving was installed on the walls. Did Tilly really have enough clothing to fill them?

"Eddie and I had them assembled in no time," he replied with a warm grin waving his hand about our room.

I cringed! Not only was he in our room, but he was here at Tilly's invitation. My thoughts seemed to spill loudly out of my mouth, "You put the shelves up? How long have you been in our room? We are already in trouble with the professors!"

"Shh," he responded to me with a frown. "No one knows I am here. No one saw us. We came in through the window."

"Thank you," Tilly said as she stood between us. Clearly she wanted to prevent our growling at each other. More importantly, she wanted his focus on her as her finger traced down the center of his chest. He was under her spell. I saw him shiver at her touch.

He was in our room and apparently a friend. I felt we should at least be introduced. I peered around Tilly and interrupted, "I'm sorry, you are?"

"Oh, Elizabeth this is Trevor. Trevor, Elizabeth." Tilly said waving her finger between us with her eyes focused on Trevor. "He is my oldest friend. I forgot you didn't know each other. Sorry."

Hmm, I thought they seemed a little chummy for friends.

"Tilly, I've got to go," he stated as they exchanged a loaded look. "You know!"

"Have a great time," Tilly responded as he pushed her roaming fingers away from him. They seemed to share a secret. I was certain it was a secret best kept between them.

He moved towards the window and my heart skipped a beat. How was he going to get down? It was a very long way down. He grabbed what looked like a rope which seemed to be hanging next to our window. Instead of going down, he went up. I moved to the window and leaned out. It was not a plain rope. It was a rickety rope ladder which went from the room above us all the way to the ground below. The view of his feet climbing was all I could see until he disappeared through a window above our room. Tilly seemed unfazed by his departure. She had begun unpacking her many purchases from her bags. I had to ask, "He knows you and somehow ended up with the room directly above us?"

"Sure," Tilly responded never looking at me. "They're guys. They don't care which room they're in. Eddie and Trevor traded with the two in the room above us today."

I wanted this room to be a sanctuary away from this unfamiliar world. Worrying about boys crawling through my window was not the peace I desired. "He's not coming down a lot?" I asked.

She turned to me with a devilish grin and stated, "Only if I ask him. Are you interested?"

"No," I quickly responded. "So the ladder hangs down all the way from their room, past ours, and to the ground?"

"Of course," Tilly stated with an annoyed tone. "Would it really have a purpose if it didn't enable us to get out of this prison?"

She turned away from me and was now stacking a pile of blue jeans on her bed. Tree limbs were more practical to crawl down and would not be noticed as escape routes. The ladder? Someone would surely notice the ladder hanging from the building. Surely they were going to conceal it somehow. I had to ask, "Tilly won't the professors see the rope ladder?"

She turned to glare directly at me, "Get a grip, Elizabeth. Be the wild thing I see as you! Why are you wiggin' out?"

"Only trying to fly under the radar," I stated, tentatively smiling, to reassure Tilly. Inwardly I asked myself, did it really matter if she thought I wasn't happy about the ladder?

"Good," Tilly sighed relieved. "I thought you were going goody tu shoes on me!" She went back to stacking clothes on her bed. "To answer your question, Trevor pulls the ladder into his room when we don't plan on using it."

I rolled my eyes and thought, just wonderful!

Tilly was too preoccupied piling the new clothes in perfect piles to notice my disapproval. There was one pile of jeans and another of pretty colored shirts. She now sat beside them stating, "You look like a denim and cotton type of girl."

I didn't understand her point. I questioned, "What?"

"These are all yours," Tilly said. Looking genuinely happy, she pointed to the three stacks of new clothing.

"For me? I asked. She nodded. In general, I needed the clothing. However, I couldn't pay for them and I didn't want to be in debt to Tilly. I couldn't accept this generous offer. "Didn't your mother wonder why you were buying these? None of them are your style!"

"She's hoping I'm turning a new corner," Tilly laughed. "She can dream on! I like the way I look."

The scene in my head of her mother noticing anything of Tilly's on me was horrifying. Her mother held a true dislike for me. "What if she sees me wearing what should be your clothes?" I hesitated.

"Whatever," Tilly said. "She won't be here. Do you always worry this much Elizabeth?"

"The clothes are expensive and she did spend a lot of money on them," I said with an emphasis on the cost.

"Money? No one uses money," Tilly stated. "Ugh! This memory thing."

"Well what do you use?" I questioned.

"As long as you work, you are entitled to any product made here. You are welcome to pick up or put your name in for any item you like," Tilly stated. "For instance, if you want a new purse, you go to the store and pick one up. If the purse you want is out of stock, you put your name on their rainy day list. Everyone here creates for pleasure and not money. The Humling maker creates for the bliss of it. The end product is up for grabs by anyone needing it."

"So the waiting list can be long at times?" I questioned.

"At times, for certain things," Tilly agreed. "My mom thrives to be on every list possible. Wanting things she doesn't need. Her excess drives me crazy! The whole idea is to only take what you need."

"It sounds a little far fetched, Tilly," I stated.

"If I need jeans and blouses for myself, I can go get more tomorrow," Tilly stated. Scouring my confused face Tilly blurted out, "Okay. Forget it! I can see this concept is over your head. Take any of the clothes from these three piles. Borrow them if that seems saner to you!"

I was on the edge of Tilly being angry with my denial of her gift. "Thank you Tilly! I feel more comfortable just borrowing."

"Just keep your borrowed clothing on your side of the room!" Tilly stated as she shoved the stack of jeans into my hands.

Our conversation was interrupted with a knock at our door. Tilly looked at the door as if she could burn it with her eyes. She opened the door and there stood a short, shapely girl with bright eyes.

"Hi! I'm Destiny," she stated. "I'm in the room next door."

"So?" Asked Tilly flatly.

I watched Destiny's eyebrows as they moved together. She then exhaled a quick gasp at Tilly's rudeness and indifference. Tilly's hand rolled in a gesture that stated, yes? Destiny's arms crossed her chest as she responded, "Professor Zirak wants to see the two of you."

Tilly turned and flung the door closed. It slammed in Destiny's face with a thud. She wasn't likely to be friends with us anytime soon. Tilly mumbled, "Nosy next door neighbor."

Tilly insisted we hang all of the clothes in our closets before going to Professor Zirak's office. She purposely wanted to tee him off. Once there, he ushered us in leaving me no time to dread what was to come. We sat down and I got ready.

"Thank you for waiting," said Professor Zirak as he rounded his desk and sat in his chair. "Elizabeth, I have not had the opportunity to tell you that your questions about Transportation Law were very well answered."

"Thank you Professor," I said looking a little puzzled and waiting for the gauntlet to fall on top of us. I did not think we would be as lucky with him as Professor Presnell. We had no Mr. Solliday to rescue us.

"The events of today has led me to believe both of you need something to fill your time," continued Professor Zirak. "This week you will be taking lessons on accessing records. I believe the two of you need to understand the proper way to access records. Here are fifty questions I would like you to answer pertaining to that!" He passed the papers across to us, "The lesson is to be turned in before the weekend. Do you have any questions?"

"No sir," I answered for both of us. Tilly angrily smacked her gum and blew bubbles. I understood her feelings. Homework before starting training in this class hardly seemed fair.

Tilly was still visibly fuming in her seat as she spewed, "Anything else for us, professor?"

"Well yes, don't pull anymore stunts like this one," stated Professor Zirak. "Your punishment from me will be more severe next time. I am no Solliday!"

"Understood," I assured Professor Zirak. I got up, pulling Tilly with me towards the door. This was no easy task as I could see she clearly had more to say. I was tearing her away from her appointed place to be rebellious. Once outside, I let go of her arm. You could almost see the steam coming out of her ears.

"Elizabeth, I don't intend to do an extra assignment for him," Tilly stated in a huff.

I understood not wanting to do it, but why get so upset. I had a more important subject to focus on. I had hoped when we returned the chapter to the Hall of Records, we could look up the name Kaswell. That hope was dashed, leaving me disappointed. Suddenly, I had a light bulb moment. I knew how to cheer her up. "Tilly, would it make you feel better to do something a little rebellious?"

"What did you have in mind?" She asked with a smile and the spark in her eyes returning. She was all ears.

I motioned for her to follow me. When we were safely alone in the conference room, "Were you aware my chapter was empty?"

"That's impossible Elizabeth," she replied with her smile fading and a serious look crossing her face.

"Impossible," I repeated and continued. "That may be, but it was empty with not one word printed. I was also curious about my locket. It had the initials E.M.K. engraved on the inside." I opened the locket and she moved close to look at the initials engraved on the inside. "I'm sure the K. refers to the name Kaswell. I want to look up any chapters for Elizabeth Marie Kaswell without others around or looming over my shoulder."

"Hmm, interesting," said Tilly. She began to pace the length of the conference room while deep in thought. The plush carpet showed the imprint of her feet. When she stopped, she looked me in the eye with a devious look. "A little detective adventure. A little probation breaking. I'm in!"

"Great," I responded. "I really need your help because I still don't remember a thing. I would never find my way there without you."

"Well, we won't be able to use the lift tonight without the fear of being caught," Tilly stated. I could see the wheels turning in her head.

"Hey, I have a plan. This is the rebellious part," I stated as we both began to grin at each other. "Can we get there by riding the subway?"

"Well, yes," Tilly replied with a puzzling look overtaking her face. "Although the platforms exist, Keepers don't usually use the subway. Do you know the location for the Hall of Knowledge platform?"

I had not considered the possibility that the Hall of Knowledge would have its own station, "No, the Hospital Station is the only one I'm familiar with!" I replied.

She contemplated for a split second with her body emanating her building excitement. "I've never been through the Hospital Station. Returning souls don't interest me. Well, life is boring without trying new things," she said with a bold but self-reliant smile crossing her face.

Night came and we were off on our rebellious adventure. Tilly had nerves of steel as she very comfortably accompanied me across the foyer and through the ornate door that led to the Hospital. It was easier to accomplish our escape acting as lookouts for each other to watch for professors. Tilly enjoyed following a Humling family as they went through the plain wooden door leading to the Hospital Station. She just blended in with their small group. She was like a chameleon and loving every moment of it. Was her cool as a cucumber persona an act?

Neither of us had any trouble entering the subway car. I followed her lead when she stated to the subway car, "Hall of Records." The ride was short and we were practically alone, due to the night hours of our adventure. Upon exiting the subway car we found the platform to be bright, but empty of benches or souls. Directly in-front of the platform a staircase lead up to the dark sky of night. We bounded up the stairs.

Stepping out of the stairwell, I was a little in awe. We were in a desolate place and the night breeze was chilling. We were standing at a small, brick building attached to the side of a huge transparent dome. The plain front of the building looked like any other commercial building with glass plate windows and a double glass door. It was odd and looked unimportant compared to the massive, grand building which stood on the other side of the dome.

I realized Tilly's feet were fixed in place as she looked at the building. Was she deep in thought, or maybe shocked? "Tilly, are you okay?"

"I just realized we are outside of the dome," she stated with huge eyes. "I really didn't think about the fact we would be outside the dome."

"I take it you have never been on this side before?" I asked trying to gage her mood.

"Actually, I have been outside the dome with my parents when my father was on official Administration duties. But, we had to have destination cards." Tilly said. "I never imagined how simple getting around the whole concept of clearance would be."

"Yeah, I told you this was the rebellious part," I replied. Actually, I had never given thought to the fact permission was needed for travel anywhere beyond the dome. But, we were here. "Let's just get inside and look up the chapter."

She snapped back from her shock and now marveled in the rules we were breaking. She walked towards me with a smile creeping onto her face, "You seem very comfortable in your rule breaking. I guess you are more like me than I thought."

Wonderful, I thought to myself.

As we stepped through the door, I was struck by the rows and rows of metal desks with computers setting upon them. Bright florescent lights hung from the ceiling with the room looking bigger from the inside.

Tilly leaned over to me whispering, "On the other... you know. We look up the chapter number and pull it from the bookshelves. Where are the chapters? Did they move them all?"

"What?" I questioned with alarm in my voice. I too, had just discovered the empty shelves. Bare white walls and empty shelving were all we saw. I shot Tilly a glance that screamed, what do we do now?

"We'll have to figure out where they moved them," replied Tilly.

"How?" I questioned as I looked at all the stark white walls. I was out of my element.

"The computer silly," Tilly said as she pointed at the rows of desks and computers. She could see my blankness and lack of knowledge. She leaned over and whispered, "We are already here. Let's at least give it a try."

I followed her. The door at the rear of this room led to the Hall of Records. Hundreds of computer stations were set up here. I chose a computer which left as much distance between us and the door as possible. I pulled out the chair and motioned for Tilly to sit at the computer next to me.

She sat and turned in her chair whispering, "I'll keep an eye on the door. You do the computer search."

I nodded. The computer screen was straightforward, asking for the name. I typed in Elizabeth Marie Kaswell. The next screen asked for the keeper number. I recalled the only keeper number I knew, which was the number printed in the chapter that Tilly borrowed for me. I typed it in and too my surprise the computer brought up a box, loading. 1% of 100%.

While I sat patiently waiting on the slow beast, my mind poured over bits of information I had acquired. I knew I was Elizabeth Kaswell. Not just because Dustin mentioned the name or the locket I wore had these initials, but because the same keeper was listed for Elizabeth Cantrell and Elizabeth Kaswell. Who was the keeper? I didn't have a clue. However, they would know me better than myself since I had no memory. 10% of 100%. And why would my name change? Was I adopted?

The single, lonely door in the back of the room opened! A gruff, young man dressed entirely in black stepped inside. Tilly and I exchanged a look. I was trying desperately to convey, stay calm. He walked casually up the isle of computers across from us, stopping at the computer facing ours. 20% of 100%.

He had the darkest, pitch black eyes which seemed to be peering through me when I glanced up at him. Equally as eye catching was his ratted, black curly hair poking out from under his black derby hat. Although I did not understand why he made me uncomfortable, I suddenly felt the need to run. He had turned his head as though listening for something when I glanced up a second time.

In my head I heard, "Yes, she is here."

I surveyed the room thinking someone else had entered, not able to pinpoint who was talking. "Tilly, did you hear someone talking?"

"No one has said a thing," she whispered back to me while turning her gaze from the young man across from us.

I knew instantly, my mind heard someone. They knew I was here. "Tilly, we need to go. Now!" I whispered. I stood in one fluid motion, pushing the chair back with my legs. The computer had only reached 25%. As I walked away the computer suddenly flashed, RESTRICTED, ACCESS DENIED. Acting calmly, I joined Tilly in the aisle.

I heard, "She is leaving, do you want me to detain her and her friend."

A female answered, "Yes, I am almost there."

Startled, I grabbed Tilly's hand and we ran. I sped towards the door. We were in some sort of peril.

"Good, I love a chase," I heard.

I felt Tilly push up against me as we both tried to exit the door at once. "I think he is following us," Tilly said.

I turned for a quick look. The gruff, young man was quickly closing in with a crooked grin across his face. I felt the panic in every bone of my body as I pulled Tilly towards the subway staircase. Whomever or whatever was coming was bad. I had inadvertently involved Tilly. Reaching the subway platform we both realized no car was in sight. In an instant, I pulled the locked from beneath my blouse. I felt the locket between my fingers. I placed my hands firmly on Tilly's arm, closed my eyes, rubbed the locket, and thought of the safety of our room in Keeper House as I whispered, "Keeper House." I heard Tilly scream but did not open my eyes until I felt a sudden, falling, hard thump.

My eyes opened to Tilly's gaze. "How… How did we end up here? And how did you do that?" Tilly questioned as she looked a little taken back and shocked.

"Do you really want to know?" I asked under my breath. Before I could answer we heard a knock at our door.

I got up to answer it finding Destiny, the girl who resided in the room beside ours, standing outside the door. "Hey, I happened to be downstairs. The professor wants to speak to the two of you immediately." She looked over to Tilly with a smirk asking, "What did the two of you do now?"

"Nothing, we have been in on our room," Tilly defiantly retorted. Then meeting my stare still sprawled out on the floor, she got up mumbling, "Nosy neighbor." Tilly shoved her way past Destiny causing her to lose balance and take a step backwards.

Since Tilly had pushed her, I mouthed, "Sorry." She gave me a fake smile and exited our door. I followed. She stood aside at her own doorway letting me pass.

"Tilly," I called as I followed her down the staircase. "Tilly."

The professor met us at the bottom asking with an amused grin, "Are the two of you having a disagreement?"

"Oh no sir," said Tilly. "Why would I have a disagreement with my best friend?" She put her arm around my shoulder and gave me a huge grin. Tilly was a natural actress and she captured the moment producing a united front. I responded by placing a smile on my face.

He gave us a look that said he could see right through us. "I just wanted to make sure the two of you were in and safe for the evening."

"Why would we not be in?" I asked trying to be coy but wondering if he knew.

"Where else do you think we would be? You know we would not want to cause anymore trouble. After all, we are officially on adult status," Tilly stated in agreement with a sticky sweet voice which was almost a giggle.

"Oh, don't push it," said the professor. "Good night."

Tilly chose not to speak to me upon arrival back at our room. Although we both crawled into our beds, I knew she too was not sleeping. I could only imagine she was taken back from the chase by the gruff young man. Maybe the use of the locket had shocked her. I wanted to tell Tilly everything, but I simply did not know where to begin. What should I tell her? Should I start with Mrs. Farris and explain my distrust for her or tell her about Dustin? Tell her I could hear his thoughts and he was being made to do something which he didn't want too. What about the fact they both seemed to know more about me than I did. After all, our adventure this evening was due to Dustin giving me the name Kaswell.

Should I tell her about my feelings for the wooden door and how it calls to me? Should I speak of my visit to Lakeland and how peaceful it had been? How about the fact I feel I belong in the world of the Humlings more than the Keepers. Would Tilly want to hear of my adventure with Emma, Anthony, and Daniel? It would certainly be of interest to her. Tilly would expect me to explain how I new about the Hospital Station and how to use it. My list of subjects seemed to never end in my mind.

Next item was the locket. This I would need to explain. But, how could I explain to her my hearing the voices? Was I a schizoid? It was crazy to say I heard one voice much less multiple voices. I knew the man wasn't just following us out the door. He was coming for me. I could hear it in my head! Was I some sort of schizoid with a bit of psychic talent mixed in?

I glanced over at Tilly who was lying on her side, staring at me. I started, "Look at my locket." I pushed it across the night stand towards her and watched as her long fingers took it in her hand. She turned it over and over looking at it.

"You used this to return us here this evening, didn't you?" Tilly asked.

"Yes," I said as I began to stare at the ceiling. "But I didn't know it worked until this evening."

"At one time this type of locket was very dangerous." She cautioned. "Hey! Look at me!" As I looked at Tilly I could see she was ready to talk it out. Tilly was unusually serious. "This type of locket…"

I interrupted, "I know. I heard the story this week from someone I met."

"Okay, you know about the possible danger," Tilly said as her demeanor lightened. "I thought they were all destroyed. Where did you get the locket?"

"I still don't have any idea about who I am." I replied. "So no, I don't know how I came to have it. The locket was just on my neck when I arrived home in the Hospital."

Suddenly Tilly sat straight up and you could see she was having a light bulb moment. "You are lucky to have me as a best friend," she said as a devious grin came across her face. "I am probably the only person who would look at this as an opportunity. The locket is our ticket to a whole new life style around here!"

"Wait a minute," I cautioned. "I don't think we should use it again."

"It certainly got us out of trouble tonight," she said. "It saved us from being caught by that stranger."

"Yes, but the danger of locket travel and its mysterious uses at one time were real. How do we know the danger won't happen again?" I questioned.

"I'm sure the Dwellers assume the lockets were all destroyed," she said. "We'll keep our little treasure a secret. Only you and I know about it. They can't use a locket against us that they don't know exists."

I held out my hand for the locket, "I don't know." She turned back over to stare at the ceiling, humming a happy curious tune. I rolled over with my back to her saving my other concerns for another time. Sleep soon overtook me.

CHAPTER EIGHT

Elizabeth

Stepping into the small conference room in Keeper House, every head turned. Our late night adventure and our oversleeping led to our being tardy. It seemed someone had an aversion to the new alarm clock Professor Zirak insisted we have. Tilly had turned the sound off after I fell asleep. I made a mental note to place it on the other side of my bed tonight.

"Thank you for joining us today," Professor Zirak said sternly as he continued writing on the board. I quickly and nervously scanned the room for seating. The room was full! Turning to look at us he stated, "Please find a seat." A moment passed while Tilly and I crossed the room of eyes and sat in the two remaining chairs. The professor continued ignoring the chaos in the conference room we caused. "Please take one and pass it around. This is your general schedule for the next twelve weeks. As your schedule notes, Monday morning we will meet here to start our week."

"Must it be this early?" Asked Tilly under her breath as she positioned herself on the edge of her chair. Her right arm was bent back with her hand on her shoulder blade. Her other hand was on her elbow. She was stretching? Then she reversed and did the other arm oblivious to the stares about her.

The professor stopped writing and turned to sternly look at Tilly and emphatically stated, "We can always make it earlier if you would like Miss Bradford!" Tilly lowered her arms and thumbed her nose when his view left her. He continued, "During the first meeting of the week, I will be assigning an activity. Our first activity will be in the form of an assignment. It will enable our group to get to know each others strengths and weaknesses."

The Professor turned back to the board to finish his writing. Tilly popped a piece of gum in her mouth and leaned over to whisper, "I don't have any weaknesses!" Really? I could name several but one stuck out in my mind, rebellion. She was the most defiant person I had ever known!

Destiny rolled her eyes wildly at Tilly's comment. The majority of the faces in the room held her in the same regard as Destiny. A snicker or two from those across the table erupted.

"Shh," I mouthed to Tilly and those across from us. Keeping us out of trouble was a job! Tilly shrugged in total disregard and glanced briefly at Trevor. He peered at her adoringly. Nonchalantly, she went back to stretching with her arms above her head, fingers interlocked, and reaching towards the ceiling. Then her arms moved to the front of her, stretching as far as she could reach, cracking her knuckles. It was a nerve wrenching sound.

"I would like each of you to write a paper on the following two questions," stated the professor as he moved to reveal what he had written on the board. "Number one. How did your life theme better Humlings? Number two. What did your life theme enable you to learn?"

The room filled with the noise of zippers, unzipping and backpacks opening. Notebooks and papers then shuffled as pens began writing the assignment questions in fresh notebooks. My focus before coming down had been my appearance. I felt like a big marshmallow in this all white ensemble. I had taken the time to throw a few of Tilly's pens into my processing bag. I was totally unprepared for this whole training thing.

Tilly was preoccupied with the young man across the table from us disregarding the professor's assignment. If she wasn't planning to jot down the questions, I knew I had better. I nudged her with my elbow. "Tilly, may I have a piece of paper from your notebook?"

"What?" Tilly questioned quickly turning to me with an annoyed tone and look upon her face.

"A piece of paper," I repeated.

Tilly reluctantly grabbed her backpack and abruptly slammed it loudly onto the table. Once more, frowns from every direction.

"Can anyone give me a definition of a life theme?" Professor Zirak questioned. Professor Zirak was beaming as hands shot up from around the room.

"Mr. Wellsey."

Tilly slowly ripped a piece of paper out of her notebook. Each metal, spiral ring made its own noise. I thought I saw a hint of a grin as she temporarily distracted everyone's attention from the professor.

A boy seated beside Trevor, with long black hair, didn't notice as he spoke and captured the group's attention, "Yo! A life theme is what you plan to learn on the Earth Plane. You know, like learning to kiss a girl! Or ride a bike… be a doctor. It's all about learning new things! "

Tilly slid the paper towards me and whispered, "That is sooo Eddie." She looked across the table at Trevor and rolled her eyes.

"Yes," Professor Zirak agreed. "The Earth Plane can be thought of as a school. Choosing to live an earth life is choosing to enroll into the school of life on the Earth Plane. Life themes are learning classes to be taken during your earth stay. Can anyone tell me a Keepers main goal in regards to their earth life?"

Again, everyone's hands shot up, except Tilly's and mine.

"Miss Cantrell?" Professor Zirak called as he pointed a bony finger at me.

Luckily, I recalled Mrs. Farris's words and answered, "To help others in the capacity of a Keeper, you must first live one earth life to develop compassion!"

"Very good," Professor Zirak complimented. "Miss Bradford, your thoughts?"

"To hop down to the Earth Plane, successfully rub shoulders and brown nose the Humlings. Throw a coin or two in the charity bucket. Learn lessons. Blah, blah, blah. Most importantly, at least for some, experience a roller coaster on the tunnel of love!"

The professor just stared at Tilly for a long, startled, awkward moment. You could cut the rooms tension with a knife. Then, the mousy girl at the end of the table raised her hand. The professor responded, "Yes, Miss Stone?"

"When is th… th… the p… paper due?" She stuttered, pointing towards the board. I was surprised to see Tilly warmly smiling at her. Then when the professor turned to the board, Tilly gave the girl a thumb up gesture. The shy girl blushed and returned her attention to the professor.

"We will have brunch together on Sunday," the Professor began. "Each of you will have an opportunity to read your paper to the group at that time."

"Excuse me Professor," Destiny interrupted as she shot us a look in contempt. "We will be late for our next class with Professor Presnell if we don't leave soon. We are late due to others not managing their time well."

The Professor responded, "Oh yes, look at the time. Does anyone need help using the lift this morning? The lift operator is a bit cantankerous." He paused and then seemed to look directly at me. I turned away from his glare while I shoved the schedule and questions into my processing bag. "Very well, by all means, get going. I wouldn't want you to be late."

As a group, we made our way down into the foyer. Then we formed a line outside the four elevators, that Tilly called a lift, awaiting the double doors to open. Tilly's head was on swivel. "Aha!" Tilly stated as her eyes found who they were looking for in the far corner of the room. She exited the line and made her way across the room, stopping in-front of the stuttering Stone girl. She appeared to be introducing herself and offering the girl a stick of gum.

I was doing a little rubbernecking of my own. My attention drifted to the sight behind me. Tiffany was snuggling up to Dustin's arm. Yuck! They were too engrossed in each other to notice the flush rising in my face. I could not blame him for obviously liking her. She was beautiful with her long curly black hair, flawless skin, amazing green eyes, and a body that most would die for. I was opposite, not a breathtaking beauty. I was a plain Jane.

I heard the ding of the lift and a swish of the doors opening which brought me back to reality. Tilly was once again at my side, closely followed by the stuttering Stone girl. The doors opened as Tilly grabbed my arm whispering, "New plan! Repeat my destination." She held my arm long enough to get her point across. Inside the door she calmly stated, "Destination One!"

I moved into the lift finding it was the size of small room. I repeated, "Destination one." I realized I wasn't talking to an invisible force as with the subway. An operator whom was no bigger than a midget was taking our request in a growling and grumbling tone. His face was strong and stern with a long nose and the deepest blue eyes. I was staring at him when Tilly pulled me further into the lift to stand behind him. He was indeed in a cantankerous fowl mood as Professor Zirak had warned.

Peering over the small man at the control panel for the lift, I saw six buttons numbered zero through five. All were labeled with the places you could take the lift. I watched as others I knew stepped on, pausing to tell him their destination. One poor soul not thinking reached to the panel to push a button. The little man instantly grabbed him by the wrist and growled, "Push my buttons and you'll be wearing your H. A. N. D. backwards!" The frightened soul backed up in the elevator until his back hit the wall behind him.

Then a young man stepped through the door and stated, "The City." This shocked me because The City was the Humling town my where my uniforms were made. I did not think we were allowed to go to the world of the Humlings.

The small man growled, "Destination Card?"

The young man seemed to dig in his pockets while trying to shuffle his books from hand to hand. He produced a key card which the small man pushed into a slot besides the number five button stating, "Thank you sir."

As the lift doors were closing, I noticed that Tiffany and Dustin were standing directly behind me. I heard Tiffany say, "Thank you for the flowers this morning, love. They were beautiful."

"Yeah, Beautiful flowers for a beautiful girl," replied Dustin with a tone of annoyance in his words.

Why did this leave a sickening feeling in my stomach? Yuck! I would distance myself from them if it weren't for the fact I wanted to hear their conversation. I felt awkward and green with envy.

"Yeah, all yellow! Just like your mother insisted." I heard Dustin's voice speak in my mind. "Too bad I couldn't have made the bouquet stink weed!"

What exactly was the meaning of that? Did he really say that? No, or Tiffany wouldn't be still hanging on him.

"Good grief, listen to that mushy," said Tilly loud enough for them to hear, interrupting my thoughts with a jab to my side and a snicker. Tilly had brought me back to reality. It was obvious they were a couple no matter what my mind seemed to think it heard.

Tiffany leaned forward and over Tilly's shoulder stated, "I'm busy now. Can I ignore you some other time?"

Luckily the door opened without Tilly being able to respond. The small man announced, "Destination one, Department of Administration Complex."

"That's us, move out of our way," said Tiffany as she pushed pass Tilly and me. She turned her nose up in a snooty condescending way as she exited the lift.

As Dustin stepped past me, his eyes met mine for a split second and his handsome face smiled directly at me. He smelled divine! On his heels, I quickly followed to be able to inhale one more whiff of his cologne. I must be crazy. I turned my face to the lift operator as I was exiting the elevator saying, "Thank you." A slight grin graced the corners of his mouth and for a brief moment his blue eyes lit up. Then his gaze went to Tilly. His demeanor instantly changed as he gave Tilly an intense dirty look. What had Tilly done to him to invoke his changed demeanor?

The Department of Administration Complex was a massive building. The roof of the three story, massive foyer was glass. The rays of the sun flooded down through the roof illuminating the room. The center of this room re-minded me of a perfectly square greenhouse. A fountain set in the middle surrounded by lush plants and exotic grass. Modern benches set on the out-skirts where the grass met the marble flooring. The marble flooring extended throughout the foyer around the centered greenhouse area, and up the stair-cases. It was shiny reflecting your image like a magnificent mirror.

This Department of Administration Complex was a bustling place with people coming and going. I followed Tilly up the grand staircase. I began to realize how preoccupied I was with the grandeur of this place. I focused on climbing the stairs to catch up to Tilly who was a few steps ahead of me. She was submerged in thought as I interrupted, "Your quiet, what's on your mind?"

"I have never heard anyone thank the leprechaun," Tilly said as she crossed her arms across her chest.

"Leprechaun?" I questioned feeling quite tired of simply not understanding.

"Yes, the lift operator," she replied. "You do remember you don't have to thank them, don't you?"

"What do you mean? Thank you is part of polite manners. Did you see his face light up when I thanked him?" I retorted. Stubbornly she gave me no response. "Is this not the point of life? To learn how to treat others as you would like to be treated? So, why would I not thank him?"

"It is just the way it has always been," mumbled Tilly as she threw her hands up in-front of her.

The leprechaun! I shook my head in disgust and decided to steer the conversation in a new direction. No way was I going to waste time angry with Tilly about the treatment of the lift operators. I was right!

Tilly had lost the puppy dog which had been following her. The Stone girl left us in the lobby. "What's up with the Stone girl?" I asked.

"What are you talking about?" Tilly questioned.

"She followed you into the lift like a darn puppy dog at your heels," I responded.

"Her name is Kim," Tilly stated with a suddenly serious look on her face. "Be nice to her. I don't think she has or will easily make friends."

"She sure is quiet," I added.

Tilly leaned over to me whispering, "Think about it. If you stuttered, you probably would be shy about talking as well."

I didn't see this coming. Tilly had a weak spot. This kindness to a stranger shot holes in her tough girl persona.

Reaching the top of the stairs we paused and faced each other. "You need to get a backpack," Tilly stated out of the blue as she rested her hands on her hips. Tilly seemed a little perturbed. I didn't know why!

"Huh?" I questioned.

"I was totally flirting with that guy this morning and you blew it for me! I had him on a line like a great fish," Tilly complained.

"When I asked for paper?" I questioned. She shrugged one shoulder. I went on, "I wanted to write down our assignment." My voice carried its tone of annoyance.

"Yes," Tilly replied. "Writing it down wasn't important! Didn't you see I was reeling him in?"

"Not important?" I repeated flabbergasted ignoring the rest of her statement.

"No! Not at that moment," Tilly replied. "If I hadn't lost his eye contact, I would have a date with him this evening. A friend knows when to back off. You blew it for me!"

I felt my face starting to flush and my temper rising. A possible date is more important than writing down our assignment. She was unreasonable! She could flirt with him some other time. Dates were not a priority. My sense of frustration with her was rising.

She interrupted the raving in my head when she threw her hands in the air saying, "Don't you see? Snagging him was important to me. It's not like we were going to do the assignment today. We should be able to remember two tiny questions."

"Can you tell me what the questions were?" I asked as I stopped dead in my tracks to call her bluff and once again ignored her references to the boy.

"You could get it from one of the other girls. My memory is just fine," Tilly declared as she continued on without me muttering and stomping her feet like a child.

My gut was telling me the other girls didn't care for Tilly. I wasn't sure

I liked her! But in reality, I seemed to be her new best friend. I shook my head while picking up my pace to close the space between us. Catching her, I asked, "Get the questions from the other girls?"

"Yes," she responded. "Couldn't you see? They were all preoccupied with writing the questions down. All were oblivious to the room full of possible dates. You have your priorities all wrong. Stupid in my opinion." The anger rose on my face. A devilish grin crossed her face and she added, "Stupid to ignore all the boys in the room. That's why I have dates and others don't!"

I was going to have to state the obvious. "Tilly, I doubt the other girls would share…"

Tilly interrupted me mid sentence throwing her right hand palm straight toward me in defiance saying, "No need to finish your thought."

An awkward silence fell between us. Tilly shrugged her shoulders and continued, "I am right! I'll get the questions from Trevor."

Tilly had stated the obvious. Trevor would give us the questions if I hadn't already wrote them down. To steer away from conflict with Tilly in the future, I did need my own backpack and school supplies. My reasoning for needing these items was much different than hers. "I prefer to write down my own assignments. I'm a stickler for doing things the proper way."

Tilly smiled warmly at me even though she had been furious with me two minutes ago. We were an odd pair. We both were able to see the true person behind the others mask. I was the girl who knew nothing and walked around as if I did. Tilly was the rebel who was not mean spirited but had a kind heart. Both of us were camouflaged by our outward personas.

We took our time in returning to Keeper House. Transportation Law at the Administration Complex had reached a whole new high for being boring. I almost nodded off to sleep. Professor Presnell was dressed brightly with her signature red glasses, deep red dress, and fuzzy red house shoes. Despite her attire, I didn't miss the fact that she was very detailed. She spoke on and on about acceptable and non-acceptable modes of transportation for Keepers. Repetition was lulling everyone to a pre sleep state. I was certain this was more for Tilly than me. She seemed to be the only one interested. If the opportunity arose, she would use the information in regards to transportation. Otherwise she wouldn't be showing such interest.

As we passed under the Department of Keeper Arch that led to Keeper House, I wondered if Tilly was still fuming about the questions and boy episode. I could feel the warm light coming through the opened windows embracing my skin. Destiny interrupted my peace as she ran down the hall towards us yelling, "Elizabeth! Tilly!" We looked up at her when she stopped in-front of us and handed over a note. "I guess Professor Zirak wants to see the two of you."

"Again? Great," replied Tilly with a huge frown upon her face.

"Thank you, Destiny," I replied as I began to try to move around her.

"So, what did he want the last time?" Destiny asked as she positioned herself to walk beside me.

I shrugged my shoulders. "He just wanted to make sure we were in our room," I replied. I had just spouted out a little white lie.

"I guess we all know why he would be checking only on the two of you," she responded as she bounced off not clarifying her statement.

Tilly and I looked at each other in mutual disbelief and disgust. It was official! I had been stereotyped into the rebellious, trouble making category with Tilly. I didn't know how I exactly felt about this. "Tilly, do you have any idea what Professor Zirak wants now?" I blurted out.

"No, I was with you all day, remember?" She replied as we stopped outside the door to Keeper House to take one long last breath of evening air.

"After we find out the trouble we are in, do you want to do some shopping?" Tilly stated calmly with a strange beam in her eye.

"Yes, I need to pick up a few items!" I replied. "Where do you go to purchase a backpack?"

"You can't pick up backpacks in any shop inside the dome," Tilly responded. "You'll have to wait for the next shopping fair. There is a little purse maker there who has mastered the art of backpack construction. You're nobody if you don't carry one of his bags."

"What is a shopping fair? And When?" My questions spilled out my mouth. "I need a backpack and supplies desperately!"

"Sorry," Tilly responded. "Once a month, vendors come into the park and hold a two day shopping fair. Everything imaginable is there. The last one was a couple of weeks ago. If you had a destination card we could travel directly to the vendor's shop." She paused as a devilish grin crossed her face. "Since you don't have a card, we could go on another adventure through the subway."

"I don't know," I hesitated. In transportation class we learned how forbidden travel outside the dome was. "Tilly what if we get caught? The consequences…"

Tilly held her hand up to stop me demanding, "Stop! Don't get caught up in the consequences. If you do, you will never be able to just go with the flow."

Silence fell between us. One more kink in my memory road blocked existence. This meant there was no hope for me to get a backpack on my own.

"Until we start our actual jobs, our families must request destination cards for us. The card enables us to go outside the dome to approved places to purchase items we need without parents accompanying us! The approval process usually takes awhile," Tilly explained.

"Tilly, I didn't think Keepers often went outside the dome. Even for shopping," I shot back.

"Look, I'll ask my Mom if she might be able to get a backpack," Tilly replied.

"Yeah, I'm sure she will want to help me out," I sarcastically replied.

Tilly simply smirked at my comment as she stepped through the front door and into Keeper House. Then we made our way to Professor Zirak's domain. I knocked on the professor's door and heard, "Ladies, please come in." The Professor was seated at his desk. His smile and eyes screamed that he got me!

"Have a seat. I would like to tell you about an opportunity I have for the two of you."

We seated ourselves and I fidgeted with my fingers trying to stay calm. Tilly just plopped down and placed her backpack on the professor's desk seeming unfazed. "We really aren't looking for any new opportunities," Tilly stated as she popped a piece of gum in her mouth. In the next moments of silence, she and I both knew this was going to be bad!

After what seemed an eternity of silence with the professor intently staring at us, he spoke, "This opportunity should leave you with little spare time. I would like the two of you to join Harmony."

"No way!" Squealed Tilly with the first hint of uncertainty I had heard from her. "I will never join Harmony! You can not make me." Her voice and posture turned to defiance in a flash.

I held my hands up, "Hold on!" Turning, I grabbed Tilly by the arm and softly repeated myself, "Hold on." I turned to the professor asking, "What is Harmony?"

Before the professor could reply, Tilly exploded. "Only a total waste of time!" Squealed Tilly, jerking her arm from me and breathing so hard her nostrils seemed to be flaring. "He wants us to sing like canaries in the choir! Just like my mother and all the other snotty high society does. I won't do it! He can't make me!"

"Oh, this is where you are wrong," spouted Professor Zirak rising to a half standing position with his hands on his desk and leaning towards us. I could see he had reached his limit of Tilly's rude remarks. He had snapped and was straining to keep his composure. "It is my belief the both of you need to be busy. I am very worried you are starting to go down a bad path Miss Cantrell. Let me tell you Miss Bradford, not only will you join the group, I will require you miss not one practice or competition." He slipped two copies of the schedule across the desk. "I'm sure you don't want to go before Professor Presnell who would be happy to share with you the consequences of not following a professor's assignment. I believe she would find pleasure in seeking to nullify your emancipation."

I watched as Tilly stood, placing her hands on the edge of the Professors desk. She leaned towards him and barked, "Threats! Is that all you have?"

"Remember those adult decisions having adult consequences?" The professor asked as he matched her authoritative stance. His skin tone was flushed and he looked extremely angry.

I could see Tilly had pushed him too far. "We will gladly accept your invitation to be apart of the Harmony," I stated as I abruptly stood. "Thank you, professor." Tilly started to add to my comment but I stomped very hard on the top of her foot. She turned her gaze upon me grabbing her backpack from the professor's desk. She was fuming! Nothing else I could have done could have made her more agitated. Grabbing her arm, I forced her out the office door closing her out. I remained inside with my weight against the door to prevent her re-entry.

The professor still shaking and standing asked, "Is there something else, Miss Cantrell?"

I scanned the Harmony schedule. It was just as I expected. Harmony practice was each and every night. I questioned, "Can we have your permission to start the lessons tomorrow evening?"

"Have a seat," the professor demanded. Reluctantly, I released my death hold on the door. Tilly had quit pushing and rattling it. I paced back and forth a couple time and then took a seat. An uncomfortable silence fell as he sat back in his chair and stared at me. "Why should I agree to that?" Stubbornness griped his voice and persona.

"If you really want us to be successful, you will understand. I will never get Tilly there this evening due to her defiant nature. In the moment you and I both can see she is out of control. I want both Tilly and I to be successful in our endeavors at Keeper House."

He did not reply but started tapping his pen impatiently on his desktop while he thought. "Fair enough, I will agree to your starting tomorrow night on one condition." His eyebrows rose, "You must agree not to leave Keeper House. Stay in your room this evening."

I instantly knew in my gut, he knew we left last night. "Agreed! Thank you! I will make every attempt to honor the chance you have given us to be successful. You can find us in our room this evening."

He nodded and gestured for me to go on with his hand. I wasted no time in making my way out the door.

The hall and common room were filling with others whom were steadily streaming in. I turned towards the stairs and quickly made my way up them. The girl's landing was quiet as I made my way past the open doors which led to the other rooms. My own door was slightly cracked as I pushed it open.

CHAPTER NINE

Tilly

I, Tilly, the self proclaimed rebel and self made anarchist was angry to the core! The door had just flung open and there she was. I turned and ignored her. I only hoped Elizabeth was smart enough not to have made any type of deal with the Professor! Boy, my gut told me otherwise! Today had not been my best day. However, my evening would make it all fade. I had a fabulous date lined up! First, I must go up to Trevor's room to tell him a brilliant plan I hatched instead of listening to Presnell drone on and on about Transportation Law. Presnell and her lecture were boring, but my plan wasn't. Who needed transportation rules? Hmm… I couldn't climb in heels. No better time than now to change into my new, loud black and white plaid tennis shoes. They screamed Tilly, skater chick. Maybe the boys would finally give in and get me a board. If they told me I was a girl one more time, I would scream! Turning and sitting on my bed to put my shoes on, I saw Elizabeth was still standing in the doorway. Apparently she was awaiting my acknowledgement of her presence.

She tentatively smiled and blurted out, "How angry are you? Let me have it!"

I stared at her till I could see it causing her to fidget. My stomped foot ached as I forced it into the plaid shoe. I was not happy about her giving the green light to join Harmony. Zirak's plan sucked! I was more angry that she had stomped my foot!

Elizabeth knelt at eye level explaining, "Tilly. I had too agree. We had too!"

Surrendering wasn't my style! It didn't matter though. I wasn't going tonight anyway. I had a date with a good looking hunk! My evening would make up for the horrible day. I smiled thinking and day dreaming a moment or two.

I heard Elizabeth take in a deep breath before she said, "Tilly, I made a deal with Professor Zirak. After you left."

Jumping up, I headed for my shoe rack. I placed my black stiletto heels onto the shoe rack. Deep within, my gut reaction as she slammed the door behind me was uneasiness. I could hear her flitting about, pacing the room. I had subconsciously understood that she had negotiated a deal for us with Zirak. This gut thing was bothersome. Was it possible that Elizabeth was causing me to consider the right thing to do! I shrugged at this thought. Truly, my worst nightmare was coming true. I looked at her hoping she didn't notice my weakness and said, "I figured as much when you slammed the door behind me and prevented me from having a say!"

"We will start practice tomorrow," Elizabeth spurted out with a weak forced smile and strained voice.

Was she counting on this delay in starting to make me happy? "I wasn't going anyway. And?" I demanded as she glanced from me to her feet. She looked extremely taught and nervous. I was reminded of when she handed her exam to the professor. Geez! Maybe I should cut her some slack.

While I moved towards the window to ponder my nights escape, Elizabeth hesitantly added, "We are to stay in Keeper House this evening. He prefers we stay in our room. It's part of the deal."

What! My brief moment of sympathy for her had ended. She shouldn't have made this outrageous deal. I wasn't hers or the professors to control. "I have a date!" I half yelled with a spiteful stance with my feet spread and hands on my hips.

Hers eyes flashed in rage as she questioned, "A date?"

Then she waited for my response. Instantly the realization came. Bottom line, I would be standing my date up this evening. I felt agitated, angry, and my nervous impulse led me to pacing. Two dates lost in one day. Ripped away! This was a scary new record for me. My flirting had been useless this morning thanks to Elizabeth. My date for tonight was my back up date. He was one of the numerous boys I could count on anytime for an impromptu outing. I would have gladly stood up my back up date for the gorgeous guy this morning. Or, I could have gone out with one for dinner and the other for entertainment. Who knows how tonight would have wrapped up! Magic perhaps! If I wasn't tied to this prison! Not going on a date at all was utterly shocking to my ego.

When I finally looked at Elizabeth, she was now perched on the edge of her bed. Obviously she had given up on my responding and seemed to be deep in thought. Noticing my pacing had halted she asked again, "Since when did you have a date this evening? I don't remember you speaking of one!"

Guess I hadn't let slip the whole back up date thing. "I always have a back up date," I answered. "You know. Someone who will go out with me on a moments notice." I frankly wasn't in the mood to do a lot of explaining.

"Oh!" Elizabeth replied.

I felt let down by Elizabeth's agreement. I would go cry on someone else's shoulder. Trevor knew me so well. He would understand or set me straight. It was time to make a break for it! Moving towards the window I told her, "I won't go outside Keeper House," I began but paused before dropping the rest of my thought. "Other than on the ladder to go up to Trevor's room, I will honor the deal you made for us with Zirak." I wanted to add she shouldn't have made a deal without me. "I'll be awhile."

"Wait! Isn't swinging outside on a rope technically outside?" Elizabeth quickly asked. I didn't answer as I heard, "See you when you come back down."

I nodded as I climbed out the window. I hugged the ledge of the building until the wooden rungs of the ladder were firmly in my grip. As I placed my feet onto the rungs the ladder began to swing. Climbing up wasn't as easy as I had thought it to be. It must be the wind I told myself. As I moved up the ladder, it swung from side to side and lifted from the building. "Whoa," I heard myself mutter. It was really swinging near the ground. I was now stepping my foot onto the boys ledge. Relief. My heart and adrenaline were sharing a rush.

Trevor appeared at the window with his face beaming. I hugged the building and shuffled to their open window. Once within reach, he clutched my hand to steady me. Suddenly my other hand was in his grasp. He pulled me into his room and onto a rocklike bed. It was actually a white cot. The first thing that struck me was how small the space was. Was it possible that this room was half the size of mine? The furniture overwhelmed the cubby hole of a room. I had to ask, "Cots?"

"Full beds wouldn't fit into this space," Trevor replied.

I raised my eyebrows. As I focused on the white cots, my attention was drawn to their legs which set upon cement blocks. Plastic containers were haphazardly shoved under the cots for storage. Someone had no taste! Their comforters were huge blue, green, orange, and white, huge plaid which made the space feel overwhelming and claustrophobic. I asked, "Which one is yours?"

"The one next to the window," Trevor pointed. "Eddie didn't want shoe prints on his bed."

My shoes had indeed left imprints on the comforter as I had entered. I walked towards the two desks that flanked the door. They were wooden like ours, only narrower. Plastic crates were stacked upon them to the ceiling. Trevor's crates held books, office supplies, and his dopp kit. Eddie's held skateboard parts, shoes, and a mess of papers. Eddie had always been unorganized.

I turned to face Trevor whose expression appeared nervous about my checking out his place. I had to tell him, "You guys got gypped! Our place is the Taj mahal compared to this!"

His grin unmistakably screamed I didn't know what I was talking about. "Yes, but the boys' floor has its own recreation room. Our dorm rooms are smaller to accommodate it."

"Oh," I quickly responded. "Guess we got gypped then."

"No," Trevor disagreed. "Boys have different priorities! Would you girls really be happy without all that room you have. The lack of closet space alone would make you crazy."

"Your right," I agreed. "You know me inside out."

"That I do," Trevor agreed in a concerned voice. He was wondering what my impromptu visit was about. "Tell me. What's wrong?"

"Zirak insists that we join Harmony," I spewed at him in my blue funk.

The damn of my emotions burst forth. I threw my hands in the air and screamed! My face flushed and I could feel the tears dropping from my eyes. I couldn't bring myself to join the group. I unwrapped and stuck a stick of gum in my mouth and plopped down on his cot wiping my eyes dry. I always enjoyed singing in the refuge of my room. It really wasn't the idea of singing which bothered me. I didn't want to follow in my mother's footsteps. The truth of it, I didn't want to be like my parents. They were arrogant, flashy, and egotistical! The makeup of their lives would never be mine. They lived a cold, superficial, phony life style.

When I glanced up briefly from my emotional gum smacking angry state, I could see Trevor studying me. He simply stated, "Tell Professor Zirak no!"

"I was doing just that when Elizabeth stomped my foot and agreed we would both join!" I grumbled at him.

"Oh Tilly," Trevor sighed. "I'm sorry." He moved to hug me and with a fast brief touch his fingers wiped the wetness on my cheek away.

My head was resting on his chest as I listened to his heart beats. His hand rubbed my back. I felt strange, warm, and fuzzy. Almost like our bodies were one, not two. The embrace felt too intimate on my part since our decision had been made. Good thing he had a girlfriend. I stepped back and told him, "Elizabeth doesn't understand how dreadful Harmony would have been tonight. That is, if I had planned to go!"

"If you weren't going tonight, why are you so bothered?" Trevor questioned as he picked up and tossed his shoes at the foot of his cot. The floor was cluttered with boy things.

"She made a deal on my behalf. I had no say," I replied. "We start tomorrow and tonight we have to stay in Keeper House. I have a date!"

He seemed to chuckle, "So, we're to the root of the problem. Your date. You always have a date!"

"Yes," I agreed. "I do always have a date. I am hot! But, this really isn't why I'm upset."

"You're a bit self centered and egotistical, but spit it out," Trevor said as I sat down on his cot. He set across from me on Eddie's bed.

"My going on a date and disobeying is different when I am responsible only for my own actions," I began. "She made me responsible to her for my actions because my actions could get her into trouble. It's like having a parent all over again!"

"Did Elizabeth agree for the two of you to join Harmony because she understood you weren't getting out of joining?" Trevor simply asked.

I hated it when he was insightful. Reluctantly, I agreed, "Yes, I suppose she was getting us out of it."

"I think she is perceptive enough to know you wouldn't have gone this evening. She realized you needed a cool off period," Trevor stated. "Could she have made the deal trying to keep you out of trouble? Perhaps thinking you would reconsider by tomorrow evening. You would have bellied up here this evening if you hadn't gone this evening."

Did Elizabeth really understand my psyche? Did she really know my intentions? Was my chosen room mate intuitive? This was something to contemplate.

Trevor interrupted my thoughts as he said, "Your silence tells me somewhere inside you know this to be true. The deal to stay in tonight may not have been a choice."

Still in an angry mood I shot back, "It's just! I would never plan something and tell anyone you would be involved without asking you first. I would give you the choice and opportunity to make your own decision enabling you to live with the consequences of that decision." Talking this out was allowing me to think a little clearer and calmer.

"This is exactly why you have never played well with the other girls," Trevor told me. Caught a little off guard I raised both my hands, palms up in a questioning gesture. He continued, "The other girls are like you. Female, talkative, complicated, can capable of scheming, manipulating, and making decisions."

"Like guys aren't capable of those exact things?" I contradicted.

"Yes, we are," Trevor began. "But when dealing with a female, we compromise and let them make the decisions. If they aren't happy, no one is. A man puts his concerns aside and lets the woman rule. You can't handle a personality like your own which is another non-compromising female."

"That sounds like my mother always dominating my father," I smirked. Just as quickly I thought, Hold on! That certainly better not be what he meant. "Don't say I'm like my mother!" I angrily retorted.

"Oh no! I would never say that!" Trevor sincerely said. "I'm just saying, back off and give Elizabeth a chance. Don't dominate the friendship! Let her lead sometimes."

Trevor always spoke it as he saw it. I would need to chew this over and consider its possibility. Right now though, I had something else to discuss and lighten the mood. "Can we change the subject?" I questioned. He nodded. "I want to tell you something over the top exciting! I don't want you to interrupt until I'm finished."

"You've got my attention! This sounds more intriguing than joining Harmony," Trevor added with big anticipating eyes.

"Oh, it is," I replied rising from his cot with excitement. "You know Elizabeth and I were discovered with her chapter. After dodging and escaping that whole mess of trouble, Elizabeth wanted to visit the Hall of Records. Let's just say to look up something that interested her. She wanted to fly under the radar. I was game and accompanied her. Her plan led us to the Humling subway." I watched as it hit his face what I was saying. He looked astonished and apprehensive all in the same expression. "Yes, we went outside the dome into forbidden territory. We visited the Humling Hall of Records. We threw all caution to the wind and the escape there was utterly exhilarating!"

"Gee, she is more like you than you give her credit for," Trevor said in astonishment. As he shook his head in disbelief, he murmured, "It was her plan?"

"This is where it gets exciting," I told him. "We didn't have a destination card to get where we were going. We just went! No one came after us from the dome! We vanished from the dome. Before, I always assumed from the tales told to me by my parents, Keepers were tracked when they left the dome. Now, I don't think this is true. It's a myth or fairy tale!"

"No guards showed up to escort you to the Council?" Trevor questioned.

"Not a single guard and no one is the wiser!" I added. I paused watching different emotions grip his face. His mouth was wide open adding to his I don't believe you look. "You see, everyone assumes Keeper hierarchy and guards know when you are out of the dome. The destination cards are supposed to tell them the trip outside the dome is authorized and where we are at all times. All myth! No one knew or cared I was gone. I don't believe they track the destination cards either. The Keepers have been brainwashed into this guards coming to get you old wives tale."

"You can't assume they don't track the cards because they didn't know you left without one," Trevor stated. "Why would this lie be created?"

"I don't know," I answered. "Maybe they would create this charade to give Keepers a sense of safety after the event or ancient locket disappearances." Who knows, maybe it was a wives tale as well. I couldn't tell him, but Elizabeth's locket worked fine! "Maybe it was to keep the Humlings out of the dome. I haven't got a clue nor do I really care what the purpose of the tale is. That is unless we can find a way to benefit from it." Trevor was deep in thought. "I'm going to try it and prove it," I stated feeling a rush of adrenaline.

"Try what?" He anxiously questioned.

"To go outside the dome with a destination card that either isn't mine or not approved," I happily and excitedly stated.

"Tilly, the risk is huge," Trevor warned. "You may think the guards won't come but then again they might. Repercussions would be more serious than having to sing in the choir!"

"I'll relish the look on your face when no one hauls me away," I added. "Think of the freedom. Come go with me Mr. Chicken!" I place my hands under my arm pits and flapped like a chicken making a puk-puk-puk sound.

Being called a chicken, his hands began to shake and he began to bite his lip in thought. I had pushed his button. After my calling him a chicken he would fall right into place as my partner. After a moment or so Trevor said, "The freedom would be great. I would love to skate board to freedom beyond the dome. If you're serious, I'm game. We need a plan."

"No plan," I shot back.

"I insist," Trevor countered. "It will take planning to get an unauthorized destination card or one that isn't yours. We should also have an escape plan if the guards shows up."

"They're not going to show up!" I assured him standing firm in his face with my hands on my hips. I knew it in my gut!

"You don't know that!" Trevor replied. "Humor me this once. If I'm right and they do show up, we must get away. This isn't our normal prank. This is serious. The consequences?"

"Don't go there," I warned him. "If you get bogged down with the consequences, it hampers your ability to just go with the flow!"

Trevor seemed appalled at my lack of concern for my safety. He quickly pulled the orientation folder out of his back pack. I could see the wheels of his mind turning and planning. He dug more in his stuff. I wasn't sure what he was looking for. Then he pulled out a thick book of yellow pages. He hunted briefly through it, stopping at a particular page. His finger skimmed the page. After a brief moment he stopped. With a grin he said, "A plan? I think I have an idea!"

"You worry! You plan! And you can consider the consequences!" I added. Hmm... I too had a plan and would need to put it into action quickly. I needed his help in a different area. Not lost in useless worrying and planning. "If you had the tools and parts, could you build a destination card machine? You know, to make cards." He seemed confused.

"Tilly, you know I can build anything," Trevor said sounding like I had slightly injured his ego by asking. "Why build a machine if your theory is correct and they don't track the cards and if you don't need cards?"

"Only you and I know that! Knowing we can freely travel beyond the dome would be our secret!" I said grinning from ear to ear. "Don't you see? Guards don't check the beyond the dome destination cards. We could black market fake ID's to suckers wanting to escape to freedom. Others like us! They will be limited to having to use our cards. They still hold to the myths and fairy tale scare stories of guards and want proper fake ID's for outside. We could be very good entrepreneurs getting paid in favors."

"What a scam! This could be our biggest escapade ever," Trevor stated with a grin across his face. "First you must prove to me your theory is correct."

In the end, he was always up for my plans. He was a follower! I was the leader. I questioned, "You will build the machine?"

"You get me the parts, the schematics, and I'm in," Trevor agreed.

It was a deal made in heaven, a divine plan. I squealed in delight and threw my arms around his neck.

CHAPTER TEN

Elizabeth

Following my fellow classmates out the door of Keeper House, it hadn't gone unnoticed that Tilly and I temporarily were not on speaking terms. Tilly was insistent on ignoring me. I had to have faith that Tilly would show up and be gracious about taking part in Harmony. The professors were sticklers for details and being on time. The group schedule required practice one hour every evening. Competitions were every third Saturday. The professor was aspiring to direct us out of troubles path. He was sure this group would do just that!

Destiny was within view at the end of this corridor, leaning against the Department of Keeper Arch. I ignored her as I briskly strolled by. A few feet past her I cringed when I heard, "Elizabeth, where's Tilly?" Destiny sprung from the wall and hurried to keep pace with me.

"She left early this morning," I truthfully answered. I inhaled a deep breath of air and an annoying smell as bad as a skunk made my nose burn. Whew! The smell was Destiny! Did she dump the whole bottle of perfume on herself?

"Really," Destiny replied with a smirk. She was totally unaware of how bad she reeked! A flower would wilt in her presence.

"She had something to do before class," I simply stated trying not to breathe. I felt the necessity to quickly find an escape from this conversation. I was the fly being drawn into the spider's web! My quick fix was a few steps in front of us. A familiar friend was descending the staircase into the foyer. I picked up my pace yelling, "Trevor!"

Destiny was on my heels in pursuit. He twisted around and over his shoulder grinned and waved. He then turned his attention back to small talk with the curly red-headed girl whom he sat along side during our entrance exam and a tall, lanky boy with longer black hair. I assumed the all arms and legs guy was his room mate. The group of three stopped and mulled around the bottom of the staircase apparently waiting for me. Once catching up with them and thinking quick on my feet, I said, "Tilly mentioned you would be willing to show me to class." With one finger I pointed to Destiny behind me and mouthed, "Help!" Then loud and clear I stated, "Tilly had something else to do this morning."

Trevor's eyes were locked on mine, peering right past the veil of my lie. He grasped the hidden meaning to my gestures and deception. He replied, "Yes, if it's what Tilly said. I would be happy for you to walk with us." The tall, lanky boy kept rubbing his nose on the back of his hand. I was amused that he thought Destiny smelled too!

Destiny let out a huge sigh as she saw I was going to walk with them. She glared at the three of them, "Later Elizabeth! I'm not walking with the losers!"

"Yo! Speak for yourself, you skank!" The lanky boy replied to her rudeness.

Destiny went around us with her nose in the air. She strolled across the foyer as I whispered to all three of them, "Thank you." Trevor's eyes flashed to mine. He got the point. I was just trying to ditch Destiny.

"No problem!" Stated the tall, lanky boy. "You won't find me parading around with her! That chick stunk!"

"She must have fallen into the whole bottle of perfume," the red headed girl whispered as she shyly looked around at all of us.

Trevor looked back at me and inquired, "Where is Tilly?"

"I don't know," I truthfully answered. A troubled look crept onto his face. He knew something I did not!

I turned to the other two holding out my hand, "Hi, I'm Elizabeth."

"I'm Ruthanne," quietly stated the curly, red-headed girl as she offered her hand for me to shake. Standing before her I looked tan next to her pasty, pale skin. Her freckles were prominent and she was wearing extremely thick glasses. She gave off an aura of kindness and a gentle heart. Earth's Mother Teresa came to mind when I considered her simple graces.

"I'm Eddie," the lanky boy with long black hair responded as he put ear plugs in.

"Nice to meet you," I added.

The doors of the lift dinged and opened. The crowd ahead of us began to load in. We hurried across the foyer. I skipped into the lift just before the door closed. I began to peer around the crowd for Tilly. Where was she? We were going to join the choir. Could it really be that bad? Apparently she thought so! She was missing and I suspected her aversion to the choir had less to do with the choir itself and more to do with the fact her mother had been apart of the Harmony. In the short time I had known Tilly, I learned she rebelled against anything her parents were involved in, or wanted her to be involved in. But, I didn't expect this treatment from her. She blew me off, today's classes, and the first session of Harmony.

The lift door dinged and the small elf-like lift operator announced, "Destination three, Department of Records."

Today was the first class in the Hall of Records with Professor Kegley. The topic was accessing Keeper records. Stepping out of the lift I thanked the lift operator and received a huge smile. When he wasn't so gruff, you could see an old soul past his emerald eyes. Outside the lift, I found myself standing in a massive library. The air was filled with the fragrance of musty books. A white and brown marbled walkway led to a long desk where employees were sorting and scanning books, or soul's chapters. To the side of the walkway were rows of white tables and chairs where unknown Keepers were seated and peacefully reading. Beyond the rows of tables, were an endless amount of shelves containing chapters in a variety of colors. It did not matter which way I looked, I could not see the walls. The chapters simply went on as far as I could see.

Ruthanne led the way with Trevor and Eddie at her heels. I kept pace with them as we dodged and wound between the rows of shelves and books. The excitement of learning how to properly use this massive library excited me. The ability to correctly use it would help me with my detective work on the name Kaswell. My mind ran wild. Maybe I need special glasses to read the text, or blank pages. Maybe I had never lived my one earth life so there was nothing to record in my chapter of blank pages. I was entirely lost as to where to start in this hall. How could Tilly have left me to navigate this place by myself?

Lost in the mazes of standing shelves, I could no longer tell which direction led back to the lift. I followed Trevor and Ruthanne. They knew their way through the labyrinth of books. They babbled along about Harmony as they walked. Ruthanne had joined too! Eddie walked beside me with ear plugs in as we began to follow a red carpeted path which ran along the outside wall. We passed one door which had a red handle and a red warning light on top. The sign read, "Do not open. Humling Hall of Records. Authorized personnel only!" I knew exactly what resided on the other side. Judging the flicker of Trevor's eyes, he did too! I had a sneaking suspicion he was aware of our previous adventure. It resonated in my gut.

The next door to the right, led to a large classroom. Blinding white light bounced off the white floor, walls, and stadium seating, rising with tears of white chairs. This extreme lighting needed some toning down. You almost needed sun glasses in here! The only color in the room popped from the old fashioned green chalkboard which ran across the front of the room. Other students were mulling around and visiting as Professor Kegley bustled through the door with a huge stack of papers in her arms. She stopped abruptly. I followed her line of sight directly to Mrs. Bradford who was sitting in the professor's chair. Shocked and frustrated, the papers flew out of Professors Kegley's hands and onto the floor. She was a nervous Nelly! Who could blame her? Mrs. Bradford certainly could cause a person trouble.

As Professor Kegley scrambled to pick up the dropped papers, another lady appeared at the doorway. I knew exactly who she belonged too. The resemblance was uncanny. She was Tiffany's mother. It couldn't get any worse!

Tiffany's mother quickly and gracefully glided to Professor Kegley to assist in picking up the papers. "Why must you be so klutzy?" Questioned Tiffany's mother with a nasty, disapproving look.

Professor Kegley's only comment was, "Thank you. Mrs. Raderton."

Stealing the attention of the moment, Mrs. Raderton briskly walked over to the desk aware every eye was upon her. The stack of papers she had retrieved she haphazardly slammed to the desk as Professor Kegley inhaled a deep, cleansing breath and turned her attention to the woman in her chair, "Mrs. Bradford, to what do we owe this pleasure?"

"Rose and I were visiting. She mentioned training was to begin today. I hope you don't mind! We couldn't help but come down and check on our girls," said Mrs. Bradford as she stood and put one arm around Tiffany's shoulder and pulled her close.

"Hi, honey," said Mrs. Raderton as she leaned over and kissed Tiffany's cheek. Tiffany was wearing an attractive orange blouse and khaki pants. Actually, her whole group was in casual clothes. Why were they not in the marshmallow uniforms?

"Give me a break," Tilly sarcastically said from behind them, rolling her eyes.

"Tilly, there you are," Mrs. Bradford said in a showy type of way not to be outdone by Mrs. Raderton's affectionate show. Tilly grudgingly approached her mother. Mrs. Bradford put her other arm around Tilly's shoulder, pulling her close. Tiffany, Mrs. Bradford, and Tilly were locked into a group hug. How dreadful!

"Professor, you keep an eye on this one for me," Mrs. Bradford said with a sneer as she looked from Tilly directly to me. "She has always needed guidance and can't seem to find the right crowd to be around!"

"Mother, that's not funny!" Tilly growled with a disgusted expression on her face. Mrs. Bradford responded to Tilly's expression with a dirty, but high and mighty look of her own. Tilly shrugged off her mother's embrace and made her way to stand beside me. She would not let our spat and my agreement for us to join Harmony effect the united front she wanted her mother to see.

"Tilly, let me know if there is anything you need during training," said Mrs. Bradford as she gave the group a little wave while exiting the premises.

"Rose, are you coming with me?" She questioned as she looked over her shoulder at her friend.

"No, I'm going to assist Professor Kegley by helping to teach this group today. They need special care!" Mrs. Raderton responded with the two of them sharing a smirk. They were up to no good! Professor Kegley's eyes closed in disbelief. With a deep exhaling of breath, her head hung for a moment over her chest. She was obviously powerless to do anything about Mrs. Raderton's imposition on her class.

The room was silent. Everyone had been engrossed in this scene! Trevor and his entourage were watching across the room from Tilly and me. The distance didn't cut the connection between him and Tilly. His eyes peered across the room into hers and hers into his. Ruthanne tried to interrupt his concentration and their connection. It worked. I took the opportunity to say, "Tilly, you know I am sorry about…"

"Don't worry about it," Tilly nonchalantly said as she flashed to Trevor and then slid a plastic card the size of a hotel key into her pocket. "We were doomed so you agreed." She shrugged her shoulders. "Next time, let me make the agreements."

Tilly making agreements was not a good idea! However, I was going to pick my battles with her.

Tilly interrupted my thoughts as she leaned in close and whispered, "Sorry I am late. It is all part of my plan. It was important that my mother and I bump into each other this morning."

"Plan?" I questioned.

"Later," she responded in a whisper.

I gave her a questioning look as I whispered, "Is Tiffany part of the plan?" She shook her head no and I continued, "Why are the administration trainees not in the all white uniforms?"

"Only Department of Keepers, Department of Ghosts, and Hall of Babies associates wear all white," Tilly whispered. "We are the only groups to have direct contact with Humlings on the Earth Plane."

"Oh," I replied. "How does your mother know Tiffany and her Mom?"

"Both of our fathers trained and now work together at the Department of Administration. They're friends. I've had to put up with that Raderton demon in curls my whole life."

"Let me guess. Your mother wants you to be friends?" I asked. I could tell they were all cut from the same elite, snob cloth.

"Don't worry about what my mother said." Tilly reassured me, "Really."

That is easier said than done. Her words echoed in my ears, "The right crowd." If Mrs. Bradford only knew how right she was! Even for Tilly, my well-meant adventures were excessive and shadowy. I not only needed to worry about Mrs. Bradford, but also Mrs. Raderton. They were two peas in a pod! "Does Mrs. Raderton work for the Department of Records?" I casually asked as we moved to climb the steps up the stadium seating.

"She actually works for the Hall of Babies," Tilly responded. "It's a branch of the Hall of Records."

"Ladies, please stop your whispering." Professor Kegley stated. "Everyone find a seat while I pass out your record cards. Who can tell me what a records card does?"

Ruthanne's shot her Lilly white arm and hand into the air. The professor called on her, "Miss Jones."

Ruthanne answered, "A records card allows you to access the Hall of Records and the Hall of Charts. It keeps track of what you have viewed, checked out, and returned."

"Professor, I didn't think you can use it to check out chapters?" I said interrupting without thinking. Everyone's gaze turned to me.

"Miss Cantrell, unless I ask you a question, please raise your hand," reprimanded Professor Kegley.

"May I," said Mrs. Raderton as she got up from the chair she was seated in. She continued before Professor Kegley could continue. You could tell the Professor was annoyed. "A chapter is never allowed to leave the hall due to the fact it is an individual record of a Keeper. It is my understanding Tilly and yourself learned this the hard way when you borrowed a chapter and got caught red-handed."

Everyone was now staring at the two of us with shock clear in their eyes. We just became gossip bait for them which made me feel uneasy. I glanced over at Tilly as she popped gum into her mouth, her answer for any stressful situation. Gum! She held her head high and displayed an indifferent attitude while I sank into my chair which was much too small to hide me. I caught the satisfying smirk on Tiffany's face. Obviously, Mrs. Raderton infiltrated this group to spy and gain revenge for her daughter through our public humiliation. They had a plan. Professor Kegley couldn't help us because she was oblivious to the friction between Tiffany and us.

The class session continued. We were instructed to take notes. Ruthanne knew the majority of the answers to any questions asked. Before this lesson ended I learned records of Humlings were also called chapters and not allowed to be checked out. More interestingly, chapters could only be opened by the person they were about unless special permission from the Council is given. Now I understood why Tilly hadn't opened mine. Finding the Kaswell chapter and being able to open it would allow me to verify what I already knew. I am Elizabeth Kaswell. I lost interest as the professor began to speak of less important history and traditional library books. They could be checked out and returned and were called simply books!

During the training session Professor Kegley asked, "I need a volunteer who can share a portion of their chapter with the class to help instruct those here on how the viewer machine works."

"Excuse me, Professor. I have already loaded the viewer with Tilly's chapter," smiled Mrs. Raderton as she turned to peer at Tilly. "Tilly, I am sure you don't mind, do you?" A rhetorical question because she did not give Tilly a chance to answer. "Please come down and open the chapter for us." Tilly strutted down the center aisle smacking her gum and blowing loud pink bubbles. Begrudgingly, Tilly cracked open the chapter and Mrs. Raderton snatched the open book from her, pushing her hands away. She flipped through quickly and seemed to know what she was looking for. When an up to no good smile appeared on her face, Mrs. Raderton entered the page into the machine. It reminded me of an old-fashioned record player. The arm came out over the chapter, skimmed the words, and threw the moving scene onto a white pull down screen which automatically came down hiding the green chalk board.

"Thank you Mrs. Raderton," said the Professor as she turned the lights down lower. "Let's watch."

Tilly was driving the brightest yellow pickup truck I had ever seen. Her window was down and she was singing away to a loud song with a thumping beat. What a voice! Listening to her was pleasant. She could really sing! As she turned the corner on the rural highway leading through the small town were she was driving, she came upon a park. It was small with old playground equipment that set next to the railroad. An old railroad station was present but no longer in use.

Her truck came to a stop in one of the six parking spaces provided in this small park. The engine rested as she popped the hood lever. What was she doing? She didn't appear to have a mechanical failure. She was still singing and in a good mood! I intently watched as she opened the truck door and bounced out. With her hands she popped the catch on the hood. It went up and was propped with the hood rod. She leaned over the engine looking at the different dip sticks. When she found the one she wanted, she pulled it out. She stopped to read it and carried it around the truck to open the cab door. She held it out behind her to control its drips. Then she opened the door and dug behind the seat. She smiled as she found the rag she was looking for. After one quick wipe of the stick, she carried it back to the engine and shoved it back into its place.

A silver car which was playing music louder than Tilly's honked form the highway. Just as quickly the car pulled into a parking space a couple down from hers. She smiled and waved. You could tell they were friends. While watching her pull back out the oil dip stick and reading its results, I couldn't help but notice that on the Earth Plane she was also popular with boys. All four doors opened on the silver colored auto and the long legs of boys appeared as their feet hit the ground and climbed out.

The driver bounded over asking her if she was having car trouble. I watched as she smiled a flirtatious smile as she held the stick for them to read, "I was just checking the oil. See, it says… check in park!" The driver and two other boys tried to hold back their laughter. One was slap stick hysterical and quickly walked away. It was the look on their faces that caused Tilly to realize her folly. They confirmed it with one boy saying, "You didn't need to check your oil in the park. It can be checked anywhere as long as the truck was in the gear of park." Then they he-hawed again but was gracious enough to check her oil for her.

The rest of her chapter was ignored. The group was laughing at Tilly's expense. Professor Kegley turned off the volume and turned up the lights. I wanted to scream at the group to stop laughing. Mrs. Raderton showed how cruel she could be with this version of public humiliation. She was presenting Tilly as an air head or bimbo. I looked over at Tilly who was not laughing, but packing her back-pack. She stood and once again made her way down the aisle popping bubbles. Head held high!

If Tilly was walking out on this show, I was too! She was my friend. I stood to follow Tilly when I heard Mrs. Raderton shout, "Miss Cantrell, may I ask where you are going?" I stood still for a moment not sure how to answer. Trevor caught my attention as he shook his head from side to side to tell me not to follow Tilly.

I heard Mrs. Raderton continue, "I will excuse Tilly since she was... embarrassed. You on the other hand. Miss Cantrell. I will not excuse from class."

I sat back down, clearly defeated and humiliated for my friend. I turned my attention to Trevor as he glanced back at me aghast. I had not noticed he was seated next to the red-headed Ruthanne. She was comforting him by rubbing his arm. I thought Trevor was Tilly's property.

The rest of the class was informative, but I had a hard time concentrating. I could not help but wonder how Tilly would feel about Ruthanne hanging all over Trevor. Also, I worried about her leaving, apparently upset.

CHAPTER ELEVEN

Tilly

I was glad to get out of there! Stuffy! I couldn't imagine sitting and wasting a whole Tuesday listening to them. Boring! What a great opportunity to escape. My dramatic, embarrassed exit looked real. Acting is a gift and I stormed out as if I was upset. I wasn't. I can laugh at myself. Laughter is good for the soul. I could see them thinking, we got Tilly good! If I were to be mad at someone or something, it would be at Mrs. Raderton for trying to embarrass me. I would think of a way to even the playing field sometime soon.

Today, I had more important issues to think about. My mother had not noticed that I swiped her lift destination card from her pocket when she hugged me. She always picked up an extra destination card on Tuesday for her Wednesday morning trip to Dad's favorite store beyond the dome to get his pastries for the week. I now had what I needed to test my theory. The card was not mine. Check! The card was not authorized for today. Check! I had a feasible alibi if I should be caught. I could simply say I was out running an errand to help my mother. Brilliant!

Before leaving the Hall of Records, I needed to dive into any book about destination cards. If all went as planned, I would need schematics. Wasting no time as I rounded the corner, I stopped at the front desk.

Mrs. Summors looked up with a genuine happy and glowing face. The warmth of her grin radiated through my whole body making me feel warm. "Good Morning Tilly! How are you doing today?"

"Fine," I casually replied as I plopped my back pack at my feet.

"Fine," Mrs. Summors repeated with a hint of a frown crossing her face. "That doesn't sound like you! Has your day presented a kink like a knot on a rope? How is training?"

"It's going okay so far," I said half heartily. Hmm… Training was going well! It was the catty girls and professors who didn't appreciate my gifts. Also, the prison I was being held captive in was the kink!

"Made any new friends?" Mrs. Summors gently asked.

I understood. Her demeanor screamed that she was worried I wasn't fitting in. "Yeah," I smiled. "My room mate and I are two peas in a pod!"

"Hmm," hummed Mrs. Summors while her eyes peered through me. "What can I help you with today?"

"I am looking for a book on destination cards," I stated and then blew a big popping bubble.

"Why would you need a book about destination cards?" Mrs. Summors questioned.

Mrs. Summors knew me too well! Everything done by me served a purpose. I hesitated. Lying to her wasn't going to become a regular habit. I liked her! How could I skirt the truth? A light bulb moment seemed to spill out my mouth, "We are studying Transportation Law with Professor Presnell. Some additional research will give me extra credit for the class. I need it!" My mind never ceased to amaze me! I was good!

The gloating in my head was cut short when Mrs. Summors asked, "Did Professor Presnell give you a note?"

My elation at my wit was plummeted. "A note?" I questioned while an uneasy feeling gripped the pit of my stomach. This could derail my plans. "I didn't know I needed one. If you will let me do my research, the next time I come I promise to get a note." One look or a few moments was all I needed with the book!

Mrs. Summors was peering at me, trying to detect a hint of any scheme I might be contemplating. "Okay," Mrs. Summors eventually replied. "I'll help you this time. However, you really need to start following the rules. Especially now that you have been given adult status. Leniency is for children."

"How did you know I was emancipated?" I asked dumfounded.

"Everyone knows after that stunt you and your room mate pulled," Mrs. Summors replied with a frown. "Tilly, consequences for your actions will be severe now that you have adult status. Please tread lightly."

"Don't worry," I reassured her. My gut was beginning to have a sinking feeling. I was definitely lying! "You know me."

"Yes I do," Mrs. Summors replied with a look that clearly stated this was the problem. She knew me inside and out and had done so since I was an infant. Sighing she said, "Stay here and I will get the book for you."

I stood and watched as she disappeared into the restricted section. If that book's home was in the restricted section, the chances of my being able to check it out weren't promising. I paced a moment or two in front of the desk, surprised at how quickly she returned. I questioned, "Can I check it out?"

"May I make a suggestion?" Mrs. Summors inquired.

"I'm all ears," I responded.

"Find what you're looking for and copy it down," stated Mrs. Summors bluntly. "I suspect you have a motive. Considering the topic of this book…" She held up her hand, palm towards me, and shook her head. Clearly she didn't want to know. "You don't want this book registered on your records card."

"Really… umm… I…" I hesitated. The gig was up! "Okay. Thank you," I stated under her peering eyes. She waved her hand to usher me away as I picked up my back pack and turned to find a place at one of the long, white tables for reading.

This book was filled with mumbo jumbo! It was like reading a mechanics catalog. Boring! Just about as boring as the guy my father wanted me to date. When he spoke of the guy it was as if he could be reading out of this manual. I flipped through the book looking for pictures. That is what I needed. I would never be able to understand the technical stuff. Finally, there the schematics were in the back of the book. They were too complicated to copy down!

The front desk had no one perched behind it at the moment. I made my way behind the desk and took one glance around. I turned my back to the room and placed the book onto the glass of the copy machine. I hit the copy button wishing the machine would hurry. Restricted books were not allowed to be copied. One more silly rule! One more broken rule! As the paper finally appeared Mrs. Summors asked from behind me, "Got what you need?"

"Sure did," I replied as I pulled the book off the glass and shut the lid. I handed the book back to her saying, "Thank you."

"I have always believed in you and done my best to act as a buffer for you here in the Department of Records. Beyond these walls, I can't help you. Please remember to tread lightly," Mrs. Summors repeated as I made my way around the desk.

"Of course," I replied to her warm, motherly grin. Why did I feel when I was in her presence that she was one of a handful of individuals who really cared for me? She gave me a warm, fuzzy feeling. My mother didn't.

"Okay," Mrs. Summors said. She appeared to be satisfied with her warning. "Have a great day!"

I moved towards the lift shoving the copied schematics into the bottom of my bag. I started to practice out loud as I headed for the lift, "Of course it's my destination card. I'm going to Bakersfield to get pastries for my father." That little leprechaun of a lift operator was sure to question me. It wasn't his job! He was just helplessly nosy! "How else do you think I would have gotten out of class today if my mother hadn't sent me on this errand?" The short guy was one of a handful of beings who made me nervous. I would not panic! I needed to use my mother's destination card to test my theory that once outside the dome they didn't register who was using the card.

I pushed the button and the lift automatically opened with no waiting. I stepped inside the door, "Bakersfield."

The midget lift operator asked, "Destination Card."

I produced the destination card from my pocket. Catching me off guard, he roughly grabbed onto the card. I tightened my grip. As we came to an impasse with both firmly gripping the card, I pulled the card far above his head. He held on and was now standing on his tippy toes. I was satisfied. Nobody snatched something out of my hands! I lowered the card and bent down to look him directly in the eye saying, "Here is my card."

Clearly disgusted at his inability to snatch the card from my grip, he turned and roughly pushed the destination card into a slot besides the number five button. I questioned, "And?"

He growled, "Thank you. Ma'am."

Wonderful! He was so mad that he wasn't about to ask questions. I moved to the back of the lift and waited until the door opened with him announcing, "Destination five, Bakersfield."

Exiting the lift, I gave him one of the nastiest look I could muster. Bakersfield was like a step back in time. Walking down the dirt road between the storefronts, I enjoyed the fragrance of apple pie mixed with freshly baked bread. Bakersfield was a quaint small town whose focus was, what else, baking! It couldn't be more obvious. Numerous times I had accompanied my mother here as a small child. She stopped bringing me with her when the Baker's son developed a hopeless crush on me. I remember him being very passionate in slipping me notes and blowing me kisses. Who could really blame him! I was an unforgettable heart throb.

As I stepped thought the bakery door, like so many other things, it had not changed at all.

"Bon jour, Mademoiselle," said the burly French baker. "How may I help you today?"

"I am here to pick up some of your super delicious pastries," I said as I smiled.

"Combien?" He inquired.

I paused while I decided how many to get. The aging baker thought I didn't understand his question as he said, "Combien is asking…"

"How much," a huskier voice questioned from the doorway. Wow! The Baker's son was more handsome than I had remembered. His simple white baker's jacket sculpted to his muscular body. His skin was a deep olive and his features... Even though he was a guy... Beautiful. It was my heart throbbing now!

"Thank you, Claude. How could I ever not recognize you?" I stated as he crossed the room to stand before me.

"Bon jour," Claude said as he grabbed my hand, pulling it to his mouth and placing a kiss upon it. Then he tilted his head down in respect. He had not forgotten me!

His father cleared his throat. I nervously said, "Two dozen." He raised his eyebrows at my request and started to fold a huge box. It was too big! "Excuse me, can you split them into two smaller boxes?"

"Quoi?" The aging baker responded.

That word I didn't know. Claude could read the expression on my face as he said, "Le Pere, I can fill her order." He then hopped over the counter trying to impress me. In a fluid motion he opened up two smaller boxes and began placing the pastries inside. "Have you been on holiday? Your absence has been long."

"Did a brief stint on the Earth Plane," I answered not wanting to say my mother forbid me from coming here. That was undignified and would insult him! The first box was filled and I questioned, "Could I have one of the boxes forwarded to my address?"

A grin crossed his face with the thought of having my address. He responded, "Yes, we can send this par delivery to your household." He dug under the counter and retrieved a delivery slip.

Hand delivery wasn't going to work since he was a Humling and not allowed in the dome. It would need to be sent via mail. "Not delivery. I want them mailed."

"Pardon, you want these mailed?" Claude questioned. I nodded and the displeased boy, now a hunk of a man, once again dug under the counter. He came up with yellowed mail packaging slips. It was obvious no one mailed pastries to themselves!

He pushed the form across for me to place my address on the appropriate lines. I hesitated. I couldn't write on the form. My mother would recognize the handwriting. Hmm… I placed the pen into my left hand. The writing would be so bad she would never recognize it as mine. Quickly I wrote the address on the outside label. On the inside I scribbled, "Thank you for your continued business! This week is covered. We will see you next week!" My father would have his pastries leaving my mother no need to get another pass. No chance of the baker mentioning my visit. Best of all, my mother would never bother to thank them next week. The thought would never cross my mother's mind. By then, it would be old hat to the baker! Once complete, I passed it back to him.

He was dismayed. Yes, my address was a postal address. All Keepers' addresses were to ensure we remained anonymous. We couldn't tell the Humlings we met that we were Keepers! He caught me off guard as he hopped back over the counter with the remaining box of pastries in his hand to where I stood. He carefully placed the box on the counter.

Just as suddenly his arms surrounded me as he whispered, "Je t'aime."

"Huh?" I sighed. He didn't notice my response as his eyes were closed and his face moving towards mine. He was going to kiss me! I ducked under his arms, grabbed the box, and swiftly headed for the door. The aging baker was now privy to what his son was doing and took his bakers hat off and swatted his son with it. Glad I couldn't understand French because the words didn't seem happy.

"Au revior," Claude called after me putting his long fingers to his lips and throwing me an exquisite kiss.

"Bye," I yelled in response while not looking back. Note to self. Stay away from French bakers. They were nuts! My mother was right about this one! Although I found him attractive, he was too much for me to control.

Despite the run in with the baker and his son, this was a successful adventure. I was re-entering the lift a little out of breath from running. No guards had been summoned to check my whereabouts or my using someone else's destination card. I stated to the normal sized lift operator, "Keeper Dome." I was glad not to have to deal with the little squirt. He was probably pretty peeved at me right now. Anger only grows when you have time to stew about it!

"Destination Card?" Asked the lift operator. Returning to the dome was always pleasant since the lift operator was different. You didn't have to look at the leprechaun midget!

I backed against the wall and could see the familiar silhouette of Claude following me down the street. The lift operator inserted the card into the appropriate slot. He then turned to hand it back to me, "Thank you ma'am."

I could only hope the door would close before Claude cornered me. He was passionate. Odd for me, but he was too persistent! I moved to the corner of the lift and could hear Claude yell at the lift operator, "Have you seen a young Mademoiselle come this way?" Thank goodness he was unable to see me!

I crossed the fingers on one hand and with the other I put a finger to my lips and mouthed to the operator, "Shh!" Then I closed my eyes as I heard the lift operator say, "Sorry."

Instantly, I opened my eyes and peered at the lift operator. He stared forward and pushed the button to close the door. The leprechaun midget would never have done that! I hesitantly said, "Thank you. I'm glad to have escaped that nutty boy!"

"No problem," the lift operator said as his eyes laughed at me. "You're not the first to run from him. You're a Keeper! He should not be pestering you."

"Oh," I said. Boy, did I feel silly. "My name is Tilly," I stated as I held out my hand to shake his.

"I'm Douglas," he said as he shook my hand. The lift dinged and Douglas announced, "Department of Administration."

"It was very nice to meet you," I said as I stepped out into the Department of Administration lobby.

Turning to look at Douglas, he said with a twinkle in his eye, "It was all my pleasure."

Time to turn my attention to the second part of my plan! As I walked towards my father's office, I couldn't help but think of the young man named

Scott whom my father wanted me to date. Forced into playing hostess for dinner, I had spent a dreadful evening under Scott's and my parent's awkward smiles. I understood my father's fondness for him. He seemed to be a genuinely good guy, but I found him to be boring. Since he could never excite me, dinner was painful to get through. The spark just wasn't there! To top off the whole night, he tripped out the back door of my house upon leaving. He appeared to be too nervous to even attempt a kiss! However, today my path to him was clearly marked. I needed him! He worked in The Department of Administration Engineering Office. I needed access to the parts necessary for the destination card maker?

I was pulled from my thoughts when I heard my father's chuckle. The conference room to the right was holding a meeting, and there sat my father. I tapped on the window while smiling and giving a little wave. He glanced over at me and turned back to excuse himself. He came out the door and pulled it shut questioning, "Tilly, what are you doing here? Why are you not in class?"

"Good morning to you too!" I retorted.

He held out his hand to gesture for us to walk down the hallway. "Is something wrong?"

The light bulb went off in my head. I had never once visited him at work. He and I had never been close. However, I would pretend we had and spill my sad story of my humiliation! "Dad, it was awful. Mrs. Raderton embarrassed me today in front of all my class."

"How did she do that?" He questioned studying my face trying to decide if I was being truthful.

I was a great actress. I inhaled a deep breath. To him it appeared I was trying to calm myself, I knew I was making myself yawn. Thus, my eyes watered. I repeated the inhale and yawn technique till I had a couple tears rolling down my cheek. "She played part of my chapter. It was the part where I checked the oil in park. Everyone laughed at me!"

"Mathilda honey, I'm sorry that happened," he stated clearly hesitating whether to hug me or not. His hand went to his chin as he thought about what to say. "Honey, I will speak to Dale about it."

"That's okay Dad," I said as I tentatively smiled. "Mr. Raderton will just take her side. You don't have to say anything." I forced another big fake tear to plummet down my face.

He leaned over and kissed my forehead. My gut told me my father would say something. I didn't really know if it would do any good. Just maybe it would level that playing field if Mrs. Raderton thought I would run to Daddy if she did not behave. Let the adults squabble!

"Dad, you won't make me go back today?" I whimpered with pleading eyes. This was too simple!

"If I don't, what will you do with your day?" He skeptically asked.

"Could I spend the day observing Administration Engineering?" I asked.

"Would that have anything to do with a certain boy?" my father asked with a grin crossing his face.

"Of course not," I replied being coy.

His desire for me to date Scott would suit my plan well. I got him! My father had just been putty in my hands. He began, "If I take you to their office, you won't tell your mother, right?"

"Keepers Honor!" I replied with a wide smile. "Not if it's what I need to do to see him! Dad, he's just fascinating!" I just obtained blackmail material on my father! Later I could use it to my advantage. Give me what I want or I'll tell my mother!

We abruptly turned a corner strolling away from the hall leading to my father's office and towards Engineering. I could break out in dance! My brilliant mind was really wasted in class. I had just talked my father into taking me to Scott, got blackmail material on my father, and hopefully got Mrs. Raderton into trouble for her stunt! My talents were wasted sitting in classes.

"I just knew you would like him," my father said interrupting my internal gloating.

We arrived at a row of staircases. Each staircase opening was like a door with a sign hanging above it. I had never seen this part of the building. We passed a few staircase door signs reading; Guard Services, Housing Office, Personnel Office, Employment Office, etc. Then the staircase we were looking for announced itself by the sign which read engineering services. My father turned to me saying, "At the top of the stairs will be a receptionist. Ask for Scott."

"Thank you, Daddy," I answered with a soft smile and giving him a quick girlish hug.

"Mathilda honey, come see me more often," he replied as he leaned over to kiss the top of my head. It almost felt like he really cared. I climbed up the stairs and out of his sight.

Just as my father promised, there sat a receptionist. She had long blond hair, amazing green eyes, and couldn't be much older than myself. She smiled asking, "May I help you?"

"I'm looking for Scott Jorgin," I responded.

"Is he expecting you?" She asked with a serious look on her face.

"No," I replied.

"Have a seat and I will let him know you are waiting," she said with a sigh as though my unscheduled visit was an annoyance.

Sitting in the chair and watching her, I had to wonder. What was her problem? Was I imagining the daggers she seemed to be staring? The longer I sat there, the more nervous she made me. To my relief, Scott walked down the hallway towards me. I noticed the receptionist brightened up as he appeared. Okay. Now I understood. She liked him and saw me as competition. She had a right to be jealous. All males loved me! I was hot!

Scott walked past her with his eyes intently focused on me. A smile radiated from his face as he warmly said, "Tilly. I'm glad to see you!"

"Hi, Scott," I replied. "I thought I might shadow you today."

"You want to work in Engineering?" Scott questioned with a chuckle.

I needed to turn on the flirting! He was easy prey because I was a man eater! Quickly, I moved and placed my hand squarely on his chest. I picked at his button and looked at him with puppy eyes, "Just thought it might be... interesting to see where you work. I'll only stay until you bore me." I kissed my fingertip and placed it on his lips. There was a lot of truth in the last statement. The moment I found my parts and could tuck them into my bag, he would be a bore to me!

"You don't have class today?" Scott asked blushing.

"No," I said and smiled. "I have the afternoon off."

"Okay, you can follow me around all day if you like," Scott said placing his hand on top of mine that was still fingering his shirt button. "And, I'll try not to bore you!" He released himself from my flirtatious stance and walked to the receptionist desk asking, "Sadie, could you get a pass for my friend?"

She cordially asked with a polite, fake smile, "May I have your name?" She was my equal and her show was as polished as mine. This meant she could be dangerous. Equal forces recognize each other.

"Mathilda Bradford," I stated directly to her, blowing a bubble and popping it in front of her.

Scott's watch beeped and he looked torn saying, "Could you make your way down when Sadie gives you your pass and catch up with me?"

"Sure," I said batting my eye lashes at him. This might be simpler than I thought.

"I'm in the work room today. The last door at the end of the hall," Scott replied. I waved him on as he hesitated but seemed to be in a hurry. "The alarm must need immediate attention. I'm sorry!"

"Not a problem!" I yelled after him.

Startling me, I heard Sadie growl, "Scott is mine. Keep your hands off!"

We might have been friends if we had met under other circumstances. As it was, I couldn't back down. "Scott is only yours if he wants you." I waited a moment for my words to sink in and then held my hand out and demanded, "My pass, please."

It was lying on the desk and Sadie didn't budge. She was steaming! I reached over and grabbed the pass and hung it around my neck. I turned on a dime and strutted down the hall.

As I slowly walked past many offices on my way to the last door, Scott suddenly appeared. "Tilly, wait for me in here. I'll be right back."

I nodded and entered the door to a rectangular shop. One of the long walls was filled with hanging tools and miscellaneous parts. Several wooden tables were in the center and one held an arrangement of saws. In the corner was a desk where a standing man was busily looking through a stack of papers. Beside the desk, along the short wall in the back, was a long table which held several computers. The other long wall was filled with locked cabinets with small labels on the outside. I sat down at the long table as the busy man found what he was looking for and rushed past me and out the door.

Alone in the large shop, I began to look at the stuff hanging around the walls. I was in the right place. This was a parts and tool room. Unfamiliar with this sort of thing, I set my backpack upon the shop table, retrieved the schematic copy, and folded the copy into a smaller size. I placed my arm through the handle of the backpack, leaving it hanging slightly unzipped from my arm. With the folded, copied schematics list as my guide, I started to roam the room to find the needed parts.

The busy man who had been fumbling through papers on the tiny desk, swiftly returned through the door. He glanced my way saying, "Please don't touch anything while you wait." I nodded with a slight shrug of my shoulders. His attitude rubbed me wrong. Don't touch anything! Ridiculous! Without paying me any further attention he sat down at the desk and began typing away on a keyboard.

I spotted the first couple of items I needed all hanging closely together. How was I to get them in my bag without being noticed? The whole not touching was silly. This shop received all these parts for free after all. Which is why I would feel no guilt in helping myself too them. They could get more for free. I was doing a little restricted shopping.

The man became preoccupied typing with his back to me. I quietly and easily slid the first couple items, multicolored wires and a small fan, into my half unzipped back pack. I finally spotted the small box for the miniature fan. Reaching above my head, I let it clank into other metal as I brought it down. Instantly, I heard the keyboard stop. He turned towards me and I turned the small box over and over in my hands pretending to be enthralled with looking at it. The man was now at my side with his hand held out to retrieve the box. To his annoyed, sour look I quickly said, "Sorry."

He opened his mouth to lecture me but was distracted. The door flung open with a lady moving inside and waving for the man to come. He placed the item back in its original position and then moved towards the door and disappeared with the lady. I jumped and rapidly shoved item after item into my back pack while keeping an eye on the door. If caught, I knew I would pretend to be looking at the parts again. Thank goodness Scott hadn't come back!

When the man reappeared, I had all the parts except the two needed computer boards. I stood still leaning against a cabinet as though I was bored. If I couldn't find the boards, could Trevor make them if given the parts? What exact parts would go into a computer board? Technical was not my niche. My head hurt as well as my arm from carrying this now heavier back pack. The busy man exited again.

Speedily, I strolled towards the cabinets and began to trace my finger down them reading labels as I went. If I were a computer board, I would be safe and secure in a dry, dust free cabinet. The cabinets were all locked with the exception of the tall one on the end. It was labeled, parts to be recycled. Startling my train of thought the man who had once more returned asked, "Who are you waiting for?"

I turned around and answered, "Scott."

"I need him too! Do you know where he went?" He questioned.

"No, he just told me to wait," I said and blew a big pink bubble acting bored.

"Let me see if I can find him for both of us," the man stated as he once again walked across the room and then out the door.

I opened the cabinet and haphazardly threw every type of computer board visible into my back pack until it was full. No time to be picky. I hoped Trevor could work with what I could get! I rapidly closed the cabinet door and shoved the schematic back into my back pack. The door was opening as I zipped the bag shut.

"Tilly, I'm sorry you have been waiting," Scott said looking disgusted as he strolled over to me.

I could see there was more. "And?" I questioned.

"It turns out I am needed to go to the Hall of Ghosts and start analyzing a problem they are having with their staircases," Scott said. "I would much prefer to spend time here with you, but it's impossible!"

I placed my hand back on his chest, "I understand. Just walk me to the exit!" I couldn't miss walking past the snooty receptionist with him in tow.

"Let me carry your bag," Scott said as he hoisted it over his shoulder. "What do you have in here?"

"Just girl things and books my father gave me for studying," I replied as I started to move towards the door.

"If I wasn't working today, I would carry this darn bag all the way back to the Hall of Knowledge for you," Scott stated sweetly. He was genuine and stepped up to open and hold the door for me.

I forced a smile onto my face as I moved through the door saying, "Thank you." For a moment I had been caught up with his gentlemanly demeanor. I couldn't deny that Scott was old fashioned, especially when in the graces of such an independent female. No way was I going to let him walk me back.

Arriving back to the reception desk, Scott took a few steps away towards another young man. I could overhear him instructing him to escort and carry my bag for me to the lift. I plopped my pass down on the receptionist desk and whispered, "The hour in the tool room with Scott was pure heaven! Of course, you wouldn't know."

Turning and stepping up to Scott, I once more kissed my finger tips and placed it on Scott's chin to annoy the receptionist.

Back at Keeper House, I plopped my bag of parts on Trevor's bed and said, "Hey guys!"

"Was' Up Tilly," Eddie stated in his usual skater laid-back attitude. He tossed his board and back-pack on his bed.

"Everything went as I planned and I have nothing but good news!" I answered.

"Good news?" Trevor questioned. "I have worried all afternoon about you and the trouble you could be in. You're not even upset about that are you?"

"What should I be upset about?" I questioned. "I do everything right!"

"How about checkin' the oil!" Eddie stated with a chuckle and a teasing voice.

Trevor glared at him but it wasn't necessary. "That incident! I learned to laugh at it long ago."

"The queen and her minions wanted to embarrass you!" Trevor stated.

"So!" I replied. "Does it matter what any of them think?"

"Rock on Tilly!" Eddie stated.

"Then why did you run out?" Trevor asked.

"It was perfect timing. A teary exit for me that no one would question! When else would I have the opportunity to go get what we needed for our plan?" I questioned.

"What plan?" Eddie questioned.

"Our biggest ever," I replied to Trevor's understanding grin.

"So this is it?" Trevor questioned as his attention focused on the parts I dumped out on his bed.

"I scored all the parts! Did a little restricted shop lifting," I replied. "It's up to you to work your electronic magic."

"What are we making?" Eddie asked peering at the parts.

My eyes flickered from Eddie to Trevor who said, "Might as well tell him. He'll know soon enough."

"A destination card maker," I replied.

"No way," Eddie replied looking shocked but impressed. "That's killer. How did you come up with the parts? Or the idea?"

"Elizabeth gave her the idea," Trevor answered.

"Do tell," Eddie said. "Isn't this a choice bit of information. I won't tell this one!"

"Sometimes you are as bad as a girl," I truthfully stated. He was always looking for gossip.

"The two of them ventured out beyond the dome," Trevor interjected.

Eddie had no response, but looked a bit awed. Then suddenly he blurted out, "Outside the dome?"

I further explained, "When we were outside the dome I realized no one knew we were gone or had left. Everyone has always assumed the destination cards work as permission and track our movement outside the dome. They don't! Everyone has always assumed guards would show up. They don't!"

"Beautiful isn't it?" Trevor stated as shocked Eddie nodded in agreement.

"The cards are useless?" Eddie questioned.

"Just a piece of plastic," I answered. "A scare technique to hold Keepers to dome slavery. Only the three of us know this. The card is just for show and brain washing. Keepers have been brainwashed to believe it's their only ticket to freedom and told fairy tales about Keepers disappearing."

"Scare techniques best describe this!" Trevor stated. "It's like telling someone a fence is electrified, but it isn't. No one wants to get shocked, so you don't touch. Keepers are told they must have a card to travel. That is the electric lie!"

"Sketchy!" Said Eddie.

Trevor continued, "The card is inserted in a blank slot. The lift operators are the guards and also determine travel by the buttons."

"Don't either of you ask how I came into possession of the parts. You don't want to know," I stated.

"I owe you an apology Tilly," Eddie replied with a tone of relief. "I wasn't sure you picked the right room mate. Elizabeth seems so dull and lost. I was wrong. She's going to hang with us well."

"Yes and no," I answered him. "Yes, I always pick my friends well. No, Elizabeth doesn't know about this particular scheme yet. I want to show her rather than tell her."

Trevor was methodically laying out the parts across his bed. He was matching them to the hand drawn diagram he sent with me to collect the parts. He appeared to then be comparing his diagram to the copied schematics from the Hall of Knowledge. Eddie seemed to be lost in his own world of thought. "Cool, a destination card maker," Eddie seemed to agree. "All the skate parks I will be able to go to. My days of limited travel are over."

"Eddie," I sweetly said to gain his attention. "You know you can't tell anyone."

"Bummer!" Eddie stated.

"I need you to agree not to tell anyone," I added in a stern voice.

"To say that to me is bogus," stated Eddie. "You can trust me! You shouldn't need to ask! I knew about all the other stuff the two of you did over time. We have a friendship pact, Trevor!"

"The three of us," Trevor corrected.

"Three of us because I'm your cousin and best friend," Eddie stated. "Bro, you are always roping me into something. I honor our pact and accept Tilly into it."

"This venture is major!" Trevor said with a raised voice. "It's Council worthy."

"You think they would send us before the Council for black-marketing destination cards?" Eddie asked.

"Absolutely!" Chimed Trevor. "This is throwing every rule the Council has made concerning Keeper travel out the window. Without rules, civilization breaks down. The world the Council has created would break down. The dome would become obsolete because Keepers would be free to venture out and live in other areas. The fake cards and guard fears keeps everyone imprisoned."

"So we are going to make and black market fake cards and get heavenly rich off the average Keepers gullibility?" Eddie asked.

"You got it!" Trevor stated. "We're going to fleece the masses of blind Keepers with the promise of freedom through our fake ID's. They still believe they must have them. Everyone would like to travel to forbidden areas. A fake card lets them travel anonymously and not be a part of their eternal record or so they believe."

"Deregulating and undermining the Council's ability to track and control us is revolution and definitely Council worthy!" I stated. Adding some drama I continued, "It would be an act of treason!"

"We are leaders of a revolution and profiting from it at the same time," Trevor said. "We are going to sell freedom!"

"Totally worth doing!" Agreed Eddie.

CHAPTER TWELVE

Elizabeth

I made my way upstairs, expecting to see Tilly, but found the room empty. I flipped on the light and threw my bag onto my bed. My eye was drawn to my pillow. A single brown envelope perched perfectly on top with my name, Elizabeth Cantrell, neatly printed in gold lettering on the outside. Another one? I grabbed it, ripping the envelope open, and plopped on my bed to read it.

Journal Entry #97

They have been found living amongst the Humlings in a town named Shell Ridge. Piper seems unable to forgive her son, Walter, for choosing his love Christy, instead of his duty to his people. My associate Trenton, Walter's guard, has been beside himself with worries of what will be. Walter has no idea the harm that is planned for him and his love. Piper's evil heart will leave no other option but to see them dealt with harshly. I worry Trenton will be dealt with harshly as well.

They were found by a neighbor who recognized them when she moved next door. She is a rough character, who once was a Keeper, but was sent to live with the Humlings due to her maltreatment of the Humlings in her care as Keeper. The Keepers should have sent her to us. She belongs with us due to her natural scheming ways. At first, she tried to blackmail Walter and Christy. I don't have any idea what she asked them for, only they did not comply with her demands. She believed they would have a healthy respect for her since she knew who they were. Only once she saw they didn't, she turned to us. I'm sure her reward from Deward and Piper will be great.

Once Piper learned of the children, her Grandchildren, she knew Walter's decision was to keep his children from our world, and their duty. Deward told me, since the beginning of my selection for training to become a guard, I was chosen and one day would guard someone valuable. And so it seems, he must have known about his Grandchildren. Looking back, this explains his ongoing obsession with finding his son and his family. Deward and Piper told me today I will guard the oldest of their Grand daughters, whose royal name will be Bethany. This is not the name she has in the Humling world, but how better to hide her than to have her assume her new royal identity.

Collin, a Royal guard about my age, has been given the job to guard the younger of the two. He has no patience, how will he deal with a child? He has openly complained about the girl whom he doesn't deem worth his time to guard. Unlike me, he came to be a guard, the normal way, by being born into the role. He has a high since of self worth and I believe always thought he would guard someone more important.

Journal Entry #100

The slave Grace has always claimed that the "girl" would one day set her free. Of course, everyone thinks her ramblings qualify her as insane. Today she caused herself to receive the full wrath of Piper, handed out by Geren. As she was scrubbing the floor, she overheard about the children and was over-joyed thinking her "girl" was coming for her. As Piper often reminds her, she is a slave and no other opportunities will ever be presented to her. She was given a brutal whipping by Geren and left where she laid bleeding and in pain. Once the others were no longer amused by her sight, I carried her back to the slave quarters in the dungeon. The others were appalled and prob-ably assumed her condition was at my hands. I am sure, retaliation was on their mind and they may have acted if it were not for their general fear of the royal guard as a whole. I know they will look after her until she heals. The poor soul radiates light and I believe this is why Piper finds her disgusting.

Well, I was confused. Who had sent this to me? And why? If they had taken the time to ensure it was so carefully placed on my pillow, it must have meaning. Who was the author?

Tilly interrupted my thoughts as she crawled through the window. "What's up with you?"

"Nothing, are you okay?" I questioned as I tucked the journal entries un-der my pillow.

"Yeah, I'm fine. Why would you ask?" She retorted as she tossed her book bag onto her bed.

"You sort of stormed out of class today. I felt they embarrassed you," I explained.

"You too?" Tilly asked over her shoulder. "I just had to calm Trevor as well. I guess my acting in the spot light was believable! I was pretty convincing!" Tilly stated with a pleased look upon her face and kicked off her shoes.

"You were acting?" I questioned.

"Hey, you take any opportunity that arises to get out of a boring class," she replied as she plopped into a big chair and began rubbing her bare feet. "They provided me the opportunity to have the day off. I put it to good use!"

"Of course you used the free time to access the Hall of Records," I replied.

"Yup," Tilly replied. Her eyes suddenly were full of life as she hopped up. I watched as she unzipped her backpack retrieving a crumpled box from the bottom of it. "My mother taught me well!" She opened the box to reveal severely smashed pastries. She pried one off the box and gave the box to me as she continued, "Speaking of my mother, was there a backpack delivered today?"

"No, but its okay!" I replied while following her lead and helping myself to a pastry. "Perhaps your mother wasn't able to get a destination card to go shopping or had the time."

"She didn't even try," Tilly quietly responded. "She told me that since I wanted to make adult decisions, I must do my own shopping. I had hoped she would try."

You could see the rejection on Tilly's face and there was nothing else to say but, "Sorry."

"In a way, it's a good thing," Tilly said as she shoved what remained of the pastry into her mouth. "Some of my best work takes place when faced with such obstacles." Before I could dive into what exactly that meant, she continued, "Now, what about you and that letter you tucked under your pillow?"

She grabbed for it as I pulled it out of its hiding place and held it behind my back, "Oh no, my eyes only."

"From your Mom?" Tilly questioned totally intrigued.

"No," I said firmly.

"Dad?"

"No."

"Other family member?" Tilly questioned.

Tilly was totally into trying to guess. "No"

"Friend?"

"Not exactly."

"Love letter?" She questioned without letting me answer. "Okay, love letters are private. I won't insist on seeing. Who is it from?" She threw herself on her bed and placed her head into her hands propped up on her elbows.

"I don't know," I answered telling the truth.

"Ooo…, an admirer," Tilly responded and I threw a pillow at her.

"We better head towards Harmony practice," I said stuffing the envelope back deep under my pillow.

"Great!" Replied Tilly as she moved to begin rummaging through her closet. "Just give me a moment. I need to find the perfect outfit."

Harmony practice assembled in the rehearsal room at the Department of Administration Complex nightly. Tilly and I proceeded their by lift after she scrutinized every item in her closet. Her compulsion to be flawless left us running close to the wire. When we finally arrived at Harmony, we found ourselves powerless to find an unlocked door to the Grand Hall. The rehearsal room lay inside Grand Hall. But where? Tilly flirted with the building guard who all but fell over himself to open the entry and lead us down a series of halls to the rehearsal room door.

Once inside the door I heard Tiffany's distinct voice say, "Look Janelle. Their back from getting their heads examined. Too bad, the doctors found nothing there."

"That explains why neither of them knew how to open a simple door," added Janelle with a clear smirk.

"Like the door to Grand Hall?" Questioned Tiffany with a sneer.

"Exactly," agreed Janelle.

"Listen twinkie morons! The doors were locked and it's obvious who did it," I responded while watching Tilly pop a piece of gum in her mouth.

"Now who would do something like that?" Questioned Tiffany with a taunt. "We came through them. Oh dear, how did we manage that?"

I grabbed Tilly's arm as her eyes became flames. My mind was screaming, Tilly don't say anything. I nodded no as I dragged her away from them before she had a chance to respond. They had deliberately made us late! We didn't need anymore trouble this evening since I was sure our lateness would not be overlooked. Professor Kegley flitted about while Tilly and I found two chairs hoping to blend in. Professor Kegley stopped and looked at us shaking her head, but didn't say anything. She continued to the podium only to meet Tiffany who was eyeing her expectantly. Professor Kegley became klutzy under Tiffany's waiting stare. Tiffany stayed planted in her spot as the Professor began, "May I have your attention? Please find a seat if you don't already have one."

Tiffany placed her arm across the podium and leaned towards the microphone saying, "I'm your new conductor."

Groans came from all around the room. Tiffany's demeanor changed as she now glared about the room. "Yes, I was chosen by the Harmony Alumni Foundation for this position."

"Rigged!" Tilly yelled. "Just say it! Your Mommy got you the position!"

Tiffany seemed intent to ignore Tilly's last comment as she continued, "As your new conductor I would like to tell you about a few decisions that I finalized for the group." Professor Kegley finally stepped aside too weak to attempt to maintain control of the group.

Tilly obnoxiously and loudly spewed, "Thank you for ruining all my future evenings while being forced to be apart of Harmony." I understood. With Tiffany in charge our evenings were not going to be fun.

"I have a simple vision for the choir," Tiffany began. "I want us reorganized into a four part harmony which sings a cap pel la."

"No accompaniment?" Questioned the mousy boy with glasses seated at the piano who looked offended. He slammed the cover lid on the keys with a thump.

"You can waist your time accompanying the choir during practice if you want, but not during my performances," Tiffany replied cutting him down. "Tonight, I want to personally place us in the order of my choice which will be the order for practices on the risers and in competitions this point on."

"May I ask how we are to be organized?" Janelle interjected. It was obviously a loaded question.

"Thank you for asking," Tiffany politely said to Janelle with a smirk upon her face. "We will be organizing the group by who looks appropriate in the front since the people in the front can be seen the best."

"Oh, please," Tilly loudly stated rolling her eyes.

"Don't worry Tilly dear, you and your friend will be in back with all the ugly choir members!" Tiffany said.

"No, everyone will stand in order," piped in Professor Kegley. "From left to right; sopranos, altos, tenors, and bass voices."

"We will see about that!" Tiffany retorted without glancing at Professor Kegley.

Professor Kegley sheepishly interjected, "You must stand in that order for everyone to stay on key."

Tiffany ignored the professor and continued, "We will hold try-outs next week for the two solos which will be the main showcase for our competitions."

Janelle moved to sit behind us.

Professor Kegley held up a stack of papers and then began to pass them down the rows saying, "The two songs you need to learn for solo try-outs are on this sheet of music. Practice, practice!"

"Like I would try out," Tilly loudly spewed.

Janelle leaned forward saying, "Like you can sing."

"I want everyone to try out," Professor Kegley firmly stated. "It will give me an idea of the range of your voices and your strong points! Yes, everyone will try out. No one will be excused."

Tiffany appeared to be seething. She defiantly said, "All a formality, choir members! No need to worry. Everyone in this room understands I will be singing all the solos. After all, I am the best singer." I could hear a snobbish giggle escape her. Did she think no one else would try? As I peered around the room my question was answered. Everyone was squirming in their chairs. They were obviously too nervous to cross Princess Tiffany!

Tilly cut the tension in the room as she stood defying Tiffany stating, "The solos will not be sung by you if I have anything to say about it!"

I pulled at her shirt and mouthed, "Sit down." Clearly she was ignoring me.

Tiffany and Tilly were locked into a dart launching stare down when Professor Kegley said, "Great! I am glad to see you are taking this serious Miss Bradford. Perhaps you will give Tiffany some competition at solo tryouts!"

Tilly glanced at Professor Kegley and curtly nodded saying, "Of course. Harmony will be such a pleasure to be apart of!"

I popped my hand on my forehead in disbelief. Tilly was going to try out, but she didn't want to belong. Tilly's sole purpose was to ensure Tiffany didn't have the pleasure of being soloist! Horror filled me when Trevor crossed the room and stood with Tilly. Trevor's eyes turned to mine with a demand beaming from him. I was to stand beside Tilly as well. Did they think we were going to stage a coupe and take over? Reluctantly, I stood and took my place along side them. Two or three others joined us.

"Elizabeth, you should make more intelligent decisions about who to become friends with and stand up for!" Taunted Janelle from behind us.

Janelle's nastiness became fuel in the room. I was surprised to see the stuttering Stone girl stand. Utter shock spread through my body. I was surprised to see the Stone girl here at all! Ruthanne stood from across the room. Then the disappointed piano player followed suit.

Janelle unfazed continued, "Your time at the Hall of Knowledge is going to be a long and lonesome journey!"

"You should know about being lonesome," I retorted as I turned to look at her. "Look around, everyone just appeases you. They are scared of you! You have no true friends beyond Tiffany."

I turned back around before she could respond only to meet the stare of Professor Kegley. I saw a hint of a smile cross her face. She had heard my reply to Janelle. She handed me a copy of the sheet music and for a moment our eyes met. Yes, she agreed with my comment. Maybe a little glad that someone would stand up to them as well. As she moved on down the row she stated, "Ladies, please sit back down. It is time to lay our differences aside for the evening and sing."

A hard, cold chair had never felt so amazing before. Relief to be out of the glares of the other Harmony members washed over me. Tilly was obnoxiously digging in her purse. Gum! She popped a fresh stick into her mouth and began to write on the inside of the wrapper with a pen. Then she handed the wrapper to me. Wrote simply was, Thank you! I saw the corners of Tilly's mouth turn up slightly concerning my loyalty to her. Like her or not, we were destined to be best friends. Perhaps I could help her with her addiction to gum. The obsessive gum snapping and popping was a bit annoying. But, we all have our quirks!

CHAPTER THIRTEEN

Tilly

Today we were embarking upon our training at the Department of Ghosts. My mother and father considered the Department of Ghosts an inferior class. Always spouting, "Tilly, you are forbidden to have anything to do with the Department of Ghosts Complex! You can't play with anyone whose parents work for the Department of Ghosts!" They simply went on and on. What a load of nonsense! All they did was spark my interest! Today, I would be paying perfect attention to my lessons in this department. Emancipation was great! My parents couldn't keep me away from this Complex anymore. I was exhilarated! My goal would be to learn all I could to throw my wonderful ghost knowledge in their faces! I loved anything that ticked my parents off.

Trevor and Elizabeth had been a few steps ahead of me as we made our way to the Department of Ghosts Complex. Their conversation bored me. First they joked about his joining Harmony. He was a follower! I was the pied piper. He joined because I had! Then Elizabeth had a million questions about the ins and outs of the Department of Records. Honestly, it was just a big library. She obviously bored Eddie too. He placed his ear plugs in and was lost in his music with his hoodie pulled up around his face.

Elizabeth's voice became silent and Eddie pushed back his hoodie and removed his ear plugs when we approached the demon in curls. Tiffany rated just as high as my mother in my book! Obnoxious described them both! Tiffany was hanging all over her brooding boyfriend. I could wretch! I didn't know his name but anyone who kept Tiffany's company I didn't like. He was bound to be repulsive.

My thoughts traveled back to an early morning encounter with this guy. He had a strange effect on Elizabeth. Was I crazy? Had Elizabeth actually sniffed at him like a dog? I blinked my eyes thinking, I didn't really see her do that! I would ask Trevor if he noticed the odd dreamy behavior of Elizabeth when Tiffany's boyfriend was around. Weird!

Stepping out into the Department of Ghosts, I found it to be plain, dull, and unpredictable. No ghosts jumping out and yelling boo! Administration, Records, and Keepers Complexes had their own distinctive grandeur in announcing themselves as awe inspiring destinations. This Complex was not comparable. We stepped out of the lift onto a concrete poured floor. All I could see was grey! The walls were cement blocks all painted a grey color. The metal roof was a darker grey color as well. The only source of color in this room came from a painted rainbow of stripes which faded from color to color as it traveled around the room. Wow! This was a depressing place!

As we stood in the center of this massive, long room, a feeling of eeriness prevailed. On the wall, across from the lifts was a huge grey cork board filled with papers haphazardly pinned to it. Stats of some kind. To each side, the walls held a series of doors and plate glass windows revealing working offices filled with cubicles and working Ghosties. What an awful name the Department of Ghost associates called themselves. Why Ghosties? I could have chosen a name that the other departments wouldn't have made fun of!

Others arrived and joined us in a mass around the lift doors. Professor Bungard exited the lift and led us to stand as a group in the corner of this massive room. He was dressed shabbily. If he was intent on wearing a uniform that resembled ours, why did he not order new ones? He looked like a stuffed tomato in his well worn white uniform and gray vest. His bald head shined under the lights making his salt and pepper mustache stand out more.

A bell rang loudly and the offices emptied out into the massive entrance to stand along the walls. Elizabeth whispered to me, "What's going on?"

I shrugged my shoulders. I had no idea! A bean pole, blond-headed boy, anxious to make his presence noticed, leaned over towards us enthusiastically saying, "The cheer!"

I rolled my eyes at Elizabeth. Elizabeth eyes flickered as we both suppressed a giggle.

"Good morning," Bungard greeted over the bustle of others around him. "Keeper trainees, Welcome to your first look at Ghost Relations. Can anyone tell me this department's mission?"

"Soul recovery," I replied.

"Very good Miss Bradford," complimented Bungard. "Can you elaborate for the group?"

"Ghosts are earth bound souls who do not believe they are dead. You know, not ready to leave the party when they hear the last call. So, the job is to recover or convince them to return." I replied to everyone's odd looks. Truly this department was my dream come true!

"You are standing in the infamous Elephant Room," Bungard began. "This room holds a lot of history and is named for the one animal that is obviously big, gray, and never forgets."

"A Ghostie never forgets to retrieve a soul," Trevor surmised speaking out without being called on.

"Yes, this room serves as a reminder each day of our mission. Does anyone know the Ghost Department cheer?" Bungard asked. The blond-headed boy's hand shot up and was waving frantically for attention!

"Oh get real," I said under my breath to Elizabeth. "How hokey!"

The blond-headed bean pole boy blurted out, "I've been practicing it!"

"Mr. Weaver, come demonstrate for those who don't know it." He happily bounced up smocked in his gray sweater vest marking him as a training Ghostie. He was sucking up, scoring points with Bungard! Someone else had game this morning. Should I consider it to be a personal challenge to beat him at his own game? Then I noticed his attempt to hide his flushed grin as he looked at me. Aha! Got him! All boys were the same. All were drawn to me and taken with my beauty. I flirted, grinned at him, and popped my gum.

I watched as he made his moves and cheered like a school girl would at a football game. Really? This was a new unattractive weird. I mumbled to anyone near me listening, "He needs to get a life!"

"Repeat for the group our motto," Bungard said to the blond-headed contortionist cheerleader in approval of his performance.

"Soul recovery is our job!" The Weaver boy repeated with a brown nose sucking up look upon his face. That silly cheer soured my view of him. I stopped flirting with him. Professor Bungard was beaming at the Weaver boy and seemed satisfied as pom-pom boy took his place with our group.

A man dressed in an all white flannel shirt and white overalls stepped to the center of the room with a microphone energetically saying, "Good morning fellow Ghosties!"

In unison everyone from around the outer walls greeted him, "Good morning!"

The man in white overalls with the microphone continued, "Had a great night last night. There were 27,202 assists and 2,803 souls recovered. This included; 2,097 hangers, 704 deniers, and 2 ghosts." The crowd erupted into cheers. "As the graveyard shift signs off we want to wager a friendly challenge to the day crew."

Again the crowd echoed with excitement. Another gentlemen in grey snow-bibs stepped out into the center challenging, "Let's hear it." Silence fell as everyone anticipated what the microphone man was going to say. What was up with the snow bibs? I sure didn't see any snow!

"If you can recover 3,000 souls by next shift, we will clean your sprayers for you. If you don't recover 3,000 you will clean the sprayers for us," the man in white overalls said and smirked into the mike.

Someone from the crowd yelled, "You're on! Nothing you can throw at us would be anything we can't handle."

"Thank you," replied the grey snow-bibbed man. "As my fellow Ghostie said, we accept. We look forward to your cleaning our sprayers."

Cheers erupted as Elizabeth quietly questioned leaning towards my ear, "Tilly, what is a sprayer?"

"Isn't that what they use to capture ghosts," Trevor loudly said ignoring the crowd.

The blond-headed Weaver boy turned, glanced at me with an intrigued but not so sure look. Then, he corrected Trevor saying, "The sprayers use water to freeze the hangers and deniers as a last resort. It enables us to gain their attention so we can convince them to come back. It is never used on a ghost."

Elizabeth whispered to me, "What are hangers and deniers?"

The blond-headed Weaver boy didn't get a chance to answer. The man with the grey snow bibs took the microphone and asked the crowd, "Who wants to help me lead the cheer this morning?"

I retrieved another stick of gum from my pocket. I unwrapped and popped it into my mouth. The more I chewed, the more I thought, no one showed me up! My light bulb turned on. I shoved the red headed Weaver boy out a few steps into the center of the room. Gasps came from Elizabeth which I chose to ignore. What appeared to be his all star, frog jump out of the crowd caught the attention of the grey snow bibbed man. He smiled and shook his head a little before asking, "You are a trainee, correct?"

"Yes sir, I am Andy Weaver," the boy said with his back to me.

This was perfect!

"Cade's boy," overall man said to snow bib man as they both nodded seeming to know exactly who Andy was.

"Mr. Weaver, it is nice to make your acquaintance," snow bib man greeted. "Professor Bungard, do you mind if your student assists me in the cheer today?"

I could not contain my giggling or snickering!

"Not at all," Bungard retorted with a proud look upon his face.

Darn. I had scored points for the kid.

The grey snow bibbed man asked for a couple more volunteers. The Weaver boy glared at me from his place beside the snow bibbed man. I happily blew huge pink bubbles. Deep inside, he didn't mean the glare. He would date me if he got the chance. I knew it. No matter how badly you treat men, they keep coming back! Pom-pom boy was no different.

Elizabeth caught my attention when she poked me and asked, "What possessed you to push him?"

"He is a horrible know it all," I responded. "A suck up!"

"But…" Elizabeth began.

I held up my hand to stop her, "He'll get over it! I didn't do him any harm. I give him two days and he'll ask me for a date!" I paused and rolled my eyes.

Elizabeth shook her head and glanced at Trevor who shrugged his shoulders.

"Just a little bogus," added Eddie in true skater slang.

"Whatever," I replied. "I'll have the three of you know, I will make a point of dating him before it's all said and done. He will be putty in my hands."

"Date him?" Elizabeth questioned aghast.

"Tilly likes a challenge," Trevor said shaking his head.

"Quiet," yelled the overall man who motioned for the bib man to start.

The ridiculous cheer was led by the grey snow bibbed man who started contortionist moves of his own and yelled with a husky, deep voice, "Give me a G!"

The crowd loudly yelled, "G!"

"Give me a H!" He yelled.

"H!" The crowd returned.

"Give me an O!" He shouted as he turned to view those behind him.

"O!" The crowd echoed.

"Give me a S!" He called.

"S!" The crowd returned.

"Give me a T!" He yelled as he turned to once again face us.

"T!" The crowd belted.

"Give me a S!" He shouted.

"S!" The crowd screeched, hurting me ears.

"What's that spell?" The man in bibs screamed raising his fist over his head.

"Ghosts!" The crowd erupted.

The whole thing was repeated with the ending question, "Who is number one?"

"Ghosts!" The crowd chanted.

Again, the whole thing repeated ending with, "What is our motto?"

"Soul recovery is our job!" The crowd exploded.

My light bulb moment plan back fired! The Weaver boy was getting high fives from the group who cheered with him. He had made a definite impression. I told my annoyed friends, "See, it worked out fine for him. Didn't it?"

"That's not the point," Elizabeth said as she shook her head. "You invaded his space by pushing him."

"Think what you want," I stated taking the time to blow a flirtatious kiss towards the blond-headed fellow who had his back to me enjoying his moment of celebrity!

"We know," Eddie said tapping his forehead with a couple fingers. "He'll date you."

I smiled warmly at Eddie as Bungard clapped to get our attention and then said, "Follow me to the training room."

We began to move through the crowd as the Weaver boy sprinted and caught up with me. He fell into a rhythm as he began to keep pace with me. I asked him pointedly, "What?"

"I didn't appreciate being pushed out like that," he said as he stepped in front of me, stopped, and looked me directly in the eye.

"You knew the cheer," I defended my actions. I quickly ran my hand down his chest flirting as I smiled and with a whine said, "Besides you really shined."

His angry eyes peered through me and then turned to a twinkle. He made his decision. "Can we start over, I'm Andy." He stepped out of my path and positioned his self along side me.

As we began to walk, I smiled a devious smile over my shoulder at my doubter friends and then introduced myself, "I'm Tilly."

"I already knew your name," Andy hesitantly said. I could hear the deep breath he inhaled. What was he building up too? "They usually pair us up to work together. Would you be interested in joining forces?"

So this was his angle? "So you want to be partners?" I questioned. He grinned. Of course he wanted to be my partner. Who wouldn't? "So you think you can keep up with me?"

"This is not your department or expertise. It may be you finding it hard to keep up with me?" Andy shot back suddenly standing tall.

Now it was personal. Nobody challenged me! I could hear Trevor clear his throat to give me a clear warning not to get involved with Andy. He was usually right. I threw all caution to the wind as I said, "I would love to work with you. It will be a great challenge." I heard Trevor let out a huge sigh. "You will eat my dust new partner!"

Andy stopped and thought about what I said for a moment as I continued to blow big bubbles with my gum. We turned into the training room. He went to sit next to his friends as Elizabeth and I found seating together.

Bungard was all business, "Before we go any further I want you to break into teams of two. Your partner will be your partner through out your training and you will accumulate points together during training. The partnership with the most points will be granted destination cards to go with the working

Ghosties on their next amusement park day. Pick the partner who will help you succeed in earning points. In addition, don't help another partnership thus helping them to earn points. It is you and your partner. So, chose well." The professor waved his hands as everyone began to move about.

Trevor and Eddie made their way over to Elizabeth who asked them, "Partners?"

"Its killer that we're partners," answered Eddie. "We always score big together."

I popped my gum a couple of times waiting for Andy. Poor Elizabeth would have to find someone else for a partner.

"Tilly, this is Mike," said Andy as he stepped up to our group. "He was going to be my partner. But as you know, I have had second thoughts."

Mike didn't look particularly happy.

"Well, this is Elizabeth. She would've been mine," I added as my hands gestured towards Elizabeth.

Elizabeth's eyes were begging, don't do this. When I didn't respond, Elizabeth reluctantly held out her hand to Mike. He reciprocated the handshake asking, "Partners then? Seems like our best friends have ditched us!"

"Sure," Elizabeth answered with no more enthusiasm than Mike.

What was their deal? Elizabeth should see this as an opportunity! Like I did. Mike was kind of cute and looked really good standing next to Elizabeth. Besides, both boys were Ghosties in training by the looks of their grey sweater vests. We could use their knowledge to our benefit! I spit out my blah, worn out wad of gum and tossed it towards the trash can. I just as quickly retrieved a fresh stick.

Trevor and Eddie introduced themselves as we sat together as a group. Bungard was once again clapping to get our attention. He began, "The best way to break into this work is to first learn how to find a ghost on the Earth Plane. I hope all of you find this task easy because I will be assigning your partnership a ghost to find. I would like each pair to write a minimum of five pages on how you found them."

One by one he called the groups down and assigned them a ghost to find. When his eyes met Andy he inquired, "Mr. Hardin is not your partner?" He glanced over at Mike stating, "You always team up!"

"No, not this time! Tilly is my partner," Andy said nervously correcting the Professor and regaining his attention.

"I thought Miss Bradford and Miss Cantrell would be..." Bungard mumbled stopping mid sentence. He sat down in his chair. Every eye in the room stared at Andy as if he had lost his mind. What was their problem? The professor told him, "If Tilly is your choice, I wish the two of you to find Mrs. Wanda Settlesome."

Returning to my seat, I watched as the remaining pairs were called up and given their names. Once everyone had been called, Bungard stood stating, "I wish to now give you a brief tour of the Complex. It is a huge place with many portals. I don't want you taking a wrong turn and getting lost."

Andy and I stood. He held out his arm in an old fashioned gentlemen way. I wrapped my arm around his and was reminded of Tiffany snuggling on her boyfriend's arm. The sick thought of her was mixed with the pleasure of Andy's strong arm. Ghost training was going to be very delightful.

Guys love to show their brains off. "Andy, can you bring me up to speed on the group cheer session this morning?" I asked humoring his ego.

"What is it you want to know?" Andy asked with a gleam in his eye. I was right. The show off was just that, a show off!

"Just about it in general," I responded as we passed through the training room door and I freed his arm.

"There are two rallies a day when the shifts change," Andy stated in a robotic manner as he smiled. "They always announce the stats and challenge the other shift."

"And the cheer?" I asked as we turned from one long hall to another.

"It's ritual," Andy declared. "My Mom and Dad are Ghosties and I have known the cheer since I could walk. Mom and Dad are the heart and driving force behind me. I owe everything to them!"

Jealousy instantly coursed through my veins. I unwrapped and shoved another piece of gum into my mouth. He was good at the cheer because he had been taught it at a young age. My parents had never taken the time to teach me anything! Obviously, he had a good relationship with his family. He was of all things, proud of them and equally as proud to be training to follow in their footsteps. I took several deep breaths and asked the first thing that crossed my mind, "Why do they do the rallies?"

"I suppose it keeps up moral and production," Andy answered studying my face.

Ghosties were everywhere. I could not help but notice their strange attire. The group passing us was wearing grey rain coats, white ear muffs, and white snow boots reminding me of the strange men who held the rally. I asked, "Who are the two men who led the rally this morning?"

"They are the day and night supervisors! You know, Big wigs!" Andy answered. "That is why I seriously could have melted when you pushed me out in the center this morning."

"Okay, I probably shouldn't have done that," I admitted.

Another pair of Ghosties wearing thick, white coats and heavy, grey boots passed us. Did any of them know it was a perfect 72 degrees outside? Would the fashion police get them if they wore any other color than white or grey? "Why is everyone dressed so oddly around here? Even the supervisors this morning were," I stated.

Andy stopped and looked into my eyes telling me, "Tilly, you won't find fancy suits and ties here. We dress to do our work."

"But why is everyone dressed ready for snow or winter?" I questioned.

"We dress warm because we might get iced," Andy stated. "The portals tend to be cold."

Did he assume I knew what that meant? I questioned, "Iced?"

Suddenly, the boy in front of me stopped abruptly. I almost toppled over him. Instantly, I grabbed Andy's warm hand and pulled him through the crowd, protecting myself and him. Once I found Elizabeth and Mike, I dropped Andy's hand feeling amazed at what streamed before us. There was a corridor which went for as far as my eyes could see. Evenly spaced down both sides, with maybe about twelve inches in between them, were golden doors. Above each door was an electronic, neon sign which listed different destinations on the earth plane. The walls were the brightest white I had ever laid my eyes on. I turned to look at Andy in amazement and realized he was already aware of what we were going to see. He had popped sunglasses on. In my amazement I asked, "Which door does a Ghostie use and how are they organized?"

"Great question, Miss Bradford," Bungard said. "The doors are organized by Earth Plane population by place. For instance, all you major cities will be some of the first doors. Then down from there to smaller populated areas." He turned his attention to the group as a whole. He then clapped and continued, "Everyone please find a door. Make sure your door is next to your partners."

I stepped up to the door just inside the corridor. Andy stepped beside me, "No, not that one."

"Why not?" I asked.

"It is occupied," Andy stated as he pointed to the electronic sign above it.

Embarrassed, I flushed a little. I didn't see what he was seeing. I cast Elizabeth a questionable look and mouthed to her, "Can you read the sign?" I secured my place at the door between Elizabeth and Andy.

Elizabeth ignored my question but leaned over to me and whispered, "Take it easy with Andy."

"Don't worry about Andy," I told her in a playful manner.

"Now that everyone is standing before a door, I want everyone…" The Professor stopped to grab an over achiever from entering a door before instructions. "Do not enter the door! Open the door and peer in."

When I opened the door all I saw was a black hole.

"Let me explain what you are looking at," Bungard began. "I assume you see a black hole. It is! In the darkness you will find six steps leading down to the Earth Plane. This is a portal between Home and the Earth Plane. As you step down you will go under an invisible shower on step three. This shields those on the Earth Plane from seeing the light of Home through the door or portal on their side," Bungard explained.

Raising her hand, Elizabeth questioned, "So when you go to the Earth Plane, you get wet?" She shivered thinking of how cold waterfalls were.

"No, the invisible shower falls right off of your skin and clothing. The only effect it will have on you is making you bone chilling cold," Bungard answered.

"Do Ghosties bring souls back up through the stairs?" A tall blond girl asked looking confused.

"They try not too," Bungard said shaking his head. "Death on the Earth Plane is simply coming Home. However, when a soul chooses not to cross over, they are simply choosing not to use their portal to the Hospital which is provided for them. That portal lingers and is always there. If the soul refuses to use the portal and becomes an established ghost, the portal becomes dimmer with time due to their insistence to ignore it. Long established ghosts are hard to persuade to come back home or see their portal." Bungard paused, "On occasion, rarely though, someone will bring a soul back through the stairs. It causes a great deal of confusion on the soul's part and not recommended."

"And Keepers?" Elizabeth asked blurting out without raising her hand.

"Keepers are like Humlings in that a Keeper soul can refuse to cross over and use their portal to come home," Bungard answered. "Although it would be rare because a Keeper's soul retrieval would be top priority. Keepers can become an established ghost. The only real difference is a Keeper's portal for re-entry takes them to the Hall of Babies instead of the Hospital. Keeper souls can be brought back through the stairs. But it's not recommended for Keepers anymore than it is recommended for Humlings due to the confusion it may cause."

"Notice the control panel with buttons to the right inside the door." He paused and waited for us to look. "You always type in the address and press save for the town you wish to visit before you enter. The door automatically locks behind you if you do not. Without a destination, you could be stuck until someone comes to look for you, or another Ghostie intends to use the door. Typing the address also puts a star on the electronic sign above the door so others know someone has gone down."

I peered over at the original door I wanted to stand before. Sure enough a star was on the electronic sign. Not wanting to get trapped, we began closing our doors.

From behind me I heard Trevor ask, "Professor. If the doors are sorted by population, what happens in high populated areas when two Ghosties need to use the same door?"

"Mr. Stillholm, a great question," The Professor complimented. "More than one address can be typed into the control panel. If you are using a door that is already occupied, you hit the duplicate button before entering the address. Then when you hit the save button, the portal provides you an opening to the address you are going and a second star lights up on the electric neon sign above the door."

Everyone gathered down the corridor into a big group. The original door I started to stand at, which was occupied, flung open. A group of men came up the stairs and exited. They seemed to be ice covered. Mike leaned over and told Andy, "They must have been hunting a tricky ghost. They've been iced!"

"Recognize him? He's not just any ghost hunter, that is Rhett," Andy replied. "He hunts the old ghost. You know the one who is as old as Albert Solliday."

"I've heard all the wild hunt stories," Mike replied. "The old ghost would still be a keeper if he hadn't decided to take a second life on the Earth Plane. Poor soul, missed his wife so much when she disappeared, he just lost it!"

I didn't want to do one life. Clearly he wasn't in his right mind. What possessed him to want to do two?

I was not sure if Rhett had heard the quick references to his ghost hunt. I could feel his intent glare as he stopped dead in his tracks, looked us all over, and said, "Good morning, you must be new trainees in the Hall of Knowledge."

"Well, yeah!" I said rather loudly, rolling my eyes.

Seeing my eye action, Rhett sarcastically retorted to me, "No doubt who you are. Your attitude is just like your mother." Every bone in my body was seething. No one called me my mother! He had steamed rolled right over my weak spot. The fatal words. Like my mother! I thought Rhett was going to say something further but it seemed his stare moved from me to Elizabeth. He focused there like he somehow knew her. Hmm… Did he know her? She had no memory, so she wouldn't know.

At lunch Elizabeth inquired about the famous ghost hunter, Rhett. Andy, the show off, led everyone in a captivating ghost tale. At least for them! Even Trevor listened intently. Not me! I was still tiffed about Rhett's remark. Andy was so wrapped up in his show-off knowledge that he forgot to pay me any attention. Any other boy in the room would have gladly taken his place next to me. I was fuming on two counts.

What was their fascination with Rhett? When I thought about him. Argh! I was miffed! You couldn't get ruder than to tell a person they were becoming their mother! He was famous because he always gets his ghost. Usually it takes a group to capture ghosts and help them cross over. The only one to ever stump him was the old ghost. Another boring story Andy was enjoying telling! Who wanted to hear about a crazy old man who wanted to live a second life who was Albert Solliday's best friend? The story goes he snuck into baby row and went back to the Earth Plane. His wife had disappeared. Probably realized he was nuts and ran off! Why would we want him back? He was now a minor criminal due to stealing someone else's turn for their earth life. He had to be insane!

We marched back to the training room where Bungard spent the rest of the afternoon explaining terminology. I learned hangers were souls who were hanging on to go visit their families one last time on the Earth Plane before crossing over to Home. A hanger's Keeper always had the first opportunity to recover the hanger. If a Ghostie got involved and aided the Keeper it was called an assist. Deniers are souls who died on the Earth Plane but don't think they are dead. They were ignoring the light to cross over because they still thought they were living. Ghosts were souls who had spent too much time as hangers or deniers, usually convincing themselves they truly weren't dead. When their tunnel, or portal, began to fade they became ghosts. Time spent as a ghost, interestingly enough, is not recorded in the Hall of Records.

I was about to cat nap in my chair. Finally we were released for the evening. I was off to Harmony practice and then on to the date I had been looking forward to all day! I was going to give Andy one more opportunity to tune in and not ignore me. Rhett and ghost hunting were not going to enter our conversation!

CHAPTER FOURTEEN

Elizabeth

❝Good Morning, Welcome to the Department of Keepers Complex," stated Professor Zirak who was waiting for us as we exited the lift.

The professor then turned to me, "Miss Cantrell, thank you for ensuring Miss Bradford and you were on time this morning." I could hear the chuckles from around us. Barely on time, I wanted to correct him. Tilly stayed out too late with Andy last night. The professor had an eager look on his face which I had not seen before.

Tilly leaned over whispering, "See the fish. He's on my line today!" She rolled her eyes towards an unassuming male.

I followed her line of sight to a mousy boy with glasses. The thought slipped out of my mouth, "Really?" I didn't particularly think he was Tilly's type.

She nodded, "When I glanced at him, he quickly looked away."

After a moment or so, the boy glanced back at us. Tilly held eye contact and smiled. He turned a slight shade of pink. Tilly said out loud as she popped her gum and threw him a flirtatious air kiss, "Gotcha!" She was off on another male seducing tangent.

She didn't seem to hold the same interest in learning as yesterday. My attention now focused on the lobby of this impressive, huge building I was standing in. The front façade was a wall of glass in which a long receptionist desk set in front of. Next to the lift we exited, stood rows of kiosk machines with long lines of Keepers in front of them. Once the Keepers dressed all in white found the information they needed from the kiosk machines, they funneled through a turn-style and waited at a row of eight lifts. This was a noisy, busy place with the users moving at fast pace.

"I have already taken the liberty to get the names of the Humlings we will be observing from the kiosk information bank," said Professor Zirak as he held his hand to indicate the kiosk machines. "Our task over the next week will be to observe a Humling, keep a log of all their requests, visualizations, and how the Keepers used these to solve their request. If you will follow me, I have one special Humling I would like to introduce you too." I thought his face seemed to be amused with that smirk plastered across it. "She is unique and I'm sure you will understand the reality of this job once viewing her."

Tilly was preoccupied with her flirting with the mousy boy who seemed to be head over heals star struck with the infamous Tilly. The group walked in a line through the turn-styles and awaited the lifts. I was surprised to find no lift operator there to assist us. In their place was a key pad in which the professor pressed a number into as he said, "When you get your assigned Humling from the kiosk information bank, you will get an office number. The number is keyed into the lift keypad. Once you punch your number in, the lift will take you directly to that office number." The doors closed, lift moved, and soon opened to reveal a huge office.

The lighting was dim and the room full of Keepers were all standing looking at a huge screen, viewing a lady who appeared to be eating a sandwich off of expensive looking china. She was retirement age with hair that had already turned snow white. She appeared to be very prim and proper and wore purple slacks and a lavender floral suit jacket.

The professor moved forward to stand in front of the screen. We followed. A young man standing in the back of the original screen viewers, turned. Seeing our group, he walked over. He was slightly taller than me and very fashionable in his white polo shirt and white slack pants. He had sandy brown hair, deep brown eyes, and olive skin. He also seemed to have a jolly personality and a natural smile. Our eyes met for a split second and he looked as if he recognized me and quickly turned away. Did I repulse him? Hmm... Actually he acted more like he had caught a glimpse of a ghost from his past.

"Professor, it is so nice to see you again. Am I to assume this is your new class?" Said the young man in a hushed voice while his eyes flashed back to me.

"Yes, it is," Professor Zirak answered in a whisper.

The young man put his finger to his lips and motioned for us to be quiet.

Then he waved for us to follow him into a conference room which set to the side of this room. As we filed in the professor continued, "Class, I would like to introduce you to Marvin Lagedge. He finished his training with me not too long ago. Can you tell us Marvin, do you work with the purple clad lady everyday?"

"Yes, I certainly do because I appreciate a challenge," said Marvin as he closed the door behind the last trainee.

"A challenge," repeated the professor. "Could you tell them why she is a challenge?"

"Well, Mrs. VanCues says she can hear us," Marvin said. "Earthlings tell her she's schizoid. Actually, her psychic door between worlds is ajar! So, when she thinks she hears us, she knows we're real, here, and starts requesting. She makes so many requests she has a permanent team assigned to her. We try not to talk when she has quiet moments. Only her radio, television, or louse noises drown our sounds out. We are an ever playing tape."

"Marvin does your team look for ways to fill her every request?" Asked Tilly while flashing her flirtatious smile. A new man in the game. Andy and the mousy boy were fading in her eyes.

"Absolutely," Marvin said with a contagious grin, glancing at me again. Then he burst out laughing for no reason. We laughed with him in contagious giggles and snorts. Sympathetic laughter.

"What is so funny?" Questioned the professor.

"Well, we finally fixed her!" He stated with humor in his voice. "She has a passion for art and talked for months about wanting to paint all summer. Although we knew she meant oil painting, she wasn't specific. This spring she also wanted to get her house painted. We fixed it so every painter she hired to paint her house, left, got ill, etcetera. Instead of oil painting, she had no choice but to spend her entire summer painting her own house with a paint brush. She indeed painted all summer!"

The professor did not look impressed but rather annoyed by him and his story. I could clearly see he wished Marvin had kept this story to himself. "This is the hardest of the studies, a psychic. Are there any volunteers who would like to stay and observe Mrs. VanCues?"

To my horror, Tilly's hand rocketed to the ceiling. "Professor, Elizabeth and I would love the opportunity!"

He smiled and looked at Marvin, "Looks like you have two overachievers on your hands for the week." Stated the professor. "Very well, I will see the pair of you back at Keeper House this evening."

I watched in horror as everyone else filed out of the conference room and into the lift giving us looks like we were mad to stay. I couldn't blame them, we were crazy. "Tilly, why did you volunteer us for this one?"

Tilly very matter of fact replied, "I don't want to be bored or have a boring Humling to study."

"You really should have asked me before volunteering..." I stopped mid sentence because I noticed Marvin standing watching the two of us with an amused look on his face.

"Hello, I am Marvin, and you are?" He stated as he held his hand out to shake mine. I thought he looked a little nervous as if he had been anticipating this for a long time.

"Elizabeth," I replied. When I touched his hand it was soft and warm, feeling like it melted my hand. He was very handsome up close. I was lost in his gaze. When Tilly leaned over with her hand outstretched. "Hello, I am Tilly." I returned from the spell he had cast on me.

"Very nice to meet the two of you," Marvin said as he quickly shook her hand. Neither Tilly nor I missed that he hardly noticed my gum popping friend. He was too enthralled in me to pay her any attention.

"If you would like to come this way, I will get you a workspace." Marvin said as he led me to a small desk while slightly touching my back with his hand. Tilly was left to make her way behind us.

The desk was simple, light wood with a pencil drawer. Under it set two crates which were being used as a filing cabinet. To one side set two small photos, a couple which we assumed were his parents, and a dog wearing a blue bandana around its neck. He quickly flung all the papers across his desk and shoved them into one of the crates.

"Elizabeth, you can have my chair," Marvin offered graciously as he reached for my processing bag.

"Thank you," I said as I sat down.

"Your dog?" I asked pointing to the picture.

"Yeah, that's Banjo," Marvin replied looking a little sheepish about the photo.

"Banjo?" I inquired as he placed my processing bag on top of the crate.

"My dad likes Banjo music. As a pup he would howl along with the music," Marvin explained.

"A perfect name," I replied.

"Excuse me," Tilly interrupted in an impatient manner. "Where do I sit?"

"The folding chairs are over against the wall," Marvin replied without looking at her. "Could you bring me one too?"

"You're a gentleman, aren't you," Tilly murmured as she stomped over to get a chair. She wasn't used to being ignored by a male much less asked to carry a chair for one.

We had embarked on what was to be a long day. To begin, Tilly was irritated with the treatment she received from Marvin. She didn't have the stomach for being anything less than the center of attention when a guy was around. He just really didn't seem to acknowledge her. He was too busy pampering me. I was certain, nobody had ever ignored her! I knew she was a little jealous but I found him to be funny and charming in a friend type of way. Marvin's preoccupation with me left the rest of his team annoyed with him. However, he was oblivious to their sour looks and rolling eyes.

Marvin explained Mrs. VanCues understood the basic principles of the law of attraction. Basically, what we think, we attract! Positive thoughts results in positive, life changing results. Negative thoughts receive negative results.

Mrs. VanCues certainly knew how to ask. She made endless requests out-loud and the room was a buzz trying to fill her generic needs, or wants. Marvin again spoke of their joke. It seemed they wished her to be clear about what she wanted. After each afternoon snack, she sat and pulled out a handwritten list of her important requests. I watched as she spoke them aloud and closed her eyes to visualize them in her head. Marvin said their job was to focus on the big items she speaks and visualizes first and then the smaller requests second.

Mrs. VanCues never doubted. She believed what she asked would definite-ly be fulfilled. When she got up from today's visualization she marched over to her china cabinet. I noticed a lace doily lying in the middle of a glass shelf with nothing on top of it. Marvin said she had asked for an antique vase to set upon the doily. It was important to her and on her list. She held the belief that her desire would be brought about. In full belief, she had made space for it in her china cabinet. Now that's faith I thought to myself.

Marvin explained the vase had been worked out because Mrs. VanCues was just as clever to recognize the channels in which her visualized requests would come and open to receiving. The vase itself would come through a se-ries of synchronistic events which had already been set in motion. It seemed she would be given a vase by a neighbor who was moving. The neighbor would present her with a box of junk and in the bottom would be a vase. Mrs. VanCues would love the vase itself but give it back when the neighbor called looking for the missing vase. The ex-neighbor on an antiquing outing with Mrs. VanCues would find a replica of the exact vase. The store owner would tell them the vase had set on the shelf for at least the last ten years. Mrs. Van-Cues would realize the fact that she came into the shop weekly. The vase only surfaced when the ex-neighbor was along with her. It was the neighbor who made her fall in love with it in the first place and part of the synchronistic events bringing it to her.

A Keepers job was split between two important, basic responsibilities that bind Keepers and Humlings. The first was fulfilling the law of attraction for the Humlings we help. Second, was communicating with the Humling to ensure we help them with their life theme and plan. Marvin didn't explain anything about how to communicate with Mrs. VanCues. He assured us this would come later in our training. She was a perfect psychic to study according to him.

Our eccentric Humling's many requests kept Tilly and me writing all afternoon. Although the concept was interesting, I was ready to leave at the end of the day. She was as demanding as a two year old. Afterwards, we had just enough time to get to Harmony practice and then I was calling it an early night. Evenings were peaceful as Tilly always crept out the window for her evening dates.

The next morning when Tilly and I bounced down the stairs, ready for another day, I was surprised to see Marvin milling around in the hall at the bottom of the stairs. When he saw us, he smiled a huge grin and waved us down to him. "Good morning," Marvin greeted us. "May I walk with you to the Keeper Complex today?"

Stepping off the last stair, Tilly started to say, "Thank you Marvin, but I…" when she was interrupted.

"Picked up a board for you! Are you sure you can ride it, newbie?" Asked Eddie who seemed to appear from nowhere. He held two skateboards in his hands. The bubble gum pink one he held out to Tilly while spinning the wheels with his hand. We were joined by several others in our training group whom also had skate boards.

"Of course I can ride it!" Tilly shot back as if he had hurt her pride. "Sorry Marvin. Sorry Elizabeth. I have other plans. You two go on without me."

Tilly had a questioning look on her face. She leaned over and asked in a whisper, "You don't mind him accompanying you alone to the Keeper Complex, do you?"

I eased her mind, "No Tilly, get some fresh air. You know me, I get lost easy. Marvin will ensure I get to training on time." I tried to give her a reassuring smile and realized she was giving me the same smile trying to reassure me.

"Thanks, Elizabeth. You know me! Some fresh air and rubbing Eddie's skate board nose in the dirt would be great!" Tilly said as she grabbed the board from Eddie. Eddie grinned at her comment and hurried off.

Marvin looked at me and bashfully smiled, "I guess that leaves us."

"Guess so," I replied as we exited the door of Keeper House. I nervously pushed my hair back making sure it was all back in my pony-tail. My blood rushed when he stood too close. Outside Keeper House we paused a moment.

"I hope you don't mind, I brought you something," Marvin stated as he took off his khaki colored backpack and handed it to me. "I thought you could use this."

"Why would you think that?" I questioned. How did he know I needed one? I looked it over, zipping it and unzipping all its compartments.

"You need a backpack, not a processing bag," Marvin stated.

A little insulted as we strolled down the corridor, I sarcastically shot back, "Maybe I like my processing bag!" He grinned at me. Granted my carry all wasn't great, but it was all I had. I hadn't been able to purchase one because no shopping fair had been announced. However, I didn't intend to tell him this. I handed him back the backpack in a snotty insulted gesture. "Thank you. But, no thank you. I can't accept this."

"I bet you can't even fit a third of your books into that flimsy processing bag," he stated holding the backpack again for me to take.

He was right. My processing bag was practically useless since it was no bigger than a purse. It clearly wasn't meant for books. "Why would you bring me a backpack?" I asked.

"You're special," Marvin said. "Perhaps I'm making you my charity case."

"Well, no thank you. I don't want to be special. Nor am I a charity case," I stated.

"You didn't let me finish," Marvin said realizing he had insulted me. His grin was gone. "I can't imagine life in training without a backpack. Remember, I just finished training. I've been there. A backpack is an absolute necessity. I'm just trying to help you."

"How and where did you get this back pack to give to me?" I questioned.

He did not answer. I could see by the frown on his face that he was now insulted at my refusal. He did not believe I was going to take his gift. Not taking it was going to hurt his feelings and alienate any relationship or friendship that could possibly develop. I did need to work with him and it was a generous offer. I reluctantly grabbed it, "Okay, thank you. But, no more unexpected gifts." He held on a minute before releasing it to me. Then his smile returned as he let it go.

"Put your stuff in, and I'll carry it," Marvin stated as I unzipped the bag. He had not verbally agreed to any more gifts. I could clearly see Dustin standing with Tiffany ahead waiting for the lift. I don't think Dustin would have noticed me if it weren't for my standing with Marvin. He smiled and to Tiffany's dismay walked casually over to us leaving her standing alone.

I could hear Dustin's mind as it spoke, "Surely, she is not going out with him."

"Elizabeth, you must introduce me to your friend," Dustin spoke aloud.

"Dustin this is Marvin and Marvin this is Dustin." I stated wondering why this was important to him.

Marvin curtly nodded to greet him and extended his hand to shake. Dustin just stood there as if trying to sum Marvin up. He returned the casual handshake.

I could see Dustin's face trying to place Marvin and hear his mind say, "I have seen him before. My training… No. Records… No. Ghost relations… Maybe."

Tiffany had given up waiting on Dustin. She walked over like chains were around her ankles in coy little steps. "Hey, what is going on?" She asked as she snuggled up and hugged Dustin's arm.

"I was just meeting Elizabeth's new friend, Marvin." Dustin said.

I heard Dustin's mind chattering, "Why must she always hang on me?"

I giggled a little due to his thoughts. All three sets of eyes turned to look at me. "Nervous giggles, sorry."

Tiffany rolled her eyes, shook her head, and bent over to whisper in my ear, "Honestly, I don't know what makes you so stupid. However, it works or you wouldn't have your new friend."

I flushed a bit realizing Dustin and Marvin heard her. The lift door dinged to my relief. I could see Marvin did not like Tiffany's smart remark! Being a gentleman he forced a smile onto his face, "Time to go."

"Tilly and I are shadowing Marvin. Will I see you later Dustin?" I said directly to Dustin to annoy Tiffany. Then I gave a small wave and walked away with Marvin.

Once inside the elevator, Marvin quietly inquired, "Do you know Dustin well?"

"Not really," I said trying to be coy. I sighed. "He's friendly enough, but I don't see what his attraction to his girlfriend Tiffany is."

"She's a charmer!" Marvin said sarcastically.

"I really don't think it is me she dislikes," I said. His eyes widened and a strange look crossed his face. "Tiffany and Tilly seem to be… I guess enemies might be the best word. She dislikes me due to my being Tilly's friend."

"Hmm," he responded which clearly meant he was assessing my relationship with Tiffany. "Since Dustin seems to be an acquaintance of yours, I will try to overlook his girlfriend," Marvin harshly stated. Hmm. Was I fly paper and Marvin a fly that was attaching himself to me? My friends were his friends? I felt both elated and uneasy at his sudden attachment.

I really did think Dustin didn't seem to enjoy Tiffany as much as he let on. I couldn't help my desire to be with Dustin. Dustin was the good smelling pied piper. I would follow him anywhere. I knew this would be something that Marvin would not appreciate or understand.

The lift door dinged as the small, elf like operator announced, "Keeper Complex."

"Thank you sir," Marvin said to the small operator as we exited the lift.

Ha! I wasn't the only one who thanked the lift operator. I walked beside Marvin through the foyer with my head on swivel. This room was massive and impressive on sheer size alone. The men and women in their nice white suits and dresses were busily getting their daily assigned office using the kiosk information machines. The lines were long today, leaving me glad I already had my assignment and Marvin to usher me through the crowd. As we headed for the long lines that led through the turn styles, I noticed Marvin looking at me oddly. When our eyes met, I asked, "What seems to be on your mind? Why are you looking at me so strangely?"

"Just thinking about the look you gave me as we exited the lift," Marvin stated. He started to say something else, but closed his mouth.

"I was just thinking, you're the first person I have heard thank the lift operator. Well, besides myself," I said smiling.

As we proceeded, it seemed a huge grin enveloped his face. We entered the turn-styles and I could once again feel his hand against my back as he led me to the appropriate lift to go up to our office.

As we stepped into the Keeper Complex lift which would take us up to our office, we turned to face the door. I looked up only to recognize the gruff, young man with the pitch black eyes and ratty, curly, black hair standing a couple feet outside the lift door. He was the same one from the Hall of Records whom I was certain wanted to detain Tilly and I when we went to look up the name Kaswell. I began to sweat! As I glanced into those black eyes, instant panic overtook me.

"Hey, are you okay?" Marvin asked as I realized I had clutched his arm with both of my hands. He looked sincerely concerned and tried to follow my gaze but the doors were closing.

I released his arm, "I apologize. I'm fine." I quickly turned my eyes from his to hide my fright. I could still feel his gaze. I knew he could see something had rattled me and hear my uneven breathing. I needed a quick fix, a story to tell him on our very short ride to our office.

"What rattled your cage?" He leaned over and whispered.

"Someone I knew from another less than pleasant encounter. The dark haired, gruff guy outside the lift," I replied. That was close enough to the truth.

The lift door dinged. He grabbed me by the arm and ushered me into the conference room on our office floor. "Spill the beans. What kind of unpleasant encounter was it?"

Marvin was relentless and not letting go of my arm. I was in deep so I might as well just tell him an overview. "Tilly and I went to the Hall of Records to look up a chapter on someone. When we left he seemed to be leaving too and we felt he was following us."

"Did he say anything to you?" Marvin questioned. "Did he touch you, chase you, stalk you?"

"No," I answered, not wanting to delve any further into the subject.

"Well, he probably was just leaving as well," Marvin concluded. "Perhaps he was having a bad day and you just picked up on some bad vibes from him."

I knew this not to be true but I was unable to tell him more. If I told him I heard voices in other people's heads, he might think I was crazy. He probably wouldn't even believe me. Some things are better left unsaid.

I believe he expected further details but gave up seeing I was deep in thought. He gently turned my chin and eyes up toward his. He reassuringly told me, "If you see him again let me know, okay?"

I nodded! Marvin seemed concerned in a protective type of way. If it weren't for my attraction to Dustin, I might even pursue him.

Once in the office, I was soon joined by an angry Tilly. She spent her morning stewing over a rope cutting incident which Trevor told her about on their ride to training today. Her anger was so focused that she went the entire day without flirting with any of the guys in our office. Fuming and getting even was her focus today. In addition, she smacked her gum loudly all day annoying everyone. She didn't even notice Marvin ignoring her. It seems the escape ladder had been cut at some point after she used it to sneak back in from her date with Andy. When Trevor pulled it up, he made the discovery. The severed ropes were cut under the rung that led to our window. She was furious and lit into me thinking I had done it out of jealousy. I defended myself. I assured her I didn't do it! She took me at my word and apologized. Now there was a new mystery!

If Tilly hadn't been so focused, I would have tried to tell her about seeing the gruff young man today at the lift. She and I shared our adventure outside the dome. She would have understood.

Beyond this, we were instantly thrown into Mrs. VanCues madness. She spent the morning demanding her desires be met. She swore she could hear Tilly smacking her gum and asked the universe to clear the static gum smacking sound from her connection. Marvin immediately made Tilly spit out the gum and threatened her if she even started to put another piece in for the day. He was batting zero in Tilly's books. Mrs. VanCues went on in her ritual meditation and visualization.

Everyone in the room was relieved when Mrs. VanCues hurried off to a baby shower for a friend's daughter. Mrs. VanCues didn't want to go but felt obligated too. Our group had worked out this synchronistic event for Mrs. VanCues! She read every night before bed and had visualized a series of books she wanted to read. The friend's daughter had read the entire same series. In getting the babies room ready, the new mom had piles of books to get rid of. Mrs. VanCues was to be given the series she wanted to read. Her answer to her request was set in motion. All she had to do was go with the flow. She would come home in a good mood! A synchronistic event! We would be relieved in our accomplishment as Mrs. VanCues Keeper.

CHAPTER FIFTEEN

Elizabeth

My Saturday did not go as planned. Tilly was anticipating her date with Andy and had been pre-occupied with finding the perfect outfit all morning. Over and over she asked for my opinion as she scrutinized every piece of clothing in her wardrobe several times. I found it hard to believe she could envision her clothing as proper attire for herself for any occasion. Finally, I persuaded her to dress in a button-up shirt which she wasted no time proceeding to unbutton. She was intent on revealing the leather camisole underneath it. The jean skirt she chose was short. Way too short! I begged her to go conservative with a skirt which almost reached her knees. Tilly had brainwashed herself into believing, since Andy worked for the Department of Ghosts and their emblem was rainbow colored, she belonged in rainbow stripped leggings. They made her look like a five year old. Then she topped it all off with her fuzzy brown boots. I found the whole ordeal repulsive, time consuming, and annoying.

Her preoccupation with the way she looked led me to believe she liked Andy. She admitted she hadn't ever been on a second or third date. There were too many men to conquer to waste time on a second much less a third date. Andy and Tilly were on their fourth. She claimed after one date, most guys bored her. Andy was holding her interest. She ignored our friendship and spent every moment outside class and Harmony with him. To top it all off, Andy had promised her adventure which in her mind equated to romance! Why had I wasted a morning doing this?

After musing in the mirror and seemingly pleased with her outrageous persona, I was set back when she commented on my own attire. I found plea-sure in wearing my old sweats, T-shirt, and flip-flop combo which I arrived in. They were comfortable. I secretly hoped somehow they would jog my memory. However, I was thankful for the clothes Tilly's mother had shopped for. They were indeed modest, fashionable, tight, stuffy, and not me. Yes, definitely not me. I couldn't be sure who I was, but I knew I wasn't uptight and stuffy. Tilly even criticized my hair which I wore pulled back into a pony-tail. Why did it matter the impression I made? I had no recollection of what my style was or aware of my style now. My face was flushed from the blunt criticisms directed at me.

Needing fresh air following Tilly's comments, I ventured to the grounds outside of The Hall of Knowledge and randomly sauntered around. The grounds were lush green and well manicured with huge, shade trees sporadi-cally spread about. A flagstone sidewalk circled the school, led to the road, and was framed with wooden benches and well-kept flower gardens. I was not alone. My fellow trainees were reaping the benefits of the perfect sunny, 72 degree weather and relaxing outdoors. Some were seated on blankets, others were settled against the base of the trees reading, and some like me were path wanderers.

My aimless walking brought me to a road. I followed it and headed for the park. My fellow trainees were a buzz about it and had been speaking of the park in an excited tone all week. I strolled past a few non-distinct homes until I came upon a wooden sign announcing Spring Park. A fern lined paved path spiraled downward. As I descended into the park's valley, I was enthralled by the view. The tall, mature hardwoods formed a massive canopy with smaller trees and foliage growing underneath. Birds, squirrels, and other small animals were all visible and scampering about. A gentle breeze brushed my skin as it rustled through the leaves. At the bottom of the hill ran a crystal clear, spar-kling river with a stone bridge spanning it. Fishermen were everywhere. They were casting, reeling-in, and sitting in lawn chairs. You could tell they were enjoying the great outdoors!

The park was a lively place and had other offerings besides the river. As I turned to the left, open grassy areas were full of individuals playing various ball games, flying kites, and picnicking. A playground divided into big-kid and little-kid fenced play area set upon white sand and was full of barefoot, happily playing children. Parents were perched on shady benches around the edges of the playground enjoying the peace of the moment. I turned to view what was to the right of the road and spied a beautiful, expansive, green golf course.

I decided to stay on the path and see where it led down past the river. As I rambled along, I happened upon a group of guys playing basketball. As I stopped to watch, Marvin caught my eye from the court. I didn't expect to run into him. He was agile as he coolly dribbled around the others, making lay-ups and baskets at will. I now took-in his strong arms and the way his sleeveless shirt enhanced his muscular build. The look was a contrast to the professional, white, stiff, collared shirts which he wore for work. Wow! He looked delicious. He was such a good-looking man and such a shame we were destined only to be friends. I stood in awe at his confidence and ease on the basketball court. I was unfamiliar with the other young men.

I must have been gawking at Marvin too intently. One of the guys picked up on my staring and motioned for Marvin to look my way. He passed the ball to another player and jogged over to the fence separating us, "Hey, what are you doing here?"

I was caught off guard by his sudden grin and attention. I blushed. "I was taking a walk and happened upon your game," I responded to his beaming face.

"Umm, are you sure you weren't tracking me down?" Marvin seriously asked with his eyebrows pushed together. How should I respond to that? I was at a loss for words. Then the sides of his mouth slowly turned upwards. I knew he was joking when he began to laugh. I was not amused.

"Who's your friend?" Asked a hairy guy who bounded over with the basketball under his arm. He scanned me from head to toe. I assumed he would find my sweats and T-shirt combo homely. Tilly's remarks had left me self conscious.

"Jessie, Elizabeth. Elizabeth, Jessie," Marvin introduced us as his hand gestured between us with his eyes hardly leaving me.

Marvin's eyes made me fidget as I waved my hand and said, "Hi." I couldn't help but stare at him. Jessie was hairy! Jet-black hair covered his arms and legs. He was indeed as hairy as an ape. He wore the same muscle shirt as Marvin, but he looked dreadful in it. All his jet-black hair protruded from under the shirt like millions of little aliens wanting to escape.

"Nice to meet you," said Jessie. Marvin seemed to shoot him a hands off glance. Jessie continued, "You don't mind if we borrow him back for the rest of the game, do you?"

"No, of course not," I responded as I gawked at Jessie. Looking beyond his hairy body, you couldn't miss the irony of his bald, shaved head. Jessie tossed the ball to Marvin and then trotted back to the awaiting group.

"Hey, will you hang around? Afterwards I could walk you back," Marvin asked with begging, bright eyes.

"Sure," I responded to his pleading eyes.

I found a seat on the metal bleachers to watch the remaining game which finished quickly. Marvin didn't engage his opponents as well because he was continually glancing in my direction. He was clearly distracted! His team mates didn't appreciate his lack of concentration. They lost and the game ended. He gave the impression he was unfazed by his teams' sour looks as he broke away from the group and jogged my way.

I climbed down from the bleachers and met a broadly smiling Marvin. He held out his arm for me to take and we began to make our way back out of the park towards the Hall of Knowledge. I casually asked, "So, do you play here often?"

"Yes, every Saturday afternoon," Marvin responded. "We all met and started playing to relieve stress during our training."

"So, were they all in Keeper House with you?" I inquired as I glanced over my shoulder at the disbursing group.

"Most, but not all," Marvin replied. "Now it's stress in our various lives that we blow away with the ball."

Stress? Hmm... My thoughts spilled out of my mouth, "What could you possibly be stressed with in your life?"

"You haven't forgotten who I'm assigned to, have you?" Marvin questioned with a chuckle.

"Good point," I responded as I shook my head in agreement.

"What stresses you?" Marvin inquired.

"Not much." I responded. "I think if you look at me as a whole, I'm kind of boring."

"Boring?" Marvin repeated as his brows pushed together. "Elizabeth you are anything but boring."

His kind words were very gracious. However, I was just plain Elizabeth in sweatpants with no memories.

"Have you done your life theme opening assignment for Professor Zirak?" Marvin inquired.

"That," I huffed.

"I'll assume No," Marvin said smiling. "Bend my ear. Tell me what you are going to say."

I paused at the center of the bridge and placed my elbows on the railing. While looking out upon the fisherman I sighed, "Why would you want to hear it? It's drab at best."

"Anything about you, I will find fascinating," Marvin assured me with a gentle grin as he leaned against the railing.

What should I say or could I say? I wished Dustin peered at me in the same manner as Marvin. Marvin gave me the impression he liked me. Who knew why! I left the rail and moved past him and once again embarked on the trek back towards the Hall of Knowledge. He joined and silently kept pace with me. Was he patiently waiting for me continue? If I were going to chase him off, why not do it now. "Marvin, I have amnesia. I'm a blank page! I remember nothing!"

"Since you re-entered?" Marvin curiously asked.

"Yes, I simply woke up in the Hospital and couldn't remember a thing about myself," I admitted.

"Lighten up Elizabeth! This is a memory fog. It will pass," Marvin assured me. Then he looked puzzled asking, "You re-entered through the Hospital?"

"Yes. Is that not normal?" I asked.

"Not really for a Keeper," Marvin admitted with a slight shake of his head. You could tell he was pondering my plight.

"Where do Keepers usually come back?" I inquired.

"The Hall of Babies," Marvin replied.

"Well, I guess I could tell the group that I'm a traveler with no sense of direction and re-entered in a strange place. At least it's interesting and a bit amusing," I said.

He chuckled. Then he whistled a woe-full lost sailor's sound.

I smiled at his whistling performance as I asked, "What about you?"

"You're not planning on copying my old assignment are you?" Marvin asked with a mischievous grin. "You don't seem like the humanitarian type."

I was appalled to think he thought I could be a cheater. "I have no need or desire to copy anyone, thank you!" I half barked at him in a slight huff.

"I was just kidding," Marvin said with an honest look on his face. He slightly shook his head adding, "Lighten up!"

"Okay," I shot back. "Tell me more."

"A life theme is always chosen before going to the Earth Plane to ensure you learn your life lessons," Marvin stated. "In my early life I was a sailor which landed me on numerous shores viewing and experiencing many Humling atrocities. I surrendered and devoted my life to improve conditions of those I had encountered along my travels. Simply, I just wanted to make their living conditions better. Along the way, I focused on improving one condition. Feeding the hungry, especially starving children."

"What did you learn from your experience feeding the Humlings?" I asked as my stomach growled thinking of food.

"I learned to appreciate small things," Marvin stated as he grinned at me, stopped walking, and briefly leaned against a tree. We had climbed the hill leading out of the park and were standing in front of the flagstone sidewalk leading to the Hall of Knowledge. Marvin spontaneously asked, "Would you want to get some ice cream? I hear your stomach growling."

This sounded like an uncomfortable, small date. My face flushed because of his reference to my stomach groan. I hesitated, "I don't know."

"Do you have something else to do?" Marvin questioned. Upon my nodding no, he continued, "Then why not? Like I said, enjoy the small things in life. Your tummy would appreciate it and there are starving Humling children who would see it as the only meal for two to three days!"

How could I answer that? I conceded, "Okay, ice cream it is."

Marvin's jolly grin returned to his face. I reluctantly followed his lead as we moved away from the Hall of Knowledge in the opposite direction. "Tell me ten things in your room?" Marvin questioned.

"Ten things," I thought out loud. I didn't own ten things. All that was in my room mainly belonged to Keeper House or Tilly. It was however, overran with one item. "Clothes, clothes, and clothes," I responded.

"Oh, you're a girly girl," he said as he playfully pulled my pony tail.

"Not really," I replied. Nothing about my appearance today could support the assumption of my being a girly girl. "Tilly has our entire room over ran with her flamboyant, wild clothes!"

"Hmm," Marvin replied. My assumption was he recognized I hadn't answered his question. Maybe he should answer his own question. I blurted out, "Okay, you tell me ten things in your room."

"A bed, desk, window, carpet…" Marvin said and paused.

I gave him a playful bored look at his answer yawning. I then asked, "No personal items?"

He chuckled at me. "Okay, I have a television."

I interrupted him, "How did you obtain one? I haven't seen a television anywhere."

"It's all in who you know," Marvin grinned. "Televisions aren't popular here. Most choose to watch real life in the Hall of Records. I actually like the Earth Plane movies. Something I learned to like with my uncle who acquired the television for me."

"So what is your favorite type of movie?" I inquired stopping to pick up a piece of litter from the path. I detested those who littered.

"When I am at home, action movies," Marvin replied. "Elsewhere my taste changes."

"You have different favorites for different places?" I questioned.

"When I'm at my uncle's house, he thinks my favorite is history movies," Marvin sighed. "Actually, it's his favorite. I enjoy our time together and thus watch his choices."

"You have never thought to tell him that history movies aren't your favorite?" I pondered out-loud shaking my head slightly.

"I guess after all these years, I should," Marvin conceded. "However, he's always so happy when we watch history together."

"What else is in your room?" I asked seeking to change the subject.

"Basketball trophies," Marvin confidently said pretending to dribble the ball and make a jump shot.

"That figures! You were a stand out in the game I saw today. However, I bet your hairy friend is better than you," I said to annoy him. After all, using starving Humling children against me to compel me to accompany him to get ice cream was equally annoying.

He smiled broadly at my half-teasing comment and began, "I started out playing basketball as a child during primary school. We played far away teams from outside the dome during secondary school. We were a fast dribbling basket dunking force. We won a lot of trophies. We were great!"

"Well, I have a processing bag hoop," I stated as I giggled. I held a pretend processing bag hoop up for him to make a pretend dunk in.

"Great hoop but poor backpack," Marvin sarcastically said.

"Yeah, yeah, yeah!" I replied pretending to tuck my processing bag away.

We continued our walk towards our destination. I felt his hand rest slightly upon the small of my back. His touch felt warm, comfortable, and completely natural. He raised his other hand pointing it towards the sidewalk leading towards a colorful, small shop nestled between two houses. A real ice cream stand. What a discovery! My thoughts slipped out my mouth as I said, "It's been so long since I've tasted real ice cream! And the shop is barely a stone's throw from Keeper House." My mouth was drooling.

"Yeah, I have a peppermint and vanilla ice cream hang up myself," Marvin agreed. "When I was in training, this was a hang out spot for sweet tooth freaks which included just about everyone."

The shop was a small, natural rock building with big plate glass windows in the front. Huge ice cream cones were painted on them. A covered porch ran across the front with a hanging swing nestled between the vine covered pillars. Two or three tables and chairs were available on the porch with red checked table cloths. As we climbed the two steps up to the porch, Marvin removed his hand. The absence of his touch left me with a bare feeling. Marvin quickly stepped in front of me to open the door which was entirely not necessary. I was perfectly capable of opening my own door. For some reason, I didn't want him to think his nice ways were scoring with me.

"Marvin," the super model, blond with too much cleavage showing behind the counter said with delight. I watched as she instantly began to scoop vanilla ice cream onto the marble, cold stone. At one point she gave Marvin a small wink ignoring me and the fact I was with him. My blood boiled. She then scooped crushed peppermint hard candies and began to mix them into the ice cream.

"You came here a lot?" I said to Marvin trying to regain his attention. He didn't have a chance to answer.

"Oh, yes! All the time. I know Marvin well," she interjected as she winked again at him. "Vanilla with his favorite candy, peppermints!"

Marvin seeing that I was annoyed at her winks, shrugged and leaned over saying, "The small things. I like ice cream and peppermints."

There was nothing worse than being out with a male who flirts with other girls in your presence. I reminded myself this wasn't a real date. Perhaps I was overreacting to her flirting. While focusing on her, I hadn't noticed Marvin watching me until he asked, "What kind would you like?"

"A scoop of Double Dutch Chocolate," I responded releasing my long hair from the pony tail grip. I shook my head so my hair was wild and free.

"Anything mixed in?" Marvin questioned with an I don't know what's happening look.

"Nope, just a scoop of Double Dutch Chocolate," I assured him licking my lips slightly and shooting the blond girl a don't mess with my man look!

The blond, super model carefully placed Marvin's ice cream into a bowl. She handed it to him with a huge smile making sure her fingers touched his hands. He didn't return her gesture. He hardly looked at her. He waited a moment and said, "I need a scoop of Double Dutch Chocolate for my date!"

"Oh," she responded. "I didn't hear her order or realize she was with you!" No doubt was left in my mind, she heard me and chose to ignore me. She scooped my chocolate and roughly slung it into a bowl. I was detecting a hint of jealousy which was unnecessary. Despite what Marvin said, this wasn't a real date. Although, I was annoyed green with her. Marvin and I were just working together. Friends.

She passed my bowl to me across the counter. I told her a weak, "Thank you." Marvin was on the way to open the door and oblivious to the daggers her eyes were emitting at me. I could hear Tilly tell me... "Either you've got it or you don't! In this moment, I had it.

Once again Marvin was a gentleman, holding open the door and waiting for me to exit first. With the door closing behind us, he asked, "Want to sit on the swing?"

"Sure," I agreed aware of her intent stare through the store windows. As I sat on the swing, I coyly teased, "You know she likes you."

"Who likes me?" Marvin questioned spooning small bites of his icy peppermint concoction into his mouth.

I quickly pointed over my shoulder with my spoon towards Blondie in the window and shook my head. Was he that oblivious or just playing dumb?

Marvin shrugged his shoulders, "You think she does, huh. Well, she does make the best bowl of peppermint delight around."

"You should date her," I replied.

He didn't answer. He shoved a huge bite of his ice cream into his mouth. My guess it was a play to delay answering me. Ignoring Blondie in the window, I turned my attention back out towards the street. The demon in curls and her sidekick came into my view. On their trek up the road, they automatically zoned in on us. I began to squirm around on the swing. My thoughts spilled out of my mouth with a hint of annoyance, "Oh, no!"

Marvin looked up from his bowl of ice cream and instantly recognized the trouble strolling towards us. He leaned over and half whispered, "Don't let them get to you."

"Do we have love birds?" Janelle asked Tiffany in a ridiculing manner as they sauntered up the sidewalk closing the distance between us.

"No," Tiffany said as she shook her head and pointed her finger at me. "Who would date someone who dressed like that? Feeding the down and out and hungry, Marvin?"

I could see Marvin's neck veins and muscles tighten. However, he continued his bowl of confection ignoring her.

"Someone really ought to give you pointers on your wardrobe Elizabeth," Janelle taunted. "The sweats and T-shirt look doesn't suit you and you are definitely unfashionable! Only Humling trailer park white-trash wears them."

I had no memories and couldn't relate to what she was saying.

Marvin placed his free hand on my knee for a moment. Then he grinned hugely at my two nemeses, "I like the way she looks. Maybe it is you who should take lessons from her. The two of you look like angels who have lost their wings!"

"Well, even a wingless angel is superior to white trash," Tiffany taunted.

"Sweat pants... White trash! White trash!" Janelle chanted with a sinister giggle.

"Don't you have anything better to do today?" Marvin growled back at them. "Karma is nipping at the heels of both of you!"

Once again, he placed his free hand on my knee. I understood the gesture, he had this one. I appreciated his facing them with me.

Tiffany's glare now read that Marvin was now their target, not me. "Guess what a little birdie told me," Tiffany asked Janelle.

"Oh, sounds juicy," Janelle said. "Share with me!"

"Seems I did a little research on trash girl's friend," Tiffany spewed in a feline voice while waving a finger in my direction, but looking directly at Marvin. "You belong with the low-form, low-class Ghosties."

"A low-life pasty Ghostie," Janelle chimed in with a teasing voice.

"There is nothing wrong with Ghosties," I interjected staring Tiffany directly in the eyes while trying to imitate Tilly with my head held high and a straightened back.

"You would say that," Tiffany retorted. "Someone has to run with the underdogs."

"You have no taste in who you associate with," Janelle added. They both giggled while walking past us and through the shop door.

Through it all, Marvin had showed composure and kept me in check with his hand on my knee. "They are incredible," I said to Marvin as I shifted my sitting position to face him.

This forced Marvin's warm hand off my knee. His placed it on the swing arm and stared at it for a brief moment. "Let's get out of here before they come back out," Marvin stated rising.

"Running from them," I half-joked, standing up.

"No," he strongly stated rubbing his forehead. "If I have to listen to them anymore, I fear getting a head ache." We exited our cozy swing area and made our way down the sidewalk to the road. Marvin's face was tense and clearly showed his contempt for what Tiffany had said in front of me. He was deep in seething thought. Finally Marvin sighed as he said, "They were referring to either my parents or uncle."

I could see his eyes were hoping for a glimmer of shared outrage and maybe my acceptance. I questioned, "The Ghosties?"

"My family all work for the Department of Ghosts," Marvin stated. "I am the only Keeper in my family."

"All work is honorable," I said placing my hand on his arm. "Ghosties work hard. They have to track and be able to convince lost souls to cross over to Home. That can't be easy!"

"Sometimes it's not," Marvin agreed as his face looked relieved that I was accepting of his family's work history.

"Why would your family's work would be a big deal to me?" I questioned.

"Ghosties are equivalent to Earth Plane psychics. Ghosties area a strange eccentric lot. Sometimes it's a deal breaker," Marvin said under his breath. "People often ridicule Ghosties and call them quacks." He was quiet for a few steps and then questioned, "Didn't you get a ghost assigned to find this week?"

"That is a long story," I sighed. "I don't know where to begin!" He walked quietly while clearly awaiting my beginning. "Tilly and I were going to be part-ners. However, she got sidetracked with a boy named Andy and agreed to be his partner dumping me. Andy was to partner with Mike who I inadvertently inherited."

"So now you are Mike's partner?" Marvin asked while holding up his hands palm up waiting for an answer.

"You've got it," I replied. "I have a complete stranger for a partner. Andy has assured Tilly the five page essay will be complete for both groups and that we have no need to worry about lifting a finger. Andy simply wants to partner with Tilly to gain her full attention so she will flirt with him. Neither boy is interested in learning or completing the essay or assignment in my opinion. We've been duped and Tilly doesn't see it!"

Marvin stopped dead in his tracks, "Elizabeth, if you don't learn to find ghosts, what will you do when you are faced with this dilemma as a Keeper? You must take this assignment seriously!"

"I know," I reluctantly stated as I threw up my hands. "That's what I've been trying to tell Tilly all week. This boy has blinded her reasoning!"

"Elizabeth you must get through to her that Keepers often assist when souls cross over or use their portal to come Home," Marvin said emphatically. "Sometimes souls get confused and aren't where they should be. It's important. A poorly educated Keeper endangers those between worlds."

We began to walk in silence. He was so comforting and delightful to be with. I easily could dismiss his maturity. I wondered how much older than myself he was.

Two people were sauntering towards us across the green lawn surrounding The Hall of Knowledge. To my horror, I knew one of them very well. I directed Marvin's attention as I pointed saying, "Get a load of that."

"Is that Tilly?" Marvin questioned. "Did she dress like that on purpose? What is all over her?" He seemed stunned at her appearance.

I was aghast. "Is it paint?" I questioned as I turned and looked at Marvin who shrugged. I continued, "She actually spent the morning picking that outfit out. Believe it or not, it did look better without the current paint splatters and streaks."

"I don't mean to offend, but I can't imagine that outfit ever looked good." Marvin said under his breath. "Your friend has zero taste!"

CHAPTER SIXTEEN

Tilly

"Tilly," I heard a voice calling my name. Spinning about I glanced over the landscape to see who it was. Then I saw her. Elizabeth yelled again and waving bounced over.

"Hey Elizabeth, Marvin." I greeted straightening my appearance. I was covered in paint. However, most of it was already dried. Orange and purple colored the hair around my face. The rest of me was covered in every color imaginable. I was a masterpiece! A true rainbow for my date. Turning my attention away from myself, I was shocked to discover Elizabeth had game after all. I caught her red-handed sneaking around with Marvin! Come to think of it, she deserved credit. Who scored dressed like that.

"Why are the two of you covered in paint?" Elizabeth demanded.

I couldn't help but laugh as I began, "When Andy told Mike we were going on another date, Mike told him I would easily become bored with him. So, Andy took me paint balling!" I leaned towards them making sure the whole world wasn't listening and whispered, "Isn't that romantic!"

Elizabeth shook her head and turned me around with both hands to look me over. Then she glanced at Marvin who said, "Probably not the best idea. You look like a bad modern art canvas. Plus you ruined a set of clothing!"

I didn't act in response to reason. Instead, I focused in on Marvin and pondered about what smart remark I could spew back at him. After all, who did he think he was? The fun police? A paint critic? Worse yet, my father? I wanted to scream at him! Instantly the realization hit me that I couldn't say a thing. He had turned from me. He was standing enchanted with Elizabeth. Boy, in that outfit she had worked a miracle! I was seething and missed my chance to zing him. I needed to breathe deeply for Elizabeth's sake. I would try not to run him off! I would strive to overlook her guy's inability to control his authoritative, spouting mouth! Ugh! Elizabeth was dating an uptight square!

Over Marvin's shoulder I caught a glimpse of a colossal problem strolling my way! My meddling father had insisted I go on a date with boring Scott tonight. Scott was coming and he was hours early. Sure, I had indulged my father. It was my selfish ways to keep Scott on the line for my own benefit, not my fathers. I needed Scott long enough to get the lift card machine in working order. Where else could I get needed parts? I glanced at my paint covered wrist watch. Oh honestly, what guy arrived hours early?

Andy casually rambled his way towards us and Elizabeth introduced him. "Marvin, this is Andy."

"Elizabeth let's head in so I can change," I interrupted as I pulled at her arm. I desperately felt the need for a quick exit. Over eager Scott was going to seriously interfere with my dating Andy. I yanked harder and with my hands spun and faced her homeward. I burst out, "I'm worried about the paint in my hair." She ignored me and turned back to Marvin.

Marvin's brows pushed together as he delivered a look of unbelief. It screamed he thought I was being rude and brainless messing up his date. Marvin held out his hand to Andy, "I'm Marvin."

Before Andy could shake Marvin's hand we all heard, "Marvin, what are you doing here?" Marvin turned to see who was speaking to him.

Scott was jogging the last few steps with a big bouquet of flowers. I dropped Elizabeth's arm as I began digging in the small pockets in my paint covered skirt. Where was my piece of gum?

Marvin greeted the rose man with a huge grin. "Hey Scott! You missed the game today."

"Yeah! Sorry I had other plans." Scott's eyes fell upon me. He looked aghast at my appearance and frowned. "Tilly, what happened to you?"

I managed an uncomfortable grin. Instantly his eyes moved to Andy who he scanned up and down. Our association was undeniable. We were both covered in paint. "Who's this?" Scott asked me with a hint of instant rage in his voice.

Marvin and Elizabeth eyes flickered as they exchanged looks of disbelief. In the same instant, Andy energetically said, "I'm her date!"

"Her date?" Scott questioned as his neck began to turn red. "Tilly, say something and it better be good!"

I hem-hawed while Elizabeth spotted my missing piece of gum hanging out the back pocket of my skirt, plucked it out, and handed it to me. Geez! I forgot about that pocket. She was smooth handing me the gum. She bought me a few moments of distraction. Time to let my mind think and plot was appreciated. I chewed slowly realizing, there was no way out of this one. The cat was out of the bag. What a shame I wasn't getting the flowers! Taking a deep breath and popping my gum I replied, "This is Andy, my Ghostie partner, and yup … my date."

Scott froze. He was an icy fool contemplating what to do. Finally, his voice cut the silence as he replied, "Your parents would be so proud!" His face was now as red as his neck. He instantly had changed from frozen to boiling. "Slumming it with the Ghosties?"

Andy stepped forward arching his back which made him stand taller. He snapped, "Back off!" Clearly, he was offended enough for both of us over the Ghostie comment. I grabbed him by the arm to bring him to a stop. He was kinda dashing standing up for me. Although, he should know I can defend myself. I'm no helpless female!

"You've been duped too!" Scott snickered as he threw the flowers into Andy's chest. Adrenaline filled his body and he suddenly shoved Andy back-wards. "I'm her date this evening."

Shock spread across Andy's face as he turned to look into my eyes and asked, "Tilly is this true?"

I nodded while I peered at my brightly painted, once brown, fuzzy boots. Neither of them owned me. I wasn't pledged to either! Scott was suddenly, aggressively moving towards Andy whose fists instantly took position. Oh no, they were going to hurt each other! Marvin hurriedly stepped between them catching Scott's arm saying, "Man, trust me. Don't say things you don't mean or do something you will regret." Marvin stood feet planted and adamantly shaking his head no. "Let it go!" I hated to admit it, Marvin was a cool mediator. Thank goodness for Elizabeth's square demonstrating and spouting his authority!

Scott angrily glared at Marvin's hand which firmly gripped his arm. As Scott pulled his arm free he told Marvin, "Hey man, no offense meant."

"None taken," Marvin countered. "Just let it go!"

I took a couple steps backwards. This sucked! All angry and shocked eyes were focused on me. What was I going to do? I blew a big bubble and popped it thinking, maybe not all was lost. Who did I need more? Andy or Scott? Scott fit in well with my parent's world, but definitely not into mine. I was appalled and there was definitely no future with someone who condescendingly looked down on others. I wouldn't be upset about loosing Scott. He meant no more than just one in the vast sea of men! Hmm… My father sticking his nose in my life was going to end with this incident. It didn't matter how many bubbles I blew and popped, they weren't helping me cope with my dilemma.

Andy on the other hand, challenged me. My choice was definitely Andy. I coyly sauntered up to Andy and proceeded to run my fingers down his chest tracing a flow of green, dried paint. He jerked his body away from my touch. I could read the hurt expression upon his face and in his peering eyes. He took a deep breath and said, "I trusted you and our relationship. My friends warned me about you!"

I tried to interject an explanation, "But…"

Andy cut me off and blurted out, "Be honest, I am just one of many!" He spun around leaving his back to face me. Then he walked away saying over his shoulder, "Save your lies for your next date."

What an insensitive jerk. I watched him walk away and sighed. I guess I could still try my hand at salvaging Scott and perhaps keep him on the line awhile longer as my easy part guy! Turning to him, he flashed an equally hurt look at me. I moved to stand in front of him, seeking a way out. I softly said, "I'm sorry. I didn't realize you wanted a commitment between us. Your receptionist said the two of you were an item!"

"Don't apologize and leave her out of it," Scott demanded. "You either run hot or cold leaving me to wonder if you were dating me because I was Daddy's choice or you were really interested. Now I know! You did me a favor by not making me waste anymore time on you."

Well, that was that! There wasn't anything left to do or words to express. Once more I looked into his eyes. I could see Scott was awaiting my response. I simply threw my hands up and screamed, "Okay! Be a jerk!" Turning to march away, I swore my father was toast for causing me this embarrassment! Being dumped twice in one day wasn't something I was accustomed too!

"Marvin, I'm going with Tilly," I heard Elizabeth say. This friend thing was going to work out with her. She was on my side supporting me. Just what a best friend would do!

I turned back to wait for Elizabeth to join me. I saw Marvin frown at her. I had given no thought to the fact that Elizabeth had worked a dating miracle. I had ruined their afternoon. Darn!

Marvin reluctantly replied to Elizabeth leaving, "Okay. Good luck on your assignment tomorrow." As Elizabeth turned to walk away, Marvin yelled, "Hey, no cheating!" Elizabeth spun around and walked a few steps backward as they both shared a huge smile and wave. How was it they already had a private joke between them? It was obvious from their smiles and hand gestures. When did this happen? Elizabeth waved goodbye again and hurried to catch up to me.

"That little encounter certainly was interesting wasn't it?" I asked and then blew a big pink bubble. "Boys! The whole ridiculous situation was over-blown!"

"Let me give you a tip," Elizabeth began as we started our journey home. "Multiple dates… not a good thing. When they run into each other, boom!" She made gestures of bombs exploding with her hands.

"Come on," I said with a shrug. "You have to admit my little run in made the day interesting."

Elizabeth shook her head in disbelief. With a concerned look upon her face she asked, "What are you going to do with Andy? He looked madder than an old dog that someone has taken his bone from, snarling and barking."

"Yeah, he was more hurt than mad," I admitted as the regret of hurting him was just setting in. I held my hand to touch my heart. Was there something serious going on there?

"It's not all fun and games," Elizabeth commented as her non relenting eyes focused on mine.

"You do know I didn't intend to hurt Andy?" I retorted.

"No matter what your intention was, Andy has become a problem," Elizabeth stated. "What are you going to do about your class partnership with him?"

"I don't know!" I snapped. What was done was done. You can't put toothpaste back in the tube! I just needed time to think out a plan. Sadly, it must also include Mike. I had messed it up for Elizabeth and myself. "You're probably in the same pickle. Mike isn't likely to be happy either."

"You're probably right," Elizabeth agreed as we entered the door to the Hall of Knowledge.

I was glad to be surrounded by others who forced silence upon us as we began to walk across the foyer. Who was I kidding? Elizabeth was right. Andy might become an unbearable partner now. As much as I didn't want to admit it, my regret centered on the fact… I liked him! And, I had hurt him. However, I couldn't wallow in regret or embarrassment. That was it! Andy was my challenge! I devilishly smiled over at Elizabeth as we climbed the staircase questioning, "What would you say if I told you I will date Andy again?"

"Tilly, he is not going to date you again!" Elizabeth blurted out with a look of bewilderment. "Totally impossible! I can't even believe you said that or can think that!"

"Don't rain on my parade," I retorted with a devious look. "All I need is a good plan!"

"Well, you just work out a plan," Elizabeth muttered under her breath sighing. "We'll see."

My doubter friend had re-emerged. Didn't she know that if I put my mind to it, I can do anything? Besides, Andy was a guy after all. No male was immune to my ways!

Elizabeth interrupted my thoughts when she asked, "Have you noticed all the stares?"

"Who's staring?" I responded as my head began to swivel around. I answered my own question while we walked down the Keeper corridor. Everyone was rudely staring at my brightly painted attire. "They're just jealous. They all secretly wish they could be free to have fun like me!"

"Hmm," Elizabeth responded. "I think you should change quickly! By the way, I'll assume Scott was your back-up date?"

"He's not my typical back-up date," I sighed to her question. "It was a sort of forced on me date by my father. Scott is an upcoming engineer and works in the Administration Complex. He's in my father's mentor program and unfortunately a star! He's perfect for me, or so my parents say."

"So, he is your father's pick," Elizabeth said while rolling her eyes in understanding. "Tilly, you could do better! I didn't like his comments about Ghosties and I found him to be rude. He reminded me of Tiffany!" Elizabeth spouted as we entered the door of Keeper House. I was pleasantly surprised by Elizabeth's first hint of a backbone giving me advice and pointing out Scott's flaws. The more time that passed, the more we were turning out to be alike in our thinking. Elizabeth was insightful. After his tirade tonight and Elizabeth pointing out his prejudice toward Ghosties, I could see him getting along well with Tiffany.

As we climbed the staircase, Elizabeth leaned over so others on the staircase couldn't hear and asked, "This plan of yours, how will you get Andy to forget and forgive you about Scott?"

"I don't know yet," I sighed. "But, don't worry. I'll take care of him." I paused a moment and thought about my destination card maker. Loosing my parts guy could be a massive blow to my operation. Much to Elizabeth's dismay I stated, "Besides, Scott is a bigger problem than Andy."

"Because of your parents?" Elizabeth questioned. When I didn't immediately answer she continued, "I didn't think you would let anyone force you into dating someone who puts others down or is chosen by your parents!"

"No one can force me into doing anything," I assured her. "I was only dating Scott because..."

"Because?" Elizabeth questioned stopping in front of the door to our room.

"Oh, he is just something I must figure out what to do about," I cut her off as we entered our room door. I was torn. I really should confide in her my reason for contemplating holding on to Scott. She had trusted me with her demons. However, I couldn't let the cat out of the bag. How would she feel knowing I had kept her in the dark concerning my destination card scheme? This was probably the biggest scheme of all times against the established rules of the land. Would she truly understand Scott was my parts guy? He was a necessity. I wanted to show her my project. Imagine, going down to the lift and going anywhere of our choice. The time wasn't now. In my pacing between our beds, I hadn't noticed her crawl onto her bed and silently watch my internal struggle unfold.

"You must have your reasons," Elizabeth gently said catching my eye.

"It's complex," I stated. "Never mind. I just don't want to talk about Scott anymore." Maybe that was a little harsh. To soften the mood I said, "Can we consider him a mistake?"

"A mistake?" Elizabeth repeated. "That's an understatement."

CHAPTER SEVENTEEN

Elizabeth

Tilly and I made our way downstairs to brunch. My stomach was growling. I hadn't eaten anything since the ice cream yesterday. Only two chairs were vacant awaiting our arrival. They weren't together leaving us unable to sit together. The stuttering Stone girl moved a book bag from the chair beside her and motioned for Tilly to sit next to her. I peered around. The only remaining seat loomed between Destiny and Trevor. Both were grinning. It appeared Destiny had saved the chair for me. I moved across the room dodging between my fellow trainees and chairs. I took my seat between friend and foe.

"Do you know Tilly's story?" Destiny whispered to me as I scooted the chair out from under the table and seated myself.

"Um, No. Not really," I replied feeling annoyed at her inquisition. Was Tilly's life upon the Earth Plane any of her business?

"I looked up part of her chapter, and we are in for quite the story," Destiny responded with a sly smile placing a small bite of eggs in her mouth.

"Is that what you spend your time doing?" Questioned Trevor who left the impression he was equally annoyed by her prying into Tilly's life.

Destiny leaned her elbows on the table and stuck out her tongue at Trevor who was seated opposite her.

"How did you open her chapter?" I questioned.

"Really Elizabeth," Destiny replied as she huffed, sloughed back in her chair, and rolled her eyes at me. Was it possible for someone, other than the owner, to open a chapter? This was a secret I wished she would share.

"Good morning," said Professor Zirak as he breezed into the room. Instantly, a mass scooting of chairs began as everyone made room for Professor Zirak at the head of the table. Professor confidently took his place and spoke, "Good morning class! I look forward to hearing about your life themes. I'm sure each of you understands the basics of our assignment. Life themes are the life lessons, or classes, we hope to ace and gain knowledge from in the school of life on the Earth Plane. Life themes are set up to perfect the soul in their particular area of focus."

Tilly distracted the group whispering something inaudible to the stuttering Stone girl. The Professor glared at Tilly, tapping his fingers on the table until he caught her eye. With her new found silence intact he continued, "Each of you will stand before the group and share your experience on the Earth Plane. In your discussion, please disclose your life themes."

"Mine were an interesting choice," mumbled an egotistic short haired blond from across the table. Everyone ignored her. Suddenly, I had the realization that this brunch marked one full week of training. To my dismay, I only knew a handful of the twenty people crowded around the table.

The professor gave the short haired blond a warm smile acknowledging her remark as he stated, "As often happens with life themes, there purpose is to help your soul progress." She glowed and basked in the short attention given her. The professor continued, "The most important part of your speech should be telling the group what you learned while perfecting your life theme."

"Excuse me professor, may I suggest we start with Tilly?" Interrupted Destiny with a sticky sweet voice.

Professor Zirak took a deep breath. He looked annoyed, maybe at being interrupted or maybe at the idea of Destiny's suggestion.

As if on cue, Tilly cut through the uncertain tension as she piped up, "Yes, I would enjoy going first." I watched my friend as she began to unwrap her gum.

"No gum," demanded the professor in a strong, stern voice. He gave her a nod and waved his hand saying, "Miss Bradford."

Tilly loudly scooted her chair back with the legs scraping the floor as she stood. In an act of compliance, she placed her open gum on the table before her and grinned at the professor. She then began, "My life theme was victim."

Immediately Tilly's statement triggered the strangers around the table to stare at each other with huge eyes. No one could visualize it! Tilly a victim? Reading the room, Tilly confidently flashed a smile and concluded, "I know what you are all thinking. The Tilly we know would never be a victim. That's why my story will captivate and intrigue you!"

I heard Destiny chuckle as Trevor leaned over my lap mouthing to her, "Knock it off!"

Tilly was a master at gaining attention. She thrived on it. Looking self-satisfied with every eye in the room glued upon her, she continued, "Everyone, especially my parents, want to dedicate their earth life to better humanity. This is exactly what I chose to do! I am so pleased to share with you my story. I was a free spirit."

"You should include something we don't already know," Destiny said under her breath. The professor pointed his finger at Destiny with a clear message not to interrupt again.

Tilly ignored the comment, "As a teenager I was hopelessly drawn to my boyfriend. He was the All-American guy. He played sports, was wealthy, handsome, etcetera. I was elated he desired to date me when he had a mile long line of other girls waiting. We dated through high school, married after we graduated, and started college. I often thought I was living in a dream.

Our problems, or earth lessons, were set in motion when he flunked out of his first semester of college. He didn't know the meaning of work. His parents consistently pampered him! Their money cured all his problems. His parents stepped in and bribed the college admissions person. He continued into his second semester with me, ending with the same results. He was never forced to face any consequences. His parents rewarded his lack of motivation with an executive position within their family business.

The next fall, he demanded I no longer attend college. My being a strong willed person, I would not let him derail my ambition and went anyway. This was the first night he brutally beat me. The beatings continued throughout the rest of our marriage progressively getting worse. Towards the end of my junior year of college, I was bewildered and heart broken to learn my best friend was sleeping with my husband. She knew how cruel he was. I didn't understand how she could find my monster husband attractive! Crushed and betrayed, I simply slipped out and left.

Even in starting my new life, I could not free myself of him. He badgered me at school, work, and my new home. The night our divorce was final, I went to bed relieved for the ordeal to be over. In the middle of the night I was awakened by him talking to me. Yes, he was at the end of my bed. The fight ensued, but I did not win. I found myself in his car and frightened. He drove me to the lake and when I tried to run, he shot me twice. However, dying by gunshot was not what he intended for me. You see, I could not swim. He knew my fear of water. He wanted to drown me and watch my panic." Tilly paused and the room viewed her shiver at her own thoughts. As she stared blankly out into the group, she continued, "I only remember being held under the pitch-black water as my hands tried to pry his grip from my shoulders while my body thrashed around. When he thought I was dead, he pulled what appeared to be my lifeless body onto the bank. Two fishermen who came at dawn were off duty paramedics and my heroes.

At his trial for attempted murder, he was convicted and sentenced for many years behind bars. You see, I chose in my earth life to put myself in the direct path of a Black Arch Dweller. I would sacrifice and be his victim to keep the Humlings out of the Dweller's hands. The rest of my earth life was consumed ensuring he never got parole. If I hadn't been able to stop him, I would have been only the first to die by his hands on the Earth Plane. He was to become a serial killer."

Tilly, with a satisfied look upon her face had finished and began to sit down in her chair. The faces around the table all led me to believe they felt the same as I. This was a dreadful story. As I glanced back at Tilly, I saw her happily finish unwrapping her gum and pop it into her mouth. She was unfazed by the looks and remarks being whispered. This was a definite insight into her psyche. No wonder she lives and breathes to dominate all males.

"Miss Bradford, well done," smiled professor Zirak. "I am impressed! Not many choose to be a sacrifice in order to stop a Dweller from hurting others. Did anyone else choose this life theme?"

Professor Zirak glanced around the table to the heads nodding no. He continued, "Indeed, rarely do any of us choose this path for our earth life. Since Dwellers have been mentioned, let's take a moment to discuss the two common life themes of Dwellers. Tilly, can you share the life theme of the Dweller you encountered?"

"Sure," Tilly said while smacking her gum. "He was a persecutor. He had no regret for his actions towards me. His theme was to torture and carry out many Humling atrocities. Each horrendous act would have built on the one before as he became a serial killer."

"You described the basics of the life theme persecutor very well," Professor Zirak complimented giving her a slight small clap of his hands.

"Thank you, Professor," stated Tilly. "It's easy to understand it when you lived it!"

"Indeed," Professor Zirak agreed giving Tilly a true look of understanding as she blew a huge pink bubble.

"Let's see if Elizabeth's story is so captivating," Destiny stated out of the blue with a snicker, jabbing her elbow into my arm.

"Miss Cantrell is welcome to go next," Professor Zirak began. "After we finish discussing the remaining common Dweller life theme."

Great! I gave Destiny the dirtiest look I could muster. She shrugged her shoulders at me as if saying, oh well! Suddenly, I was aware of how warm the room was. I was stewing in my own nervous juices!

Professor Zirak captured my attention as he said, "The other common life theme of a Dweller is a victimizer. They tend to have and use their magnetic personality to draw people to them. They often share their views which they believe everyone should share. If they are given the time, their need to dominate others grows and their views become outrageously radical. They view anyone opposing their ideology as an enemy. Usually they become mass murderers or mass dominators such as dictators or cult leaders." The professor paused and smiled at me, "Miss Cantrell. You may share now."

I was sweating with all eyes upon me. Having no paper to hand over and no life theme to break the silence, there was no need to stand. I gazed at my feet saying in a low voice, "Professor, I didn't finish my paper for today."

"Would you mind to tell the group why you did not finish?" Asked Professor Zirak.

"I just didn't do it," I retorted.

"You just didn't do it," Professor Zirak repeated clearly irritated with me. "Miss Cantrell, I'm surprised! Let me assure you, before you finish training this assignment will be completed. The purpose of our earth lives was to build empathy for those we plan to help. You must understand the struggles and accomplishments on the Earth Plane. If you didn't take this assignment seriously, then you haven't learned much and it's a reflection on your position as a Keeper."

He paused, staring me down awaiting my response. What could I possibly say to the room full of open mouths and stares? Professor looked resigned to crack down on me as he continued, "Is there anyone else in this room that did not complete this assignment?"

Heads shook side to side all around the room. I indeed was the only one. The professor paced a few times at the head of the table before saying, "Very well. If I can't motivate you, then your fellow trainees will. Every week this training class will write a brief two page essay on a life theme of my choice until Miss Cantrell turns in her essay about her one earth life." Groans came from around the room as the eyes of my fellow trainees shot daggers at me. They were getting punished for my deed.

"The first life theme will be humanitarian," Professor stated as he turned his glare to me. "Directly after brunch Miss Cantrell, you will pay a visit to my office to discuss this matter further."

As I stared at my feet, I nodded in agreement to the professor's demand. Trevor's hand tapped my leg and my eyes met his. He nodded towards Tilly.

Tilly mouthed across the group, "I will come with you." Her eyes then focused on Destiny as she spewed, "Let's hear your story, princess Destiny."

"Wrong," Destiny growled back. "I'm not the princes at the table." She paused moving her line of sight to the professor. In a sticky sweet voice she said, "But I would be happy to go next."

"Very well, Miss Nabor," Professor said.

"I was an accountant," Destiny proudly stated. "My life theme was perfectionist. I lived the true meaning of the word with everything being black and white. There was a place for everything and everything in its place. I poured countless hours into ensuring everything in my life ran smoothly. Anything less, I felt guilty!

Even though my work was a lesson in perfection, my work was sadly unappreciated. I dealt with many types of clients. Most treated me as their common peasant. You see my dual theme was patience. My clients often irritated me with their belittling and nit-picking. Learning to tolerate their criticism sharpened my ability to be patient."

Destiny started to sit as Professor Zirak inquired, "What did you learn?"

"I learned not to take my clients criticism to heart and be hard on myself and to take time to enjoy the small things in life. My work was perfection. However, I learned when something went wrong to cut myself some slack and not feel guilty."

"Thank you Miss Nabor," Professor Zirak said satisfied with her response. "Mr. Stillholm," Professor Zirak said as he motioned towards Trevor.

Trevor stood as a gentleman would and started with a nod, "Professor. Fellow trainees. I grew up in a metropolitan area where the extremely poor often faced high rates of unemployment and poor education. I grew up in a single parent home with a mother who believed I could do anything. I watched her struggle to keep a job, put food on the table, and keep a roof over our heads. She wanted to ensure I had the best ..." He made quotation marks with his fingers, "educational opportunities." Then continued, "available and often encouraged me do extra studies.

When I was a teenager my mother became ill. I watched hopelessly as she struggled with bills, sickness, and worry about me. When she crossed over to home she was not filled with peace. Watching her life end made me determined to excel in my studies and I became an advocate for the poor. I fulfilled my mother's dream. I became a lawyer working pro-bono cases for the poor trying to ensure my clients had basic rights.

You see, my life theme was an activist. I tried to ensure my clients had the basic rights that those more fortunate took for granted. I poured my heart and soul into reversing society's failure and the consequences of poverty. I prided myself in doing my job right and excelled in cases that others would fail at. I learned in time to focus on the jobs which made the most impact. Relentless describes my efforts. In summary, I was good at my job!"

"That you were," agreed Tilly speaking aloud and clapping for him.

"And how would you know?" Destiny questioned interrupting Tilly's applause.

"Tilly was one of my best repetitive clients," Trevor added with a smile directed at Tilly. Trevor then leaned across me and said under his breath to Destiny, "You should have read the whole chapter!"

There sure was more to this story! I wasn't sure any of us wanted to hear it though. What little Tilly did tell shocked us. I personally didn't want to hear anymore about blood and gore beatings.

The professor seemed intent to leave any further story untold when he called "Mr. Stillholm." Eddie stood as the professor demanded, "No hoodie! I want to be able to see your face."

Eddie reluctantly pulled the fleece sweater hoodie from his head exclaiming, "I'm stoked to tell you I spent my life dirt baggin' it!"

The professor held up his hand, "Mr. Stillholm, please speak in terms we can all understand."

"I was a skateboarder who lived a bare bone life style. My life was all about skateboarding. Dirt baggin' it!" Eddie explained to the group. "My theme was adventurer. My focus was always on the next jam, so I went from job to job, experience to experience. I easily mastered most tasks, but chose to only work to save money. Then, I would live off the money for my next skateboarding adventure. The majority of my life on the Earth Plane came down too breathing, eating, and maxing out my tricks! I would crash in my car which was usually my home. It was packed full of camping gear and coolers of beer, unless it was towed. Sleeping, skating, enjoying the company of others was my bliss. Occasionally, I would hitch rides and crash in my sleeping bag under the vast night skies peering up at the stars."

"Mr. Stillholm, did you accomplish more than skateboarding on the Earth Plane?" Professor Zirak interrupted and questioned.

"I'm getting to that Professor!" Eddie retorted. "Beyond my passion, I came across many avenues to occasionally make a positive impact on the Earth Plane. On my rest days, you know the days I didn't skate, I would volunteer at the local soup kitchens, shelters, or Salvation Army offices. I even did an unpaid stint as a Green Peace worker and one as a Feed the Children worker. Volunteering opportunities taught me the value of helping others."

"Okay, thank you Mr. Stillholm," stated Professor Zirak while holding up his hand. Eddie sat down and pulled his hoodie back over his head.

The young man seated on the opposite side of Eddie, droned on and on about his playing the trumpet. Boring! As the attention of the room rotated around the table I found most of the strangers stories interesting and boring at the same time. Eventually, all eyes were upon the short haired blond girl across from me. She lived a life of privilege. With no worries, she found herself in-debted to her own shopaholic and fast lifestyle addictions. Her life was about overcoming them and seeing past monetary pleasures.

My interest once again peaked when the Professor called, "Miss Stone."

I could see the stuttering Stone girl take a deep breath in to calm herself as she stood. As she looked out upon all the eyes staring, her eyes looked like a wild, frightened deer in the headlight. She turned to look at Tilly who was smiling a reassuring smile at her. Then Tilly nodded and motioned for her to start in a reassuring gesture. I watched as the stuttering Stone girl removed her glasses. Her attention returned to the room before her. She no longer looked as anxious. I watched as she looked down at her paper for a clue where to start. She first held it close to her face, then at arms length. Apparently, she could not see anything without those thick, coke bottle glasses! After an awk-ward few moments, she folded the paper and laid it upon the table.

One more deep breath, she began, "I was a nanny." The fact that I had never heard her actually say anything without stuttering did not pass by me, or by her! A broad smile crossed her face and her eyes watered. Another deeply inhaled breath and she continued, "I worked for several wealthy families, enabling the parents to have the freedom to make an impact on the Earth Plane. My theme was caretaker and I learned not to be selfish." Her words were short, clear, and to the point. A broad smile remained on her face until she sat down placing her glasses back on her face. Once again, seeing everyone eyeing her, she retreated back into her shell.

"Thank you, Miss Stone," replied the Professor.

I turned to see Tilly give her a thumb up. Then with her eyes Tilly spoke to Trevor and me to follow and do the same. Taking Tilly's lead, we gave the Stone girl thumbs up as she sheepishly smiled at us.

When I noticed how few people were left, the realization hit me! I would soon be handed the second portion of my punishment for today's assignment in the professor's office. As the life theme discussion finished its rotation around the table, I couldn't concentrate on anything said. What was I going to do? I couldn't turn in a paper, when I had nothing to write. Marvin joked about my cheating! Actually, it didn't sound like a bad plan at this point.

"We have learned a great deal about each other through our presentation today," Professor Zirak commented, interrupting my thoughts. "In addition to the paper due on the life theme humanitarian, I would like each of you to come next week prepared to discuss the life theme of your assigned Humling with the group. Next Sunday we will meet for dinner instead of brunch." He paused and looked directly at me, "Thank you for your time today. Everyone is free to go with the exception of Miss Cantrell."

Chair legs scooted against the floor with screeching and scooting sounds ricocheting off the walls. The room was a buzz with everyone chatting with their friends as they gathered their belongings and began to leave the table.

"Good luck," Destiny said to me as she turned to leave.

I nodded my head in response. My stomach was nervous and full of butterflies. I straightened the hair in my ponytail to release tension. I turned towards Trevor who rendered a sympathizing gaze while placing his hand on my shoulder, "Come up if you need to talk."

"Um… Okay, thanks," I sputtered. His concern was genuine as he held my gaze. Was I entering the inter-circle? A strange new sense of belonging washed over me as I flashed a nervous, goofy grin at Trevor. His facial expression didn't change leaving me to believe, he must think it was going to be bad. Maybe I would need that talk. I leaned forward and grabbed his arm. My thoughts came out in a whisper, "Wait! New ladder?"

Trevor grinned and grabbed his paper off the table. I let go of his arm and read his grin. Eddie followed Trevor towards the door. As Eddie passed, he gave me a wink and thumbs up. Laid back Eddie didn't let anything get to him. I sighed as I rose and pushed my chair under the table. Tilly approached me saying, "Let's go see what the damage is."

"Yeah," I agreed. "It's going to be bad."

Tilly had no response beyond her look of agreement. We slowly shuffled our feet down the hall. In silence we stopped and stood outside the professor's door. You couldn't help but take notice of the nasty looks I was receiving as our fellow trainees passed. No one appreciated the extra assignment. Beyond the thorn in their side that was me, they were happily disappearing up the stairs or out the door of Keeper House. They were free to go on about their day. I was doomed!

Professor Zirak caught up with us and opened the office door, ushering me inside. As I pulled out the chair to sit, the professor addressed Tilly who was waiting outside the door. I overheard Professor Zirak ask her, "Miss Bradford, may I ask why you are waiting?"

"I just thought that maybe…" said Tilly sheepishly as Professor Zirak cut her off in mid sentence.

"You would be invited into my office while I talk with Miss Cantrell?" Professor Zirak finished her thoughts. She shook her head yes and the professor continued, "I need to speak with Miss Cantrell privately about her unfinished assignment. You may wait in the common area or in your room."

He moved through the door and gave it a slight push expecting it to close. Tilly looked back at me from the half closed door and mouthed, "Sorry."

Professor Zirak was anchored in his chair apparently waiting for me to start this uncomfortable conversation with an apology. Once accepting my silence and having eyed me for what seemed an eternity, he questioned, "Can you tell me why you did not complete this assignment?"

I opened my mouth and shut it again. Words wouldn't come. Could I really tell him that I remembered nothing and that there must be a mistake? I didn't finish my test or earn my place in Keeper House. I had written absolutely nothing on my test! I needed to order my words correctly.

Catching a glimpse of the indecisiveness on my face, the professor walked around his desk to close his door. Now I was in for it! He returned to his chair and began, "Whatever it is, you can trust me. I will help you."

"Professor, what if someone told you they remembered nothing?" I asked.

His quick smirk screamed he already knew this. He stated in a sense of understanding, "A memory fog? What did you find in your chapter?"

Tilly assured me it was impossible for the chapter to be empty. She was very knowledgeable, but I had seen the blank pages with my own eyes. Would the professor believe me?

"Your silence tells me what I already suspected. The chapter contained absolutely nothing. Right?" Professor asked.

I was shocked! My thoughts came out as I asked, "How did you know that? Did you look at my chapter?" I was shocked and conflicted. Professor Kegley had assured us that only the owner of the chapters could read them. Although, Destiny claimed to have read Tilly's chapter. Did Professor Zirak also have a way to look at the chapters?

"Well, you have your answer for your assignment. Your memory fog," He said to my confusion. "I will accept no excuse for not finishing any assignment. If you know you can't complete an assignment, it would be wise to let me help you next time. Before I will give my approval for you leaving training, you must complete this assignment. I will however, modify your audience in that it will only need to be for my ears only."

"Will you help me remember?" I questioned him.

"I have already given you your answer. I am always here for my students," he pointedly stated as he began to scratch notes onto a piece of paper in front of him.

"I must have been a member of the Central Intelligence Agency as a spy who was brainwashed, remembering nothing about myself," I sarcastically stated to see if he was really listening to me.

His golden pen dropped to the desk. He leaned back in his chair and stared at me. "You're not taking me seriously! Since you don't seem thankful for my help, you and your fellow trainees will enjoy the assigned essay on the life theme of humanitarian." He turned his chair and pulled a gray book from his book shelf saying, "In addition, you will complete all end of chapter questions in the book, Theories About Choosing Your Earth Life," said Professor Zirak.

He slid the book across his desk to me. I just felt confused and did not understand the point of this whole conversation. I'm sure it must have meaning, but I just didn't get it. Maybe the answer was in the book he was forcing on me. The work was piling up.

"I would prefer you complete this assignment rather than the writing about the life theme of Mrs. VanCues," Professor stated. "The assignment for this week is a warm up for an assignment we will have in a few weeks. For you, the questions are a better learning experience for the time being."

"Thank you for not requiring both," I stated as I stood and side stepped towards the door.

"Remember," Professor said as his stern looks returned to a warm smile. "Let me know next time you need help."

I swiftly departed the office closing the door behind me. There I discovered Destiny leaning against the wall opposite the door. Destiny's face unveiled her dim view of my predicament as she asked, "How bad was it?" Then she was instantly across the hall patting my arm.

She was wrong if she believed I was in the mood to play fifty questions with her. I pointedly asked, "What do you want Destiny?"

"I was just concerned," Destiny stated looking thin skinned.

Great! Just what I needed to make my day better. A nosy and annoying clinger neighbor with pretentious feelings! "Look, I'm sorry. I simply have no desire to talk about it."

"I understand," Destiny stated as she pointed towards the stairs. "Going up?"

"Yep," I said. We climbed the stairs uncomfortably together without conversation. I couldn't pinpoint her motivation for continuing to attempt to befriend me, especially since I had repeatedly tried to ditch her. Was her true motivation to offer support or irritate me? Reaching the girl's landing, relief was waiting for me at the end of the hall. Destiny stopped at her own door. I gave her a friendly grin as I breezed past her. I quickly turned my doorknob, entered, and left Destiny behind in the hall. I breathed a sigh of relief as I fell back and leaned flat against the room-side of our door.

Tilly glanced over at me from her seated position at her desk, which she had turned into a make-up table. She was applying make-up and her curling iron was warming. It was obvious she had a date! Tilly asked, "What's the damage?"

"He wants me to answer several questions," I said as I help the book up for her to see. "Theories For Choosing Your Earth Life."

"That sucks!" Tilly retorted. "That's all you need. Another assignment." She returned to her primping. She wet her finger with her tongue and then touched it to the curling iron to see if it was hot. She flinched as it sizzled.

"Actually, I'm to do the questions instead of learning the life theme of Mrs. VanCues," I responded. "He spouted something about my needing this lesson more than worrying about Mrs. VanCues life theme."

"Why would he say that?" Tilly questioned laying down the curling iron.

"Maybe because he knows!" I squealed. "He must know that..." I stopped mid sentence. I hadn't told Tilly my test was blank! I threw myself on my bed in silence.

"So you think he's a psychic, huh? Elizabeth, he only knows what you tell him," Tilly reasoned as she sat on the edge of my bed abandoning her primping.

"He believes my chapter is blank!" I said as I turned to look at Tilly. "He went on and on about my already having my answer and memory fog. I remember nothing! How can I have my answer?"

"I think he was trying to rattle you," Tilly said as she jumped up and began to pace. "Pull yourself together! You need to learn to how to put on your poker face, pop gum, flirt, be coy, do something!"

"Well, he already knows what he knows and I'm oblivious to what it is he knows," I said to Tilly's disapproving look. "By the way, I saw through your poker face today."

"Huh," Tilly sighed caught off guard and stopping dead in her tracks.

"Your life theme! I now understand why you never go on a second date," I matter of fact stated.

"What?" Tilly questioned as if she hadn't heard me right.

I began to explain, "On the Earth Plane…" I was cut off mid sentence.

"Elizabeth, on the Earth Plane I had lots of dates," Tilly said huffy and then sighed. "And lots of trust issues."

"And that is why you usually only have first dates?" I stated emphatically.

"First dates are simple," Tilly replied. "No attachment, just go have fun. It was a habit I got into too avoid complications." Tilly fluttered around the room as she finished readying herself for her date. I got the impression she didn't want to discuss her dating habits. She was a little uptight and huffy. This was why she had a use them and leave them attitude.

Tilly sat on her bed, fully preened for the date of the day. She began to share, "Don't feel sorry for me! Time on the Earth Plane is meant to be work. I faced a great opponent and won." She got up and walked to my bed and plopped down beside me. "I eventually found a male I could completely trust.

Our connection was intense and always felt beyond the world we lived in." I thought I caught a slight grin. "We had multiple blissful dates. I do go on multiple dates if it's someone I'm really into. However, most conquests I really don't want to see after the first date. They bore me! That's about it."

"I see your point!" I said to catch her attention. "Sorry I made assumptions about your dating. And thanks for sharing."

"Yeah, yeah!" Tilly said seeming satisfied. She avoided anymore conversation about her dating habits. "Well, I must be off. My date has been waiting downstairs for awhile."

"He's been waiting?" I questioned glancing at the clock.

"Of course," Tilly replied as she swung her purse over her shoulder. "I had to hang around to hear about the private, top secret meeting of yours with the professor."

We shared a smile as she left the room. A brief moment of belonging swept over me like Déjà vu! Of course, she wanted to hear the scoop. She cared! I belonged with Tilly and her group of adventurers. Trevor and Eddie had begun to accept me as well. After only a week I had come to appreciate their friendship and discover my place in their tight knit circle. Foggy minded me finally had a wee bit of history. A weeks worth of memories with new friends. A few memories are better than none!

CHAPTER EIGHTEEN

Elizabeth

Harmony practice this coming evening, by nature, was arranged to be stressful since our upcoming performance required two solos. I grabbed a chair in the audience of the Grand Hall early and was awaiting try-outs to begin. Terror gripped me. I was completely dreading my own solo try-out. Professor Kegley, in her mission to find the best solo performer, decided each of us would be given an opportunity and must perform solos before the watching group. Professor Kegley would hand pick the optimum singer for competitions. My headache was due to my own comprehension of how poorly I sang. Soon, everyone else would be included in my secret.

I was already exhausted. Today had been a long day. Professor Presnell, from behind her signature red-rimmed glasses, had discussed the modes of transportation outside of the dome in the world of the Humlings. Apparently Keepers do adventure out if on official Keeper or personal business. Both require a destination card for travel. For personal use, a lengthy application and approval process is required to receive the prized destination card. Personal applications weren't necessarily all granted. Tilly had smirked and sounded like air was escaping from her during most of this lecture. I believe she thought anything Professor Presnell lectured didn't apply to her. She was a true rebel at heart, ignoring the professors views!

Professor Presnell spoke about the rules concerning being seen, but not seen. Like a lizard we were to be chameleons. Divulging to anyone we were Keepers was forbidden. Our secret was to be guarded since Humlings couldn't be trusted. The professor never conveyed the reasoning behind not trusting the Humlings. However, I was familiar with why from Anthony and Emma. Humlings were suspected to have betrayed the Keepers on the day of the event when the Keepers disappeared. Deep down, in the pit of my stomach, I knew this was nonsense. I didn't know where this adamant belief came from.

I was steadfast in this gut feeling. Humlings would never betray the Keepers.

Professor Kegley was on stage announcing, "Please, take your seats! We will begin momentarily." I returned to reality and abandoned my thoughts.

Tilly demanded to go first and it seemed Professor Kegley didn't have the courage to argue with her. I nervously watched Tilly strut on stage with an over-confident grin. Everyone in the room was aware Tilly only desired the solos to ensure Tiffany would not get the privilege of singing them during competitions. Grossing everyone out, Tilly took her pink wad of gum from her mouth and stuck it behind her ear. Everyone gasped aloud. Really? Was she saving it for later? I shook my head and held my breath expecting some unexpected lightening bolt from Tiffany to strike Tilly rendering her unable to sing a note.

The music started and Tilly tapped her thigh with her hand keeping the beat. When she opened her mouth to sing, the room fell quiet as she took control of the stage. She was a natural showman and belted out both songs with diva drama. Listeners cheered as she easily and naturally hit all the low and high notes. She may not have wanted to join Harmony, but she was a natural with an amazing voice range! Professor Kegley was on her feet with the auditorium crowd and cheered as Tilly held the cast note high for at least two minutes. Then the cheers faded. The bar had been set and it would be hard to out perform her!

As Tilly paraded off the stage with others smiling and congratulating her as a celebrity, Professor Kegley called, "Miss Cantrell."

Wretched nervousness overtook me as I stood and walked towards the stage. This was comparable to when I turned in my initial blank exam. I was blank and my legs felt like they had chains around them. Climbing the simple five steps to the stage was a chore. Reaching center stage, I resigned myself for my impending, embarrassing doom!

Professor Kegley met me face to face as I slumped in front of the mike. She removed the microphone, leaned over placing her hand on top the mike, and handed it to me. She whispered, "Good luck!"

"Um, thanks," I countered as I positioned myself center stage. Peering out into the crowd, my anxiety deepened when I caught a glimpse of a set of eyes watching me that I hadn't expected. Dustin was sitting next to Tiffany and she was hanging all over him. Now my coming humiliation would be complete!

The music started. However, my mind was filled with thoughts of Dustin observing my annihilating myself. I couldn't concentrate! I missed the entrance! Professor Kegley had the musicians start again. Trying to keep the beat by tapping my leg as Tilly had, I opened my mouth. The sound that broke through the stifling silence reminded me of nothing less than an animal being tortured mixed with nails sliding down a chalkboard. Raspy, short, crying squeals with no musical talent at all. I gripped the microphone tightly and much too close to my mouth. Its screeching oddly sounded like my singing. I glanced at Dustin and could see him grimace. Instantly under his look of pity, I flushed a deep red with the top of my ears burning. Top it all off, Tiffany was openly loudly laughing. I turned my eyes away from Dustin to find Tilly in the crowd. Her mouth was open wide in disbelief. Great! She was shocked too. I told her I couldn't sing!

Professor Kegley startled me from behind by tapping on my shoulder saying, "No need to finish dear." She held out her open palm for the microphone.

"I didn't sing the chorus," I quietly, half protested with the mike still in my hands. This statement left the crowd teetering on the edge of erupting into what was sure to be embarrassing laughter.

"No, no. It's okay. We've heard enough," Professor Kegley said with a warm smile that screamed I'm sorry I made you do this.

Tilly had set the record for best singer and I had set the record for poorest. I surrendered the mike and ran across the stage like a fired bullet. I was met at the bottom of the steps by Tilly. Before she could say a single word, I bravely commented, "Guess I won't be doing the solos."

"That's an understatement," Tilly replied. "Are you okay?"

"Tilly, I'm fine," I said quickly to her patronizing words. She could see right through my brave face. The fact of the matter was, I was humiliated. I had never felt more like crying! I pretended to get something out of my eye to hold back the tears.

Grabbing my arm, Tilly quickly pulled me behind the curtains and through the rehearsal room door. "My stuff is back here. Let me gather it all up," Tilly sighed as she began to gather her belongings and place them into her bubble pink tote bag. "I'll walk back to Keeper House with you."

Still fighting tears I asked her, "Don't you want to be here when they announce you will be doing the solos?"

She hesitated for a moment and I could see her internal struggle. She went back to throwing her belongs into her bag as she said, "Yes, I would like to see the look on Tiffany's face. But, I know your performance was just a tad bit embarrassing and your need for me is more important." She threw her bag over her shoulder and turned to face me. "Elizabeth, you told me you couldn't sing. You didn't tell me, you suck!" She paused a minute, grimaced at her own words, and cupped her hand across her mouth briefly. "Sorry. I haven't forgotten you stuck by me the other day..." She trailed away in thought.

"When it was embarrassing being caught by Andy and Scott," I surmised.

Tilly shook her head yes and offered me a piece of gum saying, "You were there for me!"

I grabbed it and began to unwrap it while I continued, "I deserved the I suck comment. We're even. The other day, I lectured you and didn't stop to consider you might be embarrassed. Sorry."

Tilly shrugged and turned to zip up her bulging pink bag saying, "Friends stick together through thick and thin! We stick like gum!"

"As your friend," I began as I popped the gum in my mouth. "You need to be there and enjoy staring down Tiffany when your name is announced! You deserve to see her dethroned! Bask in the glory! You are starting a coupe to take over after all!"

Tilly started to counter, "But..."

"Stay!" I repeated while I rolled my eyes chewing the sweet gum. "I'm a big girl. So big I intend to sneak out the back way."

"Seriously, you're going to sneak out?" Tilly giggled and then paused a moment. "Don't show weakness! Make a mad dash or sharks will circle!"

"Sharks or no sharks, I will manage to slide away quietly and quickly," I said to her smirk as I tried to blow a big bubble to cover my teary eyes. Turning gum into perfect popping bubbles wasn't as easy as Tilly made it look!

Tilly temporarily set her bag down and retrieved another stick and handed it to me saying, "The secret is two sticks!" Then she zipped her bubble gum pink bag closed once more and slung it over her shoulder. Tilly mused, "Isn't gum great? So calming." I smiled at her as she genuinely smiled back saying, "Okay. You're sure you don't mind walking by yourself?" She paused and waited for an answer. I nodded. "See you back at our room," Tilly said with a wave as she disappeared through the rehearsal room door.

We just had a true moment of bonding and understanding. We could identify with each other! I was warming up to the strong willed, flamboyant stranger I sat next to on the first day. She was growing on me!

I made my way through the rehearsal door and towards the back stage curtain to grab my backpack. I hadn't intended to eavesdrop, but I could hear Tiffany and Janelle arguing while standing on the other side of the black stage curtain.

"Why must we include Ruthanne?" Whined Janelle. "She is geeky, unfashionable, and homespun standing next to us. She's our red-headed step child! I'm embarrassed. She seriously makes us look bad. We are not low-class dorks, Tiffany!"

"I know," Tiffany agreed. "Ruthanne should be placed into records or ghosts." I stood still listening. There was a strange quiet and then Tiffany continued, "I have found a solution for what to do with her. We'll keep her busy! We need someone smart to do our class work and save us the trouble. If Ruthanne's at Administration House doing our work, we won't need to worry about being seen with her. Problem solved!"

"I guess it could work," Janelle stated. "We are young and beautiful! We should be out having a good time. One thing is certain, we really don't want to waste our social evenings doing school work. "

"Exactly," Tiffany agreed. "The dork was forced upon us when she was placed in our house. Let the less desirable to do our school work for us. We will give her house slave status!"

They both cackled. Then Janelle said, "One problem. We need to free up a little of her time."

"I've already taken care of it," replied Tiffany with a smug voice.

Tiffany's name was called from the stage. Tiffany and Janelle both squealed like giddy school girls as Janelle spewed, "Break a leg! Oh, and rub gothic, hell-cat Tilly's nose in your performance."

"Don't worry," Tiffany spouted. "Mommy assures me Tilly won't be al-lowed to do the solos."

Upon hearing the five steps creak when Tiffany climbed them, I tip-toed to where the curtain met the wall. My backpack was leaning against the wall just inside the curtain. I stuck my hand through the curtain as if I was a ghost, making no noise. I held my breath as my heart beat frantically! I found the backpack strap and pulled it slowly behind the curtain. Now that I was re-united with my backpack, I briskly backed away from the black curtain until my back hit the rehearsal room door. I could finally breathe again! No one saw me and I was out of here! Adrenaline filled, I quickly made my way outside.

As I walked out of the Administration Complex into the cool night air, I felt my body release the stress it had been holding. The conversation played over and over in my head. I couldn't help but feel a pang of sorrow for Ruth-anne. In my house, I only had a nosy neighbor to deal with. Ruthanne had Tif-fany and Janelle. They would be impossible to live and cope with because of their self-centeredness. They were hatching a plan and clearly up to destroying and using Ruthanne. Besides making her homework slave girl, they were up to plotting some other atrocity.

A gentle breeze blew through the darkened trees making the leaves rustle. The breeze felt cool on my skin as it blew, combating the heat of my skin and drying my tears. I had a decision to make about what action to take concerning what I overheard. Tilly couldn't stand for anyone to be picked on, especially by Tiffany and Janelle. However, I couldn't tell her about their plot against Ruthanne. The uncertainty of what she might do frightened me! For my own selfish reasons, I didn't want Tilly kicked out of training. I would confide in Trevor. He was the obvious choice since he was dating Ruthanne.

I might have fully enjoyed my cool evening trek back to Keeper House if

I hadn't been so preoccupied with my thoughts. My path wound down into Spring Park where it would eventually connect to the road to take me back to Keeper House. It was a beautiful evening with a million stars in the night sky. After a time of peacefully walking, I came upon a grand estate surrounded by a massive, six foot iron fence. It appeared I was viewing the estate from the rear. The lit-up back yard revealed a series of paths and breathtaking gardens. As I sauntered on past the end of the iron fence and estate, a small A-frame house appeared. It was run down with an overgrown yard. Little distance existed between the properties. I could only imagine that whoever lived in the grand estate and those living in the unkept house were as different as night and day.

All was quiet except for the sound of the breeze in the trees. I stopped to lazily enjoy it as it blew my hair. Suddenly, I was caught off guard by the sound of twigs breaking behind me. I spun around, but saw no one trailing me. Perhaps I was a little paranoid! As I reached the familiar Spring Park, I again heard the foot steps behind me. I spun around to find no one there. I scanned my surroundings. The playground, fields, and golf course all appeared completely empty. I was eerily alarmed and couldn't shake the feeling of being followed. As I started briskly walking, I heard footsteps behind me closing in.

"Why is she walking so fast," I heard the familiar voice in my mind.

Dustin! I turned around and waited a brief moment with my arms wrapped around myself protecting myself from a cold shiver. He came into view jogging towards me. His face seemed to sense my alarm as he asked, "Slow down, are you okay?"

"I'm fine," I replied to his concerned question. "Have you been behind me?"

"No," Dustin replied while wiping sweat from his forehead. He pointed his finger to a far away knoll as he said, "I was resting on that far bench looking at the stars."

I turned and peered at the dark silhouette of the bench Dustin had pointed too. Was he there when I scanned for who was following me? Was it him who was stalking me? "Hold on! You were at Grand Hall listening to the try outs…," I suddenly flushed at the thought of his viewing me bomb my try-out. Humiliation once more swept through me.

"I saw the first couple of try-outs. Then, I left," Dustin said casually. "I had another obligation this evening but I couldn't pass up star gazing. The planets and stars are in a special alignment tonight. Tonight is special!"

"Even the stars don't compare to you though," I heard his mind think.

Was he comparing me and my star solo failure to the two true Harmony stars Tilly and Tiffany?

"I noticed you descending the path," Dustin explained. "I watched you start to walk fast, spin around, and then walk faster. So, I jogged over thinking something had scared you."

He must think that I am a frightened wimp! I hesitantly but firmly replied, "No, I'm fine."

He bent down to look me directly in the eye. Then he placed his rock hard hand on my shoulder. Clearly he was attempting to assess whether or not I truly was fine. I hadn't realized till now how tall he was or how there was a lack of any kind of softness in his touch. "If you are okay," Dustin hesitated as I caught a whiff of his cologne. It overtook all my senses. "I'll go. I wouldn't want to interfere with your plans or draw attention to you." Dustin stepped around me. I turned to see him jogging away from me.

Quickly I hurried to his side and hem-hawed, "Actually, I know it is unfair for me to ask!" His intoxicating smell had already drawn me in and I didn't desire for us to be apart. "Dustin, would you have time to walk me home?"

"There is something she's not telling me. Something did scare her," I heard his mind say.

His eyes were once again examining me and our surroundings. He replied, "Sure." He offered me his arm and took my backpack.

Silence prevailed between us but I didn't let go of the safety of his arm. I must have been mindlessly smacking my gum as we embarked on the stroll out of Spring Park. Dustin questioned, "The gum?"

"Tilly gave it to me," I replied to his frown clearly stating his annoyance.

"Tilly always has a piece in her mouth which she obnoxiously chews like a cow," I heard

his mind say.

Suddenly, I needed to defend my misunderstood best friend. I began to correct him, "You know Tilly chews gum to relieve stress."

"So this has become a habit of yours too?" Dustin questioned.

"Not really," I replied.

"That's a relief," I heard his mind say.

"Wait," Dustin said stopping dead in his tracks. I stopped and Dustin gently pushed a fly away hair behind my ear while questioning, "Did she give you the gum because you were stressed over the try-outs?"

"Stressed out really isn't the right word," I corrected blushing and turning away from his eye contact. I had no desire to discuss my humiliation with someone I felt so drawn too. I murmured, "Even you grimaced!"

"You may not have been the best singer on the stage, but you were the prettiest girl around for miles," I heard his mind state.

I was taken back by his thoughts and was rendered speechless as Dustin countered, "I'm sorry if my reaction hurt your feelings."

The breeze caught his cologne and the full force of his intoxicating scent spread over my body as the night breeze steadily swirled it about me. I felt more drawn to him than I normally did. I closed my eyes and inhaled a deep breath, allowing his smell to delight my senses. I had fantasies of being wrapped in his arms. There was nothing else my body and mind desired. Alone with him, my feelings were magnified. I was intoxicated! As I glanced up at him, he was intently gazing back at me. I was oddly drawn to him. Ceasing to walk, I released my grip on his arm as I turned to gaze into his eyes. I place my hand on his forearm. He didn't move an inch as I coyly flirted with him. His darkened brown eyes sparkled and his deep brown hair glistened in the glow of the moon. He didn't return my advances.

"Who!" Instantly, the intrusive word snapped me back to reality. Again I heard from somewhere beside us, "Who!"

Glancing into the dark, dense trees, Dustin pointed to an owl with bright yellow eyes, perched on a limb. It was intently peering as we both considered its unique beauty. When it flew away, I suddenly remembered the sad truth about Dustin. He was dating Tiffany! Why he was here and what did he want? I had no clue. More importantly, why did he not hesitate or push me away when I stepped close? I had one question, "Why are you here stargazing instead of listening to your girlfriend's audition?"

Sensing my change in demeanor Dustin instantly took a step backwards leaving more space between us as he told me again with a hint of annoyance in his voice, "I already told you, I couldn't stay at Harmony all night. I had another obligation."

"And who cares about hearing her audition," I heard Dustin think.

How insensitive those words were concerning someone he was dating. I didn't care for Tiffany, but I was insulted for her. He was cold hearted! He interrupted my thoughts as he asked, "Do you wish to walk the rest of the way alone?"

My thoughts returned to my gut feeling of being followed. If it was Dustin following me, well… Dustin was harmless. However, if it had been the young man with those pitch black eyes and untamed hair, I was in trouble. My gut screamed he wasn't harmless. Either way, I no longer wanted to ask Dustin for favors. "You can accompany me if you're going in that direction," I said hoping he would continue to walk with me. "But, I don't wish to talk anymore. I'm tired!"

Dustin nodded. He seemed relieved with my simple request for silence. I guess he didn't care to talk either. He kept a good distance between us and didn't offer me his arm again. This did not change the affect of the breeze blowing past him and carrying his scent, leaving me feeling drawn to him. He was simply mysterious and forbidden since he was dating Tiffany. Yes, forbidden and dangerous! My nose wanted to nuzzle into his neck and stay their basking in his heavenly smell. We walked in silence to the door of the Hall of Knowledge where I curtly said, "Thank you for walking with me."

"Good night," Dustin bid me as I moved through the entrance of the Hall of Knowledge. I didn't turn back. One flirtatious moment with him and I was helpless putty in his hands. I mustn't forget his cold comment concerning

Tiffany or the fact that Dustin was rude and wouldn't shake my hand when we first met. My mind knew Dustin was unhealthy for me! However, my heart and body felt more drawn to him than I normally did. Maybe it was I who was giving mixed signals. My hand flung to my forehead. What had I done! I could hopefully keep this flirtatious moment between Dustin and myself. Tiffany would make mince meat out of me if she knew.

As I crossed the foyer deep in thought, I was caught off-guard when I noticed Marvin descending the stairs. I stopped dead in my tracks watching him. He was wearing a brightly colored red and yellow sports jersey, jeans, and sandals. Probably, the jersey represented his favorite team. It made him appear delicious as it clung to his build. He seemed to be preoccupied with his own thoughts as I had been with mine. As he stepped off the last step, he caught a glimpse of me. A huge grin spread across his face and he rushed to close the gap between us saying, "Hey, I was getting ready to meet up with you at Grand Hall."

My evening so far was filled with bewildering circumstances. First, tryouts. Second, Dustin. Now, Marvin tracking me down. What next? My thoughts fell out my mouth as I inquired, "How did you know I'd be there?"

"Professor Zirak asked me to be a body in a seat tonight," Marvin replied. "You know, give the singers a sense of having an audience. I thought maybe I'd catch your audition. I'm running a little late."

I closed my eyes, exhaled slowly, and slightly shook my head. Thank heavens he had not seen my try-out humiliation. I took a deep breath and opened my eyes. Putting one hand on my shoulder, he cautiously questioned as he peered into my eyes, "So? How'd it go?"

"Tryouts were mandatory and a waste of time. Everyone knows Tilly is a shew in to sing the solos," I sighed. "She has an incredible voice." I wanted to add all hell was about to break loose. A major confrontation, a diva war was looming like a dark threatening crowd. Tilly and Tiffany both planned to do the solos, come hell or high water. Harmony was about to implode on itself!

As I glanced back up at Marvin's face, he winked at me. It was a gesture on his part affirming what I had just told him. He changed the subject saying, "Hmm... Well, I was hoping after try-outs you would accompany me to get ice cream. I don't dare go for ice cream without you!" He was grinning ear to ear.

With a slight chuckle he added, "With you there, I won't have to ask a certain blond counter girl for a date."

"Worried about your love life, huh," I lightheartedly teased as I flippantly removed the scrunchi from my ponytail and shook my long locks free.

"More than you know," Marvin admitted as his eyes turned towards the ground and away from mine. He was momentarily lost in thought. Was he self-conscious or possibly referring to another girl? His eyes flashed back to me and he questioned, "So? Ice cream or not?"

"Keeper House trainees are to come home directly after Harmony," I divulged. Marvin was so upbeat and lifted my spirits when I was in his presence. Clearly, I was wavering between abiding by the mundane rules or throw caution to the wind. I mimicked Professor Zirak, "Be in before nightfall. Rule number three."

"Really," Marvin stated with his brows pushed together. "He must have new rules this session."

"Tilly and I are sort of on house arrest!" I replied to Marvin's comment. "We would be locked in our room long before nightfall if it weren't for our being a part of Harmony practice which often runs past the sun going down."

"House arrest, huh," chuckled Marvin. "I don't think Professor Zirak's purpose is to lock you up."

"Maybe not!" I defiantly said as I defended my exaggerated view. "With Tilly and me, the professor is always double checking on us." Of course I was leaving out our mischief and sneaking activities. The professor had his reasons. We borrowed a chapter, sneaked out, and most importantly we left the dome.

Marvin gently placed his hand under my chin, turning my face up to his. "It's probably more Tilly than you," he said breaking my train of thought.

Why did everyone bash Tilly? She didn't deserve his comment.

Before I could stand up for my best friend, Marvin countered, "I don't know Tilly well, but she has quite a reputation for being rebellious."

Tilly was rebellious! However, tonight it was me who desired to throw restrictions out the window and accompany Marvin to get ice cream. I wanted to smother all my problems in ice cream and be with this upbeat boy who seemed to enjoy me as much as I enjoyed him. The light bulb went off in my head as my thoughts spilled out my mouth, "Everyone is still at tryouts!" I paused, looked at the time on my watch, and felt mischievous as I flirtatiously said, "Sure, I'll go! You need me to keep you safe from that certain Blondie."

"Perhaps it isn't such a great idea!" Marvin now said hesitantly. "I wasn't aware you were to be in Keeper House by nightfall."

"Everyone is still at try-outs," I countered in a begging voice. "It will be midnight or so before everyone has their chance to try out. Then Professor Kegley must decide and announce who will sing the solos. Professor Zirak will never know."

Marvin slid his hands into his jean pockets and began rattling its contents. He began, "Elizabeth…"

Recalling some of Tilly's man handling techniques, I placed my index finger on his lips, looked him eye to eye, and reminded him, "Enjoy the small things in life. We have a little window of borrowed time tonight."

Totally taken by surprise he focused on me with widened eyes. "Maybe I was wrong about who the rebellious one is!" Marvin challenged.

I shrugged at his name calling comment. He didn't know the half of it! I asked as I took him by the arm, "Shall we?"

We headed in the direction of the door leading outside. Marvin continued to jingle whatever was in his jeans pocket. My rule breaking apparently made him nervous. He stepped in front of me to open the exit door saying, "I was hoping to catch your solo. I'm sure you sing like an angel."

"I wouldn't exactly say that," I huffed in answers to his wrong assumption. We exited the building into the night. I wasn't about to tell him about my humiliation. I needed to change the subject! Catching him off guard, I said, "I've got a question for you! If you were a ghost what would you haunt?"

His face showed he understood I had purposely chosen a new subject. I didn't wish to fill in the missing pieces about my audition experience. "Are you trying to distract me?" Marvin asked thinking he was being sly. "I don't mind hearing more about the try-outs."

"Drop it! I don't live and breathe Harmony!" I said in a huffy voice. Then I stopped and placed my hands on my hips.

Marvin held out his hand in a shall we keep moving gesture. We rambled in silence across the grounds of The Hall of Knowledge. Silence dampened the air. Nothing would make me spill the beans about my miserable experience. We continued walking not speaking. I was surprised when he said, "If I were a ghost, I would haunt…" Marvin swung his hands at his sides snapping his fingers as he thought. "I would haunt a film studio."

Thank God the silence was broken. I was beginning to think I had blown our evening. "Why?" I questioned totally intrigued.

"It would be a marvelous Earth Plane experience to see first hand the Hollywood stars and how they make all the movies?" Marvin matter-of-fact stated.

I grinned and hoped he could see the stars in my eyes. For Marvin, who loved television, it was fitting. "May I ask you something?" I questioned.

"Anything," Marvin assured me with a serious look upon his face. "What's on your mind?"

"I didn't take the lift back to the Hall of Knowledge this evening," I stated. "I needed a little fresh air, so I walked down the trail and made an interesting discovery."

"Alone? At night?" Marvin interrupted in an alarmed tone. "You should take the lift!"

"Marvin, I'm not scared of the dark," I bluntly assured him trailing off in thought. Then I cringed. Thoughts of Dustin crossed my mind. It would crawl under Marvin's skin if he realized Dustin had escorted me back to The Hall of Knowledge because of my fearful encounter on the path.

Marvin's voice brought me back to the moment as he stated, "The trail you went down is the Dogwood Trail. The majority of the trees along that path bloom with small intoxicating white flowers once a year."

"Yes, that's where I made my discovery!" I said as I smiled at Marvin. "I walked past a grand estate with an enormous back gate. Do you know who lives there?"

"That estate is called Dogwood House," Marvin explained as he took my hand and slipped his fingers between mine. "It's the home of Albert Solliday."

"Really," I answered absent minded while thinking our hands melted together like warm butter. Hmm… Imagine a celebrity like Albert Solliday living so close to Keeper house! "Well, I'm sure he doesn't like his neighbor."

"What makes you say that?" Marvin inquired looking perturbed.

"Dogwood House is well maintained," I explained. "The small A-frame house down the trail, just beyond his property… It's an eye sore that's falling apart. The yard is over grown and speaks of the demeanor of its owner."

"Really?" Marvin replied with a distant expression upon his face. He dropped my hand and his hand found its way back into his pocket. After a bit of silence he spoke. "It does look like it's falling down."

From behind us we heard a voice, "What looks like its falling down?"

"Hey man," Marvin turned to the rear and greeted Jessie who held his fist out. They did a macho guy handshake. "What are you doing here?"

"Your Mom said you were going to take a walk," Jessie said flashing a sly smile. "Good thing I know you like a book and how often you have a sweet tooth." Marvin laughed as Jessie continued, "When I didn't find you at the local shop, I just kind of figured I would find you at the old hot spot. In the morning I have kiddie duty."

Marvin smiled and interjected, "And I have the kiddie key."

"Kiddie duty and kiddie key?" I questioned not understanding their conversation.

"Hasn't he told you that we are coaching one of the secondary basketball teams?" Jessie questioned as his eyes shot to Marvin.

"I guess that hasn't come up," I stated as I too looked at Marvin.

"It's a small commitment," Marvin stated wanting it to appear like it was no big deal. "The children's coach was chosen to be a Humling's Keeper. We are filling in until they secure a permanent coach." Marvin pulled a key ring out of his pocket. So, the keys were what he had been jingling. He unclasped a second ring from the key ring and handed it to Jessie.

"Thanks!" Jessie said dangling the keys from his fingers.

The side walk leading to the ice cream shop from the road could be seen from where we were standing. I asked, "Jessie, why don't you hang out with us and grab a bowl of ice cream?"

Jessie's eyes instantly darted to Marvin's to see if Marvin objected to his company. Marvin briefly glared at Jessie with a hand off look leading Jessie to smile at me saying, "No that's okay. I don't want to be the third wheel."

What was Marvin's problem? There was nothing wrong with Jessie tagging along. When Marvin noticed my look of disapproval, he reluctantly said, "Come along Jessie! The more the merrier!"

As our group of three took a few awkward steps down the narrow road, we reached the sidewalk leading towards the ice cream shops stone building. Marvin's familiar touch was upon the small of my back as we turned down the sidewalk.

Once reaching our destination, Jessie plopped down on the porch rail with his hairy legs hanging over. I sat down next to Jessie as Marvin inquired with annoyance in his voice, "Shall I get the ice cream and come back out?"

"Would you mind," I said smiling up at him. I kicked off my sandals letting my freshly painted toenails glisten as I wiggled my tired toes. Tilly had painted them trying to improve my blah look.

"Great looking piggies!" Said Jessie kicking off his own sandals and imitating my toe wiggling.

Marvin removed his own shoes and placed them squarely between us marking his territory. It was apparent he didn't want to leave me sitting with Jessie. Blondie was no match for me. However, it was good for him to sweat it and be a bit green. "You can handle Blondie," I countered kicking one bare slim foot back and forth. "And I'll take…"

Marvin finished my sentence for me with a green smile, "A scoop of Double Dutch Chocolate."

I returned his smile, "Thank you."

"I'll take vanilla with peanut butter mixed in," Jessie added to the order but got no response from Marvin.

Once Marvin was inside and placing our order, Jessie casually inquired, "So you and Marvin?"

"Oh, no!" I said setting him straight. "Blondie inside is the one who has her claws out for him."

"Who?" Jessie questioned with a puzzled look.

I pointed towards the window and its view of inside activities. "The gal who scoops the ice cream, Blondie! We came here the other night and she had the nerve to make all kinds of googly eyes at him even though he was with me," I said remembering how green she made me feel as she flirted with him. Suddenly, I craned my neck around to see what was going on inside. Could she see me sitting here? More importantly, would she have the nerve to flirt with him in my presence?

Jessie chuckled at my sudden interest about the happenings inside the ice cream shop. As I turned to face Jessie, I felt flush. Jessie patiently assured me, "Marvin has no interest in the blond ice cream lady. The truth is, he already saw and met a special girl awhile back. He's been crazy about her ever since. He's a one woman man."

"You're probably right!" I agreed embarrassed. I was someone Marvin was using to forget this mystery past girl. Blondie and I both were fools! I was then committed to change the subject. "Tell me about your guy code."

"Guy code?" Jessie repeated looking lost.

231

"Something to do with Marvin's Mom," I said further.

"Oh," Jessie hesitated as if I had opened a can of worms. "It's no great secret! Marvin's Mom doesn't like for us to eat sweets. She thinks it's unhealthy." Jessie jumped up and retrieved a piece of trash from the porch and placed it into the trash can. Had he avoided the code subject using a lame story about sweets? What was he avoiding and not wanting to tell me? I intently watched him as he returned and took his place next to me. My girly pleading eyes were too much for him. He leaned over as if to tell me an earth shattering secret, "Marvin's Mom has a few quirks."

Before I could inquire about the oddities of Marvin's mom, the door opened and Marvin hurried to us balancing three bowls of ice cream. Marvin was grinning at me and plopped down between us. He obviously didn't want to leave me alone with Jessie too long. I couldn't help but pump Marvin for information as I teased, "How'd it go with Blondie? Any upcoming dates?"

"I guess you're right about her liking me," Marvin stated looking to see if he was getting any response from me.

"Why do you say that?" I questioned instantly feeling my feathers had been ruffled.

Jessie chuckled and turned his ball cap backwards so the bill was behind him. I ignored Jessie's chuckle. Marvin shot Jessie a stern look as he hem-hawed before saying, "Well, she only had one topic on her mind." Marvin offered me a taste of his peppermint delight and then went on, "You!"

"What did she say?" I pointedly asked.

"Nothing really," Marvin said. Jessie snickered and Marvin gave him a dirty look.

"Explain nothing really to me," I demanded offering Jessie a taste of my Double Dutch to annoy Marvin. I was trying Tilly's pointer on making men want you.

"She wanted to know if we were dating," Marvin reluctantly said taking the spoon of chocolate ice cream and ramming it into his own mouth. Tilly was right!

This was all good and fun but I needed to snap out of it. Marvin and I weren't really dating. Friends described our relationship! In a coy voice I said, "I told you she had the hots for you."

Marvin stood, tossed his bowl in the trash can, and said, "You know, I think you should eat your ice cream as we trek back to Keeper House. If you're too late you might get into trouble with the professor."

I reluctantly stood. I wasn't so sure if it was my impending trouble with the professor or if Jessie's presence was bothering him. I agreed, "You're probably right."

"I'll see you tomorrow at work," Jessie said as he too was now standing. "Thanks for the key. Do you mind Marvin if I go in for a bit of Blondie pleasure?"

"No problem," Marvin stated looking really annoyed with his friend.

As we left Jessie, I turned and waved at him over my shoulder. Marvin's demeanor once again turned pleasant. He began a new subject on our walk back by questioning, "Can you now tell me about your life theme?"

"You want to talk about my nightmare with Professor Zirak," I blurted out in an annoyed tone.

"Guess it didn't go well," Marvin said suddenly placing his arm around my shoulders and giving me a friendly hug.

"I should have gone with the flow and used your life theme as my own," I unhappily stated. "Cheating would have been easier."

"That bad? What happened?" Marvin questioned with his brows pushed together and a concerned look on his face.

I deliberately took a huge bite of ice cream off my spoon to give myself a moment to think. If he didn't like rule breaking, he probably wasn't going to appreciate the truth. I simply spurted out, "I didn't do the assignment." I immediately stuck another spoon of chocolate in my mouth.

"Did you confide in Professor Zirak that you remember nothing and that you couldn't do the assignment?" Marvin questioned.

"Well yes," I answered. "However, he gave me some mumbo jumbo riddle about my not remembering anything being the answer to my question. Who knows what he was talking about?"

"He's really smart and there for those who need him," Marvin seriously stated. "I'm sure whatever coded riddle of words he told you was meant to help you."

I cut him off. "Yeah. He helped me make enemies. Every week until I turn in my assignment, my entire group has to do an extra paper on one of the life themes. Can you imagine how everyone feels about me! They are paying for my blankness. I'm their nightmare or a fly in their soup."

Marvin grinned like he thought I was cute all worked up into a tizzy. Marvin in calm, reasoning voice said, "Professor Zirak must think one of the life themes in the book will jog your memory. Everything the professor does serves a purpose."

I let out a deep sigh. How could I argue with that? "Let's hope it doesn't take all fifty-two life themes in the book to discover mine!" I countered and then paused. "Marvin do you understand the professor's words to me?"

"Your not remembering anything is the answer," Marvin stated. I nodded and he took my hand in his. A fly away piece of hair was once again falling about my face. Marvin startled me as his free hand gently pushed it behind my ear. "I want to ask you something," Marvin stated in a lighter mood. "I told you earlier what I would haunt. What would you haunt?"

"I don't know," I said off the top of my head. Then I decided to answer what ever popped into my head. "Umm… Earth's Internal Revenue Service."

His head jerked back in shock. You could tell he was caught off guard. "I've got to hear this. Enlighten me!"

"I would have access to all my past records," I stated and for a moment day dreamed about massive computers holding vast amounts of information that I could use. "I could access information about myself and my family. My blank foggy days would be over. I would quickly learn who I am and whether I have a large family. I would know what occupations I had. I would know me."

His face showed empathy as his fingers gently rubbed the back of my hand. He said, "Elizabeth, you are an amazing person. Your family must have a mountain of time, space, and obligations to keep them away from you for so long. Don't be down hearted. Your memories will return once the fog clears. I'm sure your family will reenter your life when the time is right."

CHAPTER NINETEEN

Tilly

There she was! Right where I expected. She was so predictable. Elizabeth was perched at a gleaming white table diligently buried in a book studying. By the looks of the stack of books, she planned to stay awhile. What a boring bookworm! She constantly worried about our class work and all of those extra assignments that she claimed were adding up. This was eternity! What were they going to do, throw us out? All these classes were some school teacher's heaven, not mine! Having nothing else to do, I strolled over and pulled out a chair.

"You don't happen to know where Trevor is, do you?" Elizabeth questioned while motioning for me to sit.

"Trevor's brother Daniel and his wife had their first baby yesterday," I began. "Trevor and Eddie have gone home for their family's celebration of the new life. Trevor invited me. However, Presnell wouldn't give me a pass saying I wasn't family. Family isn't always who you are related to by blood!"

Unlike my dysfunctional, related by blood family, Trevor Stillholm and his family stuck together. They were always planning mammoth family celebrations. They seized any reason to celebrate their family member's accomplishments, every chance they got. The first baby in the next generation of this unique family had them in full party mode.

I cringed at the name they chose for the baby boy. Henry. Their chosen name rivaled only the chosen name for The Department of Ghosts. Ghosties! Both were terrible and not fully thought-out names. In my mind there was no way they could have picked a worse boring name? The poor baby was bound to be hum drum and dull with that name bestowed upon him. Henry sounds so stuffy and serious. Poor baby!

Elizabeth had become one of us. She had submerged herself into my world and my friends more than I had realized. Why was she was looking for Trevor? I couldn't help but wonder, "Why are you looking for Trevor?"

Elizabeth looked like the cat that ate the mouse. "Trevor and Eddie are always around," Elizabeth nervously replied. "Our group is small… a little empty without them."

"Missing them, huh," I replied as I popped a piece of double pop gum in my mouth.

"How long will they be gone?" Elizabeth asked trying to appear casual.

"A few days," I replied as I now questioned in my mind the real reason behind why she was asking.

Presnell and Mrs. Raderton strutted by our table. Mrs. Raderton didn't acknowledge me. Her nose was stuck up to the sky as she passed. If it rained she would drown. Her nose could be a gutter down spout. The professor's outfit was screaming, look at me! Even a psychologist wouldn't understand why she wanted to walk around looking like a plump, red tomato. I hate tomatoes! My extreme dislike for the Presnell rivaled my extreme dislike for tomatoes. I leaned over to Elizabeth as they were out of earshot and on the lift, "Did you notice Kegley flying solo today to teach us about accessing Humling records?" In a smug voice I added, "No Mrs. Raderton for a crutch."

"I hadn't given it a thought, Tilly. She was absent!" Elizabeth replied.

"Her absence was my doing," I smugly corrected Elizabeth as I folded up my gum wrapper and shoved it into my pocket.

"Your doing?" Elizabeth repeated perplexed still trying to read a line or two in her book between the bits of our conversation.

A boy studying a table over from us turned to us with his index finger pressed against his lips, "Shh!"

My eyes flashed to study him as I gave him a flirtatious grin and repeated his, "Shh!" Then I threw him an air kiss with a wink. Maybe my date for tonight had appeared. He winked back! I began to throw him a second air kiss when Elizabeth interrupted me, "What are you doing?"

"Have I ever told you that Mr. Raderton and my father are best friends?" I asked as I once again glanced at the next table. The boy had gone back to reading and scribbling in his notebook.

"You might have mentioned that," Elizabeth shrugged. "Maybe not."

Was something wrong with me? Any other time a guy would walk over and introduce himself when I flirted. Maybe I was becoming as boring as Henry. Did the incident with Andy affect my mojo? Who was I kidding? I was Tilly, the man-eater. I wasn't loosing my touch. Elizabeth was cramping my style in some ways. She had one real issue that annoyed me. She insisted flirting and men shouldn't supersede anything else. I was of the opposite opinion.

"What did you do, complain to Mr. Raderton?" Elizabeth asked with a giggle.

"Not Exactly. I turned on the fake tears as I complained to my father about how devastating it had been being embarrassed by Mrs. Raderton!" I giggled at my devious act pulling the wool over my father's eyes. "Even though I assured him it wasn't necessary for him to interfere, my father was intent on going to talk with Mr. Raderton about it. I got her into trouble with her stiff, domineering, and spiteful husband!"

"Don't you worry about repercussions?" Elizabeth questioned while completely astonished at my devious act.

"Before I could answer, a familiar voice chimed in, "Who are you plotting against Tilly?"

I turned to see Mrs. Summors standing behind us. "Oh, no one," I replied to her waiting stare. Hoping to change the subject I quickly motioned to Elizabeth, "Mrs. Summors, have you met my friend Elizabeth?"

"No," Mrs. Summors replied as she looked upon Elizabeth's sweats and pony tail with a less than impressed look. Mrs. Summors always sported an extremely professional appearance. Her hair was done to perfection and her makeup was flawless.

I stood squeaking my chair shrilly. "Mrs. Summors, this is Elizabeth Cantrell. Elizabeth, this is Mrs. Summors."

"Hello," Elizabeth rose and greeted Mrs. Summors and held her hand out to shake.

"Very nice to meet you," Mrs. Summors responded while shaking Elizabeth's extended hand. "I'm happy to see you girls are taking your studies so seriously."

What an unnecessary comment. Was she delusional or had Mrs. Summors forgotten I never study!

"Do you work here at the Hall of Records?" Elizabeth inquired in an over friendly voice aimed at pumping her for information.

"Yes," Mrs. Summors said with a genuine smile. "I have for many years."

"For longer than I have been around," I added briefly recalling moments of pleasure sitting on her knee as a toddler. Out of respect I grabbed Mrs. Summors and gave her a small hug.

"You know there is an area in my essay I'm writing that I am blank about and need help. I haven't found an opportunity to ask Professor Kegley," Elizabeth hesitated as Mrs. Summors patiently waited for her to spit her question out. "If all the records are kept here, isn't it fool hardy? Like keeping all your eggs in one basket. What if something happens to the building and its contents? All the records…"

"The records are all safely copied," Mrs. Summors reassured Elizabeth.

"So, there are copies of this library kept safe in another location?" Elizabeth intently questioned.

"Yes," Mrs. Summors agreed. "There are three complete copies of all the history books. You are standing in a building holding one complete set of works. The second set of works is privately owned and safe within the dome."

"And the third?" Elizabeth questioned not able to let go of it.

"One complete set has been entrusted to a private owner who specializes in information storage and history in the Humling world," Mrs. Summors stated.

"A history buff that lives and breathes history," I sarcastically added. Elizabeth's obsession for the Hall of Records was now reaching an all time low in my mind. First, fifty questions of Trevor. Now, interrogating Mrs. Summors. Why did Elizabeth not see the obvious? I could tell her anything she wanted to know! With me, it wouldn't be necessary to beat around the bush.

"There are those who appreciate history, Tilly," Mrs. Summors corrected me. "Also, there are various libraries in the Humling world. However, I don't think any one library holds a complete copy of works. Each town library tends to hold the history books that are of specific interest to the Humlings of the town."

"What about chapters?" Elizabeth inquired intently watching Mrs. Summors and pretending to take notes.

"What about them?" Mrs. Summors retorted giving Elizabeth a sudden familiar shut your mouth glare. Elizabeth's obsession with this subject left her unable to pick up on Mrs. Summors vibes.

"Are they copied?" Elizabeth continued her interrogation ignoring the change in demeanor of the sweet, elderly walking information center.

"Yes, they are backed up as well," Mrs. Summors curtly answered.

Rolling my eyes at Elizabeth's dumb questions, I thought, of course the chapters were backed up! However, speaking of this in the Hall of Records with others around wasn't smart. Elizabeth wasn't being discrete and she was asking questions she shouldn't be asking. I shot her a glare that screamed stop!

Elizabeth ignored my warning glare as she questioned, "Where?"

"Hey, look at the time," I said as I began to pull Elizabeth's arm, hoping to cut her off. Mrs. Summors was intently suspicious and staring at my best friend. I warmly smiled at Mrs. Summors, grabbed her, and hugged her to distract her. I explained, "We have Harmony practice tonight. We can't be late."

Elizabeth began to say, "Tilly, Harmony practice is…"

I stepped directly on her foot with all my weight and shot her a look that screamed, shut up! "Yeah, Harmony practice is boring," I stated, incorrectly finishing Elizabeth's thoughts. We both knew practice was a couple hours away. My message delivered to the top of Elizabeth's foot was effective. Limping, she began stacking her books to carry them. She looked like the unorganized Kegley with her hands haphazardly full. I had questioned over and over about her backpack which had been missing since solo try outs. My prodding was ignored. There was more to the story, but her mouth was sealed.

As I threw my backpack over my shoulder, Mrs. Summors placed her hand on my shoulder saying, "Tilly, before you go, I want you to know how very proud I am of you."

"For what?" I retorted, totally caught off guard with both Mrs. Summors change in demeanor and her statement.

"A little birdie told me you are going to sing the solos at the Harmony Concerts," Mrs. Summors explained with a warm motherly smile. "You have always been the sunshine of my soul, even though you aren't my child!"

For a moment I could feel the tears well up in my eyes. Of all the things to cry like a baby over! I blinked my tears away as I looked up at the ceiling. I took a deep breath and told her, "Really, it's no big deal."

"No big deal," Mrs. Summors repeated with a disagreeing look. "It's a very big deal! I can't tell you how happy I am that you have recognized your niche. I always had faith that you would. I never doubted you would be a shew –in for Harmony. I remember all those afternoons you would sit under my desk playing dolls and singing. You were always my high noted musical angel. Every time you sang, it was perfection and soul stirring!" Mrs. Summors paused and I could see the intensity of her emotion. "Look at you now… you're applying yourself and doing so well."

Mrs. Summors pulled me to her and hugged me. I felt myself melting in her warm motherly hug. I too remembered all the days under her desk. She hid me there, safely away from trouble and my parent's poor care of me. She didn't know that I sang because she would hum along with me which always left me feeling warm and safe. But Harmony… If only she knew my real reason for insisting on doing the solos. I languished in the hug longer than necessary because it plainly felt good. There was nothing else to say, "Thank you and I love you Mrs. Summors!"

Elizabeth circled us waiting. She could see the visible fought back tears in my eyes. She turned and walked away a few steps to give us a private moment. When Mrs. Summors released me, Elizabeth politely said, "It was very nice to meet you."

"Thank you," Mrs. Summors said. "It has been a pleasure to meet you too."

Elizabeth and I both gave her a little wave as we left her and walked the marble path back to the lift. "Destination two," I stated wiping my eyes on the back of my hands when no one was looking.

Elizabeth stated to the midget, "Destination four, please!" A book from the stack in Elizabeth's arms fell and landed on the floor of the lift with a thud.

"Why are we going to the Department of Ghosts?" I inquired as I bent down to retrieve the book for her. Where was her backpack? The cover of the book read, Theories About Choosing Your Earth Life. Professor Zirak's notion to pile additional homework on Elizabeth was really rotten.

"Thank you," Elizabeth replied as I placed it back on top of her stack. "I need to follow up and ensure Mike has our assignment complete for tomorrow. I promised Marvin I would do so."

She promised Marvin? Why was he so interested? It was probably a good idea but Marvin had nothing to do with our predicament with our partners in our Department of Ghosts class. A woman should never do a task, good or bad, to make their guy happy. Male dominance! I wanted to scream from the roof top. I reminded myself to breath deeply to calm down. Elizabeth liked Marvin and you couldn't get between your best friend and her man. I, on the other hand, would skip the fail safe measure since my partner was Andy. It was I making that decision and not some man making it for me!

"Tilly, may I ask you to not stomp my foot again," Elizabeth demanded. "That really hurts!"

"I'm sorry I was so rough on your foot!" I looked around and leaned over to Elizabeth, "If you wanted to know about copies of..." I threw my hands up, obviously not saying out loud chapters. "You could have asked me." Elizabeth started to say something but I held up my hand to stop her. "You need to learn discretion. The Hall of Records wasn't the place."

"If you knew about copies, but borrowed the chapter for my reading, wouldn't their have been less risk in getting the copy?" Elizabeth whispered to me.

"I grew up in the Hall of Records," I told her. "Getting anything from there is easy for me. I know the ins and outs. And Mrs. Summors…"

"She seemed very nice," Elizabeth added. "Very motherly." Her eyes flickered to me, "But in a good way!"

"She is," I agreed to my friend's natural intuitiveness. No one would ever know the countless times I had wished for her to be my mother instead of my own. "I really disliked lying to her about practice. However, you didn't leave me any choice when you were asking questions about something that's supposed to be a secret."

"Well?" Elizabeth asked.

"Well what?" I retorted watching the lift's midget leprechaun's large ears perk up.

"Where are the copies of the… you know… kept?" Elizabeth asked.

"You're not going to like this," I warned her. I leaned over, cupped my hands around her ear, and whispered, "They're kept by the Council in the Administration Complex. The part of the Complex where the guards are housed. Heavily guarded!"

"There goes that idea," Elizabeth sighed as she threw one hand up balancing her arm full of books with the other.

"I suspect you were hoping they would be easier to get to," I surmised. "Making it easier for a little private research."

"You got it," Elizabeth agreed totally dejected and her heart suddenly dropped into her stomach.

The lift door dinged. "Destination four, Department of Ghosts," the little lift operator announced wiggling his pointed ears.

Elizabeth stopped mid-door and grinned at the loudly dressed little leprechaun lift operator saying, "Thank you sir." Unbelievable! The midget could smile.

Why did she insist on thanking him? His everyday cantankerous foul mood was annoying. I pretended to flip a cootie from the unsuspecting little man's shoulder as I said to Elizabeth, "See ya later."

Elizabeth waved at me from her spot in the massive grey room with her arms full. At least one of us would have something to turn in tomorrow. Andy was mad, but he would come through with the assignment. It would be useless for me to bother checking. Andy was the no fail type.

I towered over the long nosed midget as he operated the lift and coded it to stop at Destination three and let everyone but myself off. Now was my chance and I was going to take it! I leaned over him and pressed the emergency stop button, holding it firmly down. A slight buzzing noise was set off with our stopping. The little man just as quickly pushed the emergency button. Calvary would be on the way. I growled at him, "Didn't anyone ever tell you it's not nice to eavesdrop!"

"Who was eavesdropping," the midget stated in a grumbling tone staring at me with those deep blue eyes.

"Don't give me that," I growled about an inch form his unflinching face. "I saw those dumbo ears perk up when you thought I was about to say something juicy."

"I hear all kinds of stuff without eavesdropping," the leprechaun stated looking me straight in the eye never releasing his finger from the alarm button.

"You were eavesdropping on my private conversation," I said poking him with a purple polished, long, sharp finger nail.

"Private?" He repeated. "If you wanted privacy then you need too…" He paused and flashed a devilish grin at me. "Learn a little discretion. This little moving box? This isn't the right place for that."

I was livid and right. He was eavesdropping! Most incredibly, he was mouthing me! Who did he think he was?

The look on his face was one of total satisfaction. He happily went on, "Even if I know about all your chapter antics, how would you prove to anyone else I was eavesdropping."

"Pay backs are hell," I threatened as I released the stop button. He smirked and released the emergency help button. The midget seemed unaffected by my threat. I backed to the other side of the lift and stared him down. He was incredible. No one did me dirty and came out smelling like roses.

CHAPTER TWENTY

Elizabeth

As Tilly and I breezed down the steps into the foyer, we could clearly see a massive, boisterous crowd encircling Trevor. Fellow trainees were waving fists and things while taunting him. Eddie was visible scurrying about the outer rim of the encompassing circle collecting mismatched clothes. As we got closer we could see that Trevor's hands were full of … unrelated items.

Tilly and I stepped off the stairs and pushed our way to the center of the group. We positioned ourselves shoulder to shoulder with Trevor as our fellow trainees continued to taunt him. I realized Trevor had several books shoved under his arms and his hands were full of socks, toothbrush, basically a little of everything he owned. Tilly grabbed a pair of, oh dear, holey underwear from a fellow trainee. Peering over Tilly's shoulder, I got a peek at the thing Tilly was viewing intently. Every item had a tag which read, "If found, please return to Trevor Stillholm for reward."

"Trevor, here is your Transportation Law book. I'm ready for my reward," sneered Janelle from the other side of the circle.

"I have your toothbrush! Pay me," jeered a boy I didn't recognize.

"Why are you so upset? Be glad we recovered all your belongings," declared Tiffany looking blissfully satisfied. "I will gladly fork over this family photo for my reward."

In a flash, Tilly snatched the photo out of Tiffany's hand and leaned over growling, "If you had anything to do with this…" Tilly stood shaking a fully extended, rigid finger at Tiffany while grasping the photo and worn out underwear in the other.

"I didn't get my reward," Tiffany whined as she stuck her bottom lip out pretending to pout. "Did I get the unwanted possession? What a scam!" Tiffany then moved around to stand before Trevor and gloat. She placed her hand on Trevor's arm, glared at him victoriously, and loudly stated, "Ruthanne is in our house and we don't approve of you. Remember that!" Tiffany and Janelle turned tail and marched triumphantly out of the circle with Janelle waving a sock over her head that was riddled with holes.

Tilly might have pursued after them if she hadn't saw the need to grab items out of the hands of those in the crowd. The lift door dinged and opened. The duped, empty handed crowd began to disburse. Eddie had a pile of Trevor's belongings and was diligently guarding them. Others realizing the show was coming to an end, began handing all the remaining items to Trevor, Tilly and myself as they made a dash for the open door of the lift.

Ruthanne fled the scene letting her long red hair shield her face. Clearly she was trying not to make eye contact with any of us. Her skin was lividly flushed with embarrassment. I now understood what I overheard at the Harmony solo try-outs. Their plan was to disrupt Trevor and Ruthanne's relationship, and for their own selfish reasons! Knowing Trevor was gone, I should have confided in Tilly. Also, I should have warned Ruthanne. This was my new found family and I wasn't diligent in doing my best to protect them.

"Trevor, I am so sorry. This was off the wall cruel," Tilly compassionately said. Trevor was speechless. He moved like a robot as he gathered all he could carry. When his eyes met Tilly's he reached down for a brief moment and gripped her hand in his. They shared a brief, awkward moment of understanding with unspoken words passing between them. Slowly their hands separated as he retrieved his underwear from Tilly. Their moment was eerie and surpassed this place and time.

As I gave the items in my hands a once over, I found it astounding that someone had taken time to write on each tag, return to Trevor Stillholm for reward. Knowing the amount of time necessary to write and tag each item, their room must have been raided at some point yesterday. I added the belongings in my hands to Eddie's pile in the floor.

Trevor unable to vocalize due to the shock, headed back up the stairs. Tilly was one step behind him holding her arms out to block anyone from approaching him. Their slow ascend of the stairs only communicated to everyone watching, the odd closeness of their relationship.

"You think he'll be okay?" I asked Eddie.

"I'm sure he's bummed," Eddie sighed. "This was an unexpected blow. Who would want their underwear waved like a banner? Leave the worrying about Trevor to Tilly and me. Your job will be to rain in Tilly. She's going to be amped and plotting revenge!"

"Somehow I think you're right," I sighed. "She won't stop until she finds a way."

"Whatever she dishes out is probably going to be a rad ride," Eddie smiled and pulled his hoodie up over his head. "There's nothing for you to do. Go on so you won't get into trouble by being tardy to class." Eddie paused and glanced up the stairs. "I don't think Tilly needs the extra stress today of you being in trouble."

Although this was undoubtedly true, Eddie overlooked the obvious. "And you?" I asked.

"Trevor and I were skippin' class today," Eddie stated. "We barely stepped foot into the building when…" With an eye roll he gestured his hand to the foyer where the massive circle mob of chaos had been.

"You had no warning," I deducted.

"None," Eddie admitted. "We just returned from an entire night of celebratory jamming. The new baby was the only one to sleep. Morning brought too many sleep deprived party goers and too few beds."

"So you were looking for a place to crash?" I surmised.

"We were beat down and yes, planned to catch some Z's." A broad smile crossed Eddie's face while his eyes twinkled as he began to recall, "I am stoked we jammed last night! I maxed out on the rail! My whipped bro had a moment away from his girl. You know Ruthanne doesn't…" Eddie did quotation marks with his hands as he said, "Allow…" He slightly shook his head in disgust, "Trevor to do any tricks which require his skateboard leaving the ground. When the cats away the mice will play. Trevor focused on tricks which got lots of air."

"Reclaiming your dirt baggin-it life," I teased.

Eddie had a surprised look on his face at my recalling his speech about his earth life and a skateboarding term. "Well, sleeping is probably out. Speaking of Ruthanne, I'm sure at some point Trevor will meet up with her today. She probably blames herself."

"Don't you think I should wait for Tilly and Trevor to come back down?" I questioned.

"They may not come down for awhile," Eddie sheepishly uttered. "This isn't something you cope with in twenty minutes."

"Okay, I'll go." I said. "Do you want me to turn in your assignment?"

"Trevor and I turned in our assignment to Professor Bungard before we left," Eddie stated.

"When you see Tilly, please try to encourage her to go on to class!" I begged Eddie.

"Sure," Eddie assured me as he sat down next to a pile of Trevor's belongings on the floor. "Maybe I'll catch a quickie nap with this stuff as a pillow."

The lift door dinged! I shot Eddie a smile and a wave while I ran across the foyer to catch the lift. I beat the closing door barely and quickly stated, "Destination four."

Catching my breath, I recognized no one else I knew was in the lift today. Everyone was already gone. A few strangers stood ignoring me. My partner, Mike, wouldn't be happy with me if I was late. He had completed our assignment for today, but wouldn't let me look at his work. He bitterly informed me that he had no intention of teaching or sharing with me. He completed the assignment for himself, not me. The only silver lining was the professor would believe I had helped. Tilly was in far worse shape! I was sure Andy would have completed the assignment. However, Andy might have confided in the professor his singleness of participation. He seemed to be the professor's pet.

Today hadn't started out well and wasn't likely to turn for the best throughout the day. I felt a tremendous amount of remorse for not spilling the beans about my overheard conversation. How was I too have known they would attack Trevor, not Ruthanne? Unfortunately, my questions had been answered. I now knew exactly how they planned to free up Ruthanne's time.

The conversation that was to come with Tilly was going to be uncomfortable. I vowed that I would never again keep secrets from Tilly. I had my initial, selfish reasons for not mentioning it to her. Now it was much worse. My fear of what she might do if she thought Tiffany and Janelle were going to hurt Ruthanne, was nothing compared to my fear of what Tilly would now do knowing they were interfering in Trevor's life. Pay backs were hell when Tilly's path was crossed. However, she was my best friend and we would stick together through thick and thin. Just like gum! I had no choice. However, I shuddered at the unknown, what Tilly might do.

The small lift operator interrupted my thoughts as he tugged on the bottom of my shirt. As I looked down at him, he smiled back up at me and wiggled one ear, "Destination four, Department of Ghosts."

"Oh," I said shocked at the faces watching the lift operator remind me to exit the lift in such a cordial manner. I stepped towards the lift door and said to the bright blue eyes of the lift operator, "Thank you." I winked at him and gave him a smile.

I stepped off the lift into the massive grey Elephant Room which marked my destination as the Department of Ghost Relations. Professor Bungard was mulling around the lift awaiting my arrival still wearing his worn out, tight uniform. It was evident from his demeanor and twitching salt and pepper mustache that this wasn't good. He directed me to wait for him in the corner office off Elephant Room. Two familiar figures loomed ahead! I moved forward towards the office door under the glares of Andy & Mike. Just wonderful! The two jerks ratted on us! Why had I expected anything less? I ignored them and moved past them.

As I felt a tapping on my shoulder I turned spouting, "Want to gloat in person about how you got us into trouble!" To my surprise it was Dustin and I wasn't very lady like in my outburst. I really had thought it was Andy or Mike trying to annoy me.

"You're in trouble today?" Dustin asked with a mischievous grin. "Tell me more." He shifted his feet and took a casual stance leaning against the massive gray wall.

"I would love to hear this one," Dustin's mind stated.

Regaining my composure, I took a leaning position next to him. "No thank you," I replied while trying not to breathe too deeply. I simply didn't want to inhale Dustin's cologne and loose my mind! "Where's my backpack?"

Dustin casually slid my backpack off his shoulder. In a defiant act he held the backpack firmly in his hands as though waiting for a response from me.

"It would be polite for her to say thank you. I did return it!" I heard his mind state.

Dustin had been in possession of my backpack since carrying it for me after our trek back from my solo try out debacle. I had endured all kinds of questions from Tilly in regards to its whereabouts. Why in the world did he return it two days later. I reached out and my hands brushed Dustin's as I retrieved the backpack. There was intoxication in just touching his hands as they loosened their grip. I pulled the pack free and tossed it over my shoulder as I stated, "Thank you." If he only knew how I desired to lay my head and nose on his chest, envelop him in my arms, and never let go!

"You're welcome," Dustin politely stated. With a brief smile he turned on a dime and strolled away.

I opened the designated office door, viewing a group of my fellow trainees huddled together awaiting the beginning of the cheer in the massive Elephant Room. Hopefully, they hadn't viewed my run in with Dustin. I backed through the office door in defensive mode, shut it, and whirled around to face the desk. Surprised, I discovered Rhett seated behind the massive, wooden desk. He asked, "Is Miss Bradford not with you today?"

"She will be along, she is assisting another trainee who was having… there was a situation arise this morning." I nervously said as I stuttered and stumbled for words. Since we were in trouble, I could only pray she would truly be along soon.

He nodded waving his extended hand towards the two wooden chairs before his desk, "Please, have a seat while we wait."

I reluctantly sat down letting my newly returned backpack fall to the floor at my feet. I quickly unzipped it and shoved my books inside. The two of us silently waited for Professor Bungard and Tilly. The clock ticked loudly, every long minute. Evidently, this was Rhett's office. It was a dimly lit place with a solid wooden door. The windows were covered with solid wooden blinds which blocked all light from entering. The remaining three walls were covered in wooden shelving containing history movies. Marvin's uncle and this guy would get along great! A round table set directly under the covered windows with an additional four to five chairs around it. I could only imagine that this table was the strategy center for Rhett's ghost hunting adventures.

As my eyes darted around the room nervously, Rhett's eyes never left me. The way he looked at me left me with the gut feeling, he knew me. Beyond his white clothing and gray sweater vest signaling his being a Ghostie, I recognized nothing about him. An eerie, silent, uncomfortable feeling began to settle over the room between us.

Professor Bungard knocked, opened the door, and peered in. I could hear the day and night supervisors with their microphones, challenging each other.

Rhett stood and waved the professor in, "Welcome Kendell. Take a seat. Should I have one of the trainees go and fetch some coffee for us?"

"That won't be necessary. Thank you for having me," Professor Bungard said appearing star struck and in awe of Rhett's hospitality. "Also, thank you for taking such an interest in my new trainees." The professor seated himself and then paused to ask, "Where is Miss ..."

"Right here," Tilly said as she passed through the open door. "Professor, I am sorry to be late. I was helping another trainee in the Hall of Knowledge."

"Very well," said Professor Bungard as he waved at Tilly to take the remaining wooden seat next to mine. The professor closed off the grey Elephant Room when he closed the office door. He pulled up a chair from the round table and sat down loosing a button from his vest in the process. Embarrassed he leaned over to pick it up and shove it in his pocket. Why did he not just purchase a new uniform? His was literally so old, it was falling apart!

The eerie silence returned. "The reason we are talking to the two of you separate from the group is because Rhett has requested your assistance in finding a ghost that he doesn't have time to pursue!"

"My department is always short staffed," Rhett started. "And honestly, Miss Bradford, you seem youthfully spunky enough to take on this task of finding a ghost."

I watched as Tilly drifted into deep thought and ignored the present moment's happenings. She sat blowing bubbles and popping them while she stared off into space. Maybe she hadn't heard Rhett! Perhaps, this was some type of punishment for Tilly's smart remark she made to him last week. Was Rhett determined to teach her a little respect? I felt desperate to take the light off her. She didn't need this today! With my head held high and sitting straight up, I asked, "And may I ask, do you see me as capable as Tilly?"

"You run with her, so I assume you can handle yourself," he replied with a chuckle under his breath. "Besides I don't see any real danger this task poses to either of you, unless you count getting iced as danger."

"You think getting iced is my style?" Tilly piped up speaking her mind and breaking her uncharacteristic silence.

"I'm sure you will learn about it soon enough," Rhett replied.

"What about our partners from last week? And our assignment?" I whirled around asking Professor Bungard.

"Andy and Mike will now be paired up together. You will be given credit for this week's assignment," Professor Bungard stated. "They should have been pared up to begin with!"

"Protecting your pet Andy?" Tilly challenged showing a hint of sarcasm.

Before the professor could respond, Rhett ignored her comment stating, "I would like the two of you to find Brian Stanford. This is a top priority case and I will need you to work through the weekend. Hopefully you can locate him by next week so I can send the hunters to retrieve him."

"What do you know about him?" Tilly asked with a renewed interest in the conversation. After all, the ghost was a man! Figures! Another male conquest for Tilly. This was the first and only department she actually took an interest in.

"I haven't done much research," Rhett replied. "If I had, I wouldn't be asking the two of you to assist me."

Professor Bungard was eyeing the door so I needed to take my chance, "Professor Bungard, may I ask how long we will be assigned to Rhett?"

"That hasn't been decided. We will see how it goes." Professor Bungard replied. "The track record for the two of you isn't that great."

"Professor, before you go, I would like to revisit the issue of Miss Bradford being late to today's training so we are all on the same page," Rhett piped up. I could see Tilly looking at him like he was an unexpected challenge. "I don't tolerate anyone working for me to be even one minute late. I am giving the both of you fair warning! If you are late, I will double your work for each infraction."

"We're students," Tilly grumbled. "We don't actually work for you." She commenced to cross her arms across her chest in defiance.

"Your thoughts Kendell?" Rhett politely asked.

"Since you have been forewarned about punctuality, the consequences seem fair to me," Professor Bungard agreed as he stood from his chair at the table. "Ladies, your grade this week will be based on this advanced assignment."

The professor began to move towards the door to leave as I inquired, "Who will be giving our grade?"

"Your grade will be at my discretion." Rhett stated from across the desk as he stood to bid the professor bye. They shook hands and ended their business.

Turning to the two of us the professor spoke one last time, "Ladies, I will expect you to come down to class shortly after Rhett has filled you in on your assignment details." Then he walked out the door.

Elephant room was alive with applause when Rhett rounded the desk and closed the door behind the professor. "Miss Bradford, I'm a little taken back. I was sure you would be running to Mommy by now. You are your mother's daughter!"

"I don't need her help," Tilly said clearly waking from her fog. "I fight my own battles. I'm emancipated!"

Rhett slowly sauntered back around his desk with a smirk upon his face. "Due to your slacking, I am going to assign you a total of three Humlings to find," Rhett stated as he sat. "To begin, you will find Brian Stanford who is a true ghost. Once you have located him, we will get a crew and bring him back."

Before he could continue Tilly blurted out, "You said we were slacking. What makes you think that?" She pounded her fist on Rhett's desk. "We did our assignment for last week!"

"Oh, you did?" Rhett challenged leaning forward in his chair. "I thought Mr. Weaver and Mr. Harding did the work for you."

"Did one of them tell you that?" I questioned with disbelief.

"Since the two boys have always been inseparable, I assumed you divided them to use them," Rhett stated. "Miss Bradford, enlighten me. What is the first step when finding a ghost?"

Her silence spoke volumes as he questioned me, "Miss Cantrell?" I shrugged my shoulders. "My point exactly. I will not turn you in, but I will not allow you too slide by either."

"And the other two ghosts on our list?" I pointedly questioned.

"I want you to learn to properly deal with a hanger and denier," Rhett stated. "These are common tasks or cases you will tackle as a Keeper." He paused and flipped through a long registry of names. Second Humling, Staci Diamond. Third Humling, Ryan Smith. Write the names down correctly. One letter wrong in the spelling of their name and you could waste time pursuing a different individual."

I started to stand as Rhett said, "There is one more issue for us to talk about before re-joining your group for class time today."

"Something more?" I questioned with a whine as I plopped back down. I never realized I was a whiner. I was surprised at the sound that accompanied my voice. Had I picked this up from Tilly or worse yet, Tiffany?

"There is a time line for finding the three Humlings," Rhett stated.

"Let us have it," Tilly stated while popping a piece of gum into her already full mouth. As always, she appeared to be unfazed by the impending doom.

"They need to be found by next Wednesday," Rhett stated. "You will need to work some evening hours." The gauntlet had fallen!

"That's only seven days and evenings are out!" Tilly huffed as her mouth fell open.

"This assignment was yours to complete last week!" Rhett reminded us. "The way I look at it, you are a week behind in your studies."

"Finding three will be impossible," I stated. "We won't be in the Hall of Knowledge this weekend."

"I assume you are referring to this being a weekend you can visit your home?" Rhett inquired. We both nodded as he smirked, "You can have your weekend as long as you find them by next Wednesday. Do you have any further questions?" As our heads both nodded no, from side to side, he relaxed in his chair. We could tell he was satisfied with his punishment. He enjoyed doling it out! With a smirk, he waved his hand and said, "You are free to go on to class."

I once again stood tossing my backpack over my shoulder. Tilly remained planted in her chair. Without looking at me she said, "Elizabeth, I have one more question. I'll be right behind you."

I wasn't going to argue in-front of Rhett. I reluctantly, but speedily threw my backpack across my shoulder and crossed the room to the office door. With my hand on the door knob, I looked back at Tilly and Rhett who were locked in a nasty stare and battle of the wills. I started to return to my chair but Rhett stated without looking at me, "Go on Miss. Cantrell."

I closed the office door behind me and stepped out into the grey Elephant Room. It was quiet now as the crowd had disbursed going to work and class. Rhett's team was dressed for winter all in different shades of grey and white, leaning against the wall waiting for their day to begin. They smiled at me as I passed. The man who caught my attention was the one wearing the big, worn cowboy hat. Is he really going ghost hunting in that hat? I would be worried it would be blown away.

I slowly found my way through the maze of halls to the classroom as I enjoyed the enchanting smell of my backpack. It smelled exactly like Dustin's cologne. The heavenly, mystical scent must have rubbed off him and onto my backpack. It was now mine to enjoy! I daydreamed about him all the way to class. Professor Bungard was already teaching from the front of the room. I entered regretting my inability to continue enjoying smelling my backpack while I sat in class. The professor's topic for the day obviously was built on what we should have completed last week. Rhett was correct. We unfortunately were a week behind all due to Tilly's flirtation and fiasco with Andy.

Tilly arrived shortly after me. In true Tilly fashion, she walked in like she owned the room. As she sat beside me, Tilly was uncharacteristically quiet. I knew she wasn't happy about being assigned to Rhett. She had bigger fish to fry. All day she spaced out! She doodled, popped her gum, and was oblivious to any type of conversations going on around her. I knew all her energy was focused on Tiffany and Janelle. She had whispered to me she needed time to think.

On one hand, I could skin Tilly alive. Being friends with her was not an easy path. Tilly's escapades tended to cause both her and me a lot of extra work. On the other, I was proud my best friend had the strength to stand up for the weaker like Trevor.

Andy and Mike didn't look happy about our new assignment either. They worshiped Rhett and the thought that we got to work with him made them green with envy. They were jerks, so I simply ignored their glares. They must have had their time in his office just prior to ours.

The stuttering Stone girl and I walked to Keeper House from Harmony Practice together. Tilly begged me to ensure she got back to Keeper House without anyone hassling her. Tilly took the safety of the stuttering Stone girl upon herself daily. It was a silent walk since she was tongue tied and hardly ever verbalized. It was a load off my mind to leave her before the door to her room. I breezed through my own door and flipped on the light. Our windows were standing wide open with a peaceful breeze blowing in. I scanned the room and nothing appeared to be missing. There was an addition. A perfect beige envelope with gold lettering was perched on my pillow.

The comfort of my bed called me. I kicked my shoes off and released my hair from its ponytail holder. I grabbed my backpack and crawled onto my plump, fluffy comforter placing the backpack beside me. I leaned over to breath in the lingering fumes of cologne. As my head swirled with thoughts of Dustin holding me, I grabbed the envelope off my pillow. I instantly turned the envelope over and over. It was blank with the exception of my handwritten name in golden ink. I tore open the envelope and shook it! A random journal entry fell out.

Journal Entry #123

It did not go as planned.

Deward planned for a select group of the guards to bring the Grand daughters here, assuming that Walter would follow them and come home to reclaim his place with us. Piper insisted this was not acceptable, Walter already made his choice. She wanted him dealt with. Unknown to Deward, the guards went following Piper's orders to deal with Walter brutally. I believe Geren, Deward's guard, follows Piper's orders due to his enjoyment of her vicious solutions to handle problems which arise. I suppose he enjoys her ruthlessness. Collin and I were spared going, only because we were to wait at the entry for the girl's arrival. Once they entered, we were to ensure their safety back to the family.

When they left, Collin and I went to the entry and waited two days. Only the smaller girl, whose royal name is Tina, entered. She had Piper's cold, black eyes which seemed uncertain, but not afraid. Her sharp facial features gave her an aged appearance which matched her disposition. She wasted no time telling Collin she did not require his services. She tried to dismiss him as if he were a common slave. To my surprise, this action made him chuckle as he looked at her like she fascinated him. He wasted no time whisking her away against her will while I continued to wait.

Geren eventually came for me as Bethany would not be arriving. I always feel nervous in his presence because his harsh demeanor matches no other. He began to divulge Piper's plan and how it came to pass, thinking I would be impressed. His description of how he personally took care of Walter made me feel nauseous. Walter was sent through the Black Arch inside Venema House in-front of his children. Xavier was compelled to try to fight the other guards and protect Walter. He had so vocally disagreed to the plan, that the plan was altered to include sending him through the Black Arch as well. It seems Bethany is less like us than Tina. When she discovered the guards, she did not join the ranks as Tina did. She sat and cried in a corner while the guards disappeared, leaving the two girls to take the blame for sending their Father through the Black Arch. In the end, the Humling justice only held Tina accountable for her father's demise. The council sent only her to us.

I would never tell anyone, I fear I am more like Bethany because I often don't agree with their heinous actions. I guess I am uniquely suited to protect Bethany as I am probably the only one who could deal with, what they see as weakness, a conscious.

The journal entries combined laid the foundation for the dreadful story about the young man. The individuals mentioned in the entries baffled me. The author was dwelling with a group of harsh individuals. Their descriptions reminded me of Tiffany and Janelle. They were arrogant, immoral, and wicked.

I still had no knowledge of who was secretly leaving the journal entries or why. My attention focused on the open window. Was the person leaving the entries obtaining entry into our room through the window? I sprung up and shoved the new journal entry, with the others, between my mattress and box springs. I cautiously moved to the window and peered out into the black darkness. There was no visible intruder and no ladder! If someone hadn't climbed up the ladder, how did our windows get open? Was someone on the girl's floor? Did they gain entry through the door? If so, why would they open the window? Maybe they knew about the ladder and escaped upward? Could it be that the person leaving the journal entries and the person who cut the lower ladder rungs off were one in the same!

"Hey," Tilly greeted me and interrupted my thoughts as I stood at the window. "Having any luck seeing out in the dark?"

"Tilly, did you open the windows before we left?" I skeptically questioned watching Tilly toss her bubble gum pink backpack across her bed.

"No. Did it rain or something?" Tilly asked as she sat down in her chair before her desk which acted as a makeup table. "I'm glad their open. There is a nasty smell in this room. It needs some fresh air!"

"There is a problem," I stated walking over to her primping table. "I didn't open them. If you didn't, who did?"

"Had to be Trevor or Eddie," Tilly dismissed my concern as she began to rifle through her finger nail polish case. "Elizabeth! Don't get so paranoid!"

"The ladder is not out," I countered.

"So they pulled it up," Tilly flippantly shot back as she settled on a bottle of purple passion nail polish.

Secrets eat at you. I wanted to be done keeping secrets. However, the timing wasn't right to inform Tilly that someone had been in our room to leave the journal entries. Tilly had stressed out over Trevor's room debacle. She would flip! The journal entries had to be kept a secret. Tilly had enough on her plate.

Seeing the worry and indecisiveness on my face Tilly tried to calm and reassure my frayed nerves, "A bit of flirting today on my part snagged a snitch. Trevor's enemy is Janelle's boyfriend, Rodger. He got himself invited over to the boy's recreation room for a game of pool the other night when Trevor and Eddie were gone. He didn't arrive alone. A huge boisterous and rowdy gang tagged along with him. The guys upstairs admitted they didn't watch them closely. They cleaned out Trevor's stuff. The snitch spilled all for a chance at a date with me!"

"We should put locks on our doors and windows," I spit out.

Tilly slammed the bottle of nail polish remover on the desk. "Don't be so uptight!" Tilly retorted rolling her eyes. "Everyone is aware of their prank on Trevor. It won't be so easy for them to gain entrance next time.

How little Tilly knew! I watched as she began to remove the cracked and peeling bright pink nail polish with a cotton ball soaked in polish remover. She was dabbing the cotton ball against her nails as I asked, "Are Trevor and Ruthanne still dating?"

"Yeah," Tilly responded. "He's crazy about Ruthanne. What does he see in her red hair, that pasty skin, and all those freckles? I'm sure they won't be so public with it for awhile. Nothing could keep him away from her. However, it's best not to rock Ruthanne's boat. She has to live with Tiffany and her cronies till she can hopefully obtain a house transfer. Trevor and she will keep it low key!"

"Obviously, that's a good idea," I responded.

"I'll pay them back big time for their little joke," Tilly stated as her mood instantly soured. Instead of dabbing, she was using mad, rough swoops with her cotton ball to remove the polish. "They crossed the line! A bomb will fall destroying their power trip. They drew first blood!"

"Tilly," I said trying to interrupt the subject and interject my own thoughts. No luck!

"This prank was over the top," Tilly growled. "Our parents all work together and we have known each other since we were small children. They should have never tried to humiliate one of our own!"

"I might be a target," I unhappily stated to the surprised look across her face. "I have crossed them on more than one occasion. Like Trevor dating Ruthanne, I'm on their radar. They both know I will stand up for you because you're my best friend."

"You are new, Trevor is not!" Tilly disagreed. She tossed another polish smudged cotton ball down. "They have never before picked on Trevor because truly their fight only lies with me. However, I will never put up with them attacking others because they dislike me. They drew first blood when they crossed the line with Trevor!"

She was dreadfully protective of Trevor at a level I would never understand. "I thought maybe the two of you were secretly dating," I stated hoping to lighten the mood.

"Oh no, he's not my type!" Tilly said as she quickly looked away.

There was definitely more to their relationship but Tilly was intent on hiding it from me and the world. As far as her type, I had to respond, "Tilly I didn't know you had a type."

"Only wild and fun will do for me," she matter of fact stated. Then a few words spilled out of her mouth as she seemed deep in thought, "Were not meant to be together. Trevor is a great guy but he is too quiet, thoughtful, and methodically plans everything."

"That's bad?" I asked.

"I just don't like that type!" She replied. "Quiet and thoughtful always ends with them getting attached and I don't want anything permanent. I just want to be spontaneous and have fun!"

"I see!" I replied.

"You aren't like me," Tilly said. She began to use a pink emery board to shape her nails. "Your Marvin is quiet and thoughtful."

"He's not my Marvin!" I corrected as she rolled her eyes at me. "How about you Tilly? Would you date Marvin?"

"No!" Tilly said while shaking her head. "However, I can tell you that I was a little mad the first day when we met him and he ignored me. I am always the center of any man's attention. I was insulted and green with envy over his doting on you! He likes you. You are my best friend, so I have now forgiven him."

"Well, he would be relieved to know that!" I sarcastically stated as she tossed a nail file at me.

I handed her back her Emory board as she continued to work from finger to finger. I propped myself up against my head board, not able to let go of my worry about the window and ladder. I spit out, "Tilly, I'm worried the gang of boys saw the ladder."

"You're not back to sweating the small stuff are you?" Tilly questioned shaking her head. I just stared at her. Did she not think this was a problem? Tilly smiled, "Look, Trevor will claim its use is a fire escape." She held both hands out to view her fingernails as she mumbled, "That wasn't what I was worried about them finding."

"What does that mean?" I asked as I scooted to the end of my bed. Tilly looked at me innocently, which I didn't buy. "What do you have to hide?"

"It's a good thing Trevor hid it under the floor boards," Tilly teasingly said under her breath. "How about I show you?"

"Not right now," I countered. "Someone might be watching. I have this eerie sense of being spied on!"

"I have been waiting for a chance to surprise you," Tilly genuinely smiled standing to her feet and giving me her full attention.

"Please don't let this be anything bad or trouble making for us!" I stated with a frown.

"No, it's the most amazing thing Trevor and I have ever accomplished!" Tilly excitedly stated in a girly squeal.

What did I expect? It was another escapade and male partnership of hers. Tilly grabbed a bottle of polish and began to paint her nails purple as she seemed to drift off in thought. "Earth to Tilly! Return to me!" I said waving my hand in front of her dazed look.

"Trevor said he won't let anything keep him from Ruthanne. His words have made me think about Andy," Tilly stated.

"You don't seriously want him back?" I questioned half in disbelief.

"I don't know why!" Tilly loudly said. "I just do."

"That isn't good enough!" I stated challenging her. "You admit you don't want anything serious, so you must have a reason. Do you want him back because you can't have him? You do like a challenge."

"He is a challenge," she sighed. "Usually, guys aren't for me! You are right! A serious relationship... Blah! I probably wouldn't have maintained a relationship with him past a couple of dates anyway."

"So, you want him back because you like the possibility of trying to maintain a relationship past a couple of dates." I screeched half giggly. "You want a boyfriend!"

"What!" Tilly exclaimed as she dropped her bottle of purple nail polish. "I didn't say anything about a boyfriend."

"You didn't have too!" I smugly replied grabbing some tissues to help her clean up the mess. "Maybe you should ask Andy for a second chance."

"Elizabeth, do you know anything about men's egos?" Tilly asked. "Crying and begging isn't my style. Besides, it won't work! By the way, what day does Marvin play ball with the guys?"

"Saturday," I stated standing and throwing my handful of purple smudged tissues in the trash. "Why?"

"Could you persuade Marvin to invite Andy to the game on Saturday?" Tilly asked with a devious grin.

"Can we leave Marvin out of this?" I shot back aghast at her request.

Tilly stood, placed her hands on her hips, and stared me down. "Are you going to be involved in my full-scale campaign to get Andy back? Or not?"

"I'll help you," I replied. "But, it's against my better judgment!"

Also by JJ Hull...

The Keeper Saga

Land of Angels, Part II (Book 2)
Between the Lines (Book 3)
Forever and a Day (Book 4)
Things Left Unsaid (Book 5)
Smoke and Mirrors (Book 6)
Letting Go (Book 7)

Visit The Keeper Saga

www.thekeepersaga.com
www.paranormalcrossroads.com